# DEVIL'S FOOD

# JANICE WEBER

**WARNER BOOKS**

A Time Warner Company

Warner Books, Inc., 1271 Avenue of the Americas, New York, NY 10020

w  A Time Warner Company

Printed in the United States of America
First Printing: March 1996
10 9 8 7 6 5 4 3 2 1


Library of Congress Cataloging-in-Publication Data

Weber, Janice.
    Devil's Food / Janice Weber.
        p.   cm.
    ISBN 0-446-51772-0
    1. Women cooks—Massachusetts—Boston—Fiction.   2. Actresses—
Massachusetts—Boston—Fiction.   3. Sisters—Massachusetts—Boston—
Fiction.   4. Twins—Massachusetts—Boston—Fiction.   5. Boston
(Mass.)—Fiction.   I. Title.
PS3573.E218D48   1996
813'.54—dc20                                                          95-31884
                                                                          CIP

Book design by Giorgetta Bell McRee

To John

With special thanks to
Irwin Gelber, Stanton Kessler, Rudy, Andrew, and Rosebud

DEVIL'S FOOD

# 1
_____

*I believe that my wife is having an affair. No, she hasn't bought thick, new perfume or leopard print lingerie, hasn't revamped her hair . . . There's just an energy about her that I can't place. She's restless at night and leaves our bed to sit in the atrium, where I find her staring at the pale moon beyond the glass. Sometimes she even falls asleep on the couch out there. I rarely wake her then; instead, I pour myself a scotch and sit across from her on the white wicker chair, waiting, studying, wondering what dreams could occupy that lovely head. I am fairly sure she is not dreaming about me, not in a starring role anyway. We've been married too long for that. Her face is so still that she could be dreaming of nothing at all . . . But why leave the bedroom, leave me, to dream about nothing? No, she dreams, Emily definitely dreams. Suddenly her face contracts and she sighs. It is a sexual and exquisite sound, so full of longing that I can almost feel another man there with her in the shadows. When she wakes up afterward, sees me sitting across the way, she stares at me a tiny second as if trying to remember my name. "Ross," she recollects finally. "What are you doing here?"*

*Good question, darling.*

*Could another man be running his hands, his gross thumbs, along my wife's legs? Opening her mouth with his own? No, never, I think; then she sighs again from the cold couch and I realize that this woman remains the great enigma of my life. After fifteen years, I still adore her. How many husbands could say that? None that I know. My more domesticated colleagues at the office regard their wives as permanent fixtures, dull but constant as the earth; the restless types see their wives as useful insulation against demanding mistresses; the hard-core libertines like Dana think of their wives in terms of live-in alimony. Very few of my friends have actually divorced, however; that would be economic suicide, for what? A little breathing space? Hell, we promised for better or worse. Those who ended up worse volunteer for the projects in Alaska.*

*I never liked being away from Emily longer than a week. At the beginning of our marriage, when she really wanted children, she'd come with me on the long-term jobs. We spent almost a year in Seoul while I was working on an art museum. She's come with me to Tokyo, Paris, Istanbul, not for days but for months on end. While I coaxed a building from a tremendous hole in the ground, Emily wrote articles for magazines and even began a book, which I was not allowed to read; she eventually burned it, so I never got to know what was on her mind all those long days so far from home. When she stopped writing, Emily began studying the local cuisines, saying it was easier to slice vegetables than mince words.*

*I watch the soft rise and fall of her robe as she sleeps. Over the past hour, as she's tussled with her dreams, the sash has come undone. Soon the white lace will slide from her hips. I want to wake her, take her . . . but I am a coward. If she turns me away, then I'll know there's someone else. I'm not ready for that yet. No, I'll watch, wait, try to stifle my morbid imagination. Maybe I should go back to bed, let her wake up shivering and naked alongside the rubber tree. She doesn't want to see me spying on her like this, asking anxiously what she's doing out here again . . . or does she? Maybe she comes here on purpose, forcing me to question fifteen years of conjugal harmony. Maybe she's unhappy with everything I am and do. She's going to say she's frustrated, emotionally dehydrated, bored. It happens: I know two men at the office whose wives told them just that, out of the blue, right about the time they were making their final mortgage payments.* Sorry, honey, no more interest: *Will Emily be telling me the same thing? It's crossed my mind. For all I know, she wants to start over again with someone who understands her better, someone with a little more pizzazz than an architect. Maybe she could have children with another man.*

*Maybe she's already tried. She could be pregnant now, wondering what to do about it. She wouldn't lie to me, I think. She'd not tell me a baby were mine if it weren't. Emily has more class than that. Would she have an abortion, at her age? I doubt it, not after all those years of trying. She'd have the baby no matter who sired it. Wouldn't she? I'll have to keep better track of her menstrual cycle. See if she suddenly begins wearing sanitary pads. That would be a dead giveaway: sanitary pads and no sex for three weeks. I think that's what my partner Dana said when his girlfriend had an abortion. I should have listened better.*

*Am I out of my mind? Why am I even thinking this way? Emily and I do not argue. She knows I love her madly. I have denied her nothing. And I have been entirely faithful to her. Could fifteen years of absolute devotion mean nothing? Would she feel no reciprocal obligation? Of course she would. That's why she'd keep an affair discreet. Wouldn't want to ruin my concentration at the office, destroy my fragile male ego. . . . She wouldn't want to make a cuckold of me, would she. Cuckold: I hate the thought, hate the word. Cuck, so close to cock. And old. Cock-Old.* "Ah, poor Ross. He's been cuckolded." *God! Have I?*

*Let me think. Who could it be? Any damn man at all! My wife is still beautiful. She's very smart, very elegant, and she's*

*tough. She has a laugh that breaks men's hearts. I've seen con-
versations stop when she laughs. Men pause—no, freeze—and
look at her lips with a mixture of intense animal lust and pure
helplessness. It's a laugh you just ache to put your mouth over
and try to swallow: half virgin, half smoldering ruins. She
doesn't laugh often, though. That's why it catches everyone so
off balance. Even me, even now. Two things might make her
laugh: private jokes and embarrassing situations, the type you
can't foresee and usually can't avoid. Dropping a hundred-
dollar bottle of wine, for instance. When was the last time I
heard her laugh? Months ago. We were at a backyard fund-
raiser on Beacon Hill. She wore a black sheath with tiny
straps, architecturally perfect: left nothing and everything to
the imagination. It was the first real spring night of the season
and the air was perfumed with lilacs. Emily was talking to Guy
Witten, her boss, on the veranda. He was standing as close to
her mouth as socially acceptable, as if he had a hearing problem. He looked at the hostess in the garden, muttered something, and Emily laughed: Every man within ten feet turned his
head. Later that night, I asked her what Guy had said. She
couldn't remember.*

*Could it be Guy? He's obviously infatuated with her. She
sees him five days a week. But an affair with the boss? She
wouldn't. Too tacky. She likes her job too much anyway. Nice
restaurant. The kitchen is her fiefdom. She wouldn't jeopar-
dize that for a few muscle spasms, would she? Guy's been
married twice. Emily wouldn't settle for being number two
and a half.*

*No, it's someone else. I hope it's not someone I know. If it's a
friend, I might have to kill him: I am a man of principle, after
all. Would I divorce Emily? I doubt it. Forgive her? I doubt that,
too. The moonlight has crept up her leg, past her knees, minute
by minute approaching those shadowy places I consider my very
private property. No trespassing there; violators will be prose-
cuted. Is she guilty? Even if she isn't, I might have to punish her
a bit. Move out for a few nights. I may occasionally neglect her,*

*but she has now caused me much anguish. There's a big differ-
ence in liability here.*

*Silly old man, you imagine things! She's not involved with
anyone else. How could she kiss me good morning, sit with me
at breakfast, answer my calls at lunchtime, spend her evenings
with me, and at the same time be sleeping with another man?
Could she be capable of such duplicity? I just don't the hell
know. Duplicity might run in the family. Look at her twin sister,
Philippa, the actress: voracious and cunning as a panther. Underneath, is my wife just like that? Impossible. When would
Emily have time for an affair? She works hard. She's tired when
she gets home. Weekends she spends with me. If she's seeing
anyone, it would have to be during afternoon rush hour. Or
when she says she's running a few errands. I'll have to take
more notice of those errands, inspect what she's actually
brought home. She's been doing a lot of clothes shopping
lately—and returning empty-handed. Strange that I never
thought it unusual before. I should start asking exactly where
she's been shopping, who waited on her, why she bought nothing. I'll have to watch her eyes when she replies.*

*Is something the matter at work? Does she have a medical
problem she's not telling me about? Ordinary midlife crisis, perhaps? I should suggest a long vacation far away from Boston.
She doesn't have to work. Hell, if she insists on getting out of the
house, I could buy Emily her own restaurant. Maybe that's what
I should suggest, a cozy little number on the Wharf or in Back
Bay. No, right down the street, at the foot of Beacon Hill. I'd design the interior for her. She could hire her own staff and not
worry about Guy on her back anymore. Would she like that, no
more Guy? I definitely would.*

*Her breathing is so deep and regular now, like an innocent
child's. I should go back to bed, try to sleep. It's getting chilly
out here. Where does she keep the spare blankets? I don't want
her catching cold. Ah, that face, those secret dreams, they drive
me mad. I'll have to pull myself together by breakfast.*

Ross Major, the architect, preferred to have his morning coffee on the balcony of his Beacon Hill home, where he could watch the sunrise tinge Boston's skyline first a tender pink, then a fiery red: God blessing his work. On overcast days like this one, however, he drank his coffee inside, comforted by the reflection of halogen lights on his polished marble countertop. Today he was just finishing the sports pages as his wife came into the kitchen. Almost six-fifteen: she would be late for work. "Sleep well, love?" he asked cheerfully.

"Unnnh."

She had dressed in a business suit rather than jeans; on her lapel was the pearl brooch he had bought for her in Tokyo as a tenth-anniversary present. Pouring her coffee, Ross glanced at his wife's face. Unusual makeup today, particularly around the eyes. She had outlined them with black pencil; the mascara looked way too thick. And she had never worn slate blue shadow to work before. Her eyes were still a little puffy from lack of sleep, or hyperactive dreams. Ross intuitively decided that this was not the time to mention her night on the couch; he might get a straight answer. "Toast?" he asked.

"Sure." Emily peeled a banana, chewing pensively as Ross returned to the newspaper. "What's new in the world?"

"Nothing at all. The rich are getting poorer and the poor are having triplets." He scanned a few obituaries. It was always interesting to read how people had died. Cancer and cardiac arrest got most of the old ones. The young and foolish had drowned, contracted AIDS, or tried to ride motorcycles. Ross read through to the last paragraphs, checking if he knew any of the survivors: none today. When Emily's toast popped up, he passed her the marmalade. "What's on your agenda?"

"Food." Cafe Presto, where Emily worked, was one of the busiest eateries in the financial district.

"That's all? You look very businesslike. I haven't seen that blouse before."

"I've been reading a book on power dressing," she said.

"Oh? You look pretty powerful in your regular gear."

"Aprons and T-shirts are not powerful, Ross."

"You're a chef, honey. No one expects you to look like a stockbroker."

"Just give it a chance, all right? I wanted a little change." Emily concentrated moodily on her toast as Ross waited for her to elaborate. "Busy today, sweetheart?" she asked after a few moments.

He sighed; she had deflected the conversation away from her clothing and makeup and mischief. "George Kravitz is coming in to see sketches of his new office park."

"Think he'll like them?"

"For two hundred thousand bucks, let's hope so. Then I'm taking Dagmar Pola out to lunch."

Emily stopped chewing. "Who's that?"

"Pola's Pretzels. Or should I say, the widow of Pola's Pretzels. Good old Joe checked out last week. Now Dagmar wants to build some sort of gallery for his art collection."

"What did he collect?"

"Nudes, I hear."

"Male or female?"

"Female, of course. Joe was never without a woman on his arm."

"Wife, you mean."

"No, Dagmar was his only wife. We're talking about the five hundred mistresses. All those salty pretzels must have affected his libido."

"Maybe Dagmar did." Emily brushed a few crumbs from her lapel. "By the way, you haven't slept with me in three weeks."

Eh? How did she get from pretzels to their sex life? Did she really count the days in between? He must be better than he thought. "We'll go to bed early tonight. Catch up."

"We have theater tickets tonight."

"Oh." Done with the newspaper, Ross put it aside. "Do you think you could arrange a table for Dagmar and me at lunch today? I'm sure she'd like the fish chowder you serve on Thursdays."

"Then she should have made a reservation two weeks ago." Emily didn't need to remind her husband that Cafe Presto was always packed from eleven till two. "I'll see what I can do."

He followed her to the bathroom, watching as she vigorously

brushed her teeth and applied a second layer of that heavy eye shadow. When she began painting her lips vermilion, he considered following her to work. "Are you all right?" Ross asked. "That's such strange makeup."

Finally she looked at him. "What's so strange?"

"It's a little tarty." Whoops, mistake. "Well, not tarty. It's a little strong. For the morning, anyway."

"Do you mind? I'm turning over a new leaf."

"What was the matter with the old leaf?"

"Just that. It was old." Emily again checked her watch. "Like me. Have fun with Dagmar, dear."

She grabbed her raincoat and hastily left, obviously not wanting him to walk downtown with her. As Ross was thinking about that, the phone rang. "Hello?"

Hang-up. Ross called his wife around noon, wondering if a table for two had unexpectedly turned up at Cafe Presto. The pastry chef told him that Emily had left at eleven and would not return until three.

Emily stepped onto Joy Street just as the thick, warm air coalesced into drizzle. It had been a cloudy, listless summer and she was glad it was almost over. Seven out of ten weekends had been wet, soddening getaways to their cabin in New Hampshire; by the middle of August, even Ross refused to drive two hours north to stare at a fogged-in lake and a cupboard of wilted jigsaw puzzles. Instead, they had flown to New York to see a matinee and a few exhibitions; that weekend turned out to be the sunniest of the season, of course.

Emily ducked into the subway at Park Street, avoiding the stagnant pools blotching the steps. The station smelled of yesterday's sweat and today's doughnuts. Not having slept well, she felt heavy and slow, stalked by a headache. Several commuters looked up from their newspapers as she walked to the center platform; maybe these bluish lamps fluoresced her makeup. As a wayside musician pipped into his flute, she watched a mouse scurry along the third rail. Behind her, two men discussed a local bank failure. Only as her train rumbled in did Emily finally focus on the poster across the tracks. It was a provocative close-up of Philippa, her twin sister, eating a green olive. CHOKE HOLD, the title of Philippa's new movie, splashed across the poster in green letters matching the olive. Philippa's name floated underneath in red letters matching her lipstick. Opening next week.

Emily smiled wanly; she had been thinking about her sister last night. They hadn't talked in a while. Philippa had just divorced her fifth husband. Five! Was she already considering a sixth attempt at Everest? Emily hoped not. Philippa was not made for marriage. Made for men, yes; marriage, no. Not that Philippa hadn't made a sincere attempt. In each case she had tried very hard to be a perfect wife, like Emily. Then temptation, usually in the form of another man, had tripped her up. Too bad; Philippa's first husband had been fairly decent. Thereafter, she had chosen less and less wisely. The last challenger was a total loser, all eyelash and mustache, zero brain. She had tossed him out after a few weeks. But no man held on to Philippa for long. She was a bonfire, born to emit millions of cinders, burn a few fingers . . . and move on. Ever since they were children, Philippa had attracted men who were a trifle too handsome to be reliable. And they always swallowed that line about her mother dying in childbirth, as if it explained and excused everything.

Several months ago, the last time the twins had seen each other, Philippa had been very blond. She had not been a brunette for years, perhaps in a tacit, merciful gesture to Emily, who was constantly mistaken for her famous sister. The confusion was understandable; they had the same face, the same graceful figures, the same enunciations. But their lives had taken very different paths, mostly because of the men they had met. Philippa's first lover had been an actor in soap operas; Emily's had been her aesthetics professor. On his account, she had stayed in school, earning a master's degree in art history. She had fiddled around Europe in his wake for another two years before realizing that academics rarely divorced wives to marry their pupils. Crushed, she went to New York and worked in a museum. One overcast March afternoon, she met Ross in front of a Whistler. After their first date, she knew this man could become Permanent. He was very intelligent. He worked hard and aimed high. He came from an accomplished family and was not too shy, not too confident, not too poor, not too rich, neither plain nor perilously handsome; he was one boiling mass of superb potential, in need only of a woman's refining hand. And he adored her. Marrying him had been the most positive move of her life. It wasn't a flamboyant life, like Philippa's. It wasn't a particularly fearless life either, not compared to Philippa's. Ah, always back to that famous sister. Now that their hair was different, people were always telling Emily that she reminded them of someone else, but they couldn't quite figure out whom. She had finally learned to accept it.

So *Choke Hold* had made it to the box office; last time Emily had spoken to Philippa about it, the film was throttling its third director. Emily resolved to call her sister that evening. Maybe they could meet at a health spa and exchange a few secrets, give the other a little bad advice . . . forget men for a while.

The oncoming train screeched to a halt. Emily took a seat and pulled the September issue of *Gourmet* from her briefcase. Most other commuters were reading about the Red Sox, who had startled the bejesus out of everyone last night by almost holding on to a four-run lead through the bottom of the ninth inning. Across the aisle, an Asian student was reading the *Wall Street Journal*; off in the corner sat a woman with a few bags from Filene's Basement. She was probably going to charge the Returns line the second the store opened. Emily skimmed through some recipes and left the car after two stops.

The drizzle had now amplified into rain. Along State Street, a legion of umbrellas jousted for space six feet above the narrow sidewalks. Emily could smell the ocean. She took a deep breath: This was going to be a good day, damn it. In two hours her life was going to make an abrupt about-face. Stepping over the puddles surrounding Quincy Market, she noticed that the Yuppies seemed to have stopped wearing seersucker suits; summer's lassitude was perhaps over.

As she entered the kitchen of Cafe Presto, the familiar aroma of yeast and cinnamon enveloped her. "Hi, Bert," she called to the pastry chef as he eased a tray of scones from the oven. "Everything under control?"

"You're late." He had deeply resented all eight minutes. "Start grinding the coffee. There's just so much one person can do all by himself around here."

In the seven years since she had taken over, Presto had gone from a sleepy muffin dispensary to one of the busiest cafes in Boston. Emily's pistachio twists, a recipe she had brought back from Turkey, had put Presto on the map; thereafter, hers was the typical seventy-hour-week success story. Whipping off her jacket, Emily donned an apron and prepared to face the first rush of die-hard workaholics. That was the danish and black coffee crowd. Afterward, the bran muffin and decaf contingent would start filtering in; then came the cheesecakers, who usually felt compelled to explain that they were combining breakfast and lunch. Lois, the cashier, arrived at seven-fifteen and dove into the ladies' room to apply her final two coats of hair spray and face powder; like Mass, it had been part of her morning ritual for the last umpteen years. She emerged just in time to open the registers.

"Where are Lucy and Randall?" she called, counting dollar bills.

The counter help had been fairly reliable until a month ago, when they had started sleeping together. Now they were either both late, both in a snit, or speaking a slobbery goo-goo to each other. Their co-workers, not in love themselves, were losing patience with the couple, who kept blaming everything on Not Enough Sleep Lately. "They're not here yet?" Emily cried, up to the elbows in pancake batter. "Call them at home."

"They went to the Cape yesterday," Bert reminded her. "Right now they're probably screwing on the beach as they look for whales. They couldn't care less about serving breakfast to people with clothes on."

"Call them up," Emily repeated. "Maybe they got home early."

Lois tried both numbers. "No answer."

"Then call Guy at the gym," Emily said, mounding croissants into the display cases. "Tell him to get over here and start pouring coffee."

"The boss? He's going to be furious! You know what he said last time we interrupted his workout!" Lois became so upset that she slammed the cash drawer shut on her finger. "Goddamn it!" She began dancing profanely behind the register, snapping her injured hand through the air.

The man standing first in line outside of Cafe Presto knocked on the glass and pointed at his watch. "Unlock the door," Emily ordered Lois. "You can serve, can't you? I'll take the register." As the first wave of customers tumbled in, Emily called the gym and was put on hold. She was still on hold twenty danishes later.

A fortyish woman in exhausted jeans came to the register. Her graying hair looked as if it had been blow-dried by a Boeing 747. Maybe she had been trying to polish hubcaps with the front of her sweatshirt. Odd face, disproportionately small for her neck. Emily looked again; no, the face was all right. The neck was too thick. The woman had the shoulders of an ox. "Three scones, two milks, one coffee," she rasped.

Emily's ear was beginning to burn from clamping the phone to her shoulder. "Seven-fifty, please."

The woman paid and left. Soon she was back at the register with corn muffins and orange juice. Now a dot of raspberry jam gleamed on her sleeve. She leaned toward Emily. "Aren't you usually in an apron behind the counter?"

"I got promoted." Emily finally heard Guy's voice on the phone. "Get over here," she hissed. "Romeo and Juliet are late again." She slammed the handset down, rubbed her neck, and stared at the food on the woman's tray. "That's four dollars."

The woman fished some damp bills out of her sweatpants. "Do I know you?"

"No." Emily looked pointedly at the next person's tray. "Five twenty-five."

Soon the woman was back with a couple of bagels. "Me again. When are you going on break?"

Come on! Why didn't any of this crap happen when Lois was at the register? "Never," Emily said.

Sighing, the woman placed a red business card on the counter. "Do you know the restaurant Diavolina?"

"Vaguely." In the South End. It served things like lobster with blueberries.

"We need a new chef. Tonight."

"What happened to your old chef?"

"He blew town."

Emily collected six dollars from the next person in line. "I'll keep my eyes peeled. You never know when a reject from the Cordon Bleu might wander in here looking for work."

"Very funny. I'm serious about that job."

"I'm serious about this one. Good-bye."

Shrugging, the woman left. Lucy and Randall appeared around eight-thirty, after the run on bran muffins had ended. Guy Witten, proprietor of Cafe Presto, sauntered in at nine. Taking a scone and a cup of coffee, he made the rounds of his employees, greeting Bert and Lois, chewing out the inamorati. When he stood behind Emily, who was making chicken salad, he stopped. "Good morning."

She flung a handful of walnuts into the tub. "I called you two hours ago."

"I got over as fast as I could." He leaned over the counter, brushing her back with his elbow. "Whatcha making there?"

"Bartolo ordered ninety chicken-salad sandwiches for lunch."

"And twelve cherry pies," Bert complained. "I'm not sure I can finish in time."

"Defrost a dozen," Guy told him. "That should help." He started toward his office in the back. "Emily, come with me. I need you to check the invoice we got from the dairy."

"Just pay it," she snapped.

Guy stopped in his tracks. For a moment he watcher her furiously stir the chicken salad, wondering if she was aware of the little smacking noises her wooden spoon made as it mucked through all that mustardy, meaty quicksand. "Come when it's convenient," he said finally, leaving the kitchen.

First she made the sandwiches. Then she frosted three chocolate cakes. Finally Emily went back to the office. Guy was on the phone trying to collect a few overdue invoices. Bartolo and Associates, the law firm across the street, owed him about six thousand dollars. Guy was trying to convince old man Bartolo that he'd never see ninety sandwiches and twelve pies until his bill was paid in full, preferably in cash. Fairly convinced he had won, Guy hung up. He studied Emily's face a moment. "Are those two black eyes or are you trying to look like that dog on the Miller Lite commercials?"

She remained at the door. *Say it!* she thought. No words survived the trip from brain to tongue. "Which invoices did you want me to check?"

Guy got up from the desk and inspected her eyes at close range. Suddenly he kissed her deeply, roughly. "Let's get out of here for an hour. I'll get a room at the Meridien."

She pushed him a few inches away. "Are you out of your mind?"

"What's the matter, Plum? Don't tell me you're busy."

"I just did."

They stood a moment, angrily breathing in each others' faces as his warm, heavy hands crept over her shoulders, her back, reclaiming territory that another man had usurped for a few days. It made him crazy when she went home to that proper codfish of a husband. Crazy! Guy lifted her blouse, catching his breath when he touched stomach. One hand got under her bra, ah, it was so sweet there. And there. "I missed you," he whispered, half amused, half terrified, at his own ludicrous understatement. What he really wanted to do was throw himself at her feet, beg, confess like a man, hope she'd pick him up—wrong, all wrong. What he really wanted was Emily to throw herself at his feet so that *he* could pick *her* up—wrong again. She'd never do that, not while her husband was around. The gulf between Guy's aspirations and current reality overwhelmed him with hopeless lust. He kissed her again.

Too soon she opened her eyes, back in the grim world of dishes and dishonor. "I have to go."

"Where?" He despaired as Emily's hand squeezed not him, but the doorknob. "Can't get messed up, eh? Must be lunch with your husband. That explains the suit and pearls."

Without answering, Emily left. Guy's stomach went cold. He

sat a moment wondering if he should follow her. No: Such behavior was beneath his dignity. She could be meeting a girlfriend, seeing her gynecologist, getting a facial, one of those
woman things. They always liked you to think they were doing
something more exciting with a handsome stranger. Guy returned to his accounting and made quite a few addition mistakes.

It was a craven way out, but an exit nonetheless. After leaving Guy's office, Emily took the red business card the woman
had left at the cash register. She peered at the small script. *Diavolina*: "little she-devil"—how appropriate. She left Cafe
Presto and began walking quickly toward the South End, needing air and movement away from Guy. No thinking, just movement. Suddenly the drizzle became steady, pelting rain. In her
haste to leave Cafe Presto, Emily had forgotten an umbrella.
Now she'd get her new suit wet; just a little more punishment
for her naughtiness. Stuck at a traffic light, Emily beseeched the
clouds. Give me a break, she thought. I ended it, didn't I?

She stepped into the bustling intersection. Over the past
decade, as the mezzo-affluent had renovated the brownstones
lining Tremont Street, the area had become a mecca of tony
eateries and boutiques. The new stores offered a nice contrast to
the fire-gutted churches still jagging the boulevard. Despite the
cars triple-parked on both sides of the street, traffic moved just
fast enough in the one remaining lane to outpace the kicks of
pedestrians, who felt they had the right of way, like in California. After a long, mindless walk, Emily stood outside a large
window. A red neon sign in the upper left corner spelled DI-
AVOLINA. She went in.

Nearly lunchtime and there was no manager, in fact no
human, in sight. Emily glanced over the pinkish brown walls
and aqua tablecloths: Southwestern Vulva, a style Ross detested.
It looked more like something his partner Dana would design.
The low-backed chairs would keep their occupants comfortable
for about two hours and the lighting would smooth the most
corrugated complexions. How about the food? Emily took a
menu. Diavolina offered the standard mishmash plus a few

trendy entrées involving offal and invertebrates. At the moment it was one of the hot places to be seen eating in Boston.

Calling obscenities over her shoulder, the woman in the sweatshirt burst from the kitchen and stalked to the bar. Her hair had still not touched a comb; either a bottle of ketchup had scored a direct hit on her apron, or she had been slaughtering chickens out back. As she rolled up her sleeves, Emily realized that the woman wasn't wearing shoulder pads at all; she was wearing muscles. They overlaid her body like dozens of little saddlebags. Emily watched her yank a mug from the freezer and mix herself a tremendous martini.

She walked to the bar. "Remember me? Cafe Presto?"

"Of course! The cashier! Your mascara wasn't all over your chin then."

Emily smiled pleasantly. "My name's Emily Major. Still need a chef?"

"You're looking for a job? What happened between eight this morning and now?"

Emily could feel the blood bubbling to her cheeks. Reminding herself that she was the sister of a great actress, she continued smiling. "I quit."

"Now that's handy." The woman leaned mightily over the counter, displaying forearms laced with tattoos. "What can you do besides pistachio buns?"

This was not the same beggar who had come to her cash register this morning. Emily thought of leaving Diavolina; then she thought of returning to Guy Witten at Cafe Presto. "Anything. I'm a great cook. I spent a year in Korea, a summer in Paris, a couple months in Morocco—"

"Why?" the woman interrupted. "You got something against hot dogs?"

"My husband is an architect. I went with him to his projects." It didn't sound very hip, did it. "You were fairly eager to hire me this morning."

The woman swallowed a large belt of her martini. "I've been reconsidering. This is a much bigger place than Cafe Presto, Ms. Major. What makes you think you can run it?"

"What makes you think I can't? Food is food."

"Ah, but how are you with kitchen personnel? Friendly?"

"Fine," Emily snapped, feeling her cheeks flame again. "Ask anyone at Presto."

"Diavolina's different. How good are you with knives?"

The kitchen doors banged open and a small, ferocious man strode toward the bar carrying a plate of food. His nose looked as if it had spent some time on either cheek, courtesy of a sledge hammer. "Put it there, Klepp, I'm not hungry." The woman pointed, then turned to Emily. "Eat some of that and tell me what you think. I'll consider this your entrance exam."

Emily began eating as her interviewer poured drinks for a half dozen customers who had wandered in. The food wasn't bad but the book on power dressing that she had been reading recommended force, verbal as well as sartorial, in gaining the respect of a potential employer. In case after case, starting salaries were at least ten thousand dollars higher than an ordinary wimp's. "The cole slaw's compost," she said confidently when the woman returned. "You could tile the Callahan Tunnel with these corn cakes. The chicken is burnt." She popped a pickle into her mouth. "I can't tell whether this is tomato or cranberry relish. What's for dessert?"

"Zero," the woman replied. "Your interview is over."

"Already? When do I start?"

"Never. I'm not impressed with your personality."

This particular reaction had not been discussed in her book. Emily was on her own. "This is not my real personality," she confessed. "I'm having a bad day."

"I don't think so. And I don't think you'd make a good kitchen manager. You have about as much finesse as an earthmover."

"Listen," Emily said, hunching over the counter. "I desperately need this job. I'll work very hard here."

"I've got three more interviews this afternoon," the woman replied. "Serious contenders. They won't give me any of this Korea or Morocco crap. My customers don't want to eat monkeys and camels."

Emily stood up. "I'll come back at two o'clock. You'll see who the serious contender is." She wandered around Copley Place for several hours, then walked back to Diavolina. The woman kept her waiting for a few moments before bringing a dish of apple pie to the bar and introducing herself as Ward. Maybe that was her last name; Ward didn't use, or divulge, another. They briefly discussed money. Emily was hired.

Having taken Dagmar Pola, the pretzel widow, to Legal Sea Foods instead of his wife's cafe for lunch, Ross Major returned to his office in a foul mood. Not on account of Dagmar, of course: She had hired Major & Forbes to construct the gallery of her dreams. No, Ross had acquired a sharp headache the moment he was told that Emily had left Cafe Presto at eleven and would not return until three. Where had she gone? A thousand destinations, all involving mattresses, sprang to mind. He had hardly swallowed a bite of his lobster bisque and now could barely recall a word of what Dagmar and he had talked about. Fortunately, most of it had been gas about murals and pretzels.

Ross's secretary, Marjorie, immediately saw the tension in his face. "How was Dagmar?" she asked brightly, following him to his office.

"Terrific." He rubbed the kinks forming in the back of his neck. "Any aspirin handy?"

When she returned, Ross was standing at his glazed window high over the financial district. "You can't even see Faneuil Hall from here," he complained. "Some panoramic view of Boston."

"You can see better from Dana's office." Marjorie handed him a glass of water and five aspirin, his usual dose. "Looking for something down there?"

"No." Ross backed away from the window. "Is Dana in?"

"He left around twelve. In a big hurry."

"Why? Was he seeing someone?"

Marjorie had not seen her boss so distraught since the time they received new rates for liability insurance. "I don't think so. I'll look in his appointment book." She left.

Ross went to his partner's spacious office and glanced over

Dana's desk. In the corner, he saw a vast collection of vitamin supplements and homeopathic medicines, all connected with sexual potency; Dana gobbled them like raisins. Otherwise, the desktop was cleared of everything but official correspondence. After twenty years Dana had finally learned to treat epistles from his mistresses the same as he would live hand grenades: average time from perusal to paper shredder, five seconds.

Ross was gazing out the window with a pair of Dana's binoculars as Marjorie returned. "His appointment book's blank. Sorry, Ross. I'll ask when he gets back."

Dana Forbes didn't reappear until four, fairly drunk. He told Marjorie that he had been at the athletic club, then out to lunch with Billy Murphy, who was in charge of building permits at City Hall. Dana no longer noticed the disapproving frown on Marjorie's face; over the years he had seen it so often that he thought this was the woman's natural demeanor. A shame, because she was otherwise an extremely handsome lady, expertly preserved, outstanding in high heels and Brooks Brothers suits. Dana would have asked her out years ago except that she obviously preferred his partner. "Ross in, darling?" he asked cheerfully.

Marjorie passed an envelope through the laser printer. "He's been waiting for you."

"Really? Must be good news." Tossing a few pills into his mouth, Dana went to his partner's office. "Hey, buddy! Did you ravish Dagmar?"

Ross looked up from his sketching pad. For the last hour he had been debating whether or not to call Emily at Cafe Presto and demand to know where the hell she had been. Swiveling in his chair, he faced Dana. "Where the hell have you been?"

"To a six-martini lunch. I fixed three permits with Murphy. Wasn't cheap." Dana walked to Ross's desk. "What are these?" he asked, picking up a handful of sketches. "Very nice."

"Just fiddling around." Ross cursed himself for having left them exposed. "Emily might be wanting to open her own restaurant one of these days."

"No kidding! That's great!"

Was that enthusiasm a wee bit forced? As he took the sketches back, Ross thought he smelled a whiff of perfume on his partner's white shirt. Sweet, floral. Wait: That was only the booze evaporating on Dana's breath. Right? "Tell me about Murphy," Ross said. "Where'd you eat?"

"Drink," Dana corrected. "Where we always do. The Blue Frog."

"Where did you sit?"

"Where we always do. Behind the pinball machine."

"How long were you there?"

"Long enough to take care of all current business. What is this, an inquisition?"

Ross rubbed the two deep furrows between his eyes. "Sorry. I thought we had agreed to let Marjorie know where we were at all times. In case a wife called or something." *Wife:* With the very word, lightning flashed between his ears.

Dana sighed. "What can I tell you? Murphy called at the last minute. It was a golden opportunity and I ran with it."

Of course Dana was right. Major & Forbes had not become one of Boston's preeminent architectural firms by blowing kisses at golden opportunities as they floated by. The partners had been fast friends since their first Cub Scout overnight, when Dana had awed his tentmates with a deck of pornographic playing cards. In forty years, the tenor of their friendship had not really changed: Dana despised rules, Ross despised indiscipline, and they both lived to pour concrete. While Ross attended blue-hair matinees at Symphony Hall with the Old Money, Dana engaged in heavy substance abuse with Harvard faculty and the nouveaux riches. The result had been many six-martini lunches near many city halls.

For half an hour, Dana and Ross discussed business affairs. When Dagmar Pola's name came up, Dana beamed. "Deep pockets. Joe's were, anyway. I built a little chapel for him a while ago."

"What was the occasion?"

"I didn't ask. He was probably working off a few cardinal sins. Charming man. What's Dagmar like? Young? Luscious?"

"Old and sharp." In fact, she reminded Ross of Dana's wife, Ardith. Or Ardith after another twenty years of Dana and his mistresses. Ross looked at his watch. "I'd better go. Umberto's meeting me at five." That was the plasterer, specialty restorations. "Will I see you tomorrow?"

"Don't think so. I'm taking a long weekend sailing." Dana kept a modest yacht in the harbor. Because his marriage was not in tip-top condition, he spent as much time as possible on the water, claiming that a forty-foot boat was more therapeutic than a marriage counselor. Besides, Dana knew that his wife would never ditch him until she found a richer man: no easy feat in today's economy.

"Long weekend, eh?" Ross resisted an urge to ask if Ardith would be aboard. "Remember I need you here on Monday." He put his drawing pencils neatly away.

"Going to New Hampshire?" Dana asked, swallowing a few more pills. "The weather's supposed to be perfect. Warm days, cool nights. Great for getting under the blankets with that sexy wife of yours."

Ross looked oddly at him. Why had Dana said that? "Do you ever think about anything else?" he asked irritably. "Maybe you should stop eating all those damn aphrodisiacs."

"Are you kidding? Without these, I'm dead meat."

"I'll have to remember that." Ross grabbed his umbrella. "See you Monday."

He left for a nearby sushi bar to meet Umberto, who talked as if his mouth were full of warm, setting plaster. No matter: Ross wasn't listening anyway. He was imagining himself in a white, tiled room with Emily, shining a light in her face as he asked where she had been that afternoon. The last thing he felt like doing was laughing it up at a musical with her tonight. So he stewed and drank, occasionally mouthing a few sentences at Umberto. He arrived at the theater seconds before the curtain rose. Instead of watching the chorines onstage, he kept staring at his wife as red, green, and blue lights splashed her face. Finally the cacophony stopped and they were walking along the Common, back to Beacon Hill.

"Hard day?" Emily asked as they waited for a light to change.

"Somewhat."

She paused; nothing shifted but the red light. "Tell me about it."

Ross's resistance suddenly snapped; he had never been able to deny his wife anything. "Dagmar Pola really wanted to eat at Presto today. I tried to get a table and you weren't even there." Even as he spoke, Ross realized how tortured and juvenile he sounded.

"I was at a job interview."

He stopped in the middle of Beacon Street. "What for?"

"I'm bored. Need a change." She tugged him away from on-coming traffic. "A place on Tremont Street needs a chef right away. It's called Diavolina."

"Italian?"

"Not exactly."

Ross walked uphill in silence a few minutes, absorbing the news. "What did Guy say?"

"I'm telling him tomorrow."

Now that he knew his wife was leaving a latent rival, Ross felt a rush of sympathy for him. "Isn't this a little sudden, honey? I thought you liked Presto. Thought you liked Guy, too."

"He'll find someone else in two minutes flat."

As they turned onto Joy Street, Ross held his wife's arm, guiding her over the uneven cobblestones. Although he couldn't quite put his finger on it, he knew that Emily had just made a heavy decision in his favor. Thank God he had kept his mouth shut and waited it out! Then an awful thought struck him as he unlocked his front door. "Who's your new boss?"

"Someone named Ward. She walked into Presto this morning and offered me a job."

Ross followed his wife inside. "Just like that? Isn't that a little unusual?"

"Absurdly so, thank God." Emily hung up her raincoat. "Her chef just quit. There seem to be a few maniacs loose in her kitchen. I haven't met them yet."

"Maybe you should before you sign on."

"How bad can they be?" How choosy could she be? Emily followed Ross to the den and watched as he poured two glasses of cognac. His mood had completely lifted in the last five minutes and she could guess why. Ah, adultery! At best, momentary amnesia; at worst, ruination; and in between, a thousand tiers of guilt. She never wanted to see her husband's face clouded like that again. "How's Marjorie these days?" she asked.

"Fine." Ross handed Emily her drink and sat beside her on the black leather couch. "A hell of a lot better than Dana, actually."

"What's Dana's problem?"

"He told me he was taking a long weekend sailing. Without Ardith, of course." Ross noted his wife's reaction: nothing. He was relieved yet slightly disappointed, even slightly suspicious. Emily usually rushed to Dana's defense in all matters. "He disappears for half a day, then comes back to the office with these flimsy excuses about building permits. I'm beginning to lose my patience with that."

She finished her drink in one gulp. "Does it interfere with his work?"

"Not really."

"Then leave him alone." Her voice regained a little color. "How was Madame Pretzel?"

"We got the contract. But Dagmar's one flinty old lady. I'd better be on my toes for that one." He checked his watch: almost news time.

Emily stood up to go to bed. Neither mentioned their heavy sex make-up session scheduled for that evening. After the news, Ross remembered some important reading in the library; by midnight Emily was pretending to be asleep. He did not pretend to wake her.

Early the next morning, Emily was back at Cafe Presto baking her valedictory batch of lemon danishes. At nine-thirty, as the breakfast rush piddled to a slow drip-drip-drip of truly lazy office workers, a woman wearing sunglasses, an Hermès scarf, and a fire-engine red raincoat walked in. Emily recognized Philippa at once. The small fluff of hair that Emily could see beneath the scarf was no longer blond. It, and her sister's eyebrows, were again their natural brunette: They were identical twins again. As Philippa hesitated in the doorway, Emily went quickly to greet her. "Hey, Phil! What a surprise!"

"Emmy," Philippa replied with a noncontact kiss. "Have I come at a bad time?"

"Of course not." Damn, Guy Witten would show up any moment! Emily's stomach imploded for the fiftieth time that morning. She led her sister to a corner table. "Well, well! What are you doing in Boston?"

"Interviews. And I did call yesterday morning. Ross answered so I hung up." Sighing enigmatically, Philippa removed her sunglasses and scarf. Her shoulder-length hair tumbled down. "Experimenting with your makeup?"

"I'm trying a new look for the fall."

"They're wearing golds and greens in Paris. Understated tones. I wouldn't wear that ghastly blue until Halloween." Philippa looked toward the food counter. "Have you got any hot coffee here, Em? Maybe a croissant? I'm starved."

"Sure." When Emily returned to the table, her sister was refreshing her magenta lipstick. "Why'd you change your hair, Phil? New role?"

"No, new man. This is a wig. I don't want to be recognized with him."

"Why not? Is he a priest or something?"

"He's getting divorced. Now's not the time for his wife to know he's seeing me." Philippa took a deep draught of coffee. "Ah, that's good. I'm mad about him. I've lied to everyone about where I am for the next couple of days."

"He lives in Boston?"

"You know him," Philippa said. "Dana Forbes."

Ross's partner? "Are you joking?"

"I met him at a party. He was doing some consulting for the Louvre, I think."

Last month, Ross had suggested taking that job himself. He and Emily would have four days together in Paris. She had said

no; the French capital was a pestilential sty in August. "I guess
you're the reason he had to stay an extra week in France? Sup-
plemental consulting?"

"Of course! But listen, you really must not tell anyone about
this. Including Ross. How is that lovely man, by the way?"

"Fine. Why can't I tell him? He's not going to call the *National Enquirer.*"

"Dana thinks it's a little . . . ah . . . incestuous." As Philippa
waved her hand, an emerald and diamond ring glistened in the
morning light. It had been their mother's; the twins took turns
wearing it, switching every year on their birthday. "And Ross is
such a straight arrow. Dana's sure he'd be annoyed."

"He's going to find out sooner or later. Dana is not the world's
most discreet fellow, if you haven't noticed. You're not exactly
invisible, either. Even with the wig."

"What do you mean? I'm wearing sunglasses."

"Philippa, they're covered with rhinestones. Your scarf is purple. Your raincoat is bright red. No one dresses like that around
here. Take a look outside."

A few moments' observation of sidewalk traffic led Philippa
to agree that Quincy Market was no Champs Élysées. "What am
I supposed to do, vanish? I'm meeting Dana in ten minutes at
the marina. We're going sailing for the weekend."

Emily guffawed, recalling Ross's comments about his partner's
weekend at sea. "Ardith is no fool, you know. I'd be shocked if
she hasn't hired a private detective by now."

"Bitch! And what a stupid name. You can't tell if she's Jewish
or Quaker. A private detective could be trouble."

"No kidding. Cancel the trip."

"Oh, lighten up! Haven't you ever been swept off your feet?
I've waited years for a man like this." Philippa chomped her
croissant. "Help me out."

Emily frowned. Not one day ago, she had foresworn adultery.
Now she had to help her sister commit it. More important, her
soon-to-be ex-lover would be arriving at Cafe Presto any second
now. She had to get rid of Philippa at once. "Call Dana," Emily
said. "Tell him you'll meet him in the middle of the harbor."

"That's wonderful. What am I going to do, swim out?"

"At the marina there's a little sloop. An old drunk named Stanley lives on it. He's usually on deck. Give him a hundred bucks and say you've got to deliver an important letter. He'll take you out."

Philippa smiled: melodrama. "Can I borrow your clothes?"

"What for?"

"Well, your raincoat and umbrella, at least. So I look anonymous. Like Ingrid Bergman in *Casablanca*."

Emily noticed Guy walking toward Cafe Presto. She stood up. "Hurry." Philippa followed her to the garderobe, where they exchanged coats, scarves, and sunglasses. "Go out the back," Emily instructed, pushing her sister through the kitchen. "Take the subway to Mass General. The marina's right there." She kissed Philippa. "Make sure you get Dana back to the office in one piece on Monday. Ross needs him."

"Thanks, darling," Philippa called, rushing out. "Keep the raincoat. It cost me six thousand francs."

"Who was that?" scolded Bert when Emily returned to the kitchen. "We're not supposed to bring people back here. It's against health regulations."

"That was my sister. I believe she took a bath this morning."

Coffee in hand, Guy strolled to Emily's counter. She felt the familiar heat rise as he approached. Chemical reaction, genetic; succumbing to it couldn't be entirely her fault. "What? Not done with the chicken salad yet?" he asked, brushing her shoulder. "Tsk-tsk."

"May I speak with you a moment?" she said. "In your office?"

"She's going to quit," Bert called as they left the kitchen. "Betcha fifty bucks."

"You're hilarious, Bertie," Guy responded, following Emily to his office. "One of these days, that twerp is going to find himself out of a job."

"Take it easy on him. At least he's dependable."

Guy closed the door. "What can I do for you, baby?"

Perhaps she should have sent a telegram; phoned. Feeling

herself wilt, Emily decided to amputate. "I've found another job."

He stared, then laughed, maybe hiccuped. "You're leaving?"

"Yes. Don't try to talk me out of it."

"Why? Money? I'll double your salary."

"Shut up! You know why."

Guy smiled, genuinely amused. "Don't tell me you've decided to become a faithful wife again."

"I never considered myself an unfaithful wife."

"No? You think sleeping with me is like watering the plants?" Guy stepped lightly over to her; she backed up until his desk obstructed further retreat. As he put his hands on her waist, she closed her eyes, smelling his skin. Ah, delicious. Never again?

"I'm not your wife," she said feebly.

"You don't want to be. I've asked you often enough." He kissed her neck. "Why stop? We're not hurting anyone."

"Wrong." She pushed him away.

"What, don't like my hands? You liked them well enough yesterday."

She slapped his face. Guy momentarily froze, murder in the eyes; then, after running his fingers slowly along the curves of Emily's body, he took a step backward. "You are making a big mistake."

"I don't think so."

"Then you're fired. Now. Good-bye."

She walked out.

That morning, delighted to be alive, possessed of a lovely and loyal wife, Ross Major strolled through the warm drizzle to work. He made several phone calls to clients, then told Marjorie he was going to run a few errands and would be back in an hour. After buying a dozen pink roses, Ross walked briskly toward Cafe Presto. He intended to stop in for a cup of coffee, say hello to Emily, give her a little moral support; after all, she would be terminating Guy Witten today. Ross wanted to hold her hand, suggest they dine out that evening. Then they'd go to bed early, as they should have done last night.

He was half a block from the cafe when he saw his wife hurry onto the cobblestones and begin walking swiftly away from him. His heart constricted: leaving work again? Had she told Guy off? Then he should catch up with her, help her celebrate; but something in her gait held him back. When she glanced quickly over her shoulder, checking if anyone were following her, all of Ross's blood-sucking demons returned. He watched her go to the subway, make a brief phone call, and, nearly flying down the steps, run to catch the approaching inbound train. Ross ran after her, ducking into the next car, his heart pounding as deafeningly as the rap music from a nearby boom box. She changed trains at Park Street. Keeping a careful distance, he followed her to the Mass General stop. Without looking back, she walked to the marina that Ross knew so well. He watched her say a few words to the drunk in the sloop, hop aboard, and chug into the harbor. For a long time, stupefied, he waited behind a tree. Finally the old man returned to the dock.

Ross walked onto the pier. "Hello, Stanley," he called.

"Hey! Your wife was just here. Said she had an important letter from you to Mr. Forbes."

Ross could barely breathe. Nevertheless, he smiled; no need to distress the innocent. "Did you find him?"

"Sure, he hadn't gone far. He'll drop her off at the Water Shuttle after he signs all the papers."

Years of good breeding did not desert Ross now. "I'm glad she caught him," he said, reaching into his pocket. "Here's something for your trouble."

Stanley waved a hand. "Forget it. She already gave me a hundred bucks." He tied his boat to the pier. "Care for a beer?"

"Maybe some other time. I've got to get back to work. Thanks for your help." Ross walked unsteadily back to shore.

# 2

God, I feel ill. My heart kicks, my head burns and whirls. She's ruined my life. To think that just yesterday I was a happy man, content to wake up and see her face next to mine, to cuddle her warm body, knowing that this was my wife. Wife! Partner, helpmate, confidante, lamb, home. I've carved great holes in the mud, pulled skyscrapers out of thin air, because of her. She was the bedrock of my accomplishments. How nonchalantly she has destroyed it all. I will never trust a woman again. What fatal indulgence could have made me think that my wife was more honorable than anyone else's wife? She's nothing but an animal after all, wild and amoral, incapable of domestication. For fifteen years I have worshiped an ordinary whore. The slut took everything I had. Then she began fucking Dana.

Dana! We grew up together. We were in the same Cub Scout troop, the same fraternity. . . . I don't believe he's done this to me. Did he struggle at all, try to fight her? Or did it grow gradually and reluctantly over the years, and he just happened to find himself alone with her in an elevator late one afternoon, when *the shadows got long? No matter: Lust is no excuse after all we've been through, all the midnight crunches at the office, the hundreds of times I've saved Dana's ass since he was ten years old. Now he sleeps with my wife? His treachery is infinitely more galling than hers. I'll kill him. At least I'll go to prison with some dignity intact. Without my income, Emily will have to sell the house, move to a ratty little dump in the burbs. No more cabin in the country, no more weekends in Paris. No more nice clothes. She'll have to fry hamburgers for a living, take the bus home at night stinking of grease and onions. And she'll feel bad. Which of her friends will help her out then? Guy Witten? Ha, she just trashed him! Her sister? No way. Philippa's publicist will squeeze as much mileage as possible out of my crime of passion; the moment Emily starts asking for money, Philippa will bolt with a new boyfriend.*

*The hell with Emily. What about me? I can't just move out like some pussy-whipped coward, can't just let her off the hook as if screwing my partner was all right because I knew him so well. And I have no evidence; all I saw her do was go to his boat. Maybe she really was delivering something. Maybe they were planning a surprise party for me; I'll be forty-five soon. And maybe I should tear the house apart, searching for letters and jewelry. Dana is very generous with his screwees: pearls, roses, diamonds if they're truly outstanding. I'll check the safe, root around her lingerie drawer. How many times has she changed the sheets recently? I haven't noticed. Christ, why should I? I was happy! I was confident, too. Was. Maybe I should murder both of them. Stanley could take me out to the boat at once. No, no, I don't want to kill them in bed, allow them to exit this world in each other's arms. They'd wake up together on the other side.*

*Dana's boat is just a speck on the water now. Are they already naked? Or are they sipping an aperitif first? I wonder if they talk about me. What could they possibly tell each other? Between the two of them lies my entire existence, silent and exposed as an open book. Why recite to each other from that? They already know all the words! Oh God, I'm so jealous of the sparks, the secrets, between them. Do they care about excluding*

*the only man on earth who loves them? Of course not. They pre-*
*fer me out of the way; like the crotchety schoolmaster, I wreck*
*all their fun. Dana was always big on fun. Emily was always big*
*on fulfillment, whatever the hell that means. Maybe it means fun*
*now.*

*Stanley's beginning to stare at me. I've got to get back to the*
*office. Marjorie's got people calling, meetings planned. How*
*long did they think they could get away with this? Emily has to*
*realize that Ardith will claw her eyes out. Did she think I would*
*do any less? Did she think she could just come home tonight,*
*smile sweetly at me, cook a cozy little dinner, snuggle up to the*
*dumb Old Man . . . No, I'm not going home tonight. I'm not in*
*control of the situation; the sight of her would put me over the*
*edge. I need a few days alone to think, to plan. Ah, incredible, I*
*don't believe this is happening to me. How quickly, permanently,*
*life can go down the tubes.*

<br>

After leaving Guy's office at Cafe Presto for the last time, Emily
got her sister's red raincoat and made one final pass through the
kitchen. "Bye, Bert," she called. "Remember to collect your fifty
bucks. I just quit."

"You what? How could you do this to me just before lunch!"

Had he said something like "That's awful," she might have
stayed to help him. Now she just smiled and left. From a phone
booth near Faneuil Hall, Emily called her husband's office.

"Hi, Marjorie." In the background, she heard angry voices. "Is
Ross in?"

"Not at the moment." The secretary didn't even try to mask
her impatience.

"Any idea when he's getting back?"

"None at all." Marjorie's voice rose from alto to sopranissimo.
"Mr. Busey! Put that umbrella down, please! Do *not* go into Mr.
Forbes's office!"

"This is a bad time," Emily said. "I'll try later." What was that
all about? She'd learn soon enough: Ross always discussed the

day's misadventures at dinner. She wished he had answered the
phone, wished she could have heard his reassuring voice; only
he could make the knot in her stomach go away. Emily hung up
and wandered along the old wharf buildings. She felt odd out
here at midday; normally she'd be up to her eyeballs in the noon
crush at Cafe Presto. What to do with herself? Lunch at the
Ritz, to celebrate . . . her outstanding integrity? Pfuiii. To initiate her crucifixion. Emily cabbed over. She sat alone near the
drapes and ordered a dozen oysters in memory of Guy, who
claimed she tasted like this succulent, squiggly shellfish. Well,
he would taste her no more.

Emily was on her second martini, last oyster, when a woman
wearing a large blue hat approached. The lady could have been
anywhere between sixty and eighty, depending on the skill of
her plastic surgeon. Two diamond rings, each the size of an animal cracker, sparkled on her blue gloves. Emily noticed the gold
fountain pen just a moment too late.

"I know you," the woman said. "You are Philippa Banks."

"Emily Major." She swallowed the last of her martini. "So
sorry."

"Nonsense, I know Philippa Banks when I see her. Those are
the sunglasses you wore when Roger Farquet raped you in *Pebble
Beach.*" The woman proffered her gold pen. "Please sign my
menu."

"I will not," Emily snapped. "Go back to your seat."

A waiter tiptoed over. "Hines," the woman intoned, "bring
Miss Banks an iced vodka with four dried cherries. It is her favorite drink."

Emily tossed thirty dollars on the table. "Try martini with two
olives." Damn! She should never have exchanged clothes with
her sister! Emily left the Ritz and began walking down Commonwealth Avenue. No one would notice her crying here.
After a few blocks, she felt better, nobler. Perhaps it was the
scenery. This beautiful promenade left no doubt that once upon
a time, Boston had indeed been the Athens of America. Architects had built its shoulder-to-shoulder mansions in an age when
wealth had had no relation to guilt. Today, of course, the mag-

nificent homes were diced into basement think tanks and apartments with too-high ceilings; great chandeliers now illuminated hot photocopiers. Poor America! No wonder Ross rarely walked along this orgy of granite, copper, and leaded glass without remarking that he had been born a century too late.

Emily turned on Dartmouth Street and called her husband again. Perhaps he could join her for coffee, dessert, and a tacit confession; she needed to tell him that she loved him. This time, however, an exasperated assistant told her that Ross was away, Marjorie was at lunch, and there were no pink message slips handy, so please call back later, *click*. Emily saw a movie, ate too much candy, and went home with a bottle of champagne. She made a Key lime pie because last time she had made one for Ross, about three years ago, he had said it was one of his favorite desserts. She cleaned house and took a long shower. Then she went to the balcony overlooking their steep backyard and read a book, waiting for his return. The light slowly faded and she got hungry; at eight o'clock the phone finally rang.

"Emily," said Marjorie. "Ross asked me to leave you a message. He had to go to Montreal tonight. I think he might not be home until Sunday."

"What? Is something wrong?"

"Everything possible went wrong today." As usual, Marjorie furnished no details.

"Where's he staying?"

"He didn't know. He'll call late tonight."

"Call whom, you or me?"

"You, I presume." It was the only polite thing to say. "This all came up at the last minute."

"Thanks, Marjorie. Let me know if you hear anything."

Emily uncorked the champagne before going to the bedroom closet: His overnight bag was gone. His pile of shirts was a little disheveled, as if he had hastily pulled one from the middle. When, though? Emily had been home since four; Ross must have come home before then. Hardly a last-minute emergency. No notes, no messages? She went to the answering machine:

three hang-ups. Maybe he had tried to call while she was at the movies. Unlike him to leave no parting word, though.

Emily returned to the balcony with the champagne and, as the stars pierced the cantaloupe smog, thought about the million tiny, daily details that caused her to love her husband above any other man. The essential virtues—industry, intelligence, humor—didn't qualify him for special distinction since Emily would not have involved herself with any man not possessing them. What set Ross aside was his silence; not the silence of indifference, but the silence of trust. Women who bitched about their husbands not talking to them had never tried to live with a man who needed to know all the mundane and unbrilliant details, who had to talk, talk, talk about feelings and reactions embedded in the genes or in childhood, and there, immutable, for life. Emily preferred the strong, silent man who could live with a few loose ends. Too much talk was a sign of insecurity, a misguided desire to bare all in the forlorn hope that another human being would understand, forgive . . . no way, of course.

Then the pale moon crept up to the clouds and Emily had to consider Guy, the blip in her theory. She hadn't gone looking for him, in fact, hadn't even felt a necessity for him until *wham*, there he was, water to a suddenly pernicious thirst. Ross had not caused the thirst, no no no. Time had. In retaliation she had gulped and bathed; now she was stepping away from that mysterious fountain because she no longer felt thirsty. Not tonight, anyway. Strange; the older she got, the less water she needed. Like a cactus. No doubt it had to do with survival in a vast, childless desert.

Emily put the champagne away and went to bed. Ross did not call and she worried, thinking the problem involved architecture.

Emily's phone rang as first light was graying the bedroom furniture. "Hello?"

"It's me." Didn't sound like him, though. And he didn't apologize for waking her.

"Where are you, honey? Why didn't you call?"

"Couldn't get to a phone." Ross cleared his throat but the tone remained black. "I'm in Montreal."

"For how long? Want me to come up?"

"No."

His clipped, hard voice was beginning to frighten her. She immediately knew that Ross's trouble wasn't work related. "What's the matter?"

Perhaps he tried to clear his throat again. "We'll talk about it later. I have to go now."

"Wait! When will you get back?"

"Monday maybe. Marjorie will know." He hung up.

Ross had never been cruel to his wife before; the effect was devastating. Oh God! Had he found out about Guy? Emily stared at the bedroom ceiling as guilt seeped from head to stomach. Morning coffee did unpleasant things to her digestive tract. Three hours later, she could still barely talk. Finally she called Ross's secretary at home. "Good morning, Marjorie. Did I wake you? I wonder if you could tell me where Ross is staying. I didn't quite catch the hotel when he called this morning."

"I haven't spoken with him since he left."

Damn! "Was this a consulting job?"

"I really couldn't say." Marjorie paused for effect. After a few seconds, realizing she might have overplayed her hand, she added, "It could be a big project."

"Thanks." Emily hung up, finally aware that she was staring at a bottomless weekend, and that spending it alone might ruin her. So she called her new employer at Diavolina. "Ward? You're working early."

"This is Saturday, dear. Every Romeo's big night out."

"Would you like me to come in today? My weekend plans just changed."

"Hey, new blood in the kitchen! I'll warn the troops."

Emily showered and scrutinized her face in the bathroom mirror, wondering how to present the best first impression. Today the raw materials were not promising. Her eyes looked wrinkled and small, like an elephant's. Skin positively yellow, and the frown lines appeared to have been installed by machete. Applying too much makeup to this façade would be like wearing a bad toupee; fakery verging on the comic. She curled her hair instead.

This was no morning to ride the torpid, bacterial subway. A haze redolent of carbon monoxide and dead fish already enveloped Beacon Hill: as Emily crested Joy Street, she realized that this was the hot, sunny weekend that she and Ross had been waiting for all summer. Once the sun cleared the Hancock Building, the faces of bypassing joggers deepened from pulsing, tomatoey red to a brownish purple. Even the most self-conscious pedestrians were beginning to take off their jackets and sweaters.

Ward stood at the bar polishing glasses as Emily arrived at Diavolina. Her hair looked less anarchic today but she wore a pearl in one ear and a gold ball in the other. Blood vessels furled like subcutaneous earthworms along her biceps. "Hello, Major."

"Water," the new chef croaked, slumping over the oak counter. "Air-conditioning."

Ward slid over a glass of water. "So what happened to your weekend?"

"My husband had to work," Emily replied tersely, emptying the glass. She stood up before there could be any further questions. "Okay, where's that kitchen?"

"First things first. Zoltan! Get over here!" Ward shouted.

A black-haired man emerged from the kitchen. Across the dining room, he looked a hale forty. With each approaching step, however, he aged a few years. By the time he reached the bar, Emily guessed she was staring at an eighty-year-old with a scalp full of shoe polish. It was possible he spent half his time as a vampire bat. "I am Zoltan," he announced. "The maître d'. You are Emily."

"He's been here for centuries," Ward said. "Knows everything. That doesn't mean he'll tell you everything, of course." She tucked her service towel under the counter. "Feeling brave?"

Emily stood up, nodding curtly to Zoltan, who was definitely wearing mascara and orange-tinted makeup. The effect was oddly menacing. "Bombs away."

"I told them to be on their best behavior today," Ward said, leading Emily into a clean, modern kitchen. "Attention, animals! This is our new head chef, Emily Major."

Five men and women in white aprons looked up from their worktables. A young Caucasian with a crew cut, one earring, and gender-aspecific tufts of blond facial hair stepped over. "Chef is really a sexist term, Ward. I thought we had agreed on food service manager."

Emily smiled coolly. "I prefer Chef Major, if you don't mind. What would you like me to call you?"

"Chess."

"Short for Francesca," Ward cut in. "She takes care of fruits, vegetables, and Martians." Taking Emily's elbow, Ward proceeded to a rotund black man. "This is Mustapha, our pastry chef."

Someone tittered in the corner. It was the murine fellow who had brought Emily's food to the bar the other day. "Mustapha," he muttered. "Last month it was Dwight."

Ward turned to the source of the comment. "You've already seen Klepp, the garde-manger." Then she led Emily toward an Asian who had been hacking chickens in half at the butcher block. "Here's Yip Chick, the broiler cook." Yip Chick lowered his head slightly but never stopped cleaving poultry. Ward looked around the kitchen. "Where's Byron?"

A soigné blond laden with butter and eggs walked out of the cooler. "My God!" he cried, halting. "What's all this about?"

"This is Head Chef Major," Ward announced. "She was able to begin working a few days early. Major, this is Byron, your first mate. He's been trying to keep us above water recently."

Byron bent at the knee. "I'd shake hands, but I'm just loaded with butter. You may rub my rear end instead. Whoops! I guess that's sexual harassment, isn't it! Pardon me!"

Ward sighed. "You'll get used to him."

Emily watched the cook delicately pile the blocks of butter at his station. "What are you making there, Byron?"

"Butter birds."

"He makes little sculptures on Saturday night," Klepp said in yet another accent that Emily could not place. "Puffs and shavings for the bread basket. Terribly cute."

"Stop picking on him because of his sexual orientation," reprimanded Chess, the vegetable woman.

A cloud of steam suddenly billowed from the dishwashers. "Ah, I've forgotten someone," Ward exclaimed. "Slavomir! Come here!" The slight, elderly man wielding the water hoses either heard nothing or ignored everything. He seemed to be chanting to himself as he ricocheted water off porcelain, creating a fine mist throughout the area. Ward led Emily to the corner. "Slavomir, this is Emily, our new chef."

"Hxxxi," the man said absently. Then he looked over. "Ehhh!" he cried, dropping the hose.

Ward lunged for the dancing nozzle, finally managing to turn the water off. "He frightens easily," she explained, tossing Emily a towel. "And he doesn't speak much English. Klepp can translate the Russian if absolutely necessary."

"Klepp is Russian?"

"No, Estonian. He hates Russians."

"Aha." Emily's drenched blouse adhered to her bra. "Have we missed anyone?"

"No, that about does it. You'll meet the waiters and waitresses soon enough."

"*Waitron* is the preferred term," Chess called.

A curvaceous young woman entered the kitchen. Her black halter set off, among other things, a golden tan and slender neck. She knew her face was attractive. "Good morning," she called, sailing to the coffee machine. Those in her wake sensed a light, spicy perfume.

"This is Lola," Ward told Emily. "One of the wa—serving staff."

"It would be criminal to call a woman like that a waitron," Klepp mused. "Good morning, love. Try to sell a lot of asparagus quiche for me today, would you?"

Ward looked at her watch. "Take it away, Major." She returned to the dining room.

Except for the mutters of the dishwater and indefatigable chopping at the butcher block, the kitchen was silent for a few moments after Ward had left. It was not a sympathetic silence and for a tiny second, Emily foresaw disaster here. "Please go about your business," she said finally. "Today I'll just be observing."

Byron leaped into action. "You need an apron, honey." He lowered his voice. "Come to the locker room."

Emily followed him out back, where the sous-chef removed a clean apron from a drawer. "Listen, sugar pie, this is the scoop," he said. "You're going to have trouble with Francesca. She's a bitch. Yip Chick swam over from China. He'll be all right if you let him steal an occasional side of beef. Mustapha burns about half the desserts he makes. Klepp is a homophobic maniac. And Slavomir is a walking vodka bottle. He occasionally tries to drown himself in the dishwater."

"Excellent," Emily commented, tying her apron. "What about you?"

"I'm perfect, darling." Pausing in front of a wall mirror, Byron adjusted his coiffure. "Cooking's just a sideline. I'm really an actor. People tell me I look like a blond Tom Cruise."

Emily tried not to laugh. Byron was at least fifty years old. "No kidding."

"I'm between soaps at the moment." He admired his three-quarter profile in the mirror. "Did anyone ever tell you you're the spitting image of Philippa Banks? Only your hair's different."

Smiling blandly, Emily went to the door. "What about Ward?"

"She's working out some problems through weight lifting. Need I say more?"

"No thank you. How about a tour of the premises?"

Byron led Emily down a tiled hallway. "Where did you work before, Maje?"

"Cafe Presto. Near Quincy Market."

"Oh! Is that the place that wins those awards all the time?"

"Yes." Emily followed him into a cool, dark room smelling of earth and spices. She walked slowly past the well-stocked shelves, stopping in front of a crate of mushrooms. "Chanterelles," she said, sniffing. "Where are they from?"

"A monastery. The monks pick them in the woods and bring them here. Actually, only one brings them in. He's quite cute. Much too cute to be a monk. Such a waste."

Emily eyed a small basket. "Peace Power Farm. Never heard of it. Where's Hale, Massachusetts?"

"Midstate, I think. They supply milk, butter, herbs, and the rankest goat cheese in creation. The delivery woman makes Ward look like a cream puff."

"When's she coming in next?"

"Monday. So is the monk."

Emily and Byron returned to the kitchen. Several of the serving staff had arrived and were chatting with Lola at the coffee machine. "New dictator," Byron called, "Leo's replacement." They waved.

Emily ambled to the pastry chef, who was removing a few cakes from the oven. "How's everything over here, Mustapha?"

They both stared at his dark, fissured handiwork. "Something's wrong with this oven," he said after a moment.

The nearly black cakes looked fused to the pans. Emily resisted an urge to ask where Mustapha kept his crowbar. "What are you making?"

"Burnt Molasses Cake. It's a secret recipe from my family."

"Can you serve them this way?"

"They're supposed to be a little burned. Otherwise the flavors don't come out."

Emily looked into the refrigerator. "I saw something called Chocolate Morgue on the menu. Could you tell me a little about it?"

"It's chocolate. Eat too much and you'll die."

"I see. Carry on." Emily left the pastry station and went to Chess, who was dicing eggplant. "Ratatouille?"

"Pastitsio," Chess said, sliding the eggplant into a large pot.

"Meatless. I hope you don't mind if I just call you Emily. The word *chef* is deeply offensive to me."

"Chef is gender neutral."

"But it implies that certain workers are more important than others. We're trying to make this a nonprejudicial work area."

Emily placed the lid on the eggplant pot. "Let's get something straight, Francesca. My name's Chef Major. I am now the boss here. You are not my equal. If you don't like that, then leave."

"Yeah!" cheered Klepp, stowing a few quiches into his oven.

Across the way, a modest altercation between Byron and Slavomir suddenly blossomed into an opera. "Wash it over again!" the sous-chef screamed as the dishwasher spewed a river of Russian at his tormentor.

"I'm not going to translate that, Byron-Boy," Klepp said. "But it's anatomically accurate."

Emily strode to the dishwasher, catching Slavomir's hand before he launched a cup. "What's the problem here, Byron?" she asked.

The sous-chef showed her a white dish. "Look at that."

"I don't see anything."

"You're not looking at the right angle. See that smear?"

"No. Stop this nonsense." As Emily put the plate on the outgoing stack, the dishwasher's ranting intensified. "What's he saying, Klepp?" she called.

"He says you're a devil."

No one even tut-tutted in her defense. After a moment, Emily turned to Byron. "I'd like a complete inventory of provisions. Now."

She watched him stomp off, then went to the broiler, where Yip Chick was thwacking poultry with his cleaver. "How's everything here?"

Yip Chick immediately stopped and gazed fixedly at her forehead. "Don't stand so close, lady," Mustapha called. "It makes him nervous."

Emily stepped backward, thought a moment, then went out to the dining room. She found Ward at the bar watching a col-

lege football game with a few customers. "What's the verdict,
Chef?" Ward asked, finally noticing her.

"I quit." Emily ignored Ward's little laugh. "They're lunatics."

"I told you they might be difficult. But give me specifics.
Were you insulted?"

"Not directly."

"Disobeyed?"

"No."

"Are they incompetent?"

"Probably not."

"Then what's the problem?"

"They detest each other. And me," Emily said. "How'd it get
that way?"

"What can I tell you? This is nineties America." Ward polished a few wineglasses with her service towel. "Come on, give
it a try. I'll back you up."

"I'm a chef, not the UN Peacekeeping Force."

"One week. Then you can decide. Please."

Emily still hesitated. "What happened to the other chef?"

"Leo? I told you. He disappeared on me. Come on, Major.
You said you needed this job. I believed you."

Ah, why not. It was better than waiting for her husband to
come home and beat her to death. "One week," Emily said.
"That's it. Now where's my office? I'd like to go over a few files."

After several hours, Emily returned to the kitchen. By then,
Byron had shouted himself hoarse and Slavomir was moving
with the deliberate grace of the totally drunk. Mustapha, who
had arrived at five that morning, had gone home; Klepp was
rhythmically passing a slab of prosciutto over the slicing machine. Chess shredded lettuce. In the dining room, Zoltan was
instructing the staff how to pronounce the evening's specials.
He expected a packed house: There would be no better night
this year to exhibit the summer lovers everyone had picked up
on Nantucket.

Diavolina's first customers trickled in around five o'clock,
wanting shrimp and beer. By six, every table was full. Everyone
seemed to be ordering chicken; as Yip Chick's mountain of

poultry hissed under the broiler, he gradually acquired the hue of a Peking duck. Byron became a swing cook, flying Superman-like to various stations, defeating catastrophes. The waitrons only screwed up a few orders and the kitchen didn't run out of anything but Mustapha's Burnt Molasses Cake, which Lola was pushing aggressively in the dining room. Emily slaved until midnight, then stayed another hour talking to Ward about menu changes. She took a cab home, found no messages on her machine, and dropped into bed, missing Ross dreadfully. After brutal days at Cafe Presto, he would often massage her feet and toes; it was no good trying to do that sort of thing herself. She watched a Bette Davis movie, drifting off occasionally, waking when she thought she heard her husband coming in downstairs. When the birds began to chirp, she knew she'd be alone another day.

# 3

A pale yellow haze, anemic with yesterday's residual heat, enveloped Boston. The sun drifted upward, raising the temperature of an already molten metropolis. Soon many air conditioners would die. Once again, Emily awoke dull and anxious for her husband. She was used to him there beside her in the morning; he was part of getting up and facing the day, an unacknowledged necessity like hot water and electricity, absence of which suddenly turned the simplest routines into unpleasant little ordeals. Her ankles were swollen, as she discovered with her first step out of bed: too much standing yesterday, then no foot massage. Emily pulled on some clothes and got the Sunday papers at a newsstand at the bottom of Joy Street. She bought croissants and fresh orange juice. A steady, salty breeze blew over Beacon Hill, less to cool its inhabitants than to flee a gigantic front rolling in from the Midwest; perhaps it would all accumulate into a thunderstorm this afternoon. Emily took the news and breakfast home, ate and tried to read about the same old earthquakes and assassinations. Even the crossword puzzle irritated her. Where was Ross, damn him?

She went to the garage, inflated the tires on her racing bike, and took a long ride along the Charles River. Rollerbladers eddied over the Promenade, occasionally slapping joggers with their flailing arms. The owners of expensive dogs on expensive long leashes paraded grandly along the macadam, perhaps unaware of the traffic they were forcing into the grass. Less expensive dogs, without leashes, chased ducks and children, yelping when they got hit by cyclists training for the Tour de France. The putt-putt of pleasure boats sounded lazily over the water. As she passed the marina, Emily checked for Dana's boat: gone, of course. He and Philippa were probably screwing each other blind as they drifted toward the Bermuda Triangle. Three days asea now: Were those two scoundrels cured of each other yet? There was a phone onboard Dana's boat, Emily knew; for several moments, she stared toward the harbor, needing her sister, willing her to call. Sometimes the telepathy worked.

As the haze broke, the temperature ruthlessly rose. Emily went home. Still no blinking light on her answering machine; this time, she did not check that it had somehow become disconnected. She drank a quart of water, hoping to stop the pounding in her temple. Then she showered and returned to the restaurant.

Brunch was on. Ward stood at the bar watching another football game. She looked as if she had slept in the apron drawer. "Hey Major! Back for more?" she called, noticing Emily during a car commercial.

"Right. Did you go home at all?"

"I lifted weights instead. More therapeutic."

Uncertain how to respond, Emily went to the kitchen, where Klepp, Chess, and Yip Chick grunted a hello. Mustapha was off, observing the sabbath, while Byron worshiped the flesh in Provincetown. Emily glanced over the incoming orders as Chess juiced oranges and Yip Chick attacked another mound of chickens. "Where's Slavomir?" she asked.

"Puking his brains out," Klepp replied, looking up from his

omelettes and pancakes. "He generally overdrinks on Saturday night."

The wretched dishwasher soon shuffled back from the bathroom to resume his duties. Brunch passed lethargically, as did the afternoon. Diavolina's patrons were content to chew quietly as football, America's Sunday opiate, pounded across the television at the bar. During the midafternoon lull, Emily devised new menus, tested a few recipes. When the sun eventually set and her husband had still not called, she went to the bar. "Gin, please," she told Ward. "One ice cube and two olives." She glanced at the television just as the quarterback got sacked.

Ward could guess that her new chef's anemia had nothing to do with Diavolina. "Thanks for coming in," she said, placing a large glass in front of Emily. "You inspire the kitchen."

"How so?"

"You take their minds off of killing each other. Now they're all trying to figure out how to kill you instead. I'm deeply grateful."

Not sure whether or not Ward was kidding, Emily tossed back her gin. For a few minutes, she watched chunky humanoids on television slam into each other. When a beer ad interrupted that phony war, she stood up. "When does the monk with the mushrooms show up tomorrow?"

"Six, six-thirty. He's usually first."

"I'll be here. Good night."

A few men at the bar watched her leave. "Yours?" one of them asked Ward.

"For a week," she replied, dispensing beer.

"Looks terrific. But can she cook?"

Ward guffawed softly. "Does it matter?" She half turned her attention back to the football game.

Once again, Emily returned to an empty, accusing house. Fear for her husband's safety had given way to a thought-obliterating panic. She was lying on the couch, swollen legs upraised, when the phone rang. "Hello?"

"Hi, darling," Philippa said. "Did you get to the country this weekend? So stinking hot!"

"No. Ross had a job in Montreal." Emily replaced an ice bag over her forehead. Her skull felt thick and hot as a cast-iron skillet. "Where are you?"

"Lost at sea. Aren't we, smoochkin?" For a few moments, Philippa's voice became smeared and gooey. Then her mouth returned to the phone. "You and Ross must come to dinner with us tomorrow night."

Emily sighed. "Dana's still married, Philippa."

"Did you hear that? She says you're still married!" Again Philippa's voice became momentarily overmushed. "So! How about it, Em?"

"Did you hear me? I said Ross is away. He might be away for a week, for all I know."

"Then let's the three of us go out."

"I have a new job," Emily replied. "I'll be working late."

"You mean you're not at that nice little cafe anymore?"

"No, I'm in the South End now. A place called Diavolina."

"What a cunning name! Have you ever eaten at Diavolina, poopsie?" Phil and Poopsie conferred at length. "Dana says he knows it well. Let's meet there."

"You'll have to eat without me. I won't get out of the kitchen until eleven."

"So we'll come around nine-thirty. We probably won't be getting out of bed until noon anyway."

Emily remembered Ross's comment about needing Dana in the office Monday. "Your boyfriend does plan to go ashore tomorrow, doesn't he?"

"Of course! I've got interviews. Ouch! No pinching, bubbala!" Philippa dropped the phone. "Sorry, Em. It's so beautiful out here. You should see the stars. And all these little sailboats bobbing on the water. What did you do all weekend?"

"I told you. Worked." Emily felt like crying: Suddenly, ferociously, she missed Guy.

"When's Ross coming home, poor thing?"

"Tomorrow, I guess."

"Are you all right? You sound a little funny. Emily?"

"Just tired."

Philippa knew better than that, even with Dana in her lap. "What is it, honey?"

"Nothing. Just the heat."

They talked a little about Philippa's latest movie, a little about maybe meeting next month in Paris. After hanging up, Philippa stared at the reflection of the moon upon the waves. Emily's flat voice had disturbed her. "Something's wrong there," she said to Dana.

He kissed her knees. "Maybe she needs a lover."

Philippa turned abruptly away; for the first time, he had irritated her. "Maybe she's got one, you fool." She continued to study the moon-dappled water, ignoring him, as his lips grazed her long legs.

Guy Witten had had a rotten weekend. No Emily, no life: It was that simple. He had been in love with her for years, in bed with her for one glorious night, and now she was gone, pretending that Niagara could just evaporate. She was thinking too much, as usual, fanning her guilt until it charred their smallest bliss. Now the saint had returned to her husband, sacrificing Guy on the fatuous altar of fidelity: Did she really prefer Ross and his drawing pencils? Stupid woman! Her even stupider husband didn't have the slightest clue what she had been feeling for the last few years. Husbands preferred to interpret a midlife surge in cosmetic, undergarment, and hairdresser bills as feminine pride rather than horrific desperation. Just because Emily didn't complain, Ross probably thought she was content. But women were never content. When they were twenty, they wanted rich husbands and grand careers. When they were thirty, they wanted superb children. But when they were forty, ever so slightly beginning to fatigue as husbands and children and careers wandered away from them, that genetic discontent became a roaring blaze, melting sanity, gutting caution: Then they were quivering perfection. Emily was, anyway. Guy sighed, wanting her terribly. She was perfect in bed, all soft yawls and sighs, an exquisite mesh of perfumes. Why were the most provocative women always married? To bores? Deep down, did they really want to be left alone, resuscitated every so often by an eager, disposable lover? How insulting.

Guy spent most of the weekend at Cafe Presto interviewing replacement chefs, all inferior in talent and pulchritude to Emily. He finally settled on a Swedish woman with the vivacity of a rolling pin. On Sunday, eviscerated, he went fishing. Early Monday he was back at Toto's Gym working off half a case of beer. Guy's chin was touching the mat for his ninety-eighth push-up when an instructor brought the phone over. "It's your lady."

He grabbed the handset, relieved and overjoyed, bleeding to touch her again. "Good morning."

"Sorry to disturb you," Emily said.

Only four words lasting one second, yet her voice had transmitted the necessary data: This was no kiss-and-make-up call. He clipped his voice accordingly. "No problem."

She crunched into business mode. "Have you been speaking to Ross lately?"

"You've got to be kidding. Why?"

"I think he knows."

"Acting strange, is he?" This time there was such a long silence that Guy knew he had made her cry: agony. "What happened, sweetie?"

"He left without a word on Friday and hasn't called since. He never does that."

"Where'd he go? Tokyo?"

"Montreal. I don't know which hotel. Neither does his secretary, or so she says."

"Is she covering for him?"

"Oh come on!"

He closed his eyes: Even her screeches balmed his soul. "We've been careful, Em. No one knows." She didn't hang up; maybe there was still hope. "What have you been doing all weekend, worrying about it?"

"I've been working."

"You found a job already? Why you little weasel. Where?"

She sniffled. "A place called Diavolina. In the South End. Ever hear of it?"

"It's awful." They were lapsing into ambiguous, uninterpretable silences. He had to get off the phone before he totally lost control. "I miss you, baby," Guy said. "Let me know if the old man doesn't come home." He hung up.

During the night, the heat swelled and the electricity failed. Emily awoke in a sweat, glanced at her flashing clock radio, and swore: Monday was off to a tardy start. Hastily combing her hair back, hardly bothering with makeup, screw the power dressing, she arrived at Diavolina shortly after six o'clock, as the clouds began spitting raindrops on sunburned commuters. Byron was at the back of the kitchen already swallowing his third cup of coffee as he finished today's crossword puzzle. Yesterday's sun/surf had burnished his tan and bleached his hair; a few more days on the beach and he'd look like a negative of a scarecrow. "Good morning," Emily said. "How was Provincetown?"

"Great. I haven't been to bed yet." Byron turned to the arts section and read the caption beneath a large picture. "Hey! Phil's new movie opens Friday! I've got to see that." He held the paper up. "Your resemblance is quite remarkable, you know. Have you ever thought of being a body double?"

Emily took the paper away from Byron. "Do you like her?"

"Philippa Banks? I adore her! She's made beach movies an art form!" Byron flexed his sagging biceps. "I used to be in beach movies myself. The muscle man in the bikini. Now I prefer doing the soaps. You don't catch as many colds."

"Have you ever worked with her?"

"Gad, no! Philippa's big time! I'm just skin."

"She might be coming for dinner tonight around nine-thirty." While Byron was still swallowing that ostrich egg, Emily casually added, "She's dating my husband's business partner."

"No! That's incredible! I've got to make the dinner, Maje! Please!"

Emily already regretted her moment of one-upmanship.

"Only if you don't tell anyone she's coming. I don't need a free-for-all back here. Understood?"

"My lips are sealed." Byron clanked his cup in the dishwasher. "This calls for a special menu. Everything she likes."

"Her boyfriend likes lobster."

"Forget the boyfriend!" Byron went to the pay phone near the kitchen door. "Jimmy, wake up! You're not going to believe this. I'm making dinner for Philippa Banks tonight. Do you want the table next to hers? Get here at eight, then. Wear your blue Perry Ellis. And don't tell anybody!" He hung up. "Egad! I'm not sure Ward stocks dried cherries!" He ran to the bar.

The service doorbell rang. Scowling, Emily went to answer it.

A man perhaps still in his sixties, strong of face, soft of eye, stood outside. White shirt and white hat gleamed in the sunlight, giving him the aura of a visiting angel. Seeing Emily, he stared for a long time; maybe his eyes were adjusting to the indoors. "Excuse me," he said finally, "I was expecting Leo. I'm Brother Augustine, the mushroom man." He held up his basket.

"Emily Major, the new chef." She led him to a sideboard.

He lifted the napkin covering his large basket. As he spoke, the quaver gradually left his voice. "This was a good week. We found cèpes, morels, even some grisettes. Quite rare in these parts now. You should use them as soon as possible."

Byron returned from the bar. "Hey Augie! Any truffles in that basket?"

"I brought you grisettes instead. Very special."

"I'll use them tonight. A movie star is coming to dinner."

Emily interrupted before Byron could bore the monk with irrelevant details about an actress he had probably never seen and never would. "We won't keep you, Brother Augustine," she said. "I'm sure you've got many stops to make today."

"Are you kidding?" Byron laughed. "We're his only stop. He's got to get back to his cubicle and pray. How do you do it, Augie? Fifteen hours a day on your knees—just praying?!"

"That's what hope is all about, isn't it?" the monk said. "I'll see you next week, Byron."

Emily caught up with Augustine at the door. "You'll send an invoice, then?"

"No. Your predecessor and I had an arrangement."

"My predecessor is gone."

"The debt remains." He got into his small, rusty car. "Eat those grisettes tonight. They're best with port and thyme." He backed onto Tremont Street and drove away.

Emily returned to the kitchen. "Byron, one more slip of your tongue and dinner's off. I said tell no one and I meant it."

"Sorry! I thought you meant don't tell anyone who worked here!"

A pickup truck veered into the driveway. Rock music bounced off the brick walls as it sped through the narrow passageway, halting sharply at the kitchen door.

"That's Bruna," Byron announced.

"Who?"

"Your milk and cheese lady from the Peace Power Farm. If we're lucky, she's got some quail eggs."

Someone pounded on the door. Before Emily or Byron could get to it, a woman in a tank top broke in. Her body was a thicket of even more grotesque muscles and tattoos than Ward's. Her recent journey in a pickup truck had distressed her coiffure; freed from the ribbon at the nape of her neck, mounds of screech-yellow hair frizzed into space. Cursing her burden, she staggered toward the refrigerator. "Open the door," she snapped at Byron. "This had better not be curdled or you won't be getting any more."

"You don't have a refrigerated truck?" Emily asked.

"I don't release any more fluorocarbons into the atmosphere than I have to." Done unpacking the milk bottles, she began stacking little logs of goat cheese on a shelf. "I made a batch with chives and lemon grass, like you wanted. Where's Leo?"

"Gone with the wind," Byron replied. "This is Chef Major, his replacement. Maje, this is Bruna. Makes goat cheese and other smelly things."

Bruna returned to her truck, brought in another pair of crates, and continued loading the refrigerator. Suddenly she turned her electric blue eyes on Emily. "Who did the man say you were?"

"Emily Major." She offered her hand, at the risk of getting crushed. "Pleased to meet you."

"Leo's gone? Is he sick? Where'd he go?"

"Who knows?" Byron exclaimed. "Did you bring any quail eggs for me today? I'm desperate for something special."

Bruna removed a small carton from her crate. "Black currants. Best of the season." As Byron pounced on them, she added, "Six bucks a pint."

"Are you out of your mind?"

Bruna pulled the cartons out of Byron's reach. "If you don't buy them, my next customer will."

"We'll take them then," Emily said, trying not to stare at Bruna's upper body. She had absolutely no breasts, just wartlike growths where the nipples ought to be. The last thing Emily would wear, if she had a bustline like Bruna's, would be a tank top. "If you'll come to my office, I'll write you a check."

The woman's face darkened. "I need to speak to Leo."

"You find him, you can speak to him," Byron answered. "He didn't leave a forwarding address."

Bruna hesitated a moment, then bowed toward Emily. "I'll be back Thursday."

After the door had slammed, Emily turned to the sous-chef. "Where'd she come from? Same place as Ward?"

"You'll have to ask Leo. I'm sure it's a colorful tale. He always preferred to do business with slightly irregular people. And the criminally insane, like Klepp. Said it kept him on his toes."

Emily carefully put the berries into a colander. "Where do you think Leo went?"

"Went? He probably got himself murdered, Maje. Leo was a wild man."

"Didn't he have a family?"

"If he did, they left him a long time ago. He never mentioned any personal details."

"How long was he here?"

"At this restaurant? Forever."

The doorbell rang again. Emily met a greengrocer, a butcher, and an old Italian woman who made the *biscotti*. She spoke little English, accepted no payment, and asked a dozen times for Leo, leaving only after Byron had convinced her that Leo was on vacation. Deliveries and introductions continued all morning; every single supplier was dismayed to see Emily instead of her predecessor. One by one, as the rest of the kitchen staff arrived, Byron announced that dinner that evening had better be very, very special. Since he would not explain why, everyone assumed that the restaurant critic would be coming and reacted accordingly. Klepp suggested poisoning the mashed potatoes. Chess and Byron almost came to blows over proprietorship of the new mushrooms. Mustapha began preparing an elaborate chocolate concoction, ignoring the cakes he already had in the oven, with sooty results. A hectic lunch was made even more so by two AWOL waitresses and no Slavomir. Around three, when the dining room finally emptied, Emily found Ward at the bar. "I thought Mondays were slow here," Emily said.

"Maybe there's a convention."

Zoltan, the maître d', stepped behind them. "I have forty reservations for dinner. The phone's been ringing nonstop. Everybody wants to sit next to someone named Phil or Flip. What's going on?"

"Who knows," Ward muttered. "But you'd better make sure you have enough staff tonight. I have to see my therapist at eight. Someone's got to cover the bar for me."

The phone at Zoltan's elbow rang. "Diavolina," he announced testily, then listened a moment. "For you," he told Emily. "A gentleman."

Ross! She tried to keep her voice regular, vernal, as if her husband had just returned from a brief road trip. "Hello?"

"I have to see you," said Guy Witten. "Now."

"Today is not good," Emily replied innocently. "Could we reschedule for next week?" She hung up, blinking slowly; his voice still ruffled her stomach. "My hairdresser," she explained to Zoltan.

"Of course." The maître d' smirked. By now, he could identify an affair in two syllables or less. Sometimes all the evidence he needed was the breathing on one end of the telephone.

Klepp stuck his head through the kitchen doors. "Florist's here, Major," he called. "Want me to take care of him?"

Emily left the bar. She met a few more suppliers, all asking for Leo. Just before five, she called her husband's office. "Hi Marjorie. If Ross checks in, could you tell him I'll be late tonight?"

"Tell him yourself." The line clicked; only after hearing the dial tone did Emily realize that Marjorie had hung up on her.

Early Monday morning, Dana Forbes reluctantly skippered his boat, and Philippa, back to shore. At her hotel by eight, Philippa immediately fell asleep and did not call her sister until long after Emily had left for work. Philippa would have called the restaurant had she remembered its name. Something like Diabolica. The phone company couldn't help so Philippa took a luxurious bath and prepared to meet a parade of journalists in her suite at the Four Seasons. She and Dana had arranged to meet downtown, at his office, when she finished.

Ah, Dana! Her mood fluttered between ecstasy at striking— once again—sexual lightning, and depression at knowing that— once again—the affair had already flopped. Dana would never marry her. He already had several teenage children and a wife who didn't care where he slept. He headed the Numero Uno architectural firm in a town with great restaurants. Why give that up for an over-the-hill actress who wanted a husband like Fred MacMurray? Moreover, an actress who happened to be his partner's sister-in-law? Philippa chuckled to herself: It was tragedy to be born with both brain cells and estrogen. She got out of the bathtub, uncheered by the sight of her body in the mirror. It had accommodated, hastily and cheaply, far too many men. Where were they now? Gone, like her youth. Lately she had begun to dream about herself, toothless, mustachioed, and incontinent, in a nursing home. Strangers would stare at her and whisper, "That old hag used to be Philippa Banks." Gad! She should have been a painter, a writer, a sculptress: In those professions, wrinkles connoted achievement. In hers, they meant the unemployment line. She was already beginning to feel like an out-of-print book. Philippa stared at her face in the mirror and suddenly became depressed at the thousands of dollars she had spent over the years on makeup, private exercise instructors, health spas, hairdressers, and dieticians. Even after a long bath she looked older than her twin sister, who had done nothing to preserve herself but slap on a little cold cream and an occasional pair of jogging shoes. And Emily had a husband: a license to decrepitate with dignity.

Philippa ordered a bottle of champagne and dressed in a peach silk lounging ensemble. She threw her brunette wig into a suitcase and arranged her light blond hair, which over the years had cost her about a buck a strand, into a casual tumble. She was feeling somewhat better when her first interviewer arrived. They discussed Philippa's new movie, *Choke Hold*, a romantic thriller about a woman and an acrobat. After much gossip about the movie industry, the journalist looked at his crib sheet. "And how is your husband?" he asked. "Is the *Concorde* still your preferred getaway for a few hours together?"

Philippa stiffened. "I am no longer married. That must be a very old news release."

"Your manager just faxed it to me yesterday." Flustered, the newsman looked for other items of human interest, found none, and said, "Well, I admire your courage, at least."

"Courage? Hardly." Philippa lit a cigarette and blew curtly at the gods. "I am a poor judge of men. Just like my mother. She was seduced and abandoned."

"You're illegitimate?"

Philippa shrugged philosophically. "She died shortly after I was born. An uncle brought us up."

"Us?"

"Brought me up, I mean," Philippa smoothly corrected herself. Years ago, Emily and she had agreed to leave twins out of the PR scenario. It took attention away from Philippa and undermined Emily's credibility as a normal human being. "I never knew my father. Maybe it was better that way."

"You're probably searching for your father through all these husbands," the interviewer offered.

Ass, Philippa thought as she nodded sagely. "Very perceptive." Suddenly bored with this stupid man, she glanced at her diamond-barnacled watch. "I'm afraid you must excuse me." She walked to the door, knowing that her silken entrails floated enticingly behind. "Please phone whenever you're in Paris."

The next journalist, a woman recently divorced, questioned Philippa incessantly about the ins and outs of marriage, Hollywood style. The interview ended abruptly when the lady turned her attention to the lack of good roles for middle-aged actresses.

Finally a television crew arrived. Philippa's boredom was mitigated by a handsome cameraman who was obviously fascinated with her; throughout the interview, she eyed him flirtatiously as she answered questions about the off-screen romance between herself and her *Choke Hold* costar, a liaison that everyone knew to be a fabrication of their press agents. As the crew was readying to leave, the cameraman quietly approached her with a gleam in his blue eyes. Her heart beat just a little bit faster.

"This is strange," he said, "but I know someone who looks exactly like you."

Philippa's beckoning smile froze. "Is that so?"

"Really. The lady behind the counter at Cafe Presto. I stop in every morning for coffee on the way to work." He zipped his camera case shut. "But I haven't seen her since the middle of the week. It really wrecks my day."

When the crew departed, Philippa finished the champagne. She tucked her gorgeous blond hair back under the brunette wig. Then she put on a tremendous white hat and Emily's sunglasses, found a cab, and commanded the driver to take her to State Street. Using the key Dana had given her that morning, she went in the private entrance of Major & Forbes, Architects. Her lover was alone in his stupendous office. However, he was on the phone with his wife.

". . . dinner with an important client," he was saying as he blew a kiss to Philippa. "I don't think I'll be able to make it, Ardith." There was a short pause. "Eh—I don't think you should join us, sweetheart. It would be a little awkward. No, that's the whole problem. Ross can't handle it. He's out of town. It's not my choice, believe me." He smiled again at Philippa. "I'll try to be home by eleven. Love you too." He hung up.

"You bastard," Philippa snapped.

Dana strode across the room and kissed her soundly. "She said she loved me. What am I supposed to say back, something like 'No kidding'? It doesn't mean anything anyway. It's like Please and Thank You. One phrase triggers the other. In polite society, that is." To illustrate his point, he said, "I love you."

Philippa scowled. "No kidding." She twisted out of his arms and went to a bronze bust on a pedestal in the corner. "Is this supposed to be the great you?"

"Who else? How do you like it?"

She ran a finger along its nose. "Beats a hat rack, I suppose." After perching her frilly bonnet on it, Philippa walked to the window. Pouting, she watched the sailboats in Boston Harbor. For a few hours, she had actually been happy among them. "Where's Ross?"

"Who knows? Fishing with the Micmacs. All this preaching about needing me in the office on Monday, then he doesn't even come in. The secretary says he's in Canada on some hush-hush project she can't divulge. It's her way of punishing me for not writing my whereabouts in the appointment book like a good boy." Catching up with Philippa at the window, Dana began nibbling the back of her neck. "I haven't made love with you in almost four hours." He slid a hand beneath her fluttery tunic. "Would you like to make up for lost time?"

"Here? You're an animal." But she didn't back away; the idea of misbehaving on the windowsill, in view of hundreds of strangers in the adjacent skyscraper, intrigued her.

Their oral cavities were steeply countersunk when, after two short knocks, Marjorie walked into Dana's office. "Excuse me!" she gasped, seeing them. "I thought you were alone."

"Thank you, Marjorie," said Dana, smartly disengaging himself. "I'll be right with you." The distraught woman left.

Philippa immediately pushed him away. "Damn you, I knew

that was a bad idea. Did you see the way she looked at me? This fucking wig! She thinks I'm Emily."

A slow smile spread across Dana's face. He straightened his tie. "Let's have some fun," he said. "Please, Phil. I'll never get another chance to razz Marjorie like this."

"No way. Emily would kill me."

"Are you kidding? She'd love it. Marjorie has been sending Ross anonymous Valentines for ten years."

Philippa still hesitated. "She'll be able to tell I'm not Emily." Too many wrinkles.

"I'll bet you dinner tonight she can't. Come on." He patted her clothes back in place and, taking her hand, tiptoed to the door of his office.

"What am I supposed to do?" Philippa whispered. "Really, Dana, this is so stupid!"

"Shhh!" He ushered her to the front desk, where Marjorie was furiously pounding her electric typewriter. Across the foyer, waiting for her appointment, sat a dowager wearing a black hat. She probably hunched over due to the tonnage of her pearl necklaces. With considerable pleasure, Dana noticed that the woman recognized Philippa instantly: The magazine she was reading dropped to her lap as she stared at the famous actress. Quickly realizing that an autograph request could ruin his little joke, however, Dana became very businesslike. "Marjie," he asked smoothly, "has Ross called in yet?"

"No," she snapped, glaring briefly at Philippa.

"It would be helpful to know when he's coming back. Where's my appointment book?" The irate secretary shoved it toward Dana's side of the desk. "Thank you. Nine-thirty tonight at Diavolina, darling?" he asked Philippa, writing the name of the restaurant in large block letters on the proper line. Dana was about to tell Marjorie that he'd be disappearing for a few hours when she slipped a small yellow note in front of him. *Dagmar Pola*, it said. An arrow pointed toward the woman in the black hat. *Lunch at Locke Ober.*

Dana Forbes had not risen to the apex of his profession by lunching with girlfriends instead of moneyed clients; also, with the wisdom of middle age, he had finally come to realize that bedding a femme fatale would ultimately generate less bliss than would building a new museum. So he took Philippa's arm and paraded her to the door. In the hallway, he laughed apologetically. "I completely forgot about that appointment."

Philippa stared at him a moment. "You're not standing me up, are you?"

"What can I say, tiger? Business before pleasure. Age before beauty." He kissed her forehead. "Go to the hotel. I'll be there naked in two hours."

"I won't." Philippa donned her sunglasses. Silks aquiver, she stalked toward the elevator and boarded without looking back, not because she wanted to cut Dana, but because she was afraid he might not still be standing forlornly in the hallway, watching her leave.

And in fact, he wasn't. "Madame Pola," Dana cried effusively, reentering his office. "This is a rare pleasure." He took her thin, cold hands, wondering why old ladies' diamond rings were always too large for their fingers, so that they clicked and slid like false teeth in a glass. "I'm afraid Ross was called to Washington this morning. State Department consultations. I'm delighted to have you all to myself. Come in, come in!" With a grandiose gesture, he swept her into his office. "Would you care for a drink before lunch?"

"No thank you." Dagmar peered at the bust in the corner. Its chin was barely visible beneath Philippa's fluent millinery. "Works of art should not be used as hat racks, Mr. Forbes."

"I'll scold the offending party. But I'm flattered that you would consider my likeness a work of art." Dana went to the bar. As he was mixing himself a highball, Dagmar surveyed the array of pill bottles on his desktop.

"Are you an architect or a pharmacist?" she asked.

"Ha-ha! You know the answer to that, I hope!" Where the hell was Ross, damn it? Dana hated trying to charm women who didn't excite him sexually. It was a thankless endeavor, like pitting prunes. "Have you been to Locke Ober recently, Madame Pola?" he said, sitting beside her on his sofa.

Dagmar wryly studied his face; after a lifetime with Joe Pola and his nonstop mistresses, she had no difficulty recognizing a male of the same ilk. "Perhaps we could lunch another day," she answered. "I am suddenly feeling under the weather."

Dana could not believe his good fortune. However, he forced his brow to crinkle in concern. "What a shame! This heat is just abominable. Let me call a cab."

"Thank you, my driver is waiting downstairs." Dagmar walked slowly to Marjorie's desk. "Please tell Mr. Major that I was here." Walking at a coronation pace, she left.

"She doesn't like me," Dana murmured after a moment. "I wonder why not."

Marjorie returned to her typewriter. "Because you're a schmuck."

"Ha-ha! Aren't we cute today!" Dana strode into the hallway. "At least let me show you to your car, Madame Pola." When the hell would this old bag tell him to call her Dagmar? They waited eons for an elevator. Finally, desperate to break the silence, he said, "I suppose you recognized that woman with me in the office just now."

"She looked somewhat familiar," Dagmar answered dryly.

"That was Philippa Banks, the actress. She wants me to build her a château on the Riviera."

"Is that so."

The elevator arrived and Dagmar inched aboard while Dana kept the Door Open button depressed. Slightly unnerved that his charm had failed on a veritable tortoise, Dana began to whistle nervously as the elevator plodded to the lobby. He regretted the little joke he had played on Marjorie; she might sue him for a deviant version of sexual harassment. He worried about Ross's prolonged disappearance from the office. Nothing like that had happened in the forty years he had known him. Dana helped Dagmar into her car and looked helplessly up and down the teeming sidewalks. His chest hurt: Rejection, even by a harridan, disrupted his biosystem. Then he thought he glimpsed Philippa's gossamer outfit wafting in the far-off breeze, and ran like a schoolboy after her.

                              *       *       *

It had been a bad Monday at Diavolina. Around dinnertime,
when Mustapha's oven died, the slow burn in Emily's stomach
began flaring into her abdomen. The chaos had begun this
morning, when she had told Byron that Philippa would be coming to dinner. He had been useless as a yo-yo, and the kitchen
off balance, ever since. Lunch had not gone well, thanks to a
surge of diners and a dearth of serving staff. Still recovering
from the unexpected depletion of their reserves, the cooks were
frantically preparing for a second assault that evening. Later in
the day, catching Emily completely off guard, Guy had called.
Ross had not. Then Marjorie had hung up on her: disaster. Instinctively, Emily knew that her husband had returned, and she
was afraid.

Just before six o'clock, two replacement waiters arrived. Following a Mach-3 rundown of the menu, they were sent into the
dining room, whence they often returned, looking confused. By
seven, Diavolina was full, the bar besieged. There was an unbelievable run on oysters and smoked salmon, forcing Klepp into
overdrive; he and Chess began scrimmaging over a bowl of
lemons, which she insisted on saving for her salad dressings.
Mustapha's rising batch of yeast rolls verged on collapse when
the stove repairman finally arrived. Placing his toolbox in the
busiest corridor in the kitchen, the man began a thorough
search of the lines, finally announcing that he would have to
shut off all the gas before proceeding further. As Emily was
protesting, Slavomir tripped over the toolbox. His face, and fifty
clean dishes, hit the floor.

For a second, out in the dining room, all conversation ceased.
Then everyone laughed in appreciation of someone else's inepti-
tude. At the bar, Ward shook her head and continued pouring
beer. She turned the music and the air-conditioning up a notch.
There were many new faces tonight, all ages, all types: Maybe
Diavolina had been mentioned in some trendy magazine. A
weird business, food. She called Zoltan to the bar. "It's all
yours," she said. "I've got a date with my shrink."

Meanwhile, in the kitchen, Slavomir was bleeding. Porcelain

shards lay everywhere, like shells on a beach. Mustapha, stand-ing the closest, helped the dishwasher to his feet. "You've been drinking again, man," he said, wrinkling his nose. "I thought we talked about this."

Emily rushed over. "Are you hurt?" Slavomir burbled in Rus-sian as the repairman gingerly exhumed his toolbox from the rubble. "What's he saying, Klepp?" she called.

"He's reciting poetry. Sounds like Tolstoy." Klepp glanced at a chit from one of the new waiters. "You stupid shit! One more oyster and I'll put your gonads on the plate instead!"

Byron had been standing near the kitchen doors, peering into the dining room. "Phil's not here yet," he worried. "Maybe the crowd scared her away."

"Would you do something useful?" Emily barked, binding Slavomir's lacerated wrist with a napkin. "Klepp, ask Slavomir if he wants to go home."

"Then who the hell's going to wash dishes?" he shouted back. "Look at him, Major. He's perfectly all right." Nevertheless, Klepp conferred with the injured party. "He'll stay if you let him lie down in your office for a few minutes."

"Fine! Go!"

Ward came into the kitchen just as Klepp and Slavomir were leaving. "What happened?" she demanded, seeing bandages and blood.

"He kissed the floor again, ma'am," Klepp replied. "No prob-lem."

The dishwasher peeped through the little window in the kitchen door. Suddenly, with a shriek, he reeled into the dining room. Klepp managed to catch him after a few steps and drag him back into the kitchen.

"Will you get that madman out of here?" Byron cried. "What is he carrying on about, Klepp?"

"He says there's a devil out there. Now he's putting a curse on the whole kitchen." Klepp wrapped an arm around Slavomir's frail shoulders. "Let's go lie down, Rasputin."

Ward looked at Emily. "I'll be back in two hours. Try not to burn the place down." She left.

Lola, the waitress with the body of Jessica Rabbit, torpedoed in with two plates of pasta. "Rejects," she said, shoving them toward Chess. "They say it's undercooked."

Chess ate a strand. "This is perfectly done. Take it back out and explain what al dente is all about."

"Don't give me any lip, Muffin," Lola retorted. "They're my best tippers."

"She's here!" Byron suddenly screeched from the doorway. "Oh my God! She's gorgeous!" He rushed to the stove and flamed a wide copper pan. "Everyone stay calm. Where did I put those mushrooms? Port. Where's the port?" He finally located the bottle on a shelf near the dishwashing utensils. "Christ, it's empty! That swine drank a half bottle of seventy-year-old port!" Byron stumbled into Mustapha, who was pulling a rack of very dark brown rolls from the oven. "Will you get out of my way? This is my workstation now! You had all day to bake!"

Mustapha carefully removed the rolls to a cooling rack. "What is with you, man?" he asked. "You got Queen Elizabeth out there or something?"

"I've got Philippa Banks," Byron retorted. "If you don't know who that is, you've joined the wrong religion."

"Philippa Banks," Klepp murmured, returning to his station. "That's the broad who always gets laid on beaches." He joined Byron at the door. "Now that's what I call cleavage. Who's the gigolo with her?"

"Get back to your oysters, Klepp!" Emily shouted. Her throat felt like the funnel of a blow torch. "Byron, sweep up these dishes at once. Before you start the mushrooms."

The sous-chef was fussily picking through Mustapha's rolls, choosing the four most perfect specimens to send to Philippa's table with a selection of cheeses. "Lola! Are you on Section C tonight?" he called.

"Nope, one of the new guys is. Step on it, will you, Chess? How long does it take to boil a little spaghetti?"

Malcolm, one of the new waiters, came into the kitchen.

"Hey, guess who just walked in!" he announced excitedly. "Dana Forbes!"

"Who the hell's that?" Klepp asked after a moment of silence.

"One of the most famous architects in America," Malcolm replied. "He's on a par with Frank Lloyd Wright and I. M. Pei."

"Oh for God's sake! Did you notice who he's sitting with?" Byron sputtered, rearranging four rolls for the fifth time in a bread basket.

"His wife, I guess." Picking up two plates of barbecued chicken, Malcolm left.

Finally satisfied with his still life, Byron began helping Emily clean up the broken dishes. "Does she eat fast or slow, Maje?" he whispered. "I have to time my courses."

"Depends how much she's drinking."

Eddy, the other new waiter, rushed into the kitchen. "Guess who's at my table!"

"Elvis Presley," Klepp roared.

"Just stay calm, everyone," Byron repeated yet again, placing an arm around Eddy's shoulder. "Have you brought their vodka and dried cherries yet?"

"Huh? The guy ordered champagne."

"Aha. Look, here's their bread. Serve it with this plate of cheese. Tell them dinner's compliments of the chef. They'll know what that means."

"They don't have to pay for it?" Chess called indignantly. "I'd like to know why not. They should pay for it like everyone else."

"She's my guest, you twit." Byron lobbed a slab of butter into his pan. "Eddy, after you serve the bread, go to the bar and get me another bottle of port for my mushrooms. If Zoltan gives you any shit, tell him to take it out of my paycheck. Go!"

The kitchen rattled into high gear as orders flew in, food flew out.

Philippa felt all eyes on her as she gracefully followed the maître d' to a table in the center of the crowded dining room. It was obvious that people either recognized her, or knew that they ought to recognize her, as she walked past. That evening, Philippa knew she looked better than any woman in sight. Having spent the afternoon with Dana in various postures of ecstasy, her skin glowed. She wore her favorite outfit, a floor-length tube of aqua spandex that made her feel like a mermaid. Her makeup was perfect. And she was hungry. Smiling at Zoltan, Philippa took her seat, innocently ignoring those gaping at her from adjoining tables. She was glad to see that Emily was finally working in a real restaurant with a real liquor license. Diavolina was a much larger, hipper place than that birdhouse at Quincy Market.

Meanwhile, Dana cast a practiced eye about the dining room. Recognizing no one, he moved his chair closer to Philippa's, so that their knees could touch under the table. Above the tablecloth, of course, he maintained a professional distance, just in case one of his clients, or one of his wife's tennis partners, happened to be here. "Tonight I deserve champagne," he said. "The best in the house."

Philippa smiled indulgently; over the last few hours, she had almost forgiven Dana for falling short of her expectations. "What have you done to deserve champagne?"

"One, I worked damn hard all afternoon. Two, you are buying me dinner. Remember our little bet at the office? Our little joke? You completely fooled Marjorie into thinking you were your sister."

She had forgotten. "I still don't get the point of it."

"Torment, sweetheart. It's what makes the world go round." When Eddy came to the table with the water pitcher, Dana ordered a bottle of Veuve Clicquot.

Philippa took a dainty sip of water. "Fine, you tormented your poor secretary. What do you think Ross is going to do when she tells him you've been fooling around with Emily? Laugh and keep reading the mail?"

Somehow Dana had never thought of that. "Relax! He'll know it's a joke." He chuckled, glancing at his watch. Nine-fifteen: Perhaps Marjorie was still at the office. It might be wise to call in, see if she knew whether Ross still had a gun permit. "How do you like the decor here?"

Philippa surveyed the pinkish brown walls, the aqua linen. "I've seen worse."

"It was one of my first interior commissions. For a complete lunatic. His name was Leo. I wonder if he's still around."

Eddy arrived with the champagne. "Where's the telephone, please?" Dana asked. Under the table, he patted Philippa's knee. "I'll be right back."

He called the office and got an assistant, who informed him that Ross had returned late in the afternoon. Marjorie had spent about an hour locked up with him; they were both gone now. Dana returned to the table as Philippa was autographing someone's wine list. Eddy arrived with a little cheeseboard and rolls, compliments of the chef. In fact, their entire dinner would be compliments of the chef.

"Isn't that sweet," Philippa cooed, choosing a roll. "I love surprises. Don't you, sugar?"

Dana tore his eyes from the entrance of the restaurant. "Always." His stomach was beginning to constrict unpleasantly; when provoked, Ross was more dangerous than a cobra.

Zoltan bore two glasses of vodka to the table. "How are you, Mr. Forbes?" he asked, nodding formally to Philippa. "We haven't seen you here since the renovation."

"Fine, thank you. I see everything's holding up well. What happened to the statue behind the bar, though?"

"Mr. Leo took it away. The feminists did not approve."

"What was the statue of?" Philippa interrupted, unsure whether Dana was conversing with a woman or a man. In either case, the orange makeup looked hideous.

"Diavolina," Zoltan replied cryptically. "Your drinks are from an admirer at the bar. Sitting under the television. The man in the red sweater says he knows you."

Batting her long eyelashes, Philippa searched the crowded bar and located the gentleman in question. To her surprise, she saw not adulation but disdain hardening his face. "I don't believe I recognize him," she said, moving an inch closer to Dana for protection. "But thank him anyway."

After Zoltan left, Dana stared into his vodka. "What's this floating in here? Dead beetles?"

"Four dried cherries, dear. The whole world knows it's my favorite drink."

After swallowing the vodka neat, Dana chewed on one or two, hoping to calm his stomach. "Your fans know that?"

"Of course. I'm surprised you don't." Philippa looked again toward the bar. "That man in the red sweater keeps staring so oddly over here."

"Maybe he thinks you're Emily."

Philippa scowled. This afternoon they had had a tiny argument concerning her wig. Dana had finally convinced Philippa that she should wear it this one last time, for privacy. Despising him a little, she had given in. What was the point? Obviously everyone recognized her anyway.

They finished the cheese in silence, glancing casually but repeatedly at the door (Dana) and the bar (Philippa). Finally she said, "That man, Dana. Does he look like someone's who's seen *Tropical Heat* twice?"

Dana glanced at the bar and felt his insides catapult. Christ! That was Rex, Ardith's aerobics instructor! The man waved impudently at him.

"He knows you?" Philippa asked incredulously. "The drinks were for you, not me?"

"Why not," Dana responded, feeling his gorge rise. "I'm not exactly unknown and unadmired here." The bastard had probably been taking pictures for Ardith's divorce suit. She was going to bankrupt him after all. "He's my wife's aerobics instructor."

"Look, he's leaving."

Zoltan suddenly blocked Dana's view. "How is everything?"

"Terrific," Dana croaked. Lacing those dried cherries with cyanide could save Ardith a couple hundred thousand bucks in legal fees. He'd better go to the bathroom and try to puke. "Excuse me again, darling. I won't be long."

When he returned, pale and unsuccessful, Eddy was just

ladling out the mushrooms in port. "Ah! What's this?" Philippa was asking. "Snails? Emily knows I adore snails!"

"Sorry, they're mushrooms." Eddy couldn't remember their name. "They were brought in this morning from a monastery."

Philippa tried a mouthful. "Delightful. Are you feeling all right, Dana?"

"No. Let's leave."

"You aren't serious. I can't insult my sister like that. She's probably spent the whole day making this meal for us." Philippa continued eating. "The mushrooms are very good. Try some."

Feeling his pulse skip and pound, Dana swallowed a forkful. For a few moments, they ate in silence. Then Dana thought he saw Ross at the bar. He threw his napkin to the table. "Excuse me again, doll. This is the last time, I swear it."

Her mouth stuffed with mushrooms, Philippa could only smile grotesquely as Dana left yet again. She was angrily tossing back the last of the champagne when an intense, athletic man with steely blue eyes slid into Dana's seat opposite her. His look stung, stunned: She sat paralyzed.

"Hello, Plum," he said. "I thought I'd find you in the kitchen, not the dining room."

Philippa knew immediately that this was her sister's lover. She also knew that the second she opened her mouth, this one would know she was an impostor. So she shrank away from him, trying to hide her face behind a napkin.

"I knew you were quick, but not this quick," Guy Witten continued in a soft, ironic voice. "Your husband's partner? That's getting suicidal, kitten." Reaching across the table, he smoothed her left eyebrow with two possessive, intimate fingers. "Too much makeup," he observed. Then his eyes fell, lingering on her décolletage. Philippa wanted both to cover herself and to expose herself; the conflict made her cheeks flame. "But why dress like a whore? That upsets me."

Zoltan stepped quickly to the table. "Is this gentleman bothering you, madam?" he asked.

Before Philippa could reply, Guy Witten stood up. "Of course I was. But now I'm leaving." His eyes never left hers. "I'll be in touch." With his last word, so intentionally rife with double meaning, Philippa's stomach rolled.

She recovered her voice when Guy was halfway across the dining room. "An old friend," she explained weakly to Zoltan.

The maître d' smiled discreetly. "Ah, here comes Mr. Forbes." Zoltan faded expertly away as Dana resumed his place at the table.

"False alarm," he said. "I thought I saw Ross." He took his jacket off. "Hot in here."

Diavolina was packed. A line had formed on the sidewalk, something that rarely happened in this neighborhood except at gay bars. At ten o'clock, when Ward had still not returned from the therapist, Zoltan upped the music from jazz to rock, perhaps to entertain the clientele as they waited for their meals. And wait they did: Operating without an oven, a sober dishwasher or sous-chef, and two experienced waitpersons, the kitchen never recovered its rhythm. Hopelessly behind, the new waiters began telling their tables that Diavolina was out of everything but chili, an entrée requiring only one plate, one level of doneness, and no side orders.

Fortunately, the friends whom Byron had lured to Diavolina tonight were not the type to speed through dinner, go home, and read nonfiction until the ten o'clock news. Comfortably inebriated, Byron's roommate Jimmy ambled toward Philippa's table as the waiter was clearing away her mushrooms in port. Jimmy knew from experience that the best time to intrude upon a pair of strangers was just before they received their main course. By then they would have drunk enough to be witty but not bathetic, and the lovers' quarrels would just be getting under way with a few barbs here and there: Interruptions would almost be welcome.

"Excuse me," he said, "but are you Philippa Banks, the movie star?" She smiled affirmatively. "May I please pretty please have your autograph? You're my favorite actress of all time. I've seen all your movies at least twice, then I always buy the videos."

Smiling apologetically at Dana, Philippa reached for Jimmy's pen. "Which is your favorite?"

"*Rough Sands*, definitely. That incest scene at the luau is just sublime. I broke my Replay button on it."

Philippa signed Jimmy's menu. "That's very kind."

Lola arrived bearing a bottle of chianti, compliments of a fan. Dana waited a moment, then asked, "You had an incest scene?"

"It was with a sister." Philippa toyed with a roll, thinking about the man who had recently called her Plum. His blue eyes haunted her. She glanced toward the kitchen. "I wonder if Emily's having fun back there."

"Are you kidding? This place is out of control tonight." Yet again, Dana glanced at the front door. The crowd, the noise, were beginning to make him nervous: too many witnesses. "I think we may have been better off staying on my boat. Quiet. Private." His medicine chest was there as well. He could take something for his writhing stomach. Meanwhile, maybe some wine would help. "Must we really stay?" Philippa didn't respond so he added, "On our last night together?"

Was he hallucinating, or did she seem to brighten as he said that? After all he had risked by appearing in public with her? After all those afternoon appointments he had canceled? Dana cringed, wondering how he was going to explain all of this to Ross tomorrow. And Marjorie! A fortune in roses would barely mollify her. Once again, he glanced apprehensively over the dining room. Bad vibrations here. Very bad. He wanted to escape to his ship and peel that dress off Philippa. Tie her down in the life boat, savage her a little. "I have an idea," he began.

Their waiter reappeared. "Filets mignons with horseradish sauce," Eddy announced, placing the dishes in front of them. "Compliments of the chef," he added for the fifth time.

Across the dining room, a wine bucket crashed to the floor. Conversations again paused, resuming on a buzzier note as waiters rushed to mop up the mess. "I wonder if it's like this every night," Philippa said, taking her steak knife.

Lola appeared again. "Pepper, anyone?"

"Just a touch," Philippa said irritably, anxious to rid the vicinity of a dazzling woman twenty years her junior. "Whoa! Enough! Fine!"

Lola made a brief pass over Dana's steak before pulling a felt-tip pen from her apron. "Would you mind autographing the pepper mill, Miss Banks? It would mean so much to me."

Philippa hastily scribbled on the pepper mill. "That should do. Run along now."

"Thank you so much!" Lola bowed and left.

Philippa took a bite of her steak. "Oh dear."

"What's the matter?" Dana asked.

"I might have to send this back. It's almost raw." Hell on her hemorrhoids.

"Take mine. It's medium." They changed plates. Dana poured more wine. He was beginning to feel melancholy. "Must you really catch that plane?"

"I've got to be in New York at ten tomorrow morning. Why don't you come with me? I don't want to go to the opening of *Choke Hold* with my agent. He smells like a moldy orange."

"You know I can't get away, Philippa." The mere thought of returning to his office gave Dana a spasm of indigestion. "Let's get out of here. We could spend one last hour on the boat."

To his chagrin, she didn't even hesitate. "No way. I still haven't seen Emily. How's your steak?"

Dana gamely shoved another slab into his mouth. Too much damn pepper. Burned his insides. The chianti ate into his esophagus like Drano. He now realized that somewhere between the champagne and the filet mignon, he had lost her.

They ate in silence. As he became ever more aware of people staring at Philippa, Dana felt cold, ill, used. Their final hour would be hell. He almost wished Ross would appear, with or without a shotgun. They'd all have a good laugh once Ross discovered that his wife was virtuous and his sister-in-law was a conniving harlot; with any luck, Philippa would go to the airport with Emily, sparing him a farewell under fluorescent lights. For now he could only stare at her lovely mouth, so recently his, and wonder what had gone awry.

Philippa wrapped long, cool fingers around her wineglass. "Have you seen Emily recently?"

"Emily?" He tried to think. She rarely came to the office. She didn't play bridge or tennis with Ardith like the other architects' wives. She never went out to dinner with Ross's clients because she had to get up early for work the next day. "I haven't seen her since July Fourth. We were all watching fireworks from the boat."

"How'd she look?"

Super! Unbelievable! "Pretty good," Dana said, vividly recalling the toreador pants and the black halter top that had left most of Emily's back exposed. Men kept draping their arms around her, asking if she would like to borrow their jackets. "Like a pastel version of you."

Philippa was not sure that was a compliment. "Was she with anyone?"

"Ross, of course."

As a busboy cleared their dishes, Philippa contemplatively sipped her wine. "I should have spent more time with her this trip. We never see each other enough now."

"Didn't you have breakfast with her Friday morning? At her old job?"

"It was rather hasty, if you recall. I was in a rush to get to your boat."

She sounded almost angry at him. Dana felt dizzy, as if he were being flushed to the bottom of a huge, swirling cesspool. With difficulty, he fought to recover his balance. "Let's go visit her, then," he said. "Where's that damn waiter?"

Right on cue, Eddy appeared at the table with two large bowls. "Black currants. Very rare."

"We're not hungry," Dana growled. Odd, his tongue was hobbling over simple words. No, the tongue was okay; the jaws were not moving. "We'd like to pay our compliments to the chef and leave."

"Hold on. He'll be here in a minute to say hello."

"He?" Philippa echoed. "I thought the chef was a she."

Byron, in full regalia, emerged from the kitchen. His immaculate white apron and tall hat beautified his tan. Dozens of friends began to applaud as he strutted to the bar and turned down the music. When he approached the famous actress's table, a hush came over the dining room. "Philippa Banks," he began, ignoring her dinner companion completely, "I have a confession to make. I have been in love with you my entire adult life."

With a wistful little grunt, Dana Forbes fell forward into the black currants.

Gas lamps flickered softly over Beacon Hill, inspiring the fireflies in the ivy. Nothing moved now but the clouds over the moon. As she left the cab, shutting the door quietly, Emily glanced up and saw a pale glow behind her living room window: Ross was home. A few hours ago, that light would have frightened her. Now she felt no more dread; tonight she had been traumatized by other, perhaps larger, catastrophes. She stood a long time on her stoop, digging in her purse for keys. Ross had probably heard the cab; ungallant of him not to come down and unlock the door. Ungallant of him to disappear for three days, in fact. He sure picked a great time to come home. Emily found the keys, the lock, and went inside.

A slight fear returned as she noticed his suitcase in the foyer. Such dim light, such ominous stillness, were not her usual greeting. She peered into the living room, the den, the kitchen, unwilling to call his name; to bleat into this silence. Then she heard the clink of ice on crystal: He was in the atrium.

Ross lay on the couch, watching the moon. Seeing her in the doorway, he slowly raised his glass and drank. She knew from the heavy sloshing of ice that it no longer floated in much scotch. "It's late," he said finally. "Where have you been?"

Emily dropped into a chair. "The question is, where have you been."

Ross said nothing for a very long time. Then he slowly raised himself to a sitting position and switched on the lamp next to the couch. Moonlight, forgiveness, fled; only his piercing eyes remained. She trembled, guilty forever, forever damned. Ross never blinked. "Are you having an affair with Dana?" he asked in a tight, merciless voice.

Emily made a little hiccuping noise. "Dana?" Then she

seemed to laugh. Could it be true? Was she spared? Her pulse feebly returned. "What makes you say that?"

"I saw you board his boat on Friday."

"That was Philippa, not me, you fool!"

Ross's face sagged. He shut his eyes. "I don't believe it." Emily waited, but her husband did not apologize. Instead, he went to the window and stared into the backyard. "How did that happen?"

"Remember Dana's job in Paris last month? They met there. Philippa came to Boston to spend the weekend with him on his boat. She wanted it kept quiet. They were at the restaurant tonight." Her voice faltered; Ross still refused to turn around. Emily went to the window and saw why: He was crying. "Sit down, Ross," she said as a fresh blast of guilt twisted through her. "I have some bad news."

He only shook his head and stared at nothing.

"They were at Diavolina," Emily continued, feeling her throat dry. "Just as they were about to eat dessert, Dana . . . Dana . . . "

Ross finally faced her. "Dana what?" he whispered.

"Collapsed."

Ross grasped her arm. "You're making this up!"

"I am not!" Her voice began to wobble. "It was horrible. Philippa went off the deep end. There was almost a stampede. The police came. The ambulance, the lights, oh God they made a mess! And Dana was just lying there with whipped cream all over his face. I'll never forget that."

Ross squeezed her arm. "Which hospital is he in? I have to see him."

"Hospital? He's dead! He was dead before he hit the floor!" She was becoming angry at having to explain things over and over.

"What do you mean, 'dead'? From what?" Ross shouted.

"I don't know," she shouted back. "Heart attack! Stroke! Indigestion!" This was a very bad finale to a very bad dream. Her husband should be comforting her, not shrieking as if this were all her fault. "Good of you to ask! Where the hell were you for three days? If you had been home, none of this would have happened!"

Ross stared at her a moment. Then he flung his glass against the far wall. The vicious crash dismayed them both: this room was no longer safe. In silence, they watched a dozen weak rivulets creep down the wallpaper, away from the point of impact. "You came that close, Emily," Ross whispered, holding two fingers an inch apart. "That close."

From the kitchen, where the light was cleaner, he phoned the police. Ascertaining from a reliable source that his business partner was indeed deceased, Ross hung up. "I've got to see Ardith," he said. "I don't suppose you want to come along."

Ardith? Who gave a damn about Ardith! Emily guffawed bitterly. "I'm sure she'd rather see you alone."

She was splashing her face with cold water as the downstairs door slammed.

# 4

*Dana's gone. I'll never see him again: "Never"
is too monstrous to even comprehend. And he was innocent,
after all. Well, half innocent: If he had Philippa, he half had
Emily. Damn him, he should have told me! It might have saved
his life. Might have saved my marriage as well. But Dana was
never one for confession. Hell, why confess if he didn't believe
he was erring in the first place? He was just having a little fun.
Fun! I hope he died happy, with a gut full of wine, a riveted audience, maybe Philippa crying hot tears on his hand . . . bitch.
She should have told me, too. Instead she told her sister, who
chose to keep her mouth shut.*

*Emily said he died quickly: didn't hurt for long, eh friend?
What could have passed through his mind those last few seconds? Surprise. Panic. Wonder. Remorse, not for his misdeeds,
but for their cessation. Perhaps he had time to telegraph a good-
bye to Ardith, his high school sweetheart. That eleventh-hour
whore Philippa couldn't even have figured in the last, garbled
flare inside his head. Did he think of me before the lights went*

*out? He should have. I've loved him the longest and I'll miss him the most. God! Why didn't he just tell me he was sailing with Emily's sister? In thirty years, he's never hesitated to tell me about any of his women, great or small. What the hell was so different about Philippa?*

*Aha. He must have thought he was in love with her. Then the rules would change, the secrets expand . . . and no safety net. Dana wasn't used to that. Somehow she must have infiltrated the tiny closet that held the key to his existence. I can understand his delight, his dismay; happened to me years ago with Emily, and I told no one. I couldn't. It was a private miracle, a fragile veil separating twilight from absolute darkness. As long as that veil remains, you cannot allow yourself to go down without a fight. Dana fought, I'm sure. But he had no chance: too much dissolution before he staggered into Philippa.*

*Dana! What could you have been thinking of! Remember your family? Remember that little business of ours? Am I supposed to start designing kitschy carriage houses and shopping malls now? I'd rather eat my protractor! Who's going to take care of building permits? What about your Fourth of July sailing party? What about half our skyscrapers? Major without Forbes; now that is truly a nightmare. I don't know how I'm going to live through this. I'm not sure I want to.*

*I wish she hadn't told me he died with his face full of whipped cream. Dana didn't really deserve that. It haunts me.*

⹀

Ardith was thoroughly drunk when Ross arrived at her home in Brookline. She was not alone, however; Rex, a man with muscles and a tan, answered the door. He took Ross to the living room and resumed his place on the couch next to the bereaved widow, who had evidently been crying into his khaki shorts. Each time Ardith said "bastard," she broke into fresh tears, as if Dana's death had forever besmirched her virtue. After half an hour, realizing that the woman was incapable of giving or accepting sympathy, Ross patted her shoulder and left.

When he got home, his wife was in bed but not quite asleep. She had been drinking too; unlike Ardith, however, alcohol on Emily smelled exotic and sensual, like a perfume she only wore on special occasions. Her skin was warm, hair wet: She had been in the bathtub. Filthy and acid, Ross crawled into bed. When she rolled over, wrapped her arms around him, he cried for a long time. At first he cried for Dana. Then he realized that his wife had forgiven him for his recent outbursts, and that she was all he had left now. He cried because she was still there, still his bulwark against that nameless monster borne of time and solitude, who ate all souls in the end. Finally Ross cried because he had no children. They would have made him braver, filled in some of the craters Dana had left, half answered some of the mysteries . . . but it was not to be. He would have to find consolation elsewhere. Theology? Work? He didn't know. Toward sunup he ran out of tears and slept with bleak, flitting dreams.

At seven o'clock, Emily brought his coffee to bed. She kissed his cheek. "How do you feel?" she whispered.

Then he remembered, and momentarily submerged beneath the cold waves. Daylight felt like a splash of peroxide in his eyes. "All right." He saw she was already dressed.

"I have to go to Diavolina for a while," she said. "The police are finishing up." She waited as Ross wanly swallowed some coffee. "I guess you're going to the office."

"Someone's got to tell them."

"Want me to come along?"

"No thanks. You've got problems of your own, I expect." Ross glanced at the alarm clock: morning already. Funny how hours, lives, just melted away. "Where's Philippa?"

"She left last night for New York."

He chuckled emptily. "She never was one for cleaning up her own mess. I wonder how I'm going to explain this to people."

"You don't have to explain anything. Dana died with his clothes on."

His wife still made excuses for Philippa. Ross couldn't believe it. "Do me a favor, will you? Remind your sister that Dana had a wife and kids. I'd appreciate her resisting the temptation to get a few cheap headlines out of this."

"I'll take care of it." Emily stood up. "Call you later."

As she stepped outside, a light breeze lifted her hair. A yellow-white sun hovered above the Common; this would become one of those serene September days, tinged with autumn, that broke the heart. Emily put her sunglasses on; sunshine was a particularly cruel reminder that the gods never grieved over the death of a minuscule human. They just continued frolicking with the stars.

Entering Diavolina, Emily saw Ward and a man at a corner table. Even from a distance, Ward looked more wretched than usual. Her hair lay flat against one ear, caromed off the other, as if a demon had been vacuuming her head as she slept. A Milky Way of cooked oatmeal streaked the front of her sweatshirt. Emily had not seen her smoking before. "Hi Major," Ward said in a gritty baritone voice, brushing ash from her enormous thighs. "Speak to Detective O'Keefe." She went into the kitchen.

The man shook Emily's hand, appraising her with a candor honed by forty years in morgues, courtrooms, and bars. He beckoned her to sit. On the table in front of him, a dozen ripped pink envelopes clustered a pot of coffee. "I'd like to ask a few questions about last night," he said, reaching for a notepad. "You were in charge of the kitchen and I understand you were a friend of the deceased."

"He was my husband's business partner. I've known him for fifteen years."

"Did he have any health problems that you were aware of? Allergies? Heart condition?"

"No. He was in good shape."

"What did he eat last night?"

"Rolls, goat cheese, mushrooms in port, filet mignon with horseradish sauce, Swiss chard, potatoes, black currants and cream. I think he drank champagne."

O'Keefe looked at his notepad. "Plus vodka and chianti. And dried cherries. Who made the dinner?"

"Byron Marlowe, the sous-chef."

"Why didn't you make it?"

"Byron wanted to. Dana's date was—is—a famous actress. Byron's a fan. I had more important things to do in the kitchen."

O'Keefe thought about that a moment. "Was Byron acquainted with the deceased?"

"Not that I know."

"Is he a good chef?"

"He knows his way around a stove."

"I mean mentally, what's he like? Delusional? Hysterical? Still going for his fifteen minutes of fame?"

Emily shrugged. "I've only been working here for four days. Byron was fairly normal until Dana dropped dead during his little speech. His nerves were already on edge from making dinner for Philippa Banks." Emily paused; sooner or later she'd have to make the next statement. "She's my sister."

O'Keefe nodded as if he knew that already and had just been waiting for Emily to mention it. "Were Forbes and your sister old friends, then?"

"Is this relevant?"

The detective's clear blue eyes suddenly met hers. "Insofar as it affected the dead man's pulse rate, yes."

"Then I would say that Dana's pulse rate was somewhat higher than it would be had he been out to dinner with his wife."

"Understood." O'Keefe sipped his cold coffee before returning to his original line of questioning. "Did Forbes have any addictions?"

"Wine. Women. Work."

"Any enemies?"

"What does that mean?"

"Just a routine question, Mrs. Major. A healthy man dropped dead over dinner. It doesn't happen every day."

"Why would Dana have any enemies? He hardly paid attention to his friends."

"Was your husband his friend? Business aside?"

"They've known each other for forty years. They were like brothers."

"No arguments? Business problems? Misunderstandings?"

"None that I'm aware of." She marveled at her own cool mendacity: How easily one fibbed to protect a wounded husband.

O'Keefe waited a moment. "Where was your husband last night?"

"Working."

"I see. Thanks for your help, Mrs. Major. The autopsy will probably explain everything." O'Keefe stood up. "I'll be in touch."

The kitchen doors swung open, emitting Ward. "Can I get my kitchen back on track now, Detective?" she yelled, stalking to the table. "You've got evidence up the wazoo. I've got five cooks going apeshit back here." She looked at Emily. "The cops are checking for food poisoning."

No restaurant needed that kind of publicity. "Is this necessary?" Emily asked O'Keefe. "No one else got sick here last night. My sister ate everything Dana did. She was alive and kicking when we put her on the plane."

"How is she now?" he asked.

"I would have heard if she burped wrong. You can call her and check if you like."

"Not necessary. I already have her statement from last night." O'Keefe seemed reluctant to talk in front of Ward. "You've both been very helpful. Thanks."

They followed him to the kitchen, where O'Keefe's assistant was finishing up with Byron. "I've told you again and again," the sous-chef was explaining, "this was a special meal. I didn't use recipes. I only made enough for two people. It tasted good. They ate everything. There were no leftovers. No doggie bags. Nothing."

"Not even gravy?"

"Oh Christ, especially not gravy! Sauces are my specialty! Pump a few stomachs if you still need samples!"

"Okay, okay. Who handled the booze?" the assistant detective asked.

"Zoltan. You already grilled him."

"And the waiter was . . . Henry?"

"Eddy! Eddy! Don't try to trick me!"

Klepp had been slouching in the doorway, smoking. "Just tell them about the arsenic in the mushrooms, Byron," he called, spinning the cigarette into the driveway. "Then we can all get back to work."

O'Keefe walked over to him. "Think we're joking here, Shorty?"

"Watch your language, Officer," Chess warned. "I'm about ready to file harassment and discrimination charges."

"Oh. Pardon me. I forgot." O'Keefe suddenly twisted Klepp's shirt tightly at the throat and nearly lifted him off the floor. "Think we're joking here, Mr. Altitudinally Challenged?" After a few seconds he let go. "One more crack and I'll bust your runty little ass." O'Keefe looked over the kitchen crew. "Does anyone have anything to add to the statements made this morning? No? Then we'll let you get back to your business. Thank you kindly." He and his assistant passed ominously close to Klepp on their way out the rear door.

"You should know better than to mess with cops," Mustapha muttered after a moment. "Especially when they're twice your size."

Klepp angrily rattled his sauté pans. "Leo never would have let the cops in the kitchen in the first place."

"Let them do their jobs," Emily said, looking around. "Where's Slavomir?"

Chess fluffed a few dandelion greens. "He hasn't come in yet."

"Ha!" Byron snapped out of his stupor. "He knows I'll kill him for drinking all my port last night. Wrecked my recipe. I hope you're going to take it out of his salary, Ward. Charge him for fifty broken dishes while you're at it."

"'Vengeance is mine, saith the Lord,'" quoted Mustapha. "Why are you so spiteful, Byron? They weren't your dishes anyway."

"That's enough, children," Ward interrupted. "Major, come with me. Everyone else, get to it. We're serving lunch today."

Emily followed her to the table in the dining room. Brushing aside O'Keefe's mound of pink envelopes, Ward said, "I would have appreciated knowing that Philippa Banks was your sister. It would have explained the chaos in here yesterday."

"I'm sorry. I try to keep it quiet." Emily felt intensely stupid.

"You're not proud of a sister like that? What's the matter with you?" Ward flicked a lock of hair out of her eye. "Obviously I'm not too thrilled about a stiff in my dining room, either. What happened while I was away? I have five versions already. May as well hear yours."

"You left around eight, I think. We were already jammed and the kitchen was a zoo. Philippa and Dana got here about nine-thirty. Eddy, the new waiter, served them. They ate and probably drank a lot. Byron wanted to make a little speech with dessert, so he came out after the berries. He was about to start when Dana collapsed. That's my version."

Ward lit another cigarette. Her voice was raw. "Then what."

"My sister has a great set of lungs," Emily said. "Byron's aren't bad, either. When I realized they weren't screaming at each other, I rushed to the dining room. There were one hundred people, all staring at this body on the floor. Then they stared at me because I look like Philippa. They probably thought the whole thing was a practical joke. I remember a few people laughing. It was bizarre, a dream. Dana was dead."

"You checked?"

"Any decent chef knows first aid." Emily forced her voice down. "I announced that he had fainted and had Zoltan and Eddy lug him to the kitchen."

"What did your sister do?"

"She managed to half-faint into Byron's arms." Emily guffawed. "Would have fainted entirely if she thought Byron was strong enough to carry her. Once we got Dana out of the dining room, things gradually returned to normal."

"What about your sister? Did she realize Dana was dead?"

"Why the hell do you keep asking about my sister?" Emily snapped.

Ward looked surprised. "Sorry. What happened then?"

"Zoltan and Eddy carried the body to my office. Slavomir was in there sleeping. He went nuts when he saw Dana so I sent him home. I put Philippa and Byron in your office with a bottle of brandy and told them everything would be all right. Then I called the police. To answer your question, yes, Philippa knew he was dead."

"How'd she know?"

"She saw my face as I was listening for a heartbeat." It was the only time in her life that Emily had seen Philippa look helpless. "Then the police came and took statements. They were carrying Dana out when you got back."

"Nothing like running into a body bag on the steps of your restaurant. I'll have diarrhea for a week." Ward poured herself a cup of cold coffee. "You're a cool cucumber, lady. Not everyone could have handled a corpse with such aplomb."

Emily's heart twitched: laughing Dana a corpse? "I lived in Turkey and Korea," she replied. "Bodies are part of the scenery there."

Out on Tremont Street, a redhead in a brilliant green suit was peering into the front window. "She's a little early for lunch," Ward commented suspiciously, watching as the woman tested the doorknob. "Cripes, who left the door unlocked? Hello! Can I help you?"

The woman walked to the table. Her purse matched her shoes matched her lipstick matched her eye shadow. The effect was merely humanoid. "I'm looking for the person in charge here."

Ward picked a fleck of oatmeal from her sweatshirt. "Speaking."

"My name is Wyatt Pratt. I am here representing Ardith Forbes." Seeing that neither name meant anything to Ward, she said, "The widow of Dana Forbes."

"You're a lawyer?"

Pratt's lips curved imperceptibly upward, as if she had just been given an expensive chocolate. "Mrs. Forbes believes that the negligence of this restaurant is responsible for her husband's death."

"That's pretty swift," Emily said. "He was only eating here twelve hours ago."

Pratt lay a thick envelope on the table. "This is fairly self-explanatory. I'm sure you'll consult your attorney if you have any further questions." Smiling with a saccharinity that tempted people to punch her in the teeth, she left.

Ward and Emily stared at Wyatt Pratt's envelope for a few moments, half expecting it to quiver to life, like a stunned rodent. "This is all my fault," Emily said finally. "Maybe I should have kept flipping pancakes at Cafe Presto."

Ward slit the envelope open with a fork. "I can't afford any goddamn lawyers."

"Forget it! I'll have my husband speak with Ardith. Once she knows I'm chef here, she'll drop the suit."

Ward skimmed the neat typing. Suddenly her eyes bulged at a couple of difficult words. "Is your friendship with Ardith worth ten million bucks?"

Emily's friendship with Ardith wasn't worth two cents. Ardith was one of those overhauled, anorexic wives who knew that no matter how perfectly lovely she looked, her husband would still prefer to sleep with raunchier women. "Ten million bucks?" Emily cried. "That bitch has no case!"

"Let's hope not." Ward slowly eased herself from the chair, wincing as her ankles bore the brunt of her weight. "Why don't you go talk to your husband right now. Just for my peace of mind."

Emily called home, got the machine. She called Ross's private office line and got Marjorie, whose toneless voice left no doubt that she had recently received some horrendous news. Yes, Ross was in, she told Emily. Of course, come on down.

Emily cabbed to State Street. Marjorie was not at her desk: That was like the Marines not guarding an embassy. Near the water cooler, an assistant with wet, red eyes honked into a Kleenex. When the phone rang, an apprentice answered, telling the caller that "he wasn't in right now." He politely took a number, hung up, and raked his fingers through a spiky haircut, as if to reassure himself that his head was still round. Not one word passed among a dozen employees, many of whom were staring out the windows. Others only nodded as Emily walked by.

She found Ross lying on the couch in his office. Marjorie sat at his side, holding a glass of water to his lips. It was a pose of tremendous intimacy. Emily stopped in her tracks, startled: Here was another Ross, one bound to another woman, maybe not in the same way he was bound to her, but with as deep a passion. Otherwise he would not have allowed his assistant to sit so close, to whisper to him so. Never having seen them alone, in their natural habitat, Emily had always thought of Marjorie as one of Ross's office fixtures, a professional fact of life, like withholding tax. Now she realized that Marjorie was more on the order of Ross's alternate wife, occupying a niche that Emily never could; in the near future, without Dana, that niche would probably widen to a canyon. Emily wondered if Ross slept with her. Why not, really. They had spent many years, and their most creative energies, pursuing the same rainbow. All Emily had done was cheer from the wayside at dinnertime.

"Ross?" She knocked and walked in slowly enough that, if his hands were in Marjorie's lap, he could remove them by the time she got to the couch. Emily dropped into a nearby chair, noticing that Marjorie's rear end hadn't budged more than an inch from its original position. At least she was trying to look more like a nurse now. "Rough morning, eh?"

"The worst," Ross replied. He half sat up. Emily's mouth dropped: He hadn't shaved. That was like coming to the office in his jock strap. "How was the restaurant?"

"Detective O'Keefe was in. He won't be sure of anything until the autopsy." Emily crossed her legs, wondering how they compared with Marjorie's. "Ardith is suing Diavolina for ten million bucks."

"What?" Marjorie cried, finally taking her eyes off her patient. "Why?"

"Who the hell knows? Ardith is Ardith. If you're feeling up to it, Ross, try talking to her, would you? Tell her it wasn't anything Dana ate in my restaurant."

Marjorie got professional. "Who's her lawyer? Maybe we should work on him instead."

"Her. The name is Wyatt Pratt. She's a cross between a buzzard and a gorgon."

"So Ardith hooked up with Personal Liability Pratt," Ross said. "Good luck. She cruises around town listening to the police band. Arrives at the accident with a lawsuit before the blood even dries." He smiled coldly. "Dana had a one-nighter with her a few years ago. He said it was like screwing a starfish, all bristles and slime."

Aghast, both women stared at him. Neither had heard him speak like this before. Then again, it was a man-to-man topic and Ross had no more -man. "Dana said that to you?" Emily asked finally.

"Of course. He told me everything." Wrong: nearly everything. As the phone rang, Ross put his face in his hands. "Word's getting out. Wait until the obituary tomorrow." Lurching off the couch, he went quickly to the washroom between his office and Dana's. A lot of water began gushing behind the oak wall.

"I apologize for hanging up on you yesterday," Marjorie said. "I mistook you for your sister." Seeing that Emily had no idea what she was talking about, she continued. "I walked in on Dana and that woman by mistake. In his office. I was quite upset. I'm sorry. Of course it couldn't have been you."

Emily didn't have the nerve to ask what stage of intimacy Marjorie had interrupted. "My sister plays by her own rules."

"So did Dana." Sniffling, Marjorie found a handkerchief. "Poor Ross. This is so difficult for him."

Emily listened to the plumbing a few moments. "I'm sure he'll be relying on you more than ever," she said carefully. Now what? Forbid the poor woman to rise to the occasion? How tacky. Ah, face it: She'd have to accept another contestant, a strong one, on the track now. The tired old wife would just have to run a little faster in a large, empty stadium. Was Marjorie her penance for Guy? Emily stood up, already aching, and went to the washroom. Ross was inside dragging a razor over his cheeks. "Can I do anything for you, sweetheart?" she asked. He didn't reply at once. Emily finally realized that he wasn't thinking about an answer, he was just concentrating on his shaving. "Then I'll let you get back to Marjorie."

He caught her arm as she was leaving. "Are you going back to work?"

She shrugged. "Where else?"

Bed. He'd really like to go to bed with her now, roll under the sheets and forget everything but her scented skin. Then the phone rang again. Ross heard Marjorie answer and knew he would be stuck here, playing Winston Churchill, for a few long hours. He hugged his wife, inhaled her. "I love you."

"Ross? It's Billy Murphy," Marjorie called. "Should I blow him off?"

"No, I'll take it."

Emily handed him a towel. "I'll call after lunch." She left as he was listlessly picking up the phone.

Emily's return to the kitchen at Diavolina interrupted a murky powwow at the coffee machine; she didn't need a psychic to realize that Klepp, Chess, Byron, Yip Chick, and Mustapha had been talking about her. Fighting an impulse to leave the premises, Emily helped herself to a cup of coffee. "Everyone ready to go?" she asked cheerfully. The group trudged sullenly to their stations as she tried to swallow the burning liquid.

Reflecting the mood of the kitchen, a peevish crowd came to lunch. This was one of those days when people went out less to enjoy food than to be served it. The old ladies complained about the seeds in the cucumbers and the young ladies complained about the small portions. Everyone wanted doggie bags; tips averaged 12 percent. At the bar, Ward ran out of ice cubes. Disgusted, she told Zoltan to take over and left to see her therapist again.

At two o'clock, Slavomir still had not come to work. Byron opened his mouth only to bray at imagined slights. Neglecting his baking, Mustapha called twenty oven repairmen, finally finding one who sounded Afro. He didn't trust the others. When Klepp wondered aloud for the tenth time when Leo might be coming back, Emily left the kitchen. She was lying on the couch in her office, daydreaming about Dana's great sailing parties, when Detective O'Keefe phoned.

"I'm at the morgue," he said. "Waiting for autopsy results. I pushed your sister's boyfriend to the front of the line."

"I'm sure he appreciates that."

"That isn't why I called, actually. You should know that a body just arrived. In his pocket's a paycheck from Diavolina made out to Slavomir Dubrinsky."

Emily's stomach hurt. "That's my dishwasher."

"Is he old, thin, dilapidated?"

"Yes. What happened to him?"

"I don't know. A jogger found him floating in the Fenway. He's got a head injury."

"He fell in the kitchen last night. I sent him home around eleven. Alive."

"Where does he live? Any family?"

"I have no idea. I only met the man last Friday. He didn't speak much English."

"Could you identify him?" O'Keefe heard her laugh oddly. "Could someone else? Where's Ms. Ward?"

"Barfing on her therapist," Emily said. "I'll take care of it."

"Could you bring down an address?"

"I'll try." Emily went to Ward's messy office. Bills, résumés, government notices, and brochures littered her desk; half cups of coffee kept the higher piles in place. The soggy Rolodex reeked of ouzo. Emily lifted Slavomir's file card out; as she did, an old newspaper clipping that had been stuck to the back of it slid to the desk.

TEEN FALLS TO DEATH, the small headline read. Curious, Emily turned over the brittle paper half expecting to see a recipe on the other side: no. She read on.

A South End woman plunged to her death from the fortieth floor of the newly completed Darnell Building late Saturday evening. A possible suicide note was left behind, according to police sources, who are with-holding the victim's identity pending notification of the family. "She must have made an extraordinary leap," said Dana Forbes, architect of the building, not-ing that the balcony railings were four feet high.

What was Dana doing on the back of a dead man's file card? Emily found paper and was about to write down Slavomir's ad-dress when she saw that she had pulled not a pencil but a nasty-looking dart from Ward's pencil cup. Swearing, startled, she crammed it back and got a ballpoint pen. Uneasily copying the dishwasher's address, Emily left Ward's office. "I'm going out for an hour," she called to Zoltan, who was in the dining room checking his reservation list.

She walked through increasingly tattier neighborhoods to-ward Boston City Hospital. Over the past few years, this area had become a favorite locale of Korean noodle factories; as the frost heaves proliferated on Albany Street, so had the alignment specialty shops. Rush-hour traffic was already piling off the ex-pressway onto Mass Ave, where a stream of ambulances and buses waited in ambush; at this time of day, only a few illegal left turns were necessary to create superior gridlock. A dozen nurses lounged, smoking, on the front steps of the historic hos-pital, founded a century ago for people who couldn't afford doc-tors. It was still a popular place to die, particularly of bullet holes.

As a tractor trailer thudded past, Emily rang the doorbell of the pathology building. O'Keefe admitted her to the morgue's decrepit foyer; no point spiffing up a place where the clientele saw nothing and their relatives would only be visiting once, in a hurry. Straight ahead was a short stairway flanked by two gilt sphinxes. Emily blinked her eyes; the recessed lighting made the statues glow, almost throb, as if they truly guarded the dead. The half-flight of stairs between them descended to two doors arched with gold laurel. Ross would appreciate this, Emily thought; the architectural symbolism was dignified, very Brahmin. But he wouldn't like the restoration job. The sphinxes had recently been regilded; they pounced out of the gloom, almost attacking the eye. The net effect was a bizarre clash of Radio City and the River Styx.

"You have a choice," O'Keefe said. "Would you prefer to identify Dubrinsky by video or in person? I recommend video. The camera's all set up."

"Okay." Emily wanted to do her duty and leave; the soul felt nervous here.

They went down the stairs, between the statues, to a small room with a television set. O'Keefe conferred briefly with a pathologist. "I appreciate your coming down," he said, patting Emily's cold hand as they waited for a picture.

Slavomir's still face suddenly appeared onscreen. His eyes were closed but his mouth had frozen in a ghastly rectangle. The welt on his cheek had become a violent purple. Emily stared in disbelief, waiting for the eyelids to flutter, for the mouth to burble Russian poetry; although she had known the dishwasher for only a few days, she had only known him alive. This image on the screen was some kind of fake. "That's Slavomir," she said.

O'Keefe turned the picture off and handed her a form to sign. "He drowned around midnight, we think. Blood alcohol level was off the charts."

"He drank a half bottle of port at the restaurant."

"And a couple slugs of grain alcohol afterward. How'd he get the head wound?"

"He fell over a tool case and hit his cheek."

"How about the back of his head?"

"He didn't hit the back of his head. Just his cheek. And he cut his wrist on some broken dishes."

O'Keefe studied Emily's eyes for a moment. She seemed sober and intelligent, but they all did in the beginning. "The poor bastard was an alcoholic, judging by the condition of his liver. Did he have any enemies at work?"

"How would I know?"

"Could he have committed suicide?"

"He was a simple dishwasher!"

"Not quite. He served twenty years at Dutworth for statutory rape. That was a long time ago, of course. Did he talk to you at all?"

"No. I think I frightened him."

Deciding not to press her on that point today, O'Keefe lay a small orange tassel on the table. "This was in his pocket. Recognize it?"

"No. It's not from Diavolina."

O'Keefe wrote a few words near the bottom of a document, then capped his pen. "Were you able to bring any information about Dubrinsky's next of kin?"

"No, only his address." Emily gave the paper to O'Keefe. "What if no one claims him?"

"The city will take care of it. Eventually. Care for a lift back to the restaurant?"

She followed him past the sphinxes into the soft, cruel sunshine. O'Keefe edged his car into the traffic on Albany Street and began slaloming between potholes. "Heard from your sister?"

"Not yet. She's been doing interviews all day."

"Ask how her stomach's feeling." O'Keefe stopped his car in front of Diavolina. "Forbes's lab reports should be back in a few hours."

Emily studied his eyes a moment, surprised: They were the same ice blue as Guy's. Odd she hadn't noticed them before. Maybe he hadn't looked at her like that before. For one wee second she imagined O'Keefe inside of her. It probably wouldn't be bad at all; it would just be futile. "Keep me posted," she said, leaving the car.

Ward was at the bar concluding, or perhaps canceling, her latest therapy session with a triple martini and a computer printout. Behind her, Zoltan stacked clean wineglasses on the shelves. "Hey Major," she called cheerfully. "Maybe I should sign a contract with your sister. Have her show up once a month with a—" Ward caught herself just in time. "Next time you talk with her, please say thanks. We sold more booze last night than we did on New Year's Eve."

"Thank Byron. His friends bought it."

"His friends also clipped two champagne buckets and three pepper mills." Ward swallowed an inch of her drink. "Shit-heads."

Emily wondered why Ward always returned from her therapist in a sour mood. Maybe she was sleeping with him. "Detective O'Keefe called, Ward. I was just down at the morgue identifying a body."

"Didn't you do that already?"

"I'm not talking about Dana. Slavomir drowned in the Fenway last night."

Zoltan rapidly crossed himself; Ward caught her breath. "Impossible," she whispered.

"It was the dishwasher. Believe me."

"No way. There's been a mistake." Ward stomped out.

"He was her favorite," Zoltan muttered after the kitchen doors had finally returned to a standstill. The late-afternoon sun brought out the ocher in his heavy makeup. When he looked at Emily head-on, it was like conversing with a rotting pumpkin. "Leo will be very upset as well. I would not tell anyone in the kitchen about this now, if I were you."

"Why the hell not," Emily snapped. "They're going to find out soon enough."

"First Leo, then last night, now this. Poor Slavomir! How is that possible, drowned?"

"Simple. He got drunk and swallowed a lot of water. Did he have a family? You're supposed to know everything around here."

"No family, I think. Only Leo." Then the headwaiter recalled a more relevant tragedy. "And now no dishwasher either. Excuse me. I should do some telephoning." He left the bar.

Much later, Emily found Ward on the floor of her office lifting barbells. "I'm sorry about Slavomir. Did you go to the morgue?"

"They wouldn't let me in. I didn't have an invitation."

"Did he have any family?"

"None that I know of." Ward counted five more repetitions, then let the barbells roll away. "Maybe Leo would have an idea, but he's gone. God knows when he's coming back."

"Why should Leo come back? Didn't he quit?"

"He owns the joint, honey."

Emily sat slowly in Ward's chair. "And where does that leave me?"

"Right where you are. You're the chef." Ward took her martini. "Or you're the bubonic plague. Your husband's going to muzzle that lawyer for me?"

"He's going to try."

The phone rang. After a few seconds, Zoltan's voice came over the intercom. "Emily, it's for you."

"Hello," she said warily.

"Em," Philippa bubbled, "I can come to Boston tonight!"

Emily almost felt her brain stripping gears. "Weren't you just in Boston? Things are a little tight here right now."

"That's why I'm coming. To help out."

"Forget it, Philippa. There's no way you can help." Then Emily remembered O'Keefe's question. "How are you feeling?"

"Great. I just had five fantastic interviews. I'm on Joan Rivers this Friday. And my agent Simon got me a great part in a miniseries. I'm a brain surgeon whose husband beats her up just before she operates on the President."

"I meant how's your stomach. Any indigestion? Cramps?"

"No. Why?"

"Just checking. Listen, I think it would be better if you stayed out of town for a while. Ross is not doing well. Ardith's not too happy, either."

"That's exactly why I should come! Families have got to stick together!"

"Stick to something else for a while, would you?" Emily slammed down the phone. "I need a visit from my sister like a hole in the head."

"She probably feels bad about what happened," Ward said. "Remember, her boyfriend died, too."

"Boyfriend? She's forgotten his name already. You may have noticed that she didn't mention Dana once in our entire conversation."

"Maybe she's grieving."

"Give me a break! There's something else on her mind."

"You are incredibly unfair. Maybe you're just jealous."

"Maybe I am. Tell me more about it when you have a sister like Philippa."

For a wee second, Emily thought Ward would punch her. Fortunately, Byron came pounding on the door. "Maje! That fuckin' dishwasher still hasn't turned up!"

"Wash the dishes yourself," Ward shouted back. She yawned enormously, tired to death. "Go make dinner, Emily," she said listlessly, and closed her eyes.

Around six o'clock, Detective O'Keefe returned to Diavolina, using the service entrance. He looked soggy, oily, in need of a few beers, or a young wife. Byron saw him first. "What are you doing back here?" he cried. "Don't tell me this is a courtesy call."

O'Keefe frowned only slightly. "Where's Chef Major?"

Byron pointed to the pantry, where Emily was sitting on a crate of lettuce, doodling on a shopping list. She had just called Ross's office and had been told for the third time that her husband and Marjorie were still at lunch. She was not going to call the office anymore today, perhaps anymore ever. Seeing O'Keefe in the doorway, she motioned to a box of oysters. "Howdy."

"Good news," he said, sitting. "Forbes died of substance abuse."

Well, hip-hip-hooray. "Which substance?"

"Chianti, for one. Cheese, for two."

"How can wine and cheese kill you?"

"When you're on iproniazid, easily."

"What's that? I never heard of it."

"It's an extremely potent antidepressant, no longer available in the U.S. because of its toxicity. Red wine and cheese accelerate its effect, making a small dose a megadose. The central nervous system zooms up and down like a roller coaster. Eventually the heart and lungs collapse. Dana's did, anyway. We can only assume he either wasn't told about mixing alcohol and inhibitors, or he forgot in the heat of the moment." O'Keefe glanced at Emily's doodling. It looked like a bunch of ornate little faces. "So you can stop worrying about your culinary reputation."

Not to mention Ardith's lawsuit. "But why would Dana take antidepressants?"

"Obviously, he thought he was depressed. Any idea where I might find the prescription? A little concrete proof never hurt."

"Dana had a lot of pills at his office." It still seemed so ridiculous, such an elementary mistake. "You're sure about this?"

"The medical examiner seems pretty satisfied. If your sister's got a moment, have her call, would you? Maybe she saw him take something."

Ward lurched into the pantry. She had been crying and was quite drunk. "Who killed my dishwasher, O'Keefe?"

Across the room, the detective could smell gin on Ward's breath. "I believe he drowned by accident. He had been drinking pure grain spirits, then decided to go for a little walk in a pond."

"That's ridiculous."

"He wasn't robbed or assaulted in any way. All we found in his pockets was a check from Diavolina and a little orange tassel. Looks like it came from a lampshade. You're welcome to take a look at it any time. It's in a drawer at the morgue with his other belongings."

Ward sagged against the door frame. "I hate morgues."

"There's some good news," Emily said after a moment. "We're off the hook with lawsuits. Dana died of substance abuse. He mixed antidepressants and alcohol."

"Who cares about that idiot?" Burping robustly, Ward rummaged in her pockets for a tissue. "Slavomir never mixed drinks. Whatever he started with, he stuck with. The night he drowned, he started with port." She blew her nose so hard it sounded like brains, not phlegm, avalanching through her sinuses. "You think about that, Detective." She left the pantry.

O'Keefe sighed. "On that fine note, I think I'll call it a day."

Emily accompanied him to the door and watched him pad lightly down the back steps. "So what's the verdict, Major?" Klepp called as she returned to the kitchen. "Don't keep us in suspense. Did Byron's sauce finally kill someone?"

She turned. Even Yip Chick was waiting for her reply. "Respiratory failure."

"Makes sense." Klepp sighed to his gherkins. "That broad's cleavage would choke any red-blooded man to death."

Emily left the kitchen as Chess, for the nth time, was expressing her profound outrage at Klepp's remarks; the two of them had no idea how like an old married couple they sounded.

By the time Detective O'Keefe had battled his way from Diavolina through rush-hour traffic to State Street, the traumatized employees of Major & Forbes had fled. At first, O'Keefe thought the office was empty; then he saw a purse on Marjorie's chair, so he rang again. Finally she came to the door. "Yes?"

He introduced himself. "You're an employee here?"

"I'm the executive secretary, Marjorie Fischer."

Made sense; she was the perfect cross between a mother hen and Genghis Khan. And she had great legs. "I'd like to ask a few questions about Dana Forbes."

"Then you might wish to speak with Mr. Major, his partner." Marjorie kept O'Keefe waiting in the foyer while she went to a rear office. After quite a pause, she returned. "This way, please."

Ross was at his large window, watching boats in the harbor. As he turned to face the detective, a black cloud turned with him and filled the room. "I'm Ross Major," he said, extending a hand. "How can I help you?"

O'Keefe felt bad for even thinking that Major had been back here fooling around with his secretary. "I'm sorry about your partner," the detective began. Noticing Ross's face harden, he decided to skip the eulogies. "Would you happen to know if he was taking any drugs?"

"He gave up cocaine a few years ago." Hampered his erectile tissue.

"How about prescription drugs? Pills of any kind?"

Ross's eyes glittered harshly. "Dana took plenty of them."

"Would he have left any bottles here?" O'Keefe saw Ross and Marjorie exchange an intimate, questioning glance; maybe they were sleeping together after all.

"This way," Marjorie answered not quite immediately. She led O'Keefe to Dana's office, which the setting sun had flooded with soft, red light. Baccarat decanters on the shelves sprayed a thousand blue fires along the mahogany walls. The office was so alive, so much Dana's, at this time of day; no wonder Ross couldn't bear to come in. Marjorie gestured toward the colony of bottles on Dana's desk. "They're mostly vitamins, I think."

O'Keefe poked through kelp, cod-liver oil, B-complex tablets, amino acids, and assorted dietary supplements guaranteed to achieve, if not immortality, a body that would outlast a senile mind by a good decade. After thirty bottles, he gave up. "Is that all?"

"Maybe there's something in his worktable."

Ross appeared in the doorway, watching as O'Keefe opened Dana's top drawer. "What are you looking for?"

"Iproniazid. It's an inhibitor. Cheerful little pink pills. For severe depression."

"What? Dana was never depressed a day in his life."

"That's what your wife said," O'Keefe answered, realizing too late that he had made a faux pas.

"Dana took an overdose of antidepressant pills?" Ross said.

"Not quite. He mixed them with cheese and alcohol. The combination was lethal." O'Keefe looked at Marjorie. "Did you happen to see him take any pills yesterday?"

"No."

"Did anyone?"

Marjorie suddenly scowled. "I have no idea."

O'Keefe sensed that he was standing in the crossfire of a battle that only peripherally involved the deceased. His opinion was reinforced by the sight of a large, frilly hat perched on a bronze bust in the corner. "Thank you very much," he said, heading for the door. "I think that will take care of everything."

After he had left, Marjorie turned to Ross. "Have you ever heard of iproniazid?"

"No. I thought Dana only took aphrodisiacs." He frowned; Dana had never mentioned anything about clinical depression, either. "At least Emily's off the hook."

Ross sent Marjorie home. Before leaving the office, he went to Dana's window and stood for a long time watching the sun coruscate the surrounding skyscrapers, wondering if he would ever build another.

# 5

Ardith had sent a dashing photograph of her husband to the Boston *Globe* along with his obituary. Ironically, it had been taken aboard his yacht, where he had spent his happiest hours, away from her. Ross read the article twice, yet his attention always returned to the number following Dana's name. Forty-five: That was only half a lifetime.

It was a humid, gloomy morning, appropriate for a premature burial. It was not a day to eat breakfast out on the veranda. Ross glanced across the kitchen table at Emily. " 'Died unexpectedly,' it says. There's no mention of the restaurant or your sister."

"Everyone knows that already." She tried to swallow a bite of toast. Blah: not hungry. "I wonder how many people will be at the funeral. There wasn't much in the way of advance notice."

"Word gets around. And this should help." Ross showed her the announcement in the lower left corner of page two: Major & Forbes, Architects, would be closed today in memory of Dana Forbes. Still not quite believing the words in front of him, Ross stood up. "I think I'll mow the lawn."

"It's only six o'clock, honey. You can't make any noise until seven." Emily went to Ross's chair and slid her hands behind his neck. "Come lie down. I'll give you a back rub."

Good idea. His entire body ached: adrenaline versus exhaustion. Ross couldn't remember the last time he had gone back to bed right after breakfast. Maybe on his honeymoon. He couldn't think of a better way to pass the three hours before Dana's funeral other than asleep, a half dimension closer to his departed friend. If Emily gave him a back rub, he might be able to doze for a while. He took his robe off and lay naked on the bed. One advantage of not having children: no need to wear pajamas. Emily straddled him and began kneading the knots cabling Ross's neck. Dense as elm roots; another week like this and his head might fuse to his shoulders. She pressed and pummeled his familiar body, loving it all the more fiercely and protectively as its youth faded. It was a trophy of the years they had spent together, a gentle reminder of the years they had left. How many would that be? More years than Dana had. She kissed Ross's ear. "I love you."

He smiled into the pillow. Emily, Emily . . . without her, he was just vinegar and dust. Ross rolled over, tilting her to the bed: enough back rub. Now he wanted a front rub. "In a playing mood?"

"Sure, big boy."

Several hours later, clad in black, they left for Dana's funeral. Ross wanted to be early, in case Ardith needed him. The service was in Weston, at the picturesque church where Dana and Ardith had married. Over the past twenty years, the Forbes family had returned to it at Christmas and Easter, so the minister sort of knew them, and there was still space in the graveyard.

"Lots of cars," Ross remarked as they drew up. Indeed, the front steps of the church pullulated with architects, lawyers, and accountants, all sorry to be there, but discreetly networking nonetheless. The smokers in the crowd pulled heavily on their cigarettes, taunting the gods. Just about everyone recognized Ross. As he mounted the half-dozen steps, many came over to pay their respects; he, not Ardith, was the one burying a partner today. His colleagues made small talk as best they could, careful to avoid mentioning the actual circumstances of Dana's death. Rumors involved a tryst with an actress and a spectacular finale in a posh restaurant: pure Dana. He died as he had lived. That was about as heroic as one got nowadays.

Ross and Emily gradually made their way into the church foyer, where Ardith was surrounded by family members. Neither she nor her college-aged sons were crying. Then again, Dana had not spent much time at home over the last fifteen years. Emily's grip on her husband's arm tightened as they approached: Everyone in this corner knew exactly where, how, and with whom Dana had died. They all must know that it really was her fault. Now she'd have to shake Ardith's cold hand and say she was sorry.

Feeling his wife's anxiety, Ross patted her arm. Then he embraced Dana's widow. "Hello, Ardith." Emily repeated the embrace, without the words; Ardith made the perfunctory response. They had never seen each other except on social occasions, and perhaps this was just another social occasion. All things considered, Ardith looked outstanding today. She was dressed for afternoon tea rather than her first days of widowhood. Her breath smelled like champagne.

Ross led Emily inside the sanctuary. He looked around a moment, then headed for a pew near the front. In it sat Marjorie, staring at Dana's shiny mauve coffin. At this proximity, it appeared tremendous, impenetrable as Fort Knox. Could Dana be trapped forever inside? Finally noticing Ross and Emily, Marjorie moved over. Ross sat next to her; perhaps their shoulders touched. Gradually the church filled and the service began. Observing that some people smirked when he referred to Dana as a "faithful servant of the Lord," the minister kept his sermon brief. The skies thickened as the mourners filed outside to the graveyard, stepping quietly between the headstones: Beneath their feet rested many broken hearts. More and more people began daubing their eyes with handkerchiefs. Dana was no saint, but he sinned with style. They would miss him terribly for a while.

As the minister was reading about dust to dust, a long white limousine prowled up to the church. The sound of crunching pebbles diverted the mourners' thoughts from the eternal to the temporal: Dana had been upstaged. Please, God, no, Emily prayed as the vehicle, molecule by molecule, came to a halt. Even the minister paused.

The chauffeur silently opened a rear door and helped a black-swathed figure to the curb. No one could make out face nor race: too many filigree veils, gloves, and stockings. Gender obvious, however. A silk frock rustled around her calves as she walked to a tree well away from the crowd and stood silently in its shade, as if she were too ethereal to get any closer to bestial humanity.

Emily looked at Ross and imperceptibly shook her head.

After a moment's inertia, Ross turned coolly toward the minister, who resumed his text and gradually regained everyone's attention. Except Ardith's, that is: With excruciating deliberation, Ardith glanced over, lingeringly, toward the black figure. Then her gaze traveled slowly toward Emily, who knew in that moment that Diavolina's lawsuit had just risen from the dead. Oh Christ, what could Philippa have hoped to achieve by coming here? Had she brought a photographer along? Emily's guts began to churn as she imagined the cinematic possibilities. Philippa was not above throwing herself into the open grave in an orgasm of grief.

The minister finished with a few upbeat comments about resurrection and everyone said Amen; hell, it really would be great to see Dana again. Then they all threw a little dirt on the shiny mauve coffin, about the color of Revlon Frosted Nail Polish #42, that Ardith had picked out. The service was over. Dana's colleagues bid their respects to his widow, whose eyes were not only dry but positively caustic, and returned to their cars. The solitary figure in black remained under the tree as the crowd rippled past; every man there thought about introducing himself, but she was so obviously one of Dana's mistresses that now was not really the time. Maybe they'd ask Ross about her in a week or two. Finally, when only a dozen die-hards remained at the graveside, she returned to her limousine. It rolled majestically away.

White as an egg, Ross embraced Ardith, again offered his assistance, and took Emily back to their car. As soon as he shut her door, she opened the glove compartment and lunged for a flask filled with gin, managing to swallow two good slugs before he reached the driver's seat. "Let's get out of here," Ross muttered, throwing the Saab in gear. "Are you up for lobster?"

"You bet."

Ross got jazz on the stereo and poked toward the highway. Once on Route 95, he shot north at ninety miles an hour. Then he glanced in the rearview mirror. "I don't believe it."

"The police?"

"No. Philippa."

Emily twisted in her seat. The white limousine was right behind them. "Pull over. I'll take care of this." Ross screeched into the next rest area. Emily slammed her door and stomped to the long white vehicle braking behind them. Seeing her approach, the chauffeur rolled up the bulletproof shield separating him from the passenger compartment. Emily flung open the door. "Get out," she screamed. Nothing happened. "Philippa! Get out!"

"I can't," a voice quavered. "I'm sick."

Emily peered inside. Philippa had removed her veils and gloves and was listing heavily toward the far door. She looked chartreuse; this was no act. "What's the matter?" Emily cried.

"I don't know. It just hit me. Watch out!" Philippa lurched toward the door and vomited into the grass. "God, my stomach hurts." She threw up again.

"What have you been eating?"

Philippa retched dryly. "Apple juice."

"That's it?"

"That's it since I left Boston. I ate too much at your restaurant."

Ten yards ahead of them, Ross waited in black silence. Emily sighed: caught in the middle again. "Here are my house keys," she said, tossing them to her sister. "Try to make it back to

Boston and lie down. Call Dr. Woo. He's in the address book by the phone." She took a few steps backward. "I've got to take care of Ross now."

"Where are you going? To the lake?"

"No, Maine. He needs to drive. Why the hell did you go to the funeral?"

Philippa replied with another gush of vomit. When that was over, she rasped. "It was the least I could do. When are you getting back?"

"Around dinnertime. How long will you be staying?"

"I have to be in New York tonight." Actually, she was supposed to be there now, doing interviews for *Choke Hold.*

"You can't go on a plane in that condition."

"It's just a bug. I'll get it out of the system one end or the other." Philippa retched again. "Go take care of Ross."

"Call Dr. Woo. He likes me. He'll see you right away." Emily returned to the Saab.

Ross accelerated back onto the highway. "So why was she following us?"

"Maybe to apologize. She's pretty sick. Didn't you see her throwing up?"

"No, I was watching a raccoon raid the garbage cans." Ross drifted into the fast lane. "Why'd she go to the funeral?"

"Because she felt bad! Ross, she's my sister! We just have to live with her."

He depressed the accelerator another inch. Other men had mothers-in-law. He had Philippa. Family, the surtax on marriage; you never knew the percentage until it was too late. Paying without complaint was the true test of a man's nobility. At least a mother-in-law had the grace to die twenty years before you did. Philippa would be galling him the rest of his life. "She could have hired a black Mercedes," was his final word on the topic.

Emily dozed for a while. Then she awoke, horrified: symptoms of food poisoning could appear as long as eight days after ingestion; she remembered that from cooking school. Emily imagined Philippa going to a hospital and getting her stomach pumped.

They'd discover evidence of botulism. Wyatt Pratt would find out and up Ardith's ante another million bucks. The case would drag on for months and Diavolina would lose. Then Ward would sue Emily. Ross would go bankrupt trying to defend her. They'd both end up in prison forever.

"Ross, could you please pull over?" she asked after a while. From a rest stop in New Hampshire, Emily called home. "Philippa? How do you feel?"

"Worse. My gut's killing me. I think I'm seeing double."

"Get Dr. Woo!" Emily nearly shouted. "He'll make a house call!"

"All right. I really don't know what's the matter."

"You might have food poisoning."

There was a slight pause. "From your restaurant?"

"Please don't get Diavolina into this, Phil. That's all I ask. I'll explain later."

Philippa hung up and hurried to the bathroom again, amazed at how much fecal sludge a body contained. She called Dr. Woo, who happened to be leaving downtown for his suburban office, and could stop by Beacon Hill in about fifteen minutes. Philippa returned to the bathroom and began sprucing herself up for the doctor's visit. She was applying a bold streak of eyeliner when she realized that Woo was expecting to see Emily Major, not Philippa Banks, in distress. So she washed off all her makeup and began again, much more pudently this time. Then she took some tea to the atrium and dialed her agent in Los Angeles; perhaps business would take her mind off her gastrointestinal eruptions.

"Hi, Simon, thought I'd check in. Any word on that new role?"

"This is a bad time, baby. I'm on the horn with Paris. Lemme call you back. You're at the Plaza?"

"No, the hairdresser," Philippa lied.

"What? Aren't you supposed to be doing interviews this afternoon?"

"Don't worry! Everything's under control!" Philippa hung up, regretting the call. Simon would hit the roof if he ever found out she was in Boston instead of New York. She hadn't meant to make a day of it, of course: jump on a shuttle, cruise to a funeral, make a desperate search for that man who had come to her table at Diavolina, return to Manhattan. She hadn't planned to get violently ill. And the beast hadn't even shown up!

The doorbell: Dr. Woo. He was much handsomer than his name would imply. Thank God she was wearing Emily's blue silk dressing gown! "Thanks for coming," Philippa said, leading him to the den. "I've been throwing up and my head's killing me. I can't see straight, either."

Wondering whether or not to compliment Emily on her brassy new hair color, Woo put his bag on the coffee table. "Could this be a hangover?"

"Of course not, you imbecile!" Philippa recovered herself. "Sorry. I don't know what got into me."

"Is there diarrhea?"

"Not anymore."

He looked into her mouth then checked her pulse, temperature, and pupils. "Have you been taking any drugs?"

"Absolutely not."

"What have you been eating? Anything unusual?"

Philippa had to think fast: What would Emily have had for breakfast that might have made her sick? "A couple raw eggs. And some steak tartare." She saw Woo looking at her blankly. "We ran out of granola."

"Would you have any of this food left? Could I see it?"

"I'm afraid I ate it all."

"The eggs too?"

"Ross finished the eggs."

"And how does he feel?"

"Fine! Fine! I scrambled his."

Woo nodded. "Could you get me a stool sample?"

"Not anymore. They're all in Boston Harbor."

"How about urine, then?"

"Doc, I've been peeing, puking, and shitting all morning. There's nothing left, believe me. Just give me some medicine

and get me out of here!" Philippa realized that she was not acting in the least like her sister. Maybe crying would help. "Forgive me," she sniffled. "I just don't feel well at all."

"I understand." He withdrew a hypodermic needle from his
kit.

"What's that? You're not going to knock me out, are you?"

"Of course not. I would like to take a blood sample."

"But you can't! I'm terrified of needles!"

"Since when?" Woo deftly pulled a rubber rope from his bag.

Philippa backed up a few feet. "Touch me with that thing and
I'll kick your balls to Faneuil Hall."

Woo took a step forward but hesitated when he saw Philippa's
foot rise. He put the rubber rope away. "I'll call in a prescription
right away. They deliver. Stay in bed the rest of the afternoon. If
you don't feel better, call me tonight." He glanced at his watch.
"That will be one hundred fifty dollars, please."

Great! She had just given most of her cash to the chauffeur.
Philippa had been intending to hit a money machine on the
way back to the airport. "One moment," she said pleasantly,
going to the nearest desk. It contained nothing but architectural
paraphernalia. Philippa tried to look confused. "Where could I
have left my checkbook?"

"Isn't it usually in the kitchen drawer?" asked Woo.

"Ah, of course! Wait here, I'll be right back." Philippa hurried to the kitchen. There were drawers all over the place. One
by one, she tore them open, becoming more agitated with each
wrong guess. Finally she reached a narrow drawer at the end of
the counter, near the telephone. Inside was a slim leather
checkbook. Philippa grabbed it and had almost shoved the
drawer shut again when a flyer caught her eye. It was a publicity
shot of the staff at Cafe Presto, with July's menu underneath. As
she lifted it out, her pulse began to skip. Yes, yes! There he was,
the man who had come to her at Diavolina! He stood next to
Emily in the back row, grinning impishly. Guy Witten, the caption said. Guy. What a perfect name. Smoky eyes; a face half
Marlboro man, half Valentino; his mouth was only an eight-
inch hyphen on the page, but Philippa extrapolated it to life-

size, and quivered. He would be seismic in bed. She wondered how her sister's affair had started, how long it had been going on, how often they—

"Excuse me," said Woo from the doorway. "I'm parked illegally outside."

Philippa slammed the drawer shut and quickly scribbled a check. "Thank you so much. I'm feeling better already."

"Lie down, Emily, you're sicker than you think," Woo instructed after a quick glance at the indecipherable handwriting. At least the numerals were sort of clear. "Drink plenty of fluids. Call immediately if your fever persists. And tell Ross he's due for his annual checkup." Woo hurried out, resolving never to make house calls again.

As soon as he left, Philippa returned to the kitchen and rummaged through the drawer; maybe Emily had more flyers lying around. Philippa found nothing but Indian and Chinese takeout menus and a few old shopping lists. A sudden pain lashed her gut, forcing her back to the couch in the atrium. For a while she lay on her back, wondering how to proceed with this fellow named Guy: a bit tricky, as she didn't know if he was still involved with Emily. From the few words he had said to her in the restaurant, Philippa inferred that he and Emily had recently had a fight. From the way he had touched her across the table, however, it was clear that Guy considered his affair with Emily far from over. Had they made up? Did Ross have any idea? No, Philippa was sure he didn't. Ross was a samaritan in all matters but Emily. Over the years Philippa had seen his eyes following his wife across enough crowded rooms to know that he registered every iota of gravitational pull she exerted on the surrounding Tarzans. Ross rarely interrupted her; he just observed from afar, and never forgot. This man fooling around with Emily had no idea what Ross could do to him.

The more Philippa thought about Ross, the less enthusiastic she felt about him finding her here this evening. Emily wouldn't be too thrilled, either. Discovery of that picture had salvaged her trip; after her prescription was delivered, Philippa called a cab and hobbled to the airport. She was back in her Manhattan hotel a few hours later.

After Dana's funeral, Ross and Emily drove to Maine. They ate lobster and spent most of the day walking along the beach, holding hands as the surf chased their feet. For miles they hardly spoke. After fifteen years of marriage, conversation had acquired the rhythm, the inevitability, of a body function: When it happened, it happened. Finally Ross began talking about a year off, just traveling. He'd like to spend a few months in Tahiti studying the fish. Talking about fish led him to talk about boats, about harbors, about Singapore, then about his new project there, the old projects he still had to finish up. By the time they had circled back to their car, Ross was resigned to going back to the office tomorrow and picking up the pieces.

Around midnight, they returned to an empty house on Beacon Hill. Since Emily had not mentioned the possibility of an overnight guest to Ross, she was relieved to see no sign of Philippa, not even a note of thanks next to the house keys. But Philippa was no idiot; after a lifetime of romantic entanglements, she had learned when to make a grand entrance, and when to utterly vanish. Emily resolved to call her first thing in the morning, ask how she was feeling; then she realized she had no idea where Philippa had gone. It was always like that.

Early the next day, Emily returned to Diavolina. A new menu would be in effect and she thought the staff would be at work preparing for the debut. Instead, she found everyone at the coffee machine handing Klepp money.

"Hello, Major," he called. "Have a nice day off? You got a little sun, I see."

She walked over. "What's going on here?"

"Give me ten bucks, please. You have to guess how many people are going to order the Mixed Tofu Grill tonight. Winner take all."

Chess had fought viciously to get it on the menu. "What if no one orders it?" Emily asked.

"Sorry, I already put my money on zero. You'll have to pick another number."

"Is this some sort of joke?"

"What? It's a tradition. Leo always ran a pool when he changed the menu."

Emily put twenty bucks on fifty orders and told everyone to return to their stations. She met with the day's suppliers and was about to leave the storeroom when Byron came in. "Maje," he said in an undertone, "I have something for you. Well, not for you, for Phil. Why didn't you just tell me she was your sister? I can understand you wanting to protect her privacy. But I wouldn't have told anyone. Really. Anyway, could you give these to her, with love from Jimmy?" Byron drew a handful of photographs from his apron pocket. "Souvenirs of her evening at Diavolina."

"He took pictures?!"

"It was totally discreet! Jimmy's a pro. He has a special camera."

Emily grabbed the stack and began riffling through the uppermost snapshots: all Philippa and Dana, smiling, swallowing, toasting, preening, autographing, unaware of what was about to happen to them. Emily's ribs began to fuse one to the other, squeezing her heart to a walnut.

"Great, aren't they?" Byron murmured after a long, transfixed moment.

Her eyeballs burned. "I presume Jimmy only took pictures of the living."

"You mean did he take any of the body on the floor? Gad, no! He almost fainted himself! You will deliver these to Phil, won't you, Maje? Maybe you could get an autographed head shot in return."

Ward loomed at the door. Her hair looked as if mice had nibbled away all the best parts. "You've got a monk asking for you, Emily."

Emily stuffed the pictures into her pants pocket. "Thanks."

Brother Augustine was waiting at the counter with another basket of mushrooms. As she approached, he studied her intently, quizzically, the way many people had over the years;

Emily resisted an urge to ask if he had seen Philippa in *Tropical Heat*. Under the kitchen lights he looked wise but very old; then again, he had been hearing the same hackneyed plots in the confessional for half a century.

"Hello, Emily." Augustine showed her the contents of his basket. "We've had excellent luck in the woods lately. Were the grisettes I brought you last week a success?"

"Howling," answered Klepp.

Augustine ignored him. "How's your supply of honey holding out?"

"Fine. What else can you offer me?"

"Fruitcakes and Labrador retrievers. Not to eat, of course."

"Some monastery, Augie," Byron called. "What's its name again? Saint Wal-Mart?"

Emily invited Augustine to her office. "Sorry about that," she said when her door was shut. "They're the worst eavesdroppers I've met in my life."

"You've never been in a monastery, my dear." Augustine sat in the chair across from her. "So! What can I do for you?"

"You haven't sent me a bill," Emily said.

"I thought that Leo would have told you about our arrangement."

"I've never met Leo in my life."

The monk went very still. "Leo didn't bring you here?" he asked quietly.

"No, he skipped town. I'm not quite sure why. Is he some kind of lunatic?"

Augustine took a deep breath. "I've known Leo Cullen since we were teenagers. He's had a very difficult life. Beneath his frightening exterior, he's a decent man. He's been in the restaurant business almost as long as I've been wearing a robe. Over the years, we've been able to help each other out in a number of ways."

That was a lot of free mushrooms. "What happens to the restaurant if Leo doesn't come back?"

"He always does," Augustine said with a monk's delphic smile.

After changing the topic to fruitcakes and retrievers, Emily walked Augustine to his car. "You'll be back on Monday?"

"Of course." He got in. "Do you enjoy working here?"

Again she felt that this was more than a simple inquiry, and was torn between a desire to confess all and an irritation that Augustine didn't ask the real question on his mind. "It beats watching Fellini," she replied after a moment.

He nodded and drove away. Emily went to Ward's office. "Got a minute?"

"Sure." Ward shoved a few papers aside. "How was lover boy's funeral?"

"Not fun." Emily sat on the tattered couch. "How long have you been working here?"

"Seventeen years. I started as a waitress. Waitron. Whatever. Then I was the weekend hostess, then bartender, then manager. Why?"

"So·you've known this man Leo for a long time."

"He hired me, sweetheart. I told you that already. Why do you keep asking about Leo? Did Augustine say something?"

"I don't understand why Leo just took off. He's the owner, he's the chef, Diavolina's his baby. Have you heard from him at all?"

Ward sighed, ever so slightly beginning to lose her patience. "The last I heard from him was about two weeks ago. He called at three in the morning and said an emergency had come up. He had to leave town and I might not be hearing from him for a while. He told me to do anything necessary to keep the place running. I grabbed at a few straws and you turned up. Something of a mixed blessing, I might add."

But that was the story of her life. "I see." Emily returned to the kitchen.

The new menu involved lots of pasta, fish, and late summer vegetables. Mustapha worked silently on an array of compotes and ice cream, featured prominently in this month's carte; they were hard to burn. Byron flitted around the kitchen, dispensing unsought advice. Emily went over the wine list with Zoltan and met a half dozen suppliers. At eleven o'clock, Bruna from the

Peace Power Farm arrived. "Leo back yet?" she asked, heaving a few crates onto the counter.

For a moment the only sound in the kitchen was the chitter of knives on cutting boards. Then Emily wearily said, "Not yet, Bruna."

When the supplier had left, Emily went to the bar, where Zoltan was instructing a new waitron how to pour wine. "How are your reservations for tonight?"

"Full. Ever since the accident Monday, we've been busy. In the old days, if someone dropped dead in a restaurant, it would suffer. Now, it increases business. America is a strange country." The phone rang. "Diavolina. One moment, please." With a sly smile, he handed the phone to Emily.

It was Guy. "Hello, love. How are you?"

"Fine."

"Whoever answered the phone is standing two feet away, right?" Guy switched to Yes, No, and Okay questions. "Was Dana's funeral yesterday? I thought it would be easier for you if I didn't go. Is Ross doing all right? How's Diavolina? Could we get together?" No answer. "Just to say hello?" Silence. "Please? I'd like to stay your friend, darling. Really."

Emily realized that she had made a critical mistake in leaving Guy before her lust had run its course. Had she stuck around another two weeks and let that happen, perhaps they could be friends now. But the fire was still raging, undoused by familiarity and access and the million tiny discoveries that demoted ardor to coziness to, finally, platonism. Maybe Philippa was right: screw the guy blind, then get to know him. You'd find out a lot quicker which ones really loved you for your brains. "I'll call you back," she said, hanging up.

Dinner was a smash. First there was a run on shrimp with bitter chocolate sauce. Then they moved a ton of ziti with roast squab. Even Chess's Mixed Tofu Grill sold nicely, although a lot of it came back uneaten and no one asked for doggie bags. Pink wine and sloe gin did particularly well; maybe it was the full moon. When the rush had ended, Emily turned the kitchen over to Byron and went home.

She found Ross out on the balcony. It was a clear, calm night, just a bit cool, shimmering with the music of crickets: summer's death rattles. Emily poured herself some gin and sat beside him. "Hanging in there, darling?"

"Somewhat." Major & Forbes was rebounding. Everyone who'd had a project in the pipeline with Dana had called, wanting Ross to take over. Four of the senior staff had expressed an interest in moving to Dana's office; tomorrow, the remaining three senior staff would do the same. Ross could feel the seven of them pawing the ground, preparing to stampede. He was tempted to divide Dana's projects among them, wait a year, and see if he had a business left. All day long he had been receiving condolences from the overseas accounts who had just read Dana's obituary in the *International Herald Tribune*. Bouquets were choking the office. Tomorrow he'd try to concentrate on his current clients.

"How's Marjorie doing?"

Ross finally smiled. "She's running the show. I just do what she tells me."

Emily took a long swig of gin and listened to a million crickets drone their mating calls. The loudest ones usually won. "Maybe you should put Marjorie in Dana's office."

"Now that's a great idea. I might do that."

She followed the slow lights of an airplane across the sky. "Any word from Ardith?"

"Regarding lawsuits? You don't have a thing to worry about. The accountant told me she was ecstatic with her widow's benefits. She's not going to blow thousands of dollars on a lawyer who will probably lose her case with Diavolina." Ross patted his wife's knee. Then his face hardened. "She's coming in tomorrow afternoon to clean out Dana's office. Marjorie and I will have to spend the morning getting it ready. Remove the panties from his bottom desk drawer, get a couple hats out of there, confiscate his address book, rip up all the love letters he hid in the building code manuals. Things like that."

"Why bother?" Emily said. "Ardith knows."

"Maybe. But she doesn't know how much. No need to rub her nose in it." He looked at her. "Is there?"

Danger here: Emily retreated. "No, I suppose not. Were there that many?"

"Dozens." Hundreds, actually. In retrospect, Dana was incredibly lucky. No paternity suits, no VD, no blackmail threats, nothing. Until Philippa, of course. Ross toyed with an ice cube. "How was Diavolina today?"

"Everyone keeps hoping this phantom called Leo comes back. My sous-chef's begging for a black eye and Ward's been hitting the bottle nonstop since the dishwasher drowned. Somehow it seems worse when a weight lifter loses it. All that discipline wasted." Then Emily thought of the newspaper article in Ward's files. "Do you remember anything about a girl jumping off the Darnell Building?"

Ross looked blankly at her. "What brings that up?"

"I happened to see an old clipping. Dana was mentioned."

"Naturally. He was the architect. I vaguely remember some poor girl trying to fly off the fortieth floor. Probably on drugs."

"When was this?"

"About ten years ago. Where'd you see the article?"

"On Ward's desk. Kind of strange to save a clipping like that for ten years, don't you think?"

"People hang on to all kinds of strange things for a long time. Look at you and your flannel pajamas."

The phone rang. Ross picked it up. "Hello? Sure." With a puzzled expression, he handed Emily the phone.

"How are you feeling?" Dr. Woo asked.

"Much better, thank you," she said.

"You were not really yourself yesterday, I think. Not yourself at all."

So Woo had made a house call. Emily could only guess what damage Philippa had done trying to impersonate her. "I'm very sorry if I offended you. Please forgive me. I feel fine now. Perfectly fine."

"I recommend you avoid raw eggs and steak tartare for the moment."

"I will. Thanks." Emily hung up. Crap!

"What was that all about?" Ross asked.

"Philippa saw Dr. Woo yesterday. For some stupid reason, she pretended to be me."

Ross suddenly lost his temper. "What is this, some kind of game? Why does Philippa keep masquerading as you? And you keep letting her? I hope you don't think it's some kind of reverse compliment."

Ouch. "I'm not sure what she's doing."

"Why don't you find out." Ross stalked to the balcony.

Emily wandered to the bedroom, stripped, and stepped into a brutally hot shower, trying to defrost some sanity. Events of the last few days were accumulating a little too fast for proper processing. Leaving Guy would have been disorienting enough. Pile on Dana's demise, a new job, a traumatized husband, a drowned dishwasher, Philippa serenading the whole mess like a banshee—and watch her fuses blow. Emily wished she had never left Cafe Presto. She missed the aroma of cinnamon and espresso in the morning, cranky Bert, lacquered Lois . . . and she missed Guy. The mere absence of his voice had become a major deprivation. Forget the physical attraction: For the middle-aged, that was only icing on the cake, momentarily tasty but ultimately a strain on the digestion. She missed the sound of him, the sight of him across a noisy kitchen, she missed the click of the doorknob when he got her alone in his office. She did love him, of course. In addition to, not in subtraction of, Ross. Emily hung her head under the scalding water, aware now that she should have worked things out without leaving Cafe Presto like a besieged Turandot. Now, instead of Guy, she was staring at a stuporous Charlene Atlas every morning. Instead of Bert, she had Klepp. Ah, hell.

Meanwhile, Ross stood out on the balcony, regretting his latest outburst. Two minutes ago, as he was stomping out of the room, he had seen a flicker of disgust in Emily's eyes; for the first time, he had felt some tremendous, irreversible doors begin to move shut. Terrifying. He had to stop blaming her for Dana, for Philippa; it might also help to stop suspecting her of—what? Adultery? He had already made one drastic misassumption in that regard. Fool! Ross almost ran into the bedroom. Emily was still in the shower. Noticing her clothes in a heap on the floor,

Ross picked them up. Funny, after years of yelling at him to hang up his clothes, she was becoming more and more sloppy while he was becoming neater and neater. Soon he'd have to start yelling back. Ross lovingly placed her shoes in the closet, tenderly dropped her panties into the hamper: His sweet wife had worked all day long in them.

As he was folding her trousers, thinking of massaging her feet when she came out of the shower, several photographs dropped to the floor. Ross picked them up and felt his life go black again: Dana; Philippa. Ross dropped to the bed and switched on Emily's reading light. The pictures had been taken in a restaurant. Must be Diavolina. Ross's hands began to shake as, one by one, he went through the snapshots. Unposed, unaware, Dana looked so . . . overwhelmed with Philippa. His eyes consumed her. His face reflected despair, bewilderment, delight; an idiot could see he was madly in love. Philippa, meanwhile, toyed with her food, smiled into the crowd, fixed her lipstick. Why was she wearing that wig? For a disguise? Her resemblance to Emily disconcerted Ross terribly. He brought the picture an inch from his eyes. That was Philippa, wasn't it? Yes, yes; look at the red fingernails. And the ring. He remembered that Philippa was wearing their mother's ring this year, not Emily. And Emily would never be seen in such a dress. Would she?

Ross stared at the next picture for a long time. It made no sense at first. What happened to Dana? Why was Guy Witten at Diavolina? Guy did not know Philippa. Why should he be touching her like that, with an expression exactly like Dana's? And why should Philippa be allowing it?

The truth enveloped him slowly, coldly, as a January fog. He felt the ground slip away from him all over again. Removing the picture of Guy and Philippa, Ross put the rest of the snapshots back in Emily's pocket, dropped her pants on the floor, and retrieved her underwear from the hamper. When the pile of clothes looked exactly as she had left it, he went back to the balcony and stared at the moon, feeling doomed as the crickets.

# 6

So it was Guy. I should have figured it out. He saw Emily for eight hours almost every day for the last six years. I may have spent twelve hours out of twenty-four with her, but we were asleep for most of that. He got her awake, full tilt. I got the butt end of the bologna roll. What did she see in him? Sure, he's handsome. Well, I'm no dog. He's nowhere near as rich as I am. I don't think he's any smarter. He ain't younger. Boyish sense of humor? Irresistible perfume? Maybe it was the way he ground the coffee in the morning. Maybe none of the above. Face it, Major: He screwed her brains out. That's what she was after. That's what women are always after: romance and adoration, with a soupçon of lust. And don't let me forget sensitivity. That's the ability to come home after fifteen hours at the office—during which time you've lost a million-dollar deal to the competition, fired your personnel manager, been taken to the cleaner's by your redwood dealer, had your drawings rejected by a client who couldn't tell a penthouse from an outhouse, and been derailed by a two-bit building inspector—and be able to *notice that your wife is wearing a new pair of shoes. If you were really sensitive, you'd want to cook dinner.*

*Well, I'm no match for the exquisitely sensitive Guy. But I'm no slouch in the romance and adoration department. Not enough for her? That infuriates me. No one's perfect, not even Emily. She's not the world's most supportive wife. Never brags about me in public. When I return from a road trip, she pecks me on the cheek then goes jogging. Instead of congratulating me for earning a terrific salary, she grumbles about income taxes. So what? Do I assuage my wounded dignity by jumping into bed with Marjorie? Perhaps I should; Marjorie's been available, seriously available, for years. The two of us should go on a long road trip together. Or we could stay at the office until midnight for a week running. I could come home with a few lipstick stains and see how long the pot refrains from calling the kettle black.*

*And if Emily really doesn't care, I'll divorce her. Marjorie wouldn't mind coming to Paris with me on business trips. She doesn't have an evil twin sister. And she'd be a hell of a lot more responsive when I came home at night. True, she's no Emily. But she's five years younger. We could have children. Emily can have her fucking Guy. They can make sticky buns all day, screw each other between meals, and live happily ever after in that oh-so-cute cafe.*

*Wait a moment, why should I give my wife away? I've invested half my life in her! Perhaps she's just momentarily swept off her feet. He's had the advantage of proximity for years now. He's probably been wearing her down with sensitive, caring glances while she's been making granola, following up with comments about how nice, or how tired, she looks. I'm sure they've talked his new divorce into the ground. He's probably been planting all sorts of ideas in her head about the ecstasy of independence. And he's got a body. I've been hearing for years about how much time Guy spends in the gym; Emily usually stares at my middling potbelly as she extols the virtues of exercise. I should have told her to choose between a hard stomach and a vacation home. And why the hell is he so hung up on his pectorals? Overcompensating for a microdick, perhaps? You*

*can't do anything about that in the gym, Guy. Nothing at all. And
that's not an area I have to worry about.*

*Bastard! The world is full of desperate, beautiful women. Why
did he have to pick my wife? Oh Christ, I know why. It's so obvious. But she's mine. I earned her and I'm going to keep her.
Emily's already had second thoughts: Why else would she leave
Cafe Presto to work at Diavolina? Look at that picture of the
poor sap trying to sweet-talk her back. He's so besotted that he
doesn't realize he's doing a snow job on Philippa.*

*Emily, Emily. You never told him about your twin, love? Bless
your proud little heart. That boyfriend of yours is in for a bumpy
ride.*

═

Philippa awoke in her New York hotel with a sore stomach and
a foul disposition. Last night she had had a bad dream about
Dana. He was holding on to her arm and would not let go;
meanwhile, Guy Witten was knocking at the door, passionately
calling her name. She woke up to find her silk negligee twisted
around her neck. Guy Witten was nowhere, of course. And
today she had another eight interviews for *Choke Hold*, which
was opening this weekend in a cataract of publicity. This movie
was the final Rubicon of her career; if it flopped, she'd be doing
nothing but denture commercials the rest of her life.

Simon, her agent in Hollywood, had busted a gut when he
heard about her trip to Boston yesterday. He refused to bend to
her weeping about a tragic family affair; the least she could have
done, he screamed, was take a photographer to the funeral.
Worse, Philippa had seriously offended two very important journalists who had been expecting to interview her in New York.
They didn't care who had croaked—hey, happened every day.
They didn't happen to have time for leathery old actresses every
day. By mortgaging his very soul, Simon had been able to
reschedule them first thing this morning, and Philippa had better be sharp. Simon suggested she play up the female/survivor
angle again. If she could work in a few lines about sexual dis-

crimination, so much the better. Should they ask about future projects, he advised that she look smug and say it was all terribly exciting but still terribly secret. To end his lecture on a properly sobering note, Simon told Philippa that another actress had won the role of the brain surgeon in that television miniseries. No, the other actress wasn't younger. She must have given the executive producer the mother of all blow jobs. But there were still a few roles left. Philippa could steal the show as head nurse. Simon would jump on it today. Loved her. Bye, baby.

Philippa ordered a hefty breakfast from room service and insipidly followed an aerobics workout on television. Head nurse! That was just one step above a Mother Superior! She would rather retire than play roles like that. Philippa wanted to be remembered in a bathing suit, with sand in her cleavage; she refused to bow out as some puffy Flo Nightingale in a wacko ward. Asinine profession, acting. Just when you got your chops together, they tossed you on the junk heap. What politician would try that shit on Golda Meir when she turned forty? What publisher would tell Agatha Christie to ditch Miss Marple when she was forty? Only actresses got the noose. Philippa disgustedly yanked open her door, admitting the bellboy with her breakfast.

She dug into her oatmeal. No more of this fanatical dieting either. Forget what they said about fat being a killer. It was just as life-threatening to be slim because then you got laid. Hello venereal disease, AIDS, vengeful wives, divorce and libel suits, all manner of metaphysical chancres, for what? Nothing. That episode with Dana was the last straw. No more flings, no matter how amusing. Philippa wanted someone serious, a man she could settle down with. Like Ross. Or that other one, Guy. He was definitely serious. How the hell had Emily managed to snag two of them? By being a chef? Maybe that crap about winning men's hearts through their stomachs was true after all. Philippa sighed; that was something their mother had never told them. Emily must have discovered it by mistake. The only thing Philippa had cooked in her life was contact lenses.

She ate quickly, cursing Simon for scheduling her first interview at ten-thirty. He knew damn well that her face only stopped looking like an inflated life raft after lunch. Maybe he thought it all jibed with his Battered Survivor scenario. Philippa finally pushed her plate away, disgusted that she had eaten two muffins. As she stood up, pain ripped through her abdomen. She waited a moment, then walked gingerly to the bathroom. No more puking, please; she had done enough of that over the last two days. The spasm did not return, but the headache did. Philippa took a hot bath, willing it away: No one was going to see her looking like a whipped dog yet. When the bell rang forty-five minutes later, she was pale but ready to go onstage.

Late that afternoon, she finished her eighth, and best, interview. She had polished and amplified the victim routine on seven prior journalists and was becoming very eloquent upon the screaming injustice of being a divorced white heterosexual childless American woman approaching middle age in the late twentieth century. There was no worse time in the history of earth to be alive. The interviewer, a black lesbian, couldn't agree more. Then she asked Philippa what kind of role model her own mother had been.

Philippa looked very pained. Not really an act: Her stomach was beginning to hurt again. "I never knew my mother," she replied. "She died in childbirth. I was brought up by her brother. My uncle."

"A man?"

Philippa tried to rectify her mistake. "Uncle Jasper wasn't the marrying sort," she said meaningfully.

Luckily the woman inferred that Uncle Jasper was gay, not that he had seduced half the female inhabitants of Manhattan and was currently chipping away at the other half. "Do you still see him?"

"Oh yes. But not recently. He's been hiking in India for the last three months."

The woman finally left. Philippa still couldn't remember which rag she wrote for. Probably one of those magazines that cranked out slop about movie stars, fudge-sundae diets, and Better Sex with Your Husband month after month. Maybe Simon had set up that last interview as a warning. She called him in Hollywood. "I'm done, dear."

"You saw everyone? Great."

"Any progress with the head nurse?"

"Still working on it, babe. Give me a little time. It's been total anarchy here today. Hey, your sister called a few hours ago. Wanted your number. I didn't give it to her."

"Why not?"

"How do I know that's not some crazy going to rape you?"

"Give me a break, Simon. You know Emily's voice. It sounds just like mine." A little less strident, perhaps. "Did she say what she wanted?"

"She was wondering how you were feeling. Were you sick or something?"

"Of course not! You know I've got the constitution of a mule." Damned if she was going to tell Simon about any health problem above a hangnail. He'd stop trying to get her work altogether.

Philippa heard him flick his platinum cigarette lighter and inhale deeply. "I'm taking the red-eye to New York tonight," Simon said. "That way I'll have all afternoon to put the finishing touches on the opening." Hoping for kinder press, Simon had organized the premiere of *Choke Hold* into a gala AIDS benefit. Most of Philippa's fans were gay, after all. "Go to bed early tonight. I want you looking twenty-one years old tomorrow."

Sure, pal. Bring your time machine. Philippa hung up and uncorked a small bottle of champagne, nature's own Alka-Seltzer. When her stomach unwound a bit, she called Diavolina. "Emily Major, please," she commanded. "This is her sister."

"Hi Phil," Ward replied. "You don't know me but I run the joint. Thanks for coming in the other night. Sorry about the boyfriend. I'm pretty sure he didn't mean to cause a major disturbance in my restaurant. Anyway, business has been up ever since. We finally moved our last four cases of blush wine. Your fans drink it like fish. Come up for another dinner sometime. Choose your company carefully, though." Hearing no response,

Ward said, "Hold on, I think Emily's breaking up a fight in the kitchen." She dropped the phone.

After a while, Emily came on the line. "Philippa?"

"Who was that?" her sister demanded. "I've never been so insulted in my life."

"Ward. She's been under some stress lately. How do you feel?"

"Much better. Simon says you called."

"I did. Why'd you play that trick on Dr. Woo?"

Having expected further solicitations upon her health, not an accusatory question, Philippa needed a moment to answer. "Because you said not to involve your restaurant!"

"So you pretended to be me instead? That was pretty stupid. If you got sick from Diavolina, we're in big trouble."

"Why? I'm not going to report you. Neither is Dana."

"Think, Philippa. Do you remember anything tasting funny on Dana's boat?"

"No. We stuck to champagne, smoked salmon, and sex organs."

"How about at Diavolina then? Could you give me a rundown of the dinner?"

There was a short silence as Philippa desperately tried to remember what she had eaten. When surrounded by adoring fans, she paid less attention to food than to the visual effect of delicately chewing it. "We started off with rolls, I think. Then we had—eh . . ." What the hell was that dark, syrupy appetizer? Snails? Beans? Aha! "Mushrooms in port. They tasted a little like mildew."

Emily frowned. So much for Byron's sorcery as *saucier*. "Then what?"

"A friend of Dana's sent drinks from the bar. The four dried cherries tasted awfully sour."

Great, just great. "Who was the friend?"

"I think it was Ardith's aerobics instructor. Dana was not pleased to be seen."

"Wait a moment, how did Ardith know he'd be at Diavolina with you?"

"No idea. I sure didn't tell her. I doubt Dana did. Maybe the guy just hung out there."

Emily sighed. "Then you had the main course?"

"Yes. Steak. There were potatoes and spinach, I think."

"Swiss chard. And how did that taste? More mildew?"

"No! It was great. Delicious. Perfect." Philippa didn't mention that that idiot in the kitchen had given her a nearly raw steak; Emily sounded upset enough already. "We ate everything."

"Then what?"

Then Dana left and Guy Witten had come to Philippa's table. Philippa decided to skip that detail as well. "We had dessert. Berries and whipped cream. Superb."

"Did you drink anything else?"

"We drank a lot. I don't remember exactly what. Nothing unusual, though."

"And you haven't eaten anything since?"

"No. I've been fasting."

"Why was Dr. Woo asking me about raw eggs and steak tartare, then?"

"I made it up. He had me over a barrel, Em. Then the stupid twit tried to give me a shot."

Emily could just imagine that tender scene. "Over the weekend, did you see Dana take any antidepressant pills?"

"Nothing. Never. Why?"

"He apparently died from mixing them with wine and cheese."

"How absurd. Send that pathologist back to med school. Dana didn't take any pills."

"You mean you didn't see him take any," Emily corrected. "How's your stomach feeling?"

"This champagne seems to be staying down."

Emily heard a howl; time to return to the kitchen. "What's your schedule for the next few days?"

"Tomorrow's the opening of *Choke Hold*. Interested in coming to New York? Simon's organized a bash."

"I'll ask Ross. He could use a little comic relief."

"I'm at the Plaza. Let me know."

Emily returned to the kitchen. The howl had come from Byron, who had burned himself at the stove while casting lingering glances at the new dishwasher's gluteus maximus. Emily waited until his hand was submerged in ice water before approaching. "Byron, I'd like you to take over for a few mornings. I'm going to visit all our suppliers."

He inspected two red fingertips. "What for? They all come here."

"I'd like to see their operations."

"No problem. Stay as long as you like." Byron glanced toward Slavomir's replacement, hoping he had impressed him.

Emily located Ward at the bar. "I understand you had a few words with my sister."

Ward looked wearily up from her highball. "Bitchy little number, isn't she?"

"Not really. Sounds like she's had food poisoning."

"From here?"

"I'm not sure. I'd like to check out our sources."

"What do you think you're going to find?"

"Nothing, I hope."

"Who's going to run the kitchen?"

"Byron."

"Oy." Ward chewed on a maraschino cherry for several moments. "Is this really necessary?"

"I'm afraid so."

"All right. You have two days. Beginning tomorrow." Ward returned to her bourbon and barbells.

After speaking with Emily, Philippa ate four pieces of toast and waited an hour. When no intestinal repercussions occurred, she picked up the phone and dialed the number at the bottom of the flyer she had found in Emily's kitchen drawer. "Guy Witten, please."

"Is that you, Emily?" asked the voice at the other end. "Maybe you should hold off. Guy's been on a rampage ever since you left."

"That's asinine," Philippa snapped. "Go put him on."

The phone cracked against a hard surface. "Guy! Phone!"

Footsteps. Then he roughly said, "Yes?"

"I have to see you," Philippa whispered. "Tonight."

Complete silence. "For what purpose?" Guy asked finally.

"You'll see. Ten o'clock. Tell me where." Again that long, black silence: Philippa knew he was debating whether or not to slam down the phone. "Please," she said.

"Here." Then he slammed down the phone.

Whew, Emily had latched on to a real meteor. Philippa briefly wondered if she should postpone introducing herself to Guy until he had given up on her sister. But that might take years, perhaps forever, and she no longer had the time, or the confidence, to wait. Better to make a quick foray tonight, assess her chances of acquiring the gentleman, and withdraw so she could plan her next move. Philippa went to the closet and tried on half a dozen outfits that might pass her off as Emily. She finally settled on a red scarf, heavy tortoiseshell glasses, a black cape, and high leather boots, the most subdued items on hand. Her disguise was so effective that, although many stared, not one passenger on the shuttle from La Guardia to Logan asked for her autograph. Bolstering her courage with a few glasses of champagne on the flight, Philippa took a cab to Quincy Market. As she sat under a gas lamp, waiting for ten o'clock, Philippa watched several couples walk by. How was it possible that so many plain-looking women had managed to find partners? Did the men in this town really prefer brains to beauty? With increasing melancholy, Philippa observed young couples jabbering obliviously by. Older couples, not quite as talkative, smiled genially in her direction. Not a soul tried to pick her up. Finally, when she heard the tower clock strike ten, Philippa snapped out of her reverie. Normally, she'd keep a man waiting fifteen minutes, half an hour. But Emily would definitely be on time.

Mummifying herself with her black cape, Philippa maneuvered over the cobblestones toward a narrow street behind Quincy Market. Whenever the wind let up, she could see her breath. Suddenly she felt nervous. What had possessed her to come to Boston tonight? Besides marrying her second, third, fourth and fifth husbands, this was the rashest thing she had done in thirty years. What would she say to Guy once she had him in a dark corner? What if he wasn't quite flattered at her attention? What if he was the Accept No Substitutes type? One kiss, one whiff of her perfume, and he'd know she was an impostor. A fresh wave of nausea overturned Philippa's stomach. She should find a cab, get the hell out of here; there were still two more flights to New York tonight. No one need ever know she had been mewling shamelessly at her sister's boyfriend.

"Lost?" inquired a nearby voice.

Philippa jumped. A man stood at her side, smiling warmly. "Not at all," she huffed, marching forward.

He not only kept up, but took her arm. "Need an escort? These streets get mighty deserted this time of night."

Philippa hit him square in the face with her Gucci handbag, a deceptively heavy receptacle thanks to the makeup, keys, and coins crammed therein. Its buckle snagged briefly on the man's ear before tearing free. "Go away," she screamed, digging in her pocket. "I have a gun."

"Easy now," he croaked, covering his ear. "I thought you were someone else."

The man took off. Philippa reeled into the entryway of Cafe Presto and pounded on the door. Where the hell was Guy? She rapped harder, nearly punching her knuckles through the glass. Finally she saw a figure hurry out from the recesses of the restaurant.

Guy swiftly unlocked the door. "Lose your key, dear?"

"Shut up! I nearly got mugged!" Philippa tumbled inside. "Christ, this town is full of perverts! Can't a lady go for a fucking walk anymore?"

Guy looked at her oddly. "Are you all right, Emily?"

"Yes, yes," Philippa replied impatiently, dropping into a chair near the window. Shit! The harshest word in Emily's vocabulary was probably *darn!* Philippa slipped off her red scarf, shaking her head so that her heavy wig obscured her face, and shifted her chair so that she was perfectly situated in the shadow of a street-lamp. "Well, sit down."

"Here?" Guy asked. Emily had always preferred his office. "Don't tell me you're going public."

Philippa snorted. "I don't see many witnesses, do you?"

Wondering whether he should have skipped that third vodka gimlet, Guy did as he was told. From the other side of the small table, he studied her handsome, shadowed face. Emily had never ordered him around before. Her manner vaguely confused him; by ten o'clock, Emily was usually tired, a little blue, very soft. Tonight she was all porcupine. And that silly cape! She had nearly tripped over it twice already with those mile-high heels. Obviously she was still fooling around with a new image. He studied her bemusedly for a few moments. Then Guy remembered how Emily had dressed the other night in Diavolina, and with whom she had been dining. His smile faded. "I'm surprised you're not home consoling your husband," he said finally.

"Why weren't you at the funeral?" Philippa shot back. "I could have used some moral support."

"Surely you jest. You never wanted me within ten miles of Ross. Did the ground rules change when you started screwing his partner?"

"My, my, you are a jealous boy. I never touched Dana. He called me on the spur of the moment. I simply joined him for a bite of dinner."

"In that incredibly slutty outfit? Give me a break."

Philippa smiled wanly; Guy knew nothing about her existence. Obviously, he hadn't spoken to Emily in the last few days. And he knew how to fight back. She wondered if he had ever been divorced. "Sorry you didn't like my outfit. Everyone else did. Why were you spying on me?"

"Think again, dear. I called you that afternoon and said I had to see you."

Philippa laughed lightly, groping for an appropriate reply. "It slipped my mind."

"Obviously," Guy growled. He hadn't come here to be

taunted and abused. Quite the opposite, in fact. "I just loved seeing you smeared all over the biggest schmuck in Boston."

"Dana had a number of redeeming qualities," Philippa said airily. "Only a woman would appreciate them, of course."

"Really? Tell that to the women he's trashed."

Realizing that this conversation was not taking on the cuddly overtones she had anticipated, Philippa started to cry. Throughout her life, tears had extricated her from more sticky situations than a pair of wings would have. "How can you be so cruel," she wept. "Dana was one of my oldest, dearest friends. These past few days have been horrible."

Guy was stunned; the only other occasion he had seen Emily cry was after they had made love. He immediately went to her chair and put his arms around her shoulders. "I'm sorry, sweet," he murmured in her ear. She smelled unusual tonight, gardenia instead of lemon. A slight odor of tobacco clung to her cape. Strange: Emily was fanatical about smoke. "I've missed you," he said. For once, she did not push him away. Guy's heart leaped; was she finally coming around? Oh God! Was that why she had called him here? He kissed her neck. "Take your coat off, Plum."

Philippa nearly swooned, realizing that she could have Guy now, on the floor; yet she knew that all her thespian skill would not convince him that she was Emily. She just didn't know enough about her sister's sexual style. What kind of little noises did Emily make? Did she prefer top, bottom, rear end, mouth, ear? And what the hell did Guy like? He'd smell the cigarettes on her breath, notice the bikini lines, the red toenails, the French underwear. Philippa halfheartedly pushed Guy's mouth away from her neck. "I should go." She sighed weakly.

"No you shouldn't."

Realizing how strong, how intent, he was, Philippa became frightened. "I really must. Ross will be home in ten minutes."

Guy stopped cold. His hands and his mouth left her body. He returned to his chair and stared out the front window of Cafe Presto. Then he straightened the salt and pepper shakers. Finally he chuckled. "Well, run along, dear. We wouldn't want to keep Ross waiting, would we?"

If only he had spoken with a little anger, a little sarcasm, Philippa could have ended their conversation with a zinging retort. But she didn't know how to counter resignation. For a long while she sat dumbly, trying to winnow a decent exit line from the dozens of shallow, stupid phrases running through her head. Unfortunately, what worked so well in a movie script never sounded quite as authentic in real life. Giving up, she reached for her red scarf and purse.

As she stood, Guy's eyes followed her body. "I'm not sure why you had to see me."

Philippa shrugged, momentarily defeated. "Neither am I, actually."

They studied each other's faces, searching for any glimmer of hope. Guy was kissing Philippa's hand, Philippa was stroking his head, when an old pickup truck plowed through the front window of Cafe Presto. Philippa saw it coming but didn't react; the pickup truck belonged in another movie, on another actress's lot. "Watch out!" she screamed a few seconds too late. Then she tripped over her cape. The last thing Philippa saw clearly was a table zooming into her face.

# 7

*I've been watching him for two nights now from this shadowy stoop across the street. He just sits alone at a window table in Cafe Presto. Every couple minutes he raises his glass to his mouth. Whenever a car goes by, its headlights show Guy brooding and drinking, still waiting for my wife to come back to him. So far she hasn't appeared. But he's kept up that vigil . . . why is that? Is the man utterly stupid? Just tired? Or has Emily given him reason to hope that he doesn't wait in vain? Time will tell, I suppose; meanwhile, I detest the waiting as much as he does. It's cold out here now. My knees are beginning to bother me from all the standing. Each time I hear footsteps coming down the street, I'm petrified that this time it's my wife. The terror lasts eons, until the person walks past my little alcove. Then, seeing only a stranger, I crumple in relief. The ups and downs only get worse as the hours go by and there are fewer pedestrians, but each one seems to walk more urgently. By the end of the night, I feel like I've been electrocuted a couple dozen times.*

*Guy normally hangs in there until one or two o'clock. Doesn't he know by now that Emily goes to bed at eleven? Maybe he thinks she's just pretending to sleep, and she's waiting until a few snores come from my side of the bed so that she can steal away to him. No dice, Guy: I don't snore. Hell, I hardly even sleep. I wake up when Emily leaves the bed to go to the bathroom. I wake up when she blows her nose and even when she rolls over to look at the alarm clock in the middle of the night. I know when her body no longer rests on the mattress, and she knows I know, because I've followed her often enough into the atrium now. She ain't comin', buddy. She's still a little afraid of me, I think. Go home.*

*Ah, more footsteps: I turn to cardboard. One breath would blow me down. That you, lamb? Sounds like you. The small, rushed steps get louder, then a woman I do not know flutters by. For the moment, I am saved. I withdraw into the alcove and watch Guy, because he's going to get blown down next. There, now he's picked up movement in the street. For the twentieth time tonight, he puts his drink down and leans forward. I look at his face as the poor bugger stares with all his might, wanting the woman to be Emily so badly that he's oblivious to my face in the gloom just a few feet behind her. That's dangerous, pal. Now she's gone and he's crushed. He settles back in his chair, slightly lower than he was sitting before. Serves him right. May he slump forever.*

*I blow on my frozen hands, wondering why I don't go home before Guy abandons his watch. I can't, of course, not while there's a one-in-a-thousand chance that she's going to incarnate my worst nightmares. I must see to believe. And perhaps deep down, petty and ungracious man that I am, I really do want to catch her here. Something inside me yearns to triumph in her iniquity; it's the only way a cuckold could ever feel superior. Oh God, why doesn't she just appear on the corner and put us both out of our misery? My knees are killing me. Guy's got to have the hangover of the century by now. Meanwhile, Emily's probably curled up on the sofa in her white robe, reading a book, oblivious to the havoc she's causing on the other side of Beacon*

*Hill. She's probably feeling virtuous to boot. I should go home and wring her neck.*

*Guy's had enough. He's slowly getting up from the table, going toward the back of the dining room . . . but he's not taking his drink along. That means he's only going to pee. Damn, should have known. It's much too early to quit; the Custom House clock is only beginning to strike ten. Guy's got another fifth of vodka to polish off. I've got another three hours to frost my ass and work myself into an uxoricidal frenzy.*

*I hear a woman's shoes tapping the cobblestones; once again, true hero that I am, I shrink into the alcove to await the guillotine. Whoever it is walks fast and loud, punishing her shoes. Definitely not Emily. Someone's out there with her; I think I heard a man's voice. But now she's yelling at him to go away. Christ! That sounded like Philippa! The cold's gotten to me. I'm hallucinating.*

*A man just ran past. Someone's pounding on the door of Cafe Presto. My God, it's Philippa! Right? It's not Emily pretending to act like her sister in order to confuse me, is it? The two of them have flummoxed me before. I can't ever let them do it again. No, that's Philippa. She shouts with a certain vile authority that Emily does not possess. And she's wearing another of her atrocious costumes, half Isadora Duncan, half General Schwarzkopf. Come on, Guy, open the door before she puts her fist through it. There he is finally. She stomps inside like a ton of bricks and they sit at the front table.*

*My brain's beginning to swim. She looks like Emily now. Is that a wig or is that my wife? Why should Philippa want to see Guy? Has Emily confessed everything to her sister? What the hell could they be discussing so earnestly over there? Getaway plans? Oh Christ, he's going to her side of the table. He's kissing her neck! She's allowing it! My blood's boiling over, it's filling my lungs. Who is that she-devil over there? Has the bastard seduced both of them? Ah, my head hurts. I should never have come here. Once again I've seen what I never wanted to see, the shadow of my wife first with Dana, now with Guy. Was it really Philippa both times?*

*Get hold of yourself, Major. Of course it was.*

*Now that is strange. An old pickup truck is charging up the street. Ouch! There goes the window! Get the license, Ross, the way you learned in Boy Scouts. Haul the old legs over the curb fast, before it pulls out of range. Remember that Massachusetts plate! Now it's skidding around the corner on two wheels. Driver's a maniac.*

*I'd better see if they're alive over there. Careful: glass all over the sidewalk. I'll just peep inside. Guy's out cold or dead. Fantastic! Leave him. As for the lady . . . no, I cannot bear to turn her over and see Emily. Cannot. Maybe I should just call the police. But how am I going to explain my presence here? "Gee, Officer, I was spying on my wife and her lover, cowering across the street like I do every night from ten till one." . . . Forget it. No police. Look, she just moved an arm. She's trying to sit up, cussing like a sailor. I'd better run back to my little troll's cave.*

*She's on her feet, heading for the door. Shaken up but unhurt, it seems. Whoever it is, she's in a rush to evaporate. Look at her stumbling off, abandoning Witten like a sack of rotten potatoes. That's Philippa, all right. It's got to be.*

*I'm going home.*

<hr />

At first, the jangling phone was part of Emily's dream. Then, louder, it wrenched her into dark reality. Disoriented and damp, she awoke in her bed and groped at the pale green glow on her nightstand. "Hello?"

"It's me," Philippa said. "Did I wake you?"

"You woke us."

Thank God; that meant Guy had not called Emily from some hospital after his interrupted tryst. "I wanted to make sure I got you before you left for work," Philippa explained.

Emily glanced at the clock: four-fifteen. It was an unusual hour, even for Philippa. "What's up?"

About six hours ago, Philippa had regained consciousness on

the floor of Cafe Presto. Realizing that she should probably not
be discovered amid upturned tables, broken glass, and Guy Witten, Philippa had wrapped her aching face in her cape and
bolted for the airport, where she had rented a limousine to take
her to New York. Ten minutes ago, she had arrived back at her
hotel. "I think I have to go to a hospital," she whispered.

"Why? Is it the food poisoning?"

"No. I fell."

"Fell where? How?"

"I slipped in the bathroom. The floor was wet. I hit my face
on the tub."

"You were taking a bath at four in the morning?"

"I had to get up and pee." Philippa anticipated the next question. "No, I am not drunk. My face looks like rhubarb pie! All
my teeth are loose! I can't be seen like this!"

"Phil, go to a hospital. They'll take an X ray."

"I have a few cuts as well. My outfit is drenched with blood.
Absolutely ruined."

"What outfit? I thought you said you were asleep."

"My pajama outfit!"

"How did you get cuts falling on a bathtub?"

"What is this, the third degree? Listen, Em, it doesn't matter
how I got hurt. You have to do me the favor of your life."

On the other side of the bed, Ross rolled tetchily over. Emily
knew that he'd never get back to sleep now. He had come to
bed very late, after another solitary séance on the balcony.
"What kind of favor? Make it quick," she whispered.

"Tonight is the opening of *Choke Hold*, remember? Simon's
made it into an AIDS benefit. Media coverage out the wazoo.
You have to stand in for me."

"Come on! Your fans would crucify me."

"My fans would never know the difference. You're going as
Philippa Banks."

"Forget it. No way. Never."

"Don't do this to me, Em!" Philippa wailed. "If you took one
look at my face you'd understand! Remember, I almost got poisoned thanks to you!"

"Oh, right. Now I owe you one?"

"We're sisters! Blood! Guts! DNA!" Hearing no response, Philippa tried a new tack. "You'd have a great time, Em. When was the last time you went dancing?"

With Guy, about a year ago. They were at a nouvelle cuisine convention at the Hyatt. When he drove her home that night, he had kissed her in a different way. "This is ridiculous, Philippa. I have a full day of work today visiting all my suppliers."

"I'm begging you. My career depends on it. You don't have to do anything but show up, watch a movie, smile and wave, then leave. That's it."

"What about my job?"

"What job, that stupid restaurant? You don't have to work night and day, do you? Leave Boston when you're done with the suppliers. The screening's at nine. You dance once with Simon afterward. If you have to get back to Boston, there's a late flight from Kennedy. Nothing could be simpler."

Outside Emily's window, a heavy truck lumbered up Beacon Hill, vibrating houses. After a while, she could hear the crickets again. Yes, summer was over. Soon the snow would return. "What's your agent going to say about this?"

"I haven't decided whether or not to tell him. So you can do it?"

"Let me think about it."

"Don't think too hard! This is the most important night of the second half of my life!"

"I still don't see how you could have wrecked your face and gotten full of cuts on the bathtub."

"It was a freak accident. I'll explain when you get here." Philippa hung up.

Emily quietly replaced the phone and tried to wriggle inconspicuously back under the sheets. She had just about regained her former posture when Ross said, "Let me guess. Philippa's getting married this afternoon and needs a bridesmaid."

"She wants me to take her place at a movie opening tonight in New York. She fell in the bathtub and bruised her face."

He laughed out loud. "What a crock!"

Emily snuggled up to her husband. "Could you come with me?"

"Don't tell me you're doing it."

Second by second, she felt him shrinking away from her. "What's the matter?"

Ross was totally awake now. "Emily, you don't think that you can just wear one of your sister's tasteless outfits and convince a thousand people that you're Philippa, do you? All of her friends will be there. So will her agent. The minute you open your mouth, everyone would know. What's going on? You've spent your entire life pretending you don't have a twin sister. Now you pretend to be her?"

"I thought for one fucking night I might have a little fun."

"Now you're even talking like her." Ross slid back beneath the sheets. "Go then. Have fun for one fucking night in your life."

Overcome with guilt, Emily stroked his back for a few moments. "Ross?" He didn't move. Eventually, her hand dropped away and she lay watching the light bloom on her bedroom walls. She wanted to get away from Boston, away from Ross, Guy, death, and Diavolina for a while. At breakfast, as her husband was studying the editorial page with acute fascination, Emily announced that she would be going to New York that evening. If he changed his mind and cared to come along, she would meet him on the three o'clock shuttle. He did not ask, and she did not tell, when she would return.

Byron looked up from the comics as Emily entered the kitchen at Diavolina. "Morning, Maje. Have you seen today's paper?"

Sure, reflected upside down on her husband's reading glasses. Emily poured a cup of coffee and sat opposite Byron at the table. "Am I missing something?"

He read from a two-inch story in the local news section. "'An unidentified vehicle drove through the front window of Cafe Presto late last night, injuring Guy Witten, the owner of the popular downtown caterer. According to police reports, Witten was seated at a front table, going over the day's receipts, when the vehicle hit the window. Witten, who sustained head injuries and a sprained wrist, was unable to identify the vehicle or the driver. There were no other witnesses to the apparent hit-and-run incident.'" Byron dipped an almond biscuit into his coffee. "How would you like a Toyota up your ass after a long day?"

Emily immediately called Cafe Presto. "No answer at the restaurant," she said.

"How could there be, Maje? The building inspector would have shut it down!"

She began phoning hospitals. Mass General had had a Witten in and out of the E-room last night. Emily tried Guy's gym, with no success. "I guess he's at home," she told Byron. Forget calling there; no telling who might pick up. "Look, I'm visiting a few suppliers this morning. Tonight I won't be in. Could you take over the kitchen for me?"

"Sorry, I have other obligations tonight."

"Wait a moment! You told me yesterday to stay out as long as I liked!"

"I've worked four weeks straight in this booby hatch! My nerves are in shreds!"

"Okay, okay. Never mind." That did it: no gala in New York. Emily felt surprisingly disappointed.

Ward shuffled in wearing her pink, jam-smeared jogging suit. It was getting fairly tight around the midriff these days, giving her the appearance of a stuffed bear, minus the alert, white eyes. She went immediately to the coffee machine. "Major, I thought you were paying courtesy calls on our vendors today."

"I wanted to touch base with Byron first."

The sous-chef closed his newspaper. "Ward, who's third in command here?" Before Ward could reply "No one," Byron continued. "Seems that Emily and I both have to be out tonight."

"Oh, that's terrific. Great." Ward reached in her pocket and got a dime. She flipped it in the air, tried to catch it, missed, and finally stomped on it with her sneaker as it was rolling toward the broiler. "Heads or tails?" she called to Byron.

"What for?"

"Whoever wins doesn't have to work tonight."

"You can't do that! I told you months ago about this! You promised!"

Ward thought a moment. "Today's your grandmother's ninetieth birthday? I forgot." She looked at Emily. "What about you? Silver wedding anniversary?"

"Masquerade ball." Emily sighed. "Maybe I shouldn't go."

Klepp walked in. "Eh, what lovely, cheerful faces. Starts my day off just right. What are you doing here so early, Ward? Getting a head start on our paychecks?"

Ward opened Mustapha's refrigerator and helped herself to a wedge of chocolate cake. "Klepp, you're in charge of the kitchen today. Serve whatever you want. Just try not to kill anybody. No, on second thought, try to kill everybody." She padded back to her office.

"Inspirational words," Klepp said heartily. "You two, vamoose. That's an order."

Emily drove toward Quincy Market; perhaps she'd find Guy in front of Cafe Presto with his arm in a sling, selling muffins to the regulars. She needed to see that he was all right. Correction: She just needed to see him again. A smile would do, or a wave, any indication that perhaps he might still be a friend. Emily still hoped for that. It was probably ridiculous. Maneuvering between jaywalking pedestrians, she stopped her car near a hydrant and walked to Cafe Presto. The notice on the front door said it would be temporarily closed for renovations. For several moments Emily stared at the boarded front. One lousy car had taken out all those windows? Guy was lucky to have escaped with a sprained wrist. What could he have been doing at a front table so late at night? Waiting for her, perhaps? Waiting for someone else?

Emily saw Presto's pastry chef emerge from a coffee shop across the street. "Bert!" she called, trotting over.

"What are you doing here?" he said. "What happened?"

"A car drove through the front window last night. I read it in the paper."

"But I woke up at five o'clock to get to work! Why didn't Guy tell me?"

"He was in the hospital. The car hit him, too."

Bert was not impressed. "Do I go on unemployment now?"

"If I know Guy, the windows will be replaced in a few hours."

"Does that mean I'm supposed to hang around for lunch?" Bert squinted up the narrow street. "Hey! Lois!"

Crossing over, the cashier greeted them. Bert explained what had happened. "Mr. Witten was hurt?" Lois cried. "What was he doing when the car hit him?"

"The newspaper said he was totaling the receipts," Emily told her.

"What? *I* total the receipts!"

"That's what he told the cops," Bert scoffed. "It would look pretty stupid for him to admit he was just sitting there drunk, staring out the window."

"Bert! That's not true!"

"Sure it is, Lois. The new chef drives him to it." Bert began to talk in a foolish singsong. "In Sveden ve like valnuts, not peestachios!" He looked accusingly at Emily. "Why did you leave us like that?"

"I had to help out a friend in an emergency," Emily lied, glancing up and down the street in case Guy appeared. Every few seconds, one of their regulars would stop, read the sign in the doorway, and look around for someplace else to get breakfast.

"When's this emergency going to be over?"

"Soon." Then, well up the crowded sidewalk, Emily glimpsed a familiar head, familiar gait: Ross? Of course, Ross! His office was just around the corner. Instinctively, Emily shrank behind a mailbox; he must not see her here. Even now, it might give him ideas. "What's the new chef's name?" she asked.

As Bert and Lois launched into cruel parodies of someone called Lina, Emily anxiously followed her husband's progress down the street. Her heart began to thump as he stopped at the entrance of Cafe Presto and stared at the sign on the front door for a very long time. As Ross finally turned away and resumed walking, she dared to look at his face. He was smiling, not his normal gentle smile, but that huge, euphoric grin Ross wore when contracts were clinched, competitors smashed. Emily even thought she heard him laughing. Laughing! No, impossible. That was just residual guilt playing tricks on her. She watched until Ross had turned the corner.

Having run the Swedish chef into the ground, Lois and Bert began to discuss last night's accident. "How are they ever going to find the person who did this?" Lois said. "Why couldn't the car bash into that ugly little rug shop next door? I don't understand how someone could drive through the front window without aiming for it."

"Probably some drunk without a license," Bert replied. "That's why no one stuck around afterward."

Up the street, a truck honked at meandering pedestrians. "Can you believe it? New windows!" Lois cried, pointing at the large panes of glass strapped to the vehicle. "Guy must have called the repairmen from the hospital! He's a maniac!"

The truck slowed to a halt in front of the restaurant. "Shhh. Here comes Lina." Bert indicated a stocky woman who was ordering the driver around.

Instantly, helplessly jealous, Emily saw Lina inspect the windows and direct the men to begin unloading them. Unable to look anymore, she exaggeratedly pushed back her sleeve, found her watch. "I've got to go. Give Guy my best."

She returned to her car and a bright orange parking ticket. Robotic commuters already jammed the narrow streets, battling for position with cab drivers who would rather take a fork in the eye than stop for a red light during rush hour. Emily squeezed along the expressway toward the turnpike, where she slipped behind a Corvette. They flew west in tandem, slowing down for a few patches of fog. After fifty minutes, Emily left the turnpike and headed into the hills of central Massachusetts. The leaves here had turned brilliant yellow and red; many trees had already become skeletons until spring. Only pumpkins, hay, and a few dry cornstalks remained in the fields. Misshapen carcasses, attended by large black crows, knobbed the roadside. In ten minutes Emily saw only two people, both women, both hanging laundry on clotheslines: looked sort of like the frontier days, except that these pioneers were about as wide as the satellite dishes in their backyards. Emily passed a hospital and a dilapidated gas station. Coming upon a nondescript mailbox with a cross carved in its post, she turned onto a dirt driveway. Two pheasants flapped out of her way as she drove down a rutted hill into the forest: must be a joy getting out of here in winter. Not many of the monks would even try, of course. They were supposed to be inside praying for the wretches vagrant in the twentieth century.

The woods suddenly cleared and Emily braked, staring at the granite mansion in front of her. It was thick and high, tiered with balconies and statues of angels in beneficent poses. Ross must see this, she thought immediately. He would smile at the balustrades and leaded windows, the copper roof, the sheer tonnage of this monstrosity in a meadow. He would probably even know which architect had fulfilled some demented client's dreams.

Appearing on the front steps, Brother Augustine watched Emily park the car. "You found us."

"You gave me good directions. This is quite a place."

"Not all monks live in caves." He took her arm. "How nice of you to visit. Have you had breakfast?"

Hours ago, with a monk of another sort. "Yes, but I'd love some coffee."

Augustine brought her inside to a dark foyer with a tremendous fireplace at either end. Overhead hung an iron-and-leather chandelier that looked like a ten-woman chastity belt. A sea of dark green tiles glimmered on the bare floor; one almost imagined that the room perched on a slumbering leviathan. "We'll go to the library," Augustine said. "It's warmer there."

Pushing a heavy door, he led Emily into a room overstuffed with books, rugs, and leather sofas. A fire crackled in the hearth, baking everything within ten feet. As Emily was removing her jacket, a young woman popped her head in. Had the woman not been wearing a nun's habit, Emily would have mistaken her for the lady of the house. "And what will it be, Brother Augustine?" she called cheerfully. Irish, pretty: some monastery.

"Coffee, thank you, Sister Grace," Augustine answered. He settled back in his chair and regarded Emily for a few moments. Then he smiled. "Yes, we're co-ed here."

She felt her face redden. "My knowledge of church orders is rather weak."

"This is a Benedictine monastery. The house and grounds were given by a woman who lost her husband and son in the First World War. This had been the family lodge. The widow added the statues as a last touch. We've grown rather fond of them."

"How many people live here?"

"About forty monks and nuns. There are two hundred acres on the estate. We're almost entirely self-sufficient. To make ends meet, we raise Labrador retrievers and run a small bakery."

"And sell mushrooms."

Augustine shook his head. "No, we eat the mushrooms ourselves. And give a few away."

"To people like Leo."

"Yes. Leo's always been one of our most generous supporters." Augustine fell silent until Sister Grace had poured their coffee and left. "Has anyone heard from him, by the way?"

"Not a word." Emily wasn't interested in Leo today. "Who's the mushroom expert here?"

"I am."

"Have you ever made a mistake?"

"Poisoned anyone, you mean? Only myself, and only once. I learned. Why?"

"You may have heard that we had an accident recently at Diavolina," Emily began.

"What sort of accident?"

"A woman had digestive problems after eating at the restaurant."

"I see. And now the concerned chef is checking her food sources. I appreciate your diligence, my dear, but I think I know good mushrooms from bad. Has the victim recovered?"

"Yes, I think so."

"Are you expecting a lawsuit?"

"What? No! The woman's a personal friend of mine."

"Excellent." Augustine amusedly placed his coffee cup on the table. "Who else suspects my mushrooms?"

"Just me," Emily faltered. "I apologize."

"No need. As long as you're here, would you like to see my retrievers?

Not really, but she owed him for the mushrooms. "Sure."

He led her through the cavernous foyer to a rear door. They walked along a grape arbor, pausing where a narrow path led into the woods. "This might be a bit muddy," Augustine said. "It's been raining." Smiling grittily, Emily followed him into the foliage. Who the hell wanted to see a bunch of dogs? "We're almost there," he called after a while.

The rocky path slithered up a hill. Cursing under her breath as she slipped on the damp stones, Emily followed Augustine to its crest. Suddenly the trees ended and she was gazing at a building that seemed to erupt from the hillside. It looked like a cross between the World Trade Center and a gigantic centrifuge. "That's the kennel?"

"No, that's our chapel."

"It's . . . uh . . . pretty amazing." Emily knew whose work this was. The clues were everywhere.

"The original chapel burned to the ground. We received a most generous gift to build a new one." Augustine studied her face as she stared. "Do you like it?"

No. She had never liked Dana's architecture. "It's stunning. May I look inside?"

"I'm afraid not. The monks are saying their Divine Offices. But we could walk around in front, if you like. The kennel is just over the hill. Come." Augustine went ahead.

The path ran a few feet from the cornerstone. As she walked by, Emily read the familiar credits: Major & Forbes, Architects. Ross had never mentioned the project to her. Why should he have? Dana had probably sat down one morning with a pencil and a hangover and had drawn a bunch of asymmetrical windows and shingles. Maybe, on a few nice afternoons, he had come out here in his Jaguar to supervise construction and mortify the nuns. Imagine someone commissioning Dana to design a chapel! What a joke!

She caught up with Augustine, who was walking quite fast now. They finally reached the kennel, where a dozen pups milled inside a high cage. When Augustine whistled, two trotted over. "Well, what do you think?" he asked proudly, sticking a few fingers through the mesh.

Emily knelt beside the monk. "Major and Forbes designed your chapel?"

Augustine played with a dog. "I understand they're a very distinguished firm."

Emily waited but the monk provided no further information. "They must have been very expensive."

"Our patron was very generous."

Another wait, another silence. Finally Emily said, "I read in the paper that Dana Forbes died recently."

Augustine muttered a few words in Latin. "How?"

"Drugs."

He continued maddeningly with the dog. Had Augustine asked one tiny question, made one tiny comment, Emily would have told him everything; she ached with secrets. But she couldn't begin cold. Perhaps the monk knew that; when he finally stood up, putting a hand on her shoulder, she felt that his silence had been in reality a question, and that her silence had somehow answered it.

"I'll pray for him," was all Augustine said. He took her to another path behind the kennel. In a few minutes, they were back at the main house.

"Sorry to have bothered you," Emily said, getting into her car.

"Not at all." He patted her hand. "God be with you."

Sounded like he was shipping her off to war. Emily got back to the main road and immediately called Ross's office on the car phone; she needed to ask him about Dana's little chapel in the woods. No answer on his private line, so Emily dialed the main switchboard. An assistant told her that Ross would be out all day with clients. "What about Marjorie?" Emily asked, already guessing the answer.

"She's with Mr. Major."

Why the fuck did God create secretaries? Emily nearly drove into a ditch trying to locate her position on a road map. Finally she yanked the car off the road and slapped the map around the steering wheel. Ah, there she was, on that wobbly blue line, heading north toward her second stop, Peace Power Farm. Christ! What was she doing out here chasing phantoms, wasting time, trying to appear busy while her husband got domestic with Marjorie? Emily stomped on the gas, spewing stones everywhere as she skidded back onto the road.

Twenty minutes later, she found a neat, white sign for Peace Power Farm. WE LOVE VISITORS, it said. Emily pulled into a dirt driveway with a strip of high grass in the center. It tickled her car's underbelly as she bumped toward the rundown house in the distance. Halfway there, a collie bounded off the porch and ran alongside her, yapping.

As she stopped her Saab in front of the house, a woman in a leotard emerged. She seemed about Emily's age, but floppier: Somehow the natural look didn't seem quite as natural on bodies whose elastic was shot. "The farm stand isn't open today," she called, frowning at Emily's high-octane car.

"I'm looking for Bruna," Emily shouted over the barking.

"She's busy."

"I won't be long. Would you mind calling off your dog?"

"Fidel! Come here!" The collie returned to the porch. "Who are you?"

"Emily Major." She stepped onto the grass. "I'm from Boston."

"Are you a corrections officer?"

In high heels and a red suede skirt? "No, I'm a chef. Bruna is one of my suppliers."

"She might be in the barn."

Emily walked past an archery range, where two women were intently practicing, to the dilapidated barn. There were no cows inside, just Bruna and her leviathan pickup truck. Seeing her visitor, Bruna abruptly stopped prying off a dented fender. "What are you doing here?"

"I was in the area and thought I'd drop by."

"What for? Tea and scones?"

"I'm visiting my suppliers and happened to be driving by. I like your farm."

"It's not a farm. It's a training center for battered women." With her bare hands, Bruna twisted the fender to an excruciating angle. "We teach them to batter back."

"Aha." Emily looked around at the old harnesses, scythes, and rusty implements cluttering the walls. "What happened to your truck?" she asked after a few moments, trying to sound friendly.

"It hit a phone pole."

"Was anyone hurt?"

"Yeah! My truck!" In a fury, Bruna ripped the fender off. "Look, do you mind? I have a lot of work to do. Come back some other time. Try calling first."

So much for that WE LOVE VISITORS. "See you Monday?"

"If I can get a new radiator." Bruna turned her attention to the flat front tire.

Making a hasty three-point turn across the front lawn, Emily decided to skip the remaining courtesy calls on her list and return to Boston; her next impromptu visit would be to her husband's office. Noticing not one brilliant leaf, not one pumpkin, she sped back to the turnpike. An hour later, she was wedged between a garbage truck and a hearse on State Street, inching toward the traffic light at the corner, growing hotter by the minute because she knew that neither Ross nor Marjorie would be at the office. Still, she felt she had to make an appearance, if only to gain the high moral ground. One of these days, she'd need it.

Emily parked and took the elevator to the forty-eighth floor. Summoning all her courage, she unlocked Ross's private entrance. What if she discovered him on the couch with Marjorie? Classy wives were supposed to observe for a moment before leaving in arctic silence. Emily didn't know if she could do that; the temptation to belt whomever was on top would just be too great. She counted to three, dashed open the door: empty. She walked slowly past Ross's desk. All his papers dealt with business matters. Every single piece of correspondence had Marjorie's initials typed neatly at the bottom; somehow that defeated Emily. She grabbed the phone and called Cafe Presto. A Swedish voice answered. "I would like to speak with Guy Witten. It's an emergency."

"Vun moment."

She heard hammering, scrooping, then Guy shouting, "Who is it? You have to get their names, Lina!" After a long time, footsteps approached the phone. "Yes?" he snapped.

"It's me," Emily said. "How are you feeling?"

There was a short silence. "Go to hell!" Guy replied furiously, hanging up.

Emily felt ill. What had brought that on? For the first time, she had heard genuine hatred in his voice, raising the possibility that he never wanted to see her again: horrifying thought, one she had never really entertained. Demoting him from lover to friend had been hard enough. Losing even that bittersweet friendship would throw her totally out of sync; she needed Guy to counterbalance Ross. Damn, damn, this was a very bad day. Emily ripped the top page off of Ross's daily note calendar and scribbled *Sorry I missed you. Love, E.* She didn't mean any of it, but Marjorie ought to know she had been here. Dogs peed to mark their turf, wives left little notes on their husbands' desks. How pathetically depressing.

She next called Philippa in New York. "I'm on my way."

"Great! Is Ross coming?"

"Nope." Emily drove to a salon on Newbury Street. "I need a facial right away," she told the artfully overbeautiful girl at the front desk. "Do you have an opening?"

"I don't think so." The girl took a second look. "Excuse me, but are you Philippa Banks?"

This time, Emily thought a moment. "I am."

Abracadabra: two hours, two hundred bucks later, she left the salon with a new face, new nails, and swelled head. No wonder Philippa was always in such a sunny mood: Complete strangers told her hundreds of times a day that she was beautiful, talented, and terrific. Emily floated to the ludicrously expensive boutique next door and bought an oufit to wear to New York. Already feeling better, she walked down Newbury Street with a little more swivel in the hips, more mischief in the eye, and lunched at the Ritz, this time ordering vodka with four dried cherries.

Emily took the shuttle to New York, arriving late in the afternoon at Philippa's hotel on Central Park. She knocked on the door of her sister's penthouse suite. "It's me," she called. Finally the knob turned.

For a long moment, the twins stared at each other. Emily spoke first. "What the hell happened, Philippa?"

No reply: Philippa couldn't take her eyes off Emily, who looked radiant in a dark green silk outfit. "Perfect, Em," Philippa said unsteadily. "You look just like me." What a lie: Emily looked fifty times better than Philippa ever would.

Emily strode into the room and studied her sister's purple bruises in the light. "Don't tell me a bathtub did this."

Realizing with relief that Emily still knew nothing about her accident last night at Guy's, Philippa shrugged philosophically. "All right. It was a man."

"You have to press charges. This is assault."

"I can't. Don't know who he was."

"You picked someone up? Are you nuts?"

"How was I supposed to know? He said he was a dentist."

"Where did you meet him?"

Philippa's mind went blank until she remembered the plot of one of her soap operas. "In a health bar on Park Ave. He happened to have two tickets to the ballet."

"I thought you hated ballet."

"I do, I do!" Philippa became desperate. "We only stayed for the first act. Then we went dancing."

"Dancing? You hate dancing, too. This must have been some dentist. Why did he beat you up? Didn't he know who you were?"

"No, he didn't know who I was!" Philippa exploded, for once

telling the truth. "All right, I made a mistake! This can't get in the papers, Em. I'll be the laughingstock of L.A."

"We wouldn't want that. Have you seen a doctor, at least?"

"I'm sick and tired of doctors! This is nothing. I'll be all right in a week. Maybe I can hole up somewhere." Philippa waited in vain for Emily to invite her to Boston.

"Did you tell your agent what happened?"

"Eh—another time. He's a little edgy about the opening tonight."

"He has no idea I'm doing this? What's he going to do when he finds out?"

"He's going to kiss your feet, Em. You saved his ass. And mine." Philippa poured two glasses of champagne, her fifth, Emily's first. "Listen, here's the deal. Simon's coming in the limo. You just sit through the movie and party a little afterward. Then you can go home."

"Sounds thrilling. Is this movie going to embarrass me?"

"Probably." Philippa went to the bedroom closet. "Just wait until you see what you have to wear."

Until Simon appeared, the sisters played dress-up. It was almost like being children again, but with alcohol and false eyelashes. Emily was corseted to the point of asphyxiation in a red dress that was little more than a floor-length bra with sequins. Philippa's spike heels hurt Emily's feet and her gigantic blond wig felt like an army blanket, with fleas. At least the diamonds were real: Philippa's five husbands, had, in some respects, paid off. Philippa was baptizing Emily with sickening perfume when the bell rang.

"I don't know whether I can go through with this," Emily said.

"Shut up! Just imitate me!" Philippa hissed, diving behind the couch. "Wear the white cape in the closet! Be affectionate with everyone! Wiggle! Remember, you're a star!"

Star? Black Hole was more like it. Emily staggered to the door. "Simon! Darling!"

A tanned, hypergroomed man in tails entered. When he smiled, his little white teeth glittered. Emily pegged him at sixty going on eighteen. "You look ferocious, babe," he said after a moment's appraisal. "I was worried there for a while."

"Worried about what? Looking more like my grandfather than my agent?"

Simon had to think about that one, but couldn't, because he had recently inhaled a snoutful of cocaine. "Ha-ha! That's priceless! Where's your coat, princess? Show starts in fifteen minutes." He studied himself in the smoky mirror. "How do I look? Good?"

"You'll do," Emily replied, rifling the closet. "Where's my white cape? Aha." She flung it over an arm. "I'll be right with you, Simon."

She went to the bedroom. "Where'd you find this guy, Phil?" she whispered, hastily packing her green silk outfit into a shopping bag.

"Shhhh! Be nice! He's nervous about tonight!"

When Emily returned to the foyer, Simon was anxiously studying his jowls in the mirror. They were beginning to bag ever so slightly over his collar again; time for another lift. Meanwhile, he'd just have to hold his head very high, stretching his neck as far as possible. Why had Philippa made that snide remark about a grandfather? Bitch! Forcing a smile, Simon led his famous charge to the elevator. "There's a little crowd in the lobby," he warned as they dropped ten floors.

"So should I look surprised?" Emily asked.

"What? No! You look as if you expected it! By the way, what is in that awful shopping bag?"

"My getaway clothes."

"Why do you need getaway clothes? You're not eloping tonight, are you?" Simon tetchily took the bag. "Here, I'll carry it. Really, Philippa, what nonsense."

The elevator doors whooshed open and the couple paraded through a sea of admiring glances to the limousine. It was like being a bride all over again, but without Ross. Emily banished that ugly thought and concentrated on a serene smile; these people, after all, were Philippa's customers. She tripped over her spike heels getting into the limousine. "Oooof!"

Simon shot in after her. "How many times must I tell you to go ass first into a limo? This isn't a fucking swimming pool on wheels!"

"Shut up," Emily snapped. "We're in, aren't we?"

They rode in silence up Broadway. Simon wondered why Philippa was so quiet tonight; she was usually a spitfire at her openings. He leaned over. "Need a little something to get you in the mood, sugar?"

Emily frowned. "Like what?"

"Never mind! Just trying to help! What's with you tonight?"

Oh, nothing a shotgun in the mouth wouldn't cure. Emily toyed with her sister's diamonds. "I don't have to make any speeches or anything, do I?"

"We've been through this. The committee doesn't want anything but your body there." Simon's eyes fell to Emily's jacked-up cleavage. "Oh my God! Where's your ribbon?"

"What ribbon?"

"Your AIDS ribbon! How could you forget it, tonight of all nights?!"

"Give me yours," Emily said, reaching over. "We'll share." With a little help from her teeth, she tore it in half. "Here. I get the pin. Stick yours on with one of those rhinestone button tacks."

Simon meekly obeyed. He loved it when women bossed him around. "Oh, before I forget," he said, jabbing his lapel, "I got a call from an Attorney Wyatt something in Boston. Does she have anything to do with that stiff in the restaurant?"

Perhaps the pin began pricking Emily's heart. "What did she want?"

"Just a few questions, she said. Listen, can we talk about this? I still think a dead lover makes great copy. Is there any way we can work it in?"

"Forget it," Emily said. "Forever. Period. Don't ask again."

"How the fuck am I supposed to get you any roles if you don't cooperate? People devour these details! At your age, you need all the details you can get!" Simon was dropping precipitously from his cocaine high; time to regain altitude with a few little pills. "Don't come crying to me when you're collecting unemployment checks."

"Maybe I should kill the lawyer," Emily suggested.

Scowling, Simon studied the pimps and prostitutes overrunning Broadway. After several blocks, he said, "It's got potential, but you have to do it right. I need six months' lead time."

The limousine slowed in front of a renovated cinema. Suddenly Emily felt naked and defenseless in front of so many curious strangers. She grabbed Simon's arm as the chauffeur rounded to their door. "Here we go, doll," he announced, oblivious to her terror. "Feet first and try to keep your knees together." He stepped out.

In a daze, Emily entered the packed lobby. As the applause swelled, a sixtyish woman with elephantine jewelry rushed over. "Philippa, you look ravishing," she exclaimed. "This is so exciting! We've raised a half million dollars!"

"Wonderful." Emily looked around for a bartender. "When does the movie start?"

"After another hundred thousand," the woman replied. "You know what they say about carrots and sticks. Or was that carrots and mules? Never mind!"

Emily glared at Simon, whose molars gleamed in a galactic smile. "We'll roust the troops for you, Millicent," he said. "Follow me, Phil darling." He guided Emily toward the bar, beaming omnidirectionally as his eyes raked the crowds. "Crap," he muttered under his breath. "There's not one movie producer here. What a bomb."

An impossibly impeccable man with pen and paper stepped in Emily's path. She stared at him a moment, admiring the Vermeeresque attention to detail: must have taken him a month to dress. "Could I have your autograph, Miss Banks?" he asked. "To Raphael, it could say."

"Sure. It'll cost you five thousand bucks, though."

He actually paid. But this was New York, where five thousand bucks amounted to only a couple of cab rides. When Raphael receded into the crowd, three other people took his place. Emily had scribbled fifty thousand dollars' worth of autographs when an ornate fountain pen slid into view. "To Byron," a familiar voice said. "After that, it's up to you, sugar pie."

"Byron!" Emily croaked, recoiling into Simon. "What are you doing here? Sugar?"

The sous-chef looked pained. "You don't remember, Phil?"

Damn it! Philippa had said nothing! "Ah—refresh my memory, darling."

"You promised to introduce me to your manager," Byron whispered in her ear. "That night you came to my restaurant."

"Right! Of course!" Emily squeezed Simon's arm, eventually weeding him from a wayside palaver. "Simon, I'd like you to meet Byron Marlowe, a great friend of mine."

Simon extended a noncommittal hand; he could smell an aspiring actor across a sky-high garbage dump. "Pleased," he said in a bored, I'm-all-booked voice.

An awkward silence was finally interrupted by a waitress asking if they would care for anything to drink. "Vodka with four dried cherries," Emily answered on cue. Yuk! "Would you like a drink, Simon?"

Simon had already seized the opportunity to commence talking with someone else. However, spying the attractive redhead waiting for an order, he broke off in midsentence. "What's good here, darling," he asked, "besides you?"

"The wine's okay. You're Simon Stern, aren't you? The famous agent?"

"Correct. Who are you?"

"Agatha."

On the sidelines, Byron looked like he might cry. "Just get some wine, dear," Emily interrupted, waving Agatha away. Simon immediately returned to his previous conversation.

"Guess that didn't work too well," Byron said glumly. "And I have to be back to work at six o'clock tomorrow morning."

"We'll try again later."

Byron's lover Jimmy struggled through the crowd carrying two glasses of wine. "Philippa darling! Did you get my pictures, love?"

Emily vaguely remembered shoving some snapshots into a rear pocket. "Yes."

"You'll send me a personal thank-you note for my collection?"

"Of course."

The waitress returned with their drinks. Emily's was warm. Jimmy babbled about the weather as Byron anxiously watched Simon, waiting for a break in oral traffic. Of course, Simon kept his conversation going on and on. Eventually the lights in the lobby flicked up and down: time to go in and watch *Choke Hold*. Emily finished her vodka, leaving the four dried cherries. "Well, here goes nothing."

Jimmy perked up. "Is this a violent film, Phil? Like *Blood Tide?* I've got to get us good seats, Byron. Meet you inside." He left.

Emily looked for the waitress. "Where do I park this drink?"

"Give it to me." Byron looked at the four shriveled mounds in the bottom of the glass. "You don't want your dried cherries?"

"No. They give me gas."

"May I? Maybe some of your luck will rub off on me."

"Be my guest. But prepare to loosen your belt."

As Byron swallowed the cherries, Simon finally ended his prolonged offside spiel. "Shall we go?" he asked Emily, ignoring Byron's overhopeful smile.

Holding Simon's arm, she walked up a winding, carpeted staircase. "Couldn't you spare him two sentences, you colossal shithead?"

"Are you out of your mind?" Simon waved to a friend. "I'm here to get you work, not to scrape it up for some other klutz." He ushered Emily into the loge nearest the stage, where queens, mayors, and executive producers generally sat, where Millicent awaited them now. The trio made themselves ostensible as the theater filled. Scanning the auditorium, Emily found Byron and Jimmy sitting nearly beneath them. She waved, they waved, kisses were blown. Then the movie began.

As Philippa appeared onscreen in a wet suit, the audience broke into cheers. The camera followed her along a perfect beach, panning occasionally into the woods or the rippling ocean while the music became darker and clouds scudded symbolically over the sun. Philippa sat on the sand, slowly unzipping her wetsuit. The camera lingered on her better body parts as she lay on her back and pretended to sunbathe. A bird flew overhead, then a man slowly arose from the breaking surf. He was carrying a bright blue nylon noose. The audience began to hoot and scream as he approached Philippa, raising the rope over her lily throat. The music swelled, then the scenery suddenly shifted to a bedroom. Philippa was in a lovely white negligee, clutching her neck. "What's the matter, doll," murmured a man on the other side of the mattress. Philippa gulped eloquently and tried to look scared. "Guess I had a bad dream," she whispered.

The audience went crazy.

After half an hour, Emily could still not decide whether her sister was the greatest comedic actress, or the worst dramatic actress, of all time. Whatever she was, her fans adored her. Several times, Emily saw the wisp of a self-deprecating gleam in Philippa's eye; it was a tiny gesture that only a twin would notice. Perhaps Philippa knew that *Choke Hold* was a terrible, trite movie, a phenomenal waste of miles of celluloid. Emily looked over the auditorium: two thousand people out there. The movie was two hours long. That meant a conglomerate dissipation of four thousand hours, and that was just tonight; by the time *Choke Hold* had finished its run, it would have consumed several lifetimes of otherwise productive human effort. Thereby Philippa had become a legend and a millionaire? Incredible.

Emily slowly became aware of extraneous noise in the seats beneath her loge. Peering down, she saw two ushers hauling a limp form toward the aisle. Another beach shot flashed on-screen, illuminating the auditorium: That was Byron! She leaned toward Simon. "I'll be right back."

Emily arrived at the side exit as two ushers were lugging Byron to a musty old divan in the hallway. Jimmy followed distressedly two paces behind. "He passed out!" he cried. "I knew we shouldn't have skipped dinner."

Byron groaned as the ushers hustled him into the men's room. Emily waited near the door, smiling at the constant in/out traffic. Finally, after five minutes, one of the ushers emerged. "I'd better call an ambulance. We've got to get him out of here before the raffle starts." He hurried to the lobby.

The ambulance did not arrive before Simon came huffing down the stairs. "What are you doing down here, babe? You're supposed to be watching a movie!"

"Byron's sick. Go in there and tell me how he's doing, will you? I'm not leaving until you do."

"Jesus, Phil, this isn't the senior prom! Don't tell me that poofter's your new boyfriend!"

Emily almost threw Simon into the men's room. He emerged a minute later, straightening his bow tie, trying to keep his withered neck as stretched as possible. "No problem. He's going to be all right. Just a little messy, that's all. They're waiting for a new suit." Simon firmly took Emily's arm. "You have got to get back upstairs, Philippa. Now."

A harsh edge in his voice commanded obedience. Emily returned to the loge and sat through the rest of *Choke Hold*, which ended with Philippa sailing out to sea on a yacht that looked remarkably like Dana's. The audience cheered, Emily bowed. Then there was a raffle while a band assembled in the foyer. Byron and Jimmy never reappeared. After a few conspicuous turns around the dance floor, Emily told Simon she was going home. She said good-bye to Millicent, who gave her kisses and her business card.

Simon walked Emily to the limousine parked on Broadway. "Good show, doll," he said. "I think we'll get some mileage out of this. I did a little horse-trading with some critics. Good reviews in exchange for exclusive interviews."

"Great! With me?"

"Ah—we're working on the details. I'll call you in the morning."

Just to irritate Simon, Emily entered the limousine headfirst. She blew a kiss at him as it pulled away. The moment he turned, Emily yanked off her three-hundred-degree-Fahrenheit wig. Then she rapped on the chauffeur's partition. "Take me to Kennedy Airport as fast as you can." While the limousine was running lights and bombing through potholes, Emily changed back into her green silk outfit. After she had stuffed Philippa's gown into the shopping bag, she picked up the car phone. "Hi, Phil. I'm on my way to the airport."

"How was it? Tell me! Did you fool Simon?"

"Easily. Observation is not his strong suit."

"Not without his glasses. So were there lots of people? How was the movie?"

"Your fans ate it up. Listen, have you been in touch with Byron, my sous-chef at Diavolina?"

"Oh, I forgot to tell you. He wanted to meet Simon."

"Then he wasted his time."

"What can I tell you? Si's an A-one schmuck. Did you meet anyone else interesting? Men?"

"No. Sorry. What should I do with your clothes?"

"Tell the chauffeur to drop them off at the hotel."

"What about the diamonds?"

Philippa thought a moment. "Maybe I should come to Boston and pick them up."

"Again? Do you realize you've made more trips to Boston in the last two weeks than you've made in the last five years?"

Philippa laughed lightly. "Strange, isn't it?"

The limo thudded through a lunar-sized crater on the Van Wyck Expressway. On the other side of the partition, the chauffeur shouted that he was going to sue the city. That reminded Emily of something. "Phil, Simon told me that Wyatt Pratt, that awful lawyer, is trying to reach you."

"Again? I've told her three times to shove it."

"Tell her again, would you? What do you think she wants?"

"Money, of course. Don't worry, I'll take care of her."

"But she's such a shark."

"She's a piece of cake compared to Simon. Speaking of whom, he's going to call in the morning. Give me a quick rundown of what happened tonight. I don't want to make too big a fool of myself tomorrow."

Emily reconstructed the evening as accurately as possible, glossing over details concerning Byron: Philippa needn't know

she had spent half the night pacing outside the men's room instead of watching *Choke Hold*. "And what about your story,
Phil? You're supposed to be falling in the bathtub now?"

"As we speak. Ouch! My face!"

Pulling off the expressway, the limousine entered an unlit, barb-
wired area: the DMZ between Kennedy Airport and the terror-
ists of Jamaica, New York. At the terminal, Emily gave the
chauffeur Philippa's bag, instructing him to return it to the hotel
at once. "Should I wait for you, Miss Banks?" the confused
driver asked. No one had said boo about driving way the hell
out here. The lady was not carrying any luggage, so she wasn't
flying anywhere. When had she changed clothes? Why? Aha,
she was meeting an illicit boyfriend. At least she had the decency to fornicate elsewhere than the back of his limousine, like
everyone else.

Emily took a hundred-dollar bill from her purse. "No need to
wait. Would you mind dropping these clothes off at the hotel?"

"My pleasure. Thank you very much, Miss Banks."

Emily entered the deserted terminal. The arrivals/departures
board was blank. No Muzak: Emily's shoes clicked like castanets
as she went to the check-in counter, there to deal with someone
nameplated Malunka whose bilingualism consisted of the words
*hello* and *go there*. She had no idea what to do with Emily's
frequent-flyer card. Emily walked to the rear of the terminal,
passing a janitor who looked like Klepp, but fifty times more
malignant. His scowl, so unlike the adoring glances she had received all evening, jolted her: This terminal, unfortunately, was
the real world. Emily hurried to a rest room and removed all of
Philippa's diamonds. She felt observed, perhaps hunted.

In the far corner of the terminal, Emily saw four people waiting on dull vinyl cushions. "Is this the flight to Boston?" she
asked the white man.

"I hope so." He returned to his laptop.

Eventually Malunka commuted to the counter, collected five
ticket stubs, and said, "Bozz-tone." The group followed her
down a flight of steps and into a twelve-seat propeller airplane.
Yawing and buzzing, the aircraft took off. Inexplicably demoral-

ized, like Cinderella, Emily got to Beacon Hill around one-fifteen. This had been a long, trying day, accomplishing little, complicating much. Emily had some scotch, glanced through a magazine, then tiptoed to her dark bedroom, grateful that a warm, lumpy husband slumbered therein.

The bed was empty. Emily stared at the flat sheets, trying to re-create her breakfast conversation with Ross. He knew she was coming back to Boston tonight, didn't he? Emily couldn't remember; it hadn't been a pleasant chat. Was he still working? Lying near death in a hospital? He wasn't out drinking with Dana. Sleeping with Marjorie? Emily called the office; no answer, of course. So she called Marjorie, hanging up after the hello. Marjorie didn't sound at all sleepy. A bad sign. Two o'clock! Bastard!

Emily was dozing on the couch when the lock downstairs clicked. Obviously alive: Ross had better have one hell of an alibi. She glared at him as he came into the living room. Maybe he glared back.

"Still up, darling?" Ross asked. "How was New York?"

"It's past three. Where have you been?"

"Out walking. I couldn't sleep."

"Ever hear of sleeping pills and a warm bath?"

"I needed to walk."

"Again? Where'd you go this time?"

"Watertown." That was miles up the Charles River. But he had needed a lot of time to think about trucks driving through windows, dead partners, antidepressant pills, errant wives, and unerrant secretaries.

"Were you alone?"

"That's a pretty stupid question, Emily."

"So answer it."

"Of course I was alone. Who else would be with me?"

She shrugged. "Marjorie."

"I spent the whole day with the woman. I wasn't about to spend the whole night with her as well. You don't think there's anything between us, do you?"

An infuriating question, one that accused the accuser. Emily despised Ross for even asking it; a real man would have either confirmed or denied the original allegation. She decided to change the topic. Were Ross innocent, he would not leave the issue of Marjorie unresolved. "Why couldn't you sleep?" she asked.

Her heart sank as he said, "Digging out from Dana is much more complicated than I thought. He hadn't told me much about his projects this past year. We were more or less doing our own thing on opposite sides of the office. Just like an old married couple."

For a moment, Emily gave up on Marjorie; the subject, like low tide, would always return. "Did he ever tell you about a chapel he built for the Benedictines? I saw it today."

Ross rubbed his sore feet. "Vaguely. It was a job for Joe Pola. Dana probably gave the project to an apprentice then tacked on a few finishing touches. Looked like a spaceship with a steeple, right? How'd you come across it?"

"I was visiting the monastery that supplies Diavolina with mushrooms. There it was on the side of a hill. Why would anyone commission Dana to build a church?"

"Why? He was a great architect, Em. One of the best." Ross sighed, reminded of the fall of an empire, and of the woman who had destroyed it. His voice soured. "How is your dear sister?"

"Awful. You were right. She was making up that story about falling in a bathtub."

"Oh? What really happened?"

"She got beaten up by a dentist. Her face looks like a blueberry."

Ross burst into metallic laughter. "First a bathtub, then a dentist!" After a while, sensing his wife's fury, he quieted down. "How was your little escapade in New York?"

Emily told her tale, omitting Byron, whose connection to Dana still smoldered. So Ross heard mostly about Simon, a man he would never meet, and *Choke Hold*, a movie he would never see. Damn! She yearned to tell him about the poor sous-chef, about the marauding lawyer Wyatt Pratt, Philippa's battered face, that chapel in the middle of nowhere, the Peace Power Farm, hell, even about Marjorie. But all current events seemed to spring from Dana dying in her restaurant, on her watch. It was a no-win situation and would remain so for a long time. Perhaps she should move out for a while, get away from her husband and this garroting guilt. She was no longer sure that he loved her, or she him. They were old, true friends, maybe more. But they were weary.

Emily stood up. "Oy, I have to be back at work in three hours."

"Why don't you quit that job?" Ross asked suddenly.

She studied Ross's small, stockinged feet. Years ago, she used to play with his toes. "Because I have nothing else to do, my dear." Emily went to bed.

## 8

After two hundred minutes of unfulfilling sleep, Emily rolled slowly out of bed. The *Choke Hold* gala was over; time to return to Diavolina. Her body felt like cement and her thoughts clung gooily to the inside of her forehead, like silt after a flood. On the other side of the bed, Ross didn't budge, so Emily reset the alarm for seven, dressed, and left the house. Although the brisk morning air and painfully brilliant sunshine revived her, she knew that the system would crash around noon; at her age, pulling an all-nighter was about as invigorative as inhaling from an exhaust pipe.

As she walked into the kitchen at Diavolina, Klepp was finishing his toast. "Good morning, Major. Glad I've got some company today."

"No one else is here?"

"We are alone, *madame*. Shipwrecked. Have some coffee."

Emily poured a cup. "Where's Byron? He usually opens the place."

"You got me. Maybe he's still at his grandmother's ninetieth-birthday party. A fine story. I don't think he remembers that day he took off last winter to attend his grandmother's funeral. Obviously, she rose from the dead."

"He took a personal day," Emily said. "Why don't you leave it at that. How did it go here yesterday?"

"Super. Except for Ward. She went on a small drinking spree. That lady's reminding me more and more of our dear departed dishwasher." As Klepp was bringing his cup to the sink, Mustapha came in. "*Bonjour*, Dwight! You're late. Should have had your apple pies in the oven by now. Don't tell me your sunrise service went overtime again."

Mustapha neatly tied his apron. "It did. Three whole minutes, I think. Where's the sous-chef?"

"Staring at you," Klepp replied. "All right, let's get to work here. I have some terrific ideas for lunch, Major. Listen."

Two more prep cooks arrived as Klepp was detailing a masterpiece involving beets, turnips, and tongue. Finally Emily stood up. "Sounds great," she said, waving as a supplier arrived. "Do it."

As she was meeting with the old woman who made *biscotti*, the phone rang. Klepp answered. "It's your sexbomb sister, Major. Sounds highly agitated."

Emily went to her office and picked up the phone. "What's up, Phil?"

"Why the hell didn't you tell me," her sister almost screamed. "I made a complete ass of myself!"

Philippa's agitation was contagious. "What are you talking about?" Emily screamed back.

"Oh Christ, you are thick! The police just left! They wanted to know all about your wannabe actor friend who dropped dead last night! That guy Byron! The story I made up had more holes than my fishnet stockings!"

"Byron's dead?"

"Would you mind telling me what happened? In detail? The police are coming back in half an hour to grill the shit out of me!"

Emily slumped onto a chair, fear swelling into panic. "What did they tell you?"

"Nothing except that Byron died in the men's room. They're expecting me to fill in the details. Rather impossible, of course. Crap! I knew it was too good to be true!"

"Listen," Emily said. "Simon and I were in the lobby before the show. I was signing autographs and he was schmoozing the sponsors. Byron and his friend Jimmy came up to me expecting to be introduced to Simon. You know all about that, of course," she added sarcastically. "Anyway, Byron stood with a thumb up his nose while Simon tried his best to ignore him. We had a drink, the lights went off, then we all had to go into the theater. The movie started and next thing I know, Byron is being carried out. He happened to be sitting right under my balcony so I had a good look. I left—"

"You left my movie? How could you do that?"

"Don't get me started, Philippa! He wouldn't have been there at all if you hadn't egged him on!" Emily resumed after a moment of hypercharged silence. "Two ushers carried him to the men's room. Jimmy went in with them. I waited outside. After a while, Simon came down to get me. Before we returned to the balcony, he checked out the situation and told me that Byron was all right. Liar."

"He was just trying to protect you. Me."

"Very touching. I'll never forgive him."

"Emily, be fair! Lying's his job! Anyway, you were supposed to be concentrating on other things. What happened then?"

"Nothing. We watched the rest of the movie. I never saw Byron or Jimmy again. After the raffle and a few dances, I went home. End of story."

"Hmmm, I guess things aren't as bad as they seem," Philippa commented relievedly. "The story I gave the police was pretty much the same as the one you just gave me."

"Not bad? What about Byron? He's dead?"

"Em, that's water over the dam. What I have to do now is sic the cops on Simon. He knows more about this than I had thought."

"Did you at least ask what Byron died from?"

"No, I forgot. The interrogation caught me totally unprepared. Quite cheeky, now that I think of it. I should lodge a formal complaint."

"You do that, Philippa. Then everyone in the world will know you got beaten up by a dentist." Emily hung up as Philippa began sputtering indignantly.

She was sitting motionless, hand still resting on the phone, as Ward came into her office. The manager wore sunglasses, a bad sign, and sweatpants, a worse sign. Six feet away, Emily smelled beer, cigarettes, and Listerine. The bright pink lipstick added a nice professional touch, though.

"Where the hell's Byron?" Ward fumed. "This is the last time he gets a personal day from me. Somehow it always expands into a hangover day as well."

"Can't Klepp run the show?"

Ward squinted keenly at Emily. "What are you trying to tell me, Major? Ah, let me guess! That last phone call! Byron fell ten thousand feet out of a birthday balloon! He's not coming back." When Emily did not reply, Ward rushed to the desk. Now the odor of soiled clothing mingled with her other aromas. "You haven't killed off another one of my crew, have you?"

Emily returned Ward's even stare. "I have no idea what you're talking about. Would you like to hear about my visits to our suppliers yesterday? Or would you rather go home and take a shower?"

"Neither." Ward grabbed the phone and punched in a number. "I keep getting Byron's answering machine. Something's wrong. I can smell it."

Emily did not have the courage to confirm Ward's suspicions. "Give him another hour," she said. Then the phone rang. Emily cringed as Ward picked it up.

"Hi, Jimmy," Ward said. "Where's your boyfriend?" She listened a moment, then cried. "How is that possible? When? Where? How did he get to New York? What for? Who?" Awful silences interspersed the questions. Finally the squawking on the other end of the phone ended. "Thank you for telling me,"

Ward said rather calmly. "Let me know if I can help in any way." After hanging up, she turned to Emily. "You know what that was all about, don't you."

"Not really."

Ward considered that a moment. "Well, I'll tell you. My sous-chef is dead." She walked toward the door, then paused. "And you're fired. Get out of my restaurant. I don't ever want to see you again."

She left.

⚌

*Tossing dirt on my husband's coffin was the greatest triumph of my life. The soft spritz of earth against steel was like a slap in the face, waking me from a long sleep; at that moment, I knew I had finally won. Free at last! I had not felt so ecstatic, so alive, since—since the day I married him. But that was many years, many women ago, and I was an innocent bursting with love and dreams. And he was so handsome. . . . May you rot in hell, my dear. I will not mourn you at all. I'll keep your money, of course: I earned it, cent by cent, every time you crawled into bed at two in the morning smelling of another woman's soap, and I pretended to be asleep. I earned it when you stopped bothering with even that courtesy and came home reeking like a goat, then had the gall to pat my bottom before you turned out the light, oh so grateful the sleepy little woman was there warming your bed, keeping your house, depending on your talent and largesse. Made you feel like a hero, didn't I? You would need to feel noble, of course; every louse does. And you would need to believe that you were cleverer than I, that I suspected nothing because you eventually came home every night, so tired from work, poor fellow. It all comes out in the end, you see; I finally did collect a dime for every time I bit my tongue, smiled, and allowed you to continue your pathetic little charade. Now that you're dead, I lie awake at night wondering why I let you get away with it for so long. Pure laziness, perhaps. I didn't want to leave my house. You were hardly in it anyway. And, after the first couple dozen of your whores, I truly didn't care how clever or noble you thought you were. I didn't care whether you smiled or cried, bumped your head or met the President, as long as you left me alone. An intelligent woman can always find ways to keep herself busy as she waits and hopes for her husband to die. In the beginning, every time you came to bed tinged with another woman's perfume, I bought myself a nice piece of jewelry. Soon I realized that I had no place to wear it all, so I joined arts councils and hospital boards, where I noticed many other women with clever husbands and heavy jewelry. I saw how artfully they used their worthless spouses' names to get what they wanted: money for a new dialysis machine, support for an exhibition . . . and I saw how they kept themselves terrifically fit for their lovers. I learned, and kept my own secret garden. You never had a clue, of course. The possibility of your own inadequacy never crossed your mind.*

*My house feels so different now that I know you'll never be intruding again. You won't be clunking around the bathroom at two in the morning, just when I've fallen asleep. Your girlfriends won't be hanging up when I answer the phone. Best of all, I'll never have to hear you call me darling or love as you make excuses for missing dinner. Good riddance, dear. The only thing about you I'm going to miss is my birthday present, or should I say, your annual gesture of atonement. But now I can buy my own. This year I might throw myself a party instead, invite all my friends. Or I might go to Europe. I'm certainly going to redecorate my house. I've been waiting for years to get rid of your awful den and that billiard table. I might even get rid of your dog.*

*Just one thing puzzles me: Now that our farce of a marriage is history, I don't understand why I'm not sleeping better. Somehow, I still feel robbed. And I keep seeing Philippa Banks every time I shut my eyes. You loved her much more than you ever loved me, didn't you? How could you help it? She's a beautiful woman, really, so confident, almost godlike. But she should never have gone out to dinner with Dandy Dana. I caught that slut fair and square. Removing her would amuse, perhaps heal, me; I don't want anything you cherished to remain. A widow's bitterness burns forever, and I've always had a terrible need for revenge. Now I've finally got the money to support the appetite. "Don't you dare touch her!" I can almost hear you scream from the grave. Ah, how you make me laugh, my dear. Go feed the worms.*

≡

Fired: After Ward left her office, Emily took the picture of Ross off her desk and tucked it into her purse. She spent a few moments rooting around her drawers for other personal items that she had brought to Diavolina: a few recipe cards, fountain pen, spare T-shirt. . . . She hadn't been here long enough to accumulate much. Where the hell were those snapshots Jimmy had taken of Philippa and Dana last week? Not here; she must have brought them home. After stuffing everything into a tote bag, Emily glanced one last time around her office, memorizing it for her bad dreams. Since her arrival a week ago, three people had died. Guy and Ross, the only men she loved, were inexorably slipping away from her. Funny that all this dissolution no longer made the slightest dent on her emotions. What she really wanted to do was go home and watch television.

"Good-bye, gentlemen," she called to Klepp and Mustapha, cruising through the kitchen and patting them both on the back. "It's been a blast."

Klepp stopped breaking eggs into a large bowl. "What's this all about?"

"Ward will explain everything." Emily pushed open the rear door.

Oof: Detective O'Keefe, standing outside, stumbled backward. Only by lunging for the rusty handrail did he prevent himself from toppling to the driveway. Emily caught up with him in the middle of the stairs. "I'm sorry! Are you all right?"

"Sure." He inelegantly regained his feet and brushed a swath of red dust from his shirt. "Going somewhere?"

"Home. I just got fired."

"You did? What for?"

"Ask Ward." Emily walked hastily to Tremont Street, O'Keefe at her heels. "Let's not be coy, Detective. I just spoke with my sister in New York. I'm aware that Byron died last night. If you know how, please tell me."

O'Keefe pulled a fax from his pocket. "An inquiry from the NYPD. Looks like your friend Byron had a serious drug overdose."

"That's ridiculous." Byron had been sober as an owl when he was trying to meet Simon. But Emily couldn't tell that to O'Keefe, of course. She snatched the fax and read a postmortem fact sheet concise and mundane as a speeding ticket. "Byron didn't do drugs," she said finally, handing it back.

"Whatever you say. After all, you knew him for—what was it—nine whole days." O'Keefe studied her face. "I guess he swallowed eighty cc's of high-grade heroin by mistake."

"Swallowed?"

"That's what the report says. He seems to have ingested it with some kind of dried fruit. Cherries or cranberries or something. Couldn't hack needles, apparently. What was Byron doing at that party?"

"I have no idea," Emily croaked. Heroin in the cherries? "He was a fan of my sister's. Used to be an actor himself."

"So he drove two hundred miles to New York for a movie opening? That's what I call real devotion. Did anyone from Diavolina know he was going to this bash?"

"Byron told everyone he was going to his grandmother's ninetieth-birthday party."

"Why would he keep something like that a secret? Especially from you?"

Because Byron knew better than to take sides between his boss and his idol. "I don't know." Emily stopped at Exeter Street. "Why did you come looking for me with such lousy news? I had nothing to do with Byron's death."

"No. Maybe your sister did, though. Did she and Byron go back a long way?"

"I think they went back one week. But I could be wrong. Why?"

"Your sister was at the scene of two—shall we say—sudden deaths. That's rather unusual."

Just fishing or was he circling like a buzzard overhead? Emily briefly considered telling O'Keefe all about the *Choke Hold* masquerade, then decided against it: too many deceptions involved. "Philippa has a flair for melodrama."

O'Keefe took Emily's arm as they passed through a cluster of rowdy teenagers, not letting go until half a block later. When he did, he dropped the topic of Philippa as well. "How well did Byron get along with people at the restaurant?"

"Well enough to get food out of the kitchen."

"Did he aggravate anyone in particular?"

"No, he aggravated everyone equally. Why?"

"I've been doing some research on the employees at Diavolina," O'Keefe said. "Are you aware that Klepp, Mustapha, and Yip Chick have all been convicted of felonies? That little girl Francesca's served ten years for armed robbery. Ward has a file of assault-and-battery charges about a mile long. Apparently she enjoys getting comments about her physique, then kicking the person's head in. About thirty years ago, the maître d' was acquitted by a hair of murdering his wife. As for your friend Byron, before becoming a chef, he was a rather popular prostitute in the Combat Zone. Calling himself an actor would be stretching his CV, to say the least. That useless dishwasher served twenty years for statutory rape. Looks like a prison term is a prerequisite for working at Diavolina."

Stunned by O'Keefe's information, Emily remained silent. After another block, he asked, "How did you get your job there?"

"Ward hired me."

"On what grounds?"

"She needed a chef, I needed a job. What are you trying to say?"

"I'm telling you that something's odd and I'm glad you're out of there. Promise me you won't go back."

"I won't." Should she tell him about the dried cherries she had given to Byron? Yes. Now. No. Later? Gad, lies were so confusing! Emily and O'Keefe walked in silence past the pristinely restored brownstones of the South End. Cars chugged by, hemorrhaging rock and rap. It was another perfect autumn morning, when crinkly brown leaves on the sidewalk inspired thoughts of cider and chestnuts rather than of the drear winter ahead.

The detective's beeper went off. He was needed at a break-in on Milk Street. "Stay in touch," he said to Emily. "What are you going to do, look for another job?"

Try look for another life. "I might go on a little vacation first."

O'Keefe noticed the *I* rather than the *we* and, having seen Ross Major at his black best, was not surprised that Emily might want to run away from it all for a while. "I'll let you know if anything comes up. Meanwhile, be careful. Call me if anything seems unusual." He cut off toward the Common.

Emily walked quickly on, shuddering. Death by cherries? Very clever, except the wrong person had swallowed them. How had they gotten into that last round of drinks? *Think.* Close bursts of laughter, clinking glasses, the smell of roses and chicken teriyaki came back to her, then the redhead Agatha, swooning over Simon, carrying a small tray with just their drinks on it. Emily remembered that her vodka had been oddly warm, almost room temperature; at the time, she had attributed it to bartender overload. With a bovine smile, Agatha had served them; two seconds later, she was gone, an inconsequential speck in a silly charade. An accident?

Emily wandered toward Chinatown, picking her way between stuporous, befouled bodies. Unnamed odors emanated from the Asian markets. Had Byron really been a hot number here, as O'Keefe had said? It wasn't beyond belief. At last, a telephone: Emily called her sister in New York. "Philippa? Did you survive your interrogation?"

"Barely. Your friend swallowed about a pound of pure heroin."

"So I hear. Detective O'Keefe just told me."

Philippa didn't react to Emily's information, but listening had never interested her. "My nerves are shot," she said. "Maybe we should just tell the police everything."

That meant going to New York and trying to square three generations of fibs. For what? Byron would remain dead. "Does Simon know about our switch last night?"

"I didn't get a chance to explain before the police woke him up. Now he's a basket case. He called a minute ago, sobbing. He regrets not telling you that Byron was dead in the men's room. Our stories didn't match and now he thinks the police suspect him of murder."

"Serves him right. Do you have to stick around, Phil? What's your schedule for the week?"

Philippa's schedule was fairly blank for the next month. She had some kind of denture endorsement in November, then nothing until January. "Simon set up a few interviews last night, didn't he?" she asked hopefully.

"Not for you. Listen, I want you to get on the first plane to Boston. Pay cash and use a different name. I'll pick you up at the airport. You've got to disappear for a while."

Boston! Great! Then Philippa realized that Emily's invitation probably had nothing to do with Guy Witten. "Why?" she asked warily.

"I think someone's trying to kill you."

After a short silence, Philippa cackled hysterically. "For Christ's sake, Emily! Forget that dentist! He was harmless!"

"I wasn't even thinking of the dentist. How's your face, by the way."

"A mess. So who's trying to assassinate me?"

"This isn't a joke, Philippa. Were you told how Byron took an overdose? In a couple of dried cherries. Guess where they came from."

Philippa thought a moment. "Uh—Portugal?"

"Oh come on! They came from my drink! Your drink! Your stupid vodka with four dried cherries! Byron thought eating them would bring him luck so I gave him my glass before we went into the theater. Half an hour later he was dead. I think someone meant those cherries for you."

Philippa was about to cry "Bosh!" when she suddenly recalled a pickup truck screaming through the front of Cafe Presto two nights ago. Had that not been an accident after all?

"Phil?" Emily said. "You there?"

"No. I'll call you from the airport." Philippa stuffed three suitcases with absolute necessities and fled without notifying Simon. Odd, now that she thought about it, him not telling Emily that Byron had kicked the bucket in the men's room. The great joy of Simon's life was passing along bad news.

Emily waited for her sister at Logan Airport. As usual, Philippa wasn't hard to spot; she wore the same head-to-toe black veils and lace that she had worn to Dana's funeral, plus a floor-length sable coat, perhaps unaware of the fundamental distinctions between herself and a Stealth bomber. "We really stepped into it, haven't we?" she cried to Emily as they walked toward the baggage claim. "To think that I could have been dead this morning! Or you, if you had really played the part and swallowed those cherries! How horrifying!"

"That dentist saved your life. Maybe you should get beat up more often." Emily noticed men staring at them as they passed. First they looked at Philippa, a specter in impenetrable black. Then they looked at Emily in jeans and sweater. Invariably, their eyes returned to Philippa: What they couldn't see was obviously much more intriguing than what they could. Inwardly, Emily sighed; even in veils, Philippa outdid her. She stopped at the baggage carousel. "What color's your suitcase?"

"Midnight blue. There are three." Noticing Emily's frown, Philippa added, "I wasn't sure what the weather would be."

"Cold. Where you're going, anyway."

"What do you mean? Aren't we going to your house?"

"No. You're going to the cabin in New Hampshire for a few days." Emily pulled Philippa's first suitcase off the carousel. "I hope you didn't pack too many ball gowns."

Philippa did not reply; her brain was already churning through ways to lure Guy Witten up to a remote cabin in the woods. There was a fireplace, she remembered. Fantastic. "I guess you can't come up because you have to work," she said, trying to sound disappointed.

"I got fired this morning," Emily said, retrieving the second suitcase. "But that's neither here nor there. I don't think we should both be at the cabin. Your whereabouts should be a secret. I might not even tell Ross." She got the last, heaviest suitcase. "You didn't tell Simon what you were doing, I hope."

"God no! I just left a note that I had to get away for a few days. He'll presume it's a man."

"What about the police?"

"I'm done with the police. They don't need any more statements from me. Here, let me take that bag." Philippa grabbed the smallest one. They loaded the car and began driving north. "This is going to be fun," Philippa said, removing her hat and heavy veil. "I haven't been camping in years."

Emily edged into the fast lane. "This is not a camping trip, Philippa. I'd be pretty worried if I were you. Who would want you dead?"

"I was thinking about that on the plane. I came up with about twenty names. People I've seriously offended over the last few years. Most of them are actresses I edged out of roles."

"They'd kill you for that?"

"Hey, I'd do the same if I had the chance. Then there are eight other women."

"Like who?"

"Mostly wives of men who have befriended me. Vicious bitches."

Emily glanced at her sister's purpling face. "Did you include Ardith in that list?"

"Who? Oh, Dana's wife? Of course not. She doesn't count."

"Why not?"

Philippa threw her hands into the air. "Because Dana didn't count! Come on, Emily, you don't think she'd put me on a hit list because I spent a few days fishing, do you?"

"You're not entirely blameless in her husband's death."

"Get serious! She should be sending me a commission!"

Emily blew past a busload of leaf peepers. "What about this

dentist? Is he a psychopath? He did a real job on your face, Phil."

"How many times must I tell you to forget the dentist? Besides, he wasn't even in New York the night of the party. I know that for a fact."

"Yeah? Where did he tell you he was?"

"At his aunt's funeral in Wyoming," Philippa lied. "His favorite aunt. Auntie Annie."

"All right, all right. So who else is on your enemies list?"

"A few talent agents. But they would never kill me. There's no money in it."

"Any of your ex-husbands, maybe? Looking to save a little alimony?"

"Emily, only one would have the panache for such a thing. And *I* pay *him* alimony."

They drove in silence for quite a while. "Maybe I'm mistaken," Emily said finally. "Maybe it wasn't the cherries and Byron did OD on something else. He was pretty depressed after Simon got through with him. I really didn't know him that well, as the detective reminded me this morning. Maybe some nutcase was tampering with food. Maybe you weren't a target at all."

Philippa wondered again about that truck crashing through the window of Cafe Presto. How could she have been the target? No one alive knew she had flown to Boston that evening to see Guy Witten. If anyone had been following her, it would have been much easier just to shoot her as she sat on that bench at Faneuil Hall. Why wait until she was inside Cafe Presto? Wreck an innocent man's storefront? Aha, maybe the problem was on Guy's end. Philippa tried to remember her phone conversation with him. It had been short but not sweet: They had agreed to meet at ten. Then he had slammed the phone down. Anyone eavesdropping with dire intent would have shown up after ten at Cafe Presto . . . looking for Emily.

"Tell me, Em," Philippa said innocently, "who knew you were going to New York?"

"Ross. Why?"

"I guess your husband would have no reason to kill you, right?"

"Of course not! Good Lord, Philippa! What a thought!"

"Well, you have to look at all the angles. I was just thinking that if someone wanted to knock you off, not me, the *Choke Hold* party would have been the perfect opportunity." Philippa observed the scenery for several miles, waiting for her sister's confession. Finally she became impatient. "Are you sure you haven't ticked Ross off somehow?"

Emily went cold: Did Ross know about Guy? She didn't think so. He would confront her with it, wouldn't he? The way he had confronted her with Dana? "I can't believe you would seriously think that my own husband would kill me, Philippa."

"Well, maybe someone else," Philippa replied. "Can you think of anyone who might want you out of the way?"

Guy Guy Guy. "Afraid not."

Damn! Why wouldn't Emily just spill the beans? Didn't she realize that affairs were as respectable as prenuptial agreements? Both helped to focus husbands and wives on the permanence of marriage. "I guess we're back where we started, then," Philippa said testily. "On the face of it, looks like someone's after me. What are you going to do?"

Emily wanted to throw everything into O'Keefe's lap and run away. But then he'd wonder why she hadn't told him about Philippa's stomach ache, her bruised face, their little switch in New York, the cherries . . . little details adding up to a suspicious whole. Eventually he'd discover her affair with Guy. No, better keep O'Keefe out of this. "First I'll try to find the waitress who served Byron that drink," Emily said. "Then I'm going to get the guest list from the lady who organized the AIDS benefit. Maybe you'll recognize an enemy or two there. Then I think you should ask Simon for a list of everyone who's called about you over the last few months."

"I could answer that myself, dear," Philippa said. "No one."

"Come on, you don't have a fan club? People don't ask for your autographed picture? Maybe we'll find some sort of correlation."

Philippa grabbed her seat belt as the car swerved down the exit ramp. "How long is this going to take, Em? Am I supposed to stare at the lake until you find out?"

"Why not? The weather's beautiful. You can't be seen with a face like that. I thought you had nothing else to do anyway." Emily pulled onto an uneven country road. "It won't take more than a few days."

"Maybe we should explain everything to the police. Let them take care of it. You don't have the time for this."

"I just lost my job, remember? How the hell else am I going to amuse myself?" Emily pulled into the parking lot of a shopping mall. "I wouldn't involve the police. They'll tell the newspapers."

Philippa perked up. "Hey, that might be just what Simon needs."

"Sure. Have him plant the story in every rag he can. Then some wacko slasher can read about it and decide to join the fun. Stay here, Phil. I'll be back in ten minutes."

Emily bought groceries. When she returned to the car, her sister was listening glumly to a rock station, hoping to hear a capsule review of *Choke Hold*. She snapped the radio off as the deejay read a capsule review of Julia Roberts's new movie instead. "Your cabin has a bathtub, doesn't it?" Philippa asked finally as they entered an unpaved driveway. "I can't live without a bathtub."

"Sorry. Showers only. You can bathe in the lake, of course. Very invigorating this time of year. The quiet will grow on you, Phil. Read a book. Watch television. Contemplate life."

"God! That would drive me to suicide!"

Emily stopped the car in front of the cabin. Beyond the rear deck, protected by tall spruce, the black lake gleamed in the midday sun. She had thought many times of coming up here alone with Guy. She still thought about it. It was one of her fondest fantasies, right up there with having children and being twenty again. "Don't give me this suicide crap, Phil. You have it all."

"*Had* it all! You have no idea how wretched it is to outlive your usefulness!"

"No, I wouldn't have any idea. That's because I've never been useful in the first place."

"You are a spoiled brat," Philippa snorted. "Women would die to be in your shoes. You've got a great house, a great husband, a job you don't need, total freedom. . . . You're set for life. What the hell else could you want?"

Having again provided Emily with the perfect opening, Philippa waited to be told all about Guy Witten. Instead, after a long silence, Emily said, "Children, maybe."

"Not that again! You're too old! You'd be senile before they went to their first prom! Ross would have a heart attack trying to play touch football with his six-year-old! Be realistic, Emily. There are certain things that neither of us is ever going to have. A mother, for one. Children, for two. Just let it go." Philippa sighed. "Go back to your husband. Get a life. He's your best friend."

Emily looked oddly at her sister. "What do you mean, *go back* to your husband?"

"I meant drive back to Boston," Philippa lied quickly. "Bake Ross a cherry pie."

"So he doesn't kill me?" Emily asked sarcastically.

"That's right." Philippa opened her door and stretched in the sunshine. "I hope you got some decent food for me. My stomach's still upset from that food poisoning."

Emily started unloading groceries. "Your stomach might feel better if you went on the wagon for a few days." She carried two heavy bags over a rocky path as Philippa followed gingerly in her high-heeled boots. "When was the last time you were here?" Emily asked, unlocking the cabin door. "Was it with Gary?"

That had been Philippa's fourth husband, the one who plucked his eyebrows and pretended to be British. "I think so," Philippa said, looking around the living room. Pure Ross: simple yet extravagant. "Hasn't changed a bit, has it?"

Warmed by the sun, they ate lunch on the deck. As Philippa talked about hemlines and Paris, polishing off the half bottle of wine she had found in the refrigerator, she gradually noticed that her sister was not really listening. "Is something on your mind, Em?" she asked finally.

Emily flushed. She had been imagining herself swimming in the lake with Guy. "I was just wondering what I'd do for a job now," she fibbed.

Philippa pounced on her speck of opportunity. "What happened to your old job?"

"Told you. I got fired."

"No, the one before that. Did you get fired from that, too?"

"I quit."

"Why'd you do that? You're not a quitter." Philippa nonchalantly chewed some spaghetti, unable to swallow, waiting: If Emily confessed her affair with Guy Witten, it was probably over. If she said nothing, it was still smoldering. After a few seconds, Philippa studied her sister's face and was disheartened to see a rigid mask, the sort that women clamped on only when affairs reached life-or-death altitudes.

"I left because I was bored," Emily said at last, standing up. "Are you sure you'll be all right here by yourself?"

"Of course! I'm a big girl!" Philippa slurped the last of her spaghetti and followed her sister into the kitchen. "I presume I can use the phone."

"To call me, yes. But no one else. You've disappeared, remember. The whole point of this exercise is that no one knows you're here. Could you go over your enemies list one more time? Maybe there are some people you've left out."

"What a delightful thought. By the way, have you considered that someone was trying to knock off Byron, not me or you?"

"It's possible. O'Keefe tells me he used to be a prostitute. And he didn't get along with the people at Diavolina." Emily put her plate into the dishwasher. "But he swallowed those four cherries by accident. Let's both think about it some more." Emily showed Philippa how to operate the microwave and the alarm system. "In case you finish all the books in the house, there's a general store a mile that way. I'll call you tonight. Just stay put."

"Where would I be going? You didn't leave me any wheels."

"My hiking shoes are in the closet." Emily got into her car. "Bye-bye."

After she had driven away, Philippa helped herself to another bottle of wine and returned to the deck, sipping thoughtfully as ducks honked over the lake. It felt strange to be so far away from cigarette smoke and sycophantic laughter and the omnipotent, carnivorous media: Mother Nature was no substitute for thieving, conniving humanity. For a long while, Philippa considered her enemies. She was halfway successful, so there were plenty. But which of them would risk killing her? It was a compliment she knew she did not deserve. After carefully rehashing her last dozen movies, and all the people she had shafted thereby, Philippa concluded that only two people on earth would have the guts to kill her: Emily, when she found out about Philippa pursuing Guy Witten; and Guy Witten, when he found out about Philippa impersonating Emily.

The afternoon suddenly seemed eerily quiet and cold. Philippa shivered, sure that thousands of unseen animals were staring at her from the bushes, getting angry about her fur coat. She thought about the horror movies she had made about women alone in wooded cabins; now those ludicrous scripts seemed all too realistic. Hastening inside, she checked that the doors and windows were locked. She activated the alarm system. Then she got the biggest carving knife from the kitchen and took a long shower, thinking about her immediate future. Obviously, she would have to call Guy very soon and beg for his cooperation and silence. It would be humiliating beyond words; however, confessing to Emily would be even worse. Unthinkable, in fact. Philippa flipped on the television and stared zombielike at the screen as more complex scenarios played in her head.

Rush-hour traffic stalled on the Tobin Bridge as the police tried to clear the last splinters of a runaway boat/trailer from the highway up ahead. Joining thousands of inbound commuters on the hoods of their cars, Emily passed the time watching ships chug in and out of the harbor. When a gorgeous yacht floated by, gleaming in the late afternoon sun, she thought of Dana. No more Fourth of July sailing parties; that would leave a big hole in the summer. How would she and Ross watch the fireworks now? Emily wondered if Ardith had sold Dana's boat yet. No question it would be one of the first things she'd get rid of; for too many years, what had been recreation to Dana had been nothing but a huge, bobbing slap in the face to Ardith. Why had she let him get away with it for so long? One affair, maybe, a wife could swallow. Several hundred was a different story. Emily tried to imagine how she'd feel if Ross slept with a new woman every week. The first betrayal would be horrendously upsetting, a taste of death. But the second betrayal would be the last. No, she couldn't imagine beyond two. But she had never related to Ardith.

Traffic way up front began squeezing past the tollbooths: obstruction removed. Emily went back to her car and slogged to Beacon Hill. It was nearly six; Ross was still at the office sharpening pencils with Marjorie. God only knew when he would remember to come home. Emily may as well play detective meanwhile. She found the business card that Millicent had given her as she was leaving the *Choke Hold* gala last night. Park Avenue address, Emily saw, unimpressed: Nowadays, it meant only that the doorman carried an Uzi instead of a handgun. After two rings, the housemaid answered.

"This is Philippa Banks," Emily announced. "Is Millicent in, please?"

"Oh! Miss Banks! Yes! Certainly!"

Millicent picked up the phone next to the bathtub. "Philippa, darling. Thank you for last night. It was a tremendous success. We collected over eight hundred thousand dollars. Your film was magnificent, your acting superb. And I must apologize for that sickening accident. It cast a pall over my whole party. I understand the police had to ask you a few questions this morning. I hope they were not rude."

"Not at all. They visited you too?"

"Of course, darling. Heroin is such a sloppy drug! I wish people would have the decency to overdose at home. Not at charitable functions."

"I agree." Emily delicately cleared her throat. "Millicent, I met several . . . ah . . . intriguing men at your gala. Would you mind faxing me a copy of the guest list? Just to refresh my memory? I'm so bad with last names."

"Certainly. But you ought to be aware that some of them would not be interested in women."

"Only one way to find out." Emily gave her Ross's office fax number. "Thanks, darling. And don't breathe a word of this to anyone, particularly Simon. He's so possessive."

"My lips are sealed." Millicent asked several salacious questions regarding three well-known actors. "Don't be coy, Philippa," she said. "I know you've slept with them all."

Emily made up silly answers then asked which caterer Millicent had used for the gala. "Ditzi's, of course! Weren't those canapés stupendous?"

"Out of this world. Did Ditzi's also supply the serving staff?"

"Everything. Don't tell me you saw a cute waiter, now!"

Emily giggled ambiguously and soon got off the line. Then she called Major & Forbes. "Hi Marjorie. Do me a favor? You're going to get a fax soon. Nothing but a list of names. Could you put it in an envelope for Ross to take home?"

"Of course."

Was that voice just a tad smug? Vaguely possessive? Emily stomped into the bedroom to change into running clothes; talking just a few seconds with the competition had flooded her bile ducts. She'd have to jog all the way to Hopkinton to detox. Emily ripped some shorts out of a drawer. Damn! No clean T-shirts! Remembering the spare that she had brought back from Diavolina that morning, she went to the front hall. Her tote bag lay in a heap next to the umbrella stand, where she had left it before rushing to the airport to fetch her sister. Emily pulled on the T-shirt and swore again: Something had scratched her.

She yanked it off. Someone had pinned a tiny envelope inside. *To Emily*, it said in irregular block letters, *A secret from Slavom.* The *m* in his name ended in a long streak.

She couldn't have been more stunned had the dishwasher's ghost appeared in the hallway. Emily tore the envelope open. A key: USPS DO NOT DUPLICATE. Why had Slavomir given her a postbox key? He hadn't said three words to her in his life. She was surprised that he even knew her name. Emily turned the key over: Below the serial number she saw 274 etched faintly, carefully, on the metal. She peered again into the envelope, looking for an address, a ZIP code; instead she saw an old photograph of a young girl. It was tattered and a little damp, as if Slavomir had carried it around in his pocket. Who was the girl? When had he put the key and picture in her drawer at Diavolina? The only time she recalled him being in her office was the night he had tripped over the toolbox and bashed his head. She had told him to go there and lie down awhile. That had been the night of Dana's accident. It had also been the night Slavomir had drowned. He had gone to a lot of trouble to pin the envelope inside her T-shirt, out of sight. A secret? Had someone interrupted him as he was signing his name, before he got to an address? She upended the tote bag, hoping to find more clues among her office scraps: nothing, of course. Cryptography required forethought and sobriety.

Now what, call O'Keefe? She'd have to think about that. Again. Emily tried to recall Slavomir's address; she had looked it up in Ward's files the day she had identified the dishwasher's body at the morgue. Although no street came to mind, a seedy area behind South Station did. In the morning, when she got tired of figuring out who was trying to knock off Philippa, she'd visit a few post offices in that area. Then, depending on what she found, she'd consider involving the detective, who was obviously interested in anything having to do with the inmates of Diavolina. Of course he would wonder why Slavomir would leave Emily, of all people, the key to a postbox and a picture of a girl. She could just see his eyes as she replied, "No idea." Ah, just what she needed: another man convinced she was a liar. Emily smeared on some sunscreen and jogged slowly toward the Promenade. She missed Guy terribly.

# 9

The morning after the *Choke Hold* gala, Ross had pretended to be asleep as Emily quietly kissed his ear and left the bed. While she dressed, he lay motionless, listening to the rustle of her clothing, wondering what she was wearing to work today. How did she even have the energy to get up? Emily had only gone to bed at four o'clock, after returning to Boston from her glitzy party in New York. Poor dear: last night a movie star, this morning a galley slave. Ross remembered a strained conversation before she had gone to bed. Over what this time? Oh yes, his midnight strolls; Emily didn't like them. Well, that was too bad. There would be more.

Feeling none too swift himself, having gone to bed as late as his wife, Ross dragged into the shower. Emily had left him about seven minutes of hot water, barely enough to steam out the cricks in his neck. And she had used his razor again. Damn! Soaking, Ross pawed around the medicine chest for a new blade. He found none, of course; that was why Emily had used his. Swearing, he stepped back into the shower. When he

slammed the door, the shampoo fell to the floor. Ross ate breakfast alone, which dejected him further. He was used to starting
the day with coffee, the obituaries, and his wife across the table
crunching toast. Instead of eating on the balcony, he stayed inside, his back to the blinding sunshine. Ross paged absently
through the newspaper, trying not to imagine himself facing
every morning like this. He put his dishes in the sink, then
smiled bleakly: Were he divorced, they'd still be waiting for him
when he returned home tonight. Ross put on his coat and left
for work, beginning to understand why grown men at the office
had been useless for years after their wives had left them.

He perked up as Marjorie smiled at him from her desk; she'd
give him a lot of stupid little chores to keep him occupied all
day long. "Good morning," Ross said, looking over her shoulder
at his appointment calendar. "Leave me any time to blow my
nose?"

"Sure," Marjorie replied, glancing up. "And I left time to
shave. I suggest doing it now. Umberto's coming in three minutes." The plasterer. "He wants to discuss the Glazer renovation.
Apparently Mrs. Glazer is changing her mind again. Now she
wants to drop the cornices and add another curved wall."

Ross had little patience with Dana's clients, who viewed architecture not as frozen music but as petrified mammon. "I
thought I gave that project to Peters."

"You did. Mrs. Glazer fired him." Marjorie followed Ross to
his executive washroom, ticking off two-sentence summaries of
his appointments as he hastily shaved. "Ardith's coming in to
pick up the rest of Dana's things. We still have some clearing
out to do."

Ross hadn't seen Ardith since the funeral. Already he felt
guilty about not taking better care of her; God knows if he had
died, Dana would be consoling Emily twenty-four hours a day.
Bah. Ross splashed his face with cold water as Marjorie churned
through his agenda. "You're meeting Dagmar Pola at ten to
check out her art collection," she said. "So you can get inspired
to design a space for it."

"I'm already inspired. She tells me they're all nudes."

Blushing, Marjorie left to send a few faxes. As soon as she had gone, Ross phoned Billy Murphy, their contact at City Hall. Yesterday, requesting a small favor, he had given Billy the license number of the truck he had seen crashing through the window of Cafe Presto. "Good morning," Ross said. "Any luck with your friend at the Motor Vehicle Agency?"

"No problem. The vehicle's registered to Peace Power Farm, Hale, Massachusetts. Whatever the hell that is." Billy knew better than to ask why Ross had needed the identification. Nine times out of ten it involved mistresses, paramours, or cuckolds. "You didn't tell me they were commercial plates."

"Sorry. I wasn't thinking." Commercial plates? Ross was lucky he had even been able to read the damn numbers as the pickup truck sped away from Cafe Presto. He and Billy talked a while about building permits. Then Marjorie buzzed: Umberto had arrived. "My plasterer's here," Ross said. "Thanks a million, Billy."

He had a short, soothing conference with Umberto, who was on the verge of pouring a ton of wet plaster over Mrs. Glazer. Then Ross met a young couple who wanted to build a tree house with flushing toilet for their adorable six-year-old. He talked to a CEO who had visions of a corporate Taj Mahal on Route 128. Then he and Marjorie went into Dana's office: Ardith would be showing up any minute to collect the last of Dana's personal belongings.

"I'll take the shelves and closet," Marjorie directed, veering toward the far wall. "You finish the desk. What should I do about that hat?"

"Put it in my closet." Ross tossed Dana's "All-Star Nude Midgets" calendar into the wastebasket. When Marjorie returned, he asked, "How did Dana take care of Billy Murphy? Besides cash, of course."

She removed a bright blue condom from Dana's copy of the *Massachusetts Building Code*. "He sent a case of Cutty Sark to Billy's brother-in-law in Stoneham. I have his address. Never send any gifts to Billy at City Hall or at home."

"Could you do that for me? Thanks." Ah, Marjorie. Without her, this office was Babel. Ross pulled open a drawer full of vitamins and miracle potions. "Do you think Ardith really wants these?" He squinted at several labels. "This one's guaranteed to produce a twelve-hour erection. This one's supposed to promote the growth of thick, luxurious hair from head to toe." He lobbed that bottle into the trash. "Just what Ardith needs."

After placing the last of Dana's books in a large cardboard box, Marjorie opened his closet. The faint smell of Dana's cologne brought tears to her eyes; for a tiny moment, his residual vapors had tricked her into believing that he was still alive. Thank God she hadn't allowed Ross over here! Inside hung Dana's dark blue suit, the one he always looked so dashing in, and a raincoat. On the shelf were spare shirts and a few unfavorite neckties. Marjorie hastily folded everything into two shopping bags and was about to shut the door when, high in the corner, she spied a white box.

"Can't reach something?" Ross asked as she was dragging over a chair. "Here, I'll get it."

Ross immediately recognized the embossed box: It came from an expensive shop on Newbury Street. Once upon a time, Emily had bought him little nothings there. The box felt empty, but Ross knew better than that. Suddenly losing his courage, he handed it to Marjorie and watched as she lifted the lid.

Beneath the tissue paper they saw purple silk. "Take it out," he whispered.

Marjorie removed a pair of bikini briefs. "Why would Dana keep this atrocious thing? There's a note. Should I read it?" Silence. "Ross?"

He had become extremely pale. "Go ahead."

Marjorie removed a small card. "'Madly.'"

He waited a moment. "That's all? No signature?"

"Nothing."

Ross snatched the card away. As he was examining the handwriting, comparing it to his wife's, the door of Dana's office swept open. Ardith strode in wearing a black suede suit, terribly exquisite makeup, and more gold chains than a professional athlete. "Good morning."

Ross slid the note into his pocket as Marjorie expertly crumpled the briefs, then the box, down her skirt. With her jacket buttoned, the bulge could be mistaken for a potbelly. "Hello, Mrs. Forbes," she replied. "You're looking well. May I get you some coffee?"

"No, no," Ardith waved, jangling her ten bracelets. "I won't be staying long." She eyed the shopping bags next to Ross. "What's in there?" she asked caustically. "A gross of condoms?"

Marjorie pretended to have misheard. "A blue suit, a rain-coat, and some neckties."

"Give them to the Salvation Army." Ardith looked quickly over Dana's books. "You can keep these, too. I have nowhere to put them." She walked to her husband's desk. "What are these?"

"Vitamins," Ross said.

Ardith noisily upended the entire box into the wastebasket. "Have I missed anything?"

Marjorie opened the top drawer of Dana's desk. "A beautiful antique Waterman," she said, removing a thick, gold pen. "Dana loved it." Actually, he hated it, but Marjorie remembered Dana mentioning that it had been an anniversary gift.

Ardith stared at the pen. On one hand, she wanted to snap it in half, on the other hand, it had cost her two thousand bucks. She could probably get two and a half for it now. "Thank you," she said finally, tucking the pen into her purse. Then Ardith noticed the bronze bust of Dana across the office. "Good God! I had completely forgotten about that thing!" She circled the statue with an appraising eye. "Not a bad likeness, really."

"We'll have it sent to your home," Marjorie said.

Ardith smiled coldly at the other woman. "You can send it out the window." She placed a key on Dana's bare blotter. "I won't be needing this anymore. Ross, I'm going to Europe tonight. Call when the lawyers have finalized the business arrangements, would you?"

"Of course." He took the key. "Ardith, do you recall Dana ever taking antidepressant pills?"

"You too? Detective O'Keefe spent a morning going through the house and the boat looking for them. He didn't believe me when I told him that Dana's boat was one huge antidepressant pill." Ardith was just about out the door when she noticed a plaque on the wall. "'Architect of the Year,'" she read aloud.

Marjorie gave it one last try, for Dana's sake. "That's an important award, Mrs. Forbes."

"Really?" Ardith lifted the plaque off the wall. "It's all yours, then. Good-bye."

The door clicked shut. After a long moment, Marjorie exhaled. "Why did she even bother coming in?"

Drained by point-blank female rage, Ross slumped into Dana's favorite chair. "She was obviously making some kind of statement. Any idea what it was?"

"Good riddance, I'd say. After that performance, the feeling is mutual." Marjorie eased the white box from under her skirt. "Would you care for a purple bikini?"

"I'd prefer a dozen aspirin."

Marjorie left, returning shortly with the pills and a glass of water. "Dagmar Pola's expecting you in ten minutes, you know."

Oh joy! More merry widows! He swallowed a fistful of aspirins. "Tell me something, Marjie. Do you think Ardith caused Madly or Madly caused Ardith?"

"That's a question only a man would ask." She sounded somewhat disgusted.

"What do you mean?"

"I mean Dana caused everything." Marjorie left.

Ross could tell from the *chuff chuff* of her shoes against the carpet that she was angry. What the hell had brought that on? He would never understand women. They blew hot and cold and tepid and deadly and they never, ever gave you an inkling which face was going on next. A man agonized his life away trying to choose between retreat and conquest, and in the end, if he guessed right maybe half the time, his reward was not even adoration but a benign, maternal tolerance. Was that what all love and lust boiled down to? Tolerance? Maternity? Ross sighed; he must be getting old. For a moment there, he would have given anything to be back on his mother's lap, nodding blissfully as she read a bedtime story. He wondered if he had ever been truly happy since.

Ross returned to his office and picked up his overcoat. "Where does Dagmar live?" he asked Marjorie, stopping at her desk.

"Commonwealth and Clarendon." She gave him a slip of paper with his exact destination. "Your eleven o'clock appointment's back here. Try to call if you're going to be more than fifteen minutes late."

"Thanks." Had Marjorie forgiven him for that stupid question about Madly? Ross wasn't sure; better bring a dozen roses when he returned. He caught a cab, arriving just a few minutes behind schedule at a palatial building on Commonwealth Avenue. "Ross Major. I have an appointment with Mrs. Pola," he told the doorman. As the fellow called upstairs, Ross wistfully admired the brass-and-marble foyer, envying those born shortly after the Civil War, when there had been a better connection between hard work and just reward, and when wives cleaved to their husbands till death did them part. On the other hand, Plexiglas hadn't yet been invented.

The doorman nodded toward a small elevator. "Tenth floor, Mr. Major."

Dagmar was waiting for him as the door whooshed open. She wore a white wool suit and, here and there, several hundred pearls. On her tiny feet were tiny red high heels. Dagmar had very slim, fine legs. Ross stared a moment at her wavy white hair. He had never seen her without a hat; the effect was oddly intimate. "Hello, Mrs. Pola," he said. "You're looking wonderful."

Her diamond rings tinkled as she offered Ross her hand. "My condolences upon the death of your partner. He was a talented man." She turned toward a long hallway. "But a wastrel."

Ross paused only momentarily, thinking he had misheard her. What could she have said, though? *Fossil? Rascal?* He trailed Dagmar through the hallway, past an exquisite series of watercolors of a woman with flowing red hair. Naked, of course. Was that tiny signature at the bottom Degas? Now was not the time to inspect; Dagmar was already half a dozen paces ahead of him.

Ross followed her into a salon with a stunning view of the

Charles River. Sculptures and paintings of lush, inviting female anatomies filled the room. Ross hastily sat beside Dagmar on a settee with orange pillows. "This is quite something," he remarked, glancing casually about, crossing his legs to camouflage the willful lump in his pants.

Dagmar poured two cups of coffee from a silver pot. "Poor Mr. Major, don't blush on my account. What's here is sedate compared to the other rooms. Milk or sugar?"

Try cold shower. "Milk, thank you." Something about this place was extremely odd. There were just so many of *them* begging for attention. A man could sit here all day, staring at nothing but navels and the river. Ross silently sipped his coffee, waiting for his brain to revert from rolling flesh to more rigorous architectural forms. It didn't. Finally he said, "Have you been living here for a long time?"

She laughed curtly. "I live in Weston, Mr. Major. I was unaware of the existence of this apartment until after my husband's death."

Terrific, a fornicatorium. What was Ross supposed to say now, What a nice surprise? He pitied Dagmar having to walk through here alone after the son of a bitch had checked out, robbing her of the catharsis of divorce or murder or even a scornful glare. Ross impulsively put his cup aside and took Dagmar's hand. "May I ask a stupid question? Why put this in a gallery?"

"Because it's worth a fortune."

"Doesn't it bother you that your husband collected nothing but nude women?"

Dagmar's sharp blue eyes mocked him. "Why should I mind? None of this fluff did him any good whatsoever." She removed her hand from Ross's grip. "Joseph was impotent."

Mortified, Ross hid his face behind a coffee cup. When they chose to be direct, Yankee dowagers could outscore a torpedo. "Forgive me."

"Nonsense. Thank you for rushing to my defense." She lit a cigarillo. "By the way, do call me Dagmar. Would you be interested in seeing the rest of the collection? Or have you had enough for one day?"

Perhaps she cast an oblique glance at his erection; it could have been just smoke in her eyes. "How much more is there?" Ross asked.

"This apartment covers the tenth floor. You've been in just one room." Dagmar extended an aristocratic hand. "Don't be shy, Ross. I'm sure you've seen it all before."

He had, but not in so many positions. Jesus! Was any creature more powerful than a naked woman? Joe Pola's collection spanned five centuries, fifty cultures, and although the bodies were different, the women all had the same dreamy, omniscient expression as if, instead of being observed, they were the observers, waiting as the obsessed artist crashed and burned in a futile attempt to capture their souls. As he trailed Dagmar from room to room, losing track of the time and his purpose in coming here, Ross began to wonder what had impelled Joe Pola to surround himself with this chimerical sea. He wondered how much time Joe spent here, whether he came alone, and what he did here if he was impotent, as Dagmar had claimed. Perhaps Joe was only impotent concerning Dagmar.

She walked past a heavy door. "What's that?" Ross asked.

"The bedroom. It's of no consequence."

"I'd like to see it. Please."

Joe Pola's unauthorized bedroom contained a four-poster bed, two fabulous armoires, and a life-size marble sculpture in front of the window, oddly blocking the view. Then Ross realized that if Joe were lying on the bed, looking at the statue, he would see a woman profiled against blue sky, forever gazing at the river. Lovely playful body; like Emily's. Suddenly Ross wanted to see the statue's face. He stepped toward the window.

"You actually like that? It's pure kitsch."

On the contrary; it was pure Emily, or he was hallucinating. Even in marble, the curve of her lips made his heart thump just a little faster. "Who did this, Dagmar?"

She remained at the door. "I don't know. The initials in the pedestal say 'S.D. 1950.'"

"Aha." So it wasn't Emily, then. Greatly relieved, feeling a little foolish, Ross stepped away. "Maybe we should put it in front of a window in your new building."

"Actually, I'm thinking of selling that one. It's extremely vulgar." Dagmar returned to the hallway. "Come along," she called as if he were a schoolboy.

She took him through Joe's remaining rooms, watching impassively as Ross went from canvas to collage, trying his best to look as if twenty inches of space between a woman's knees signified nothing more than a study in perspective. Dagmar finally rounded back to the settee with the orange pillows. This time, she offered Ross whiskey. "Well?"

"It's overwhelming," Ross said, desperate for the liquor. "I don't know whether I'm in Disneyland or hell. Typical male response. Sorry, Dagmar."

"Don't apologize. I expect you'll be inspired to design an appropriate building for it all now." Dagmar lit another black cigarette. "Try to do a little better than that chapel your partner built for Joseph. That is truly a monstrosity."

Ross's head began to throb; so Dagmar knew about that. He wondered if she had found out about the chapel the same way she had found out about this place. "I'll do my best," he said. Ross glanced at his watch and nearly choked: one o'clock. He had missed five appointments. "Dagmar, I must be going."

She reached for a straw hat. "My driver is waiting downstairs. We can drop you off."

They left the apartment. Neither spoke for a while after Dagmar's car had pulled into the street. "Who else has seen that apartment?" Ross asked finally.

"Just you. Who might have seen it with Joseph, of course, I would not know."

The car stopped at State Street. Ross lingered a moment, dreading the prospect of an office full of women with blouses and shoes and crossed legs. "Thank you for letting me see it."

She shrugged, shifting pearls. "I try not to go there alone."

Ross kissed Dagmar's gloved hand. "I'll get to work on the gallery right away." Troubled, he watched her car roll away. How was it possible that someone as smart as Dagmar had known nothing of her husband's apartment or his art collection? Hadn't she signed joint tax returns, talked to their bankers, lawyers, and accountants? Where had Joe found all that stuff anyway? Acquiring such a collection involved research as well as money; did Dagmar really believe her husband had been making pretzels all day and all night? What had they talked about at dinner? And he thought his marriage was in bad shape!

In the lobby of his office building, Ross bought a dozen roses. "I couldn't get away," he blubbered the second he saw Marjorie. "Dagmar went on and on."

Marjorie's smile exuded honey and acid. "Here are your messages."

"I'm sorry. Really. Did you have to cancel everyone?"

"By no means. I shifted them all after five. You weren't planning on an early dinner, were you?" She halfheartedly sniffed the roses.

Ross accepted his punishment. For the rest of the afternoon, he toiled obediently at his desk, bothering Marjorie only once for coffee. When she brought it, he stared doggedly out the window, trying to gaze at anything but the warm female at his elbow. If Marjorie came one inch closer, he might have to convert her into one of Joe Pola's canvases. "Could you do a little research for me, Marjie? Dana built a chapel for Joe Pola a while ago. Find out what it cost, what it looks like, why Joe built it, everything you can. I'm curious. Thanks."

When she had left, he called Diavolina to tell his wife he'd be working late. "Emily Major, please. This is her husband."

Either a high-pitched man or a low-pitched woman laughed at him. "She doesn't work here anymore."

"Is that so? Since when?"

"Since nine o'clock this morning." She finally quit, Ross thought. Then the voice said, "She got fired."

Ross immediately called the front desk. "Marjorie! Did Emily call while I was out?"

"I would have told you, Ross."

He dialed home and got the answering machine. Goddamn

it! What had his wife been doing since nine o'clock this morning? Furious, Ross redialed Marjorie. "I'm leaving," he growled.

"I'm afraid that's not possible. Mr. Levin just arrived. I've been thanking him for coming in twice today. Follow me, sir."

No way out: A few seconds later, Ross's secretary ushered Levin in. "Hello, Irving," Ross said, extending a hand. "Very sorry about this morning." Marjorie he ignored completely; maybe she'd go home. Fat chance! She stuck him with four more meetings, each time opening his door with a smile prissy and goo-goo as the Avon Lady's. Finally, around eight o'clock, Ross's last client left. After the doorknob had clicked, he stood a moment listening to the drone of the overhead fluorescents. The office was eerily still; even the divorced employees had gone home. All that remained of Marjorie was a note to turn out the lights and a sealed envelope marked *Fax for Emily*. What the hell was this? Ross held it up: opaque as cardboard. She had sealed it on purpose. Throwing it in his briefcase, he locked up and walked home.

"Emily?" he called, tossing his coat over a chair in the kitchen. No answer: Ross's heart constricted a little. Then he smelled mesquite. He went to the balcony, looked down, and saw his wife in the backyard grilling lamb chops.

"Hi, darling," she said. "Have a good day?"

No, but the sound of her voice had salvaged it. "I'll be right there," he replied, backing into the kitchen for a major dose of wine. Looked like she had already polished off the upper half of the bottle: excellent. He lost his tie. Ross went to the backyard and put his arms around her, not letting go for a long time. "I missed you today," he said, kissing her neck.

Emily gently broke away to turn over the lamb chops. "I got fired this morning."

"Thank God. That place was beneath your dignity. What was the reason?"

"Byron, the sous-chef, died unexpectedly. Ward holds me responsible."

"How so? You didn't boil him in oil, did you?"

Emily felt a familiar tension cramp her heart: mention cherries or *Choke Hold* or Philippa and Ross's good mood would cinderize. "He overdosed on heroin."

"Another real winner. That place was full of them. How does Byron's OD get you fired?"

"Ward's superstitious. Said I was killing off her kitchen crew." Ross chuckled. "You bought that?"

Sort of, yes. "I didn't care enough to argue."

"Good." He swallowed a slug of wine. "So what did you do the rest of the day?"

"Cleaned the house. Baked a pie. Thought about you."

Her voice always went a little white when she was lying, and this time was no exception. Ross played with her apron strings, sifting through tonight's priorities. First and absolutely foremost, he was going to fuck her. Nothing was going to get in the way of that. Then maybe he would ask her again what she did all day. The truth could wait a few hours; other necessities could not. "Really? What kind of pie?"

"Blueberry." Emily took the chops off the grill. "Hungry?"

With her, always. Ross watched the soft sloshing of her buttocks as she preceded him up the steps to the balcony. As they ate, he told her about his day, touching on all appointments but Dagmar's; he wasn't ready to share her humiliation, or all those naked women, with Emily yet. Instead Ross told her about Ardith's vicious little visit, but not about Dana's purple silk bikini. Neither mentioned Marjorie or Philippa; that might prick this precious, convivial bubble. Emily seemed slightly elsewhere tonight: temporary unemployment benefits? After dessert, Ross took her hand. He had just embarked on some serious foreplay when the phone rang. Sighing, he followed his wife to the counter, continuing to unbutton her shirt as she answered.

"Em? I think there's a bear outside," Philippa whispered.

"I wouldn't worry about it," Emily replied cautiously, not wanting Ross to overhear too many details.

"I'm scared shitless! What if it breaks in and tries to eat me?"

"That sort of thing just doesn't happen."

"Easy for you to say! You're in downtown Boston! And it's so damn dark up here! What a stupid idea this was. I should never have listened to you. Forget someone trying to murder me. The animals are going to finish me off first."

"Philippa, have a hot toddy and go to sleep. You're perfectly safe."

"Did you get hold of Millicent? Did she send you a list of names?"

"I'm working on it. Look, I've got to run," Emily said. Ross had several vagrant fingers in her pants. "I'll call you first thing in the morning." She hung up.

"What was that all about?"

"Philippa's up at the cabin for a few days." That was the truth. "She needed someplace to hang out until her face returns to normal." That was part of the truth.

Ross's insinuating fingers paused. "You took her up there? Why didn't you tell me?"

"I didn't want to get you upset."

"I'm not in the least upset." On the contrary, he was delighted: If Emily had been driving back and forth to New Hampshire all day, she hadn't had time to get into mischief with Guy Witten. "How long is she going to stay up there? Until all my booze is gone?"

"Very funny. You mustn't tell anyone. Not even Simon knows about this."

His fingers resumed their delicious invasions. "She called just now because she couldn't sleep?"

"Thought she heard a bear."

Ross turned out the kitchen lights. "Come with me," he whispered, seeing Dagmar's canvases.

As daylight was just beginning to iridesce the windows, Ross opened his eyes and listened: Something was not right. Then he heard Emily swallow. "You awake, honey?" he asked, slithering over to her.

"Yes."

"Something on your mind?"

Guy, Slavomir, Byron, O'Keefe, Philippa, Marjorie, marriage, murder, and postbox keys. "No."

"Can I get you anything?"

"No thanks." For a time Emily lay warm and taut beneath his caresses. Then she asked, "Did you get a fax for me at the office yesterday?"

"Marjorie got something," Ross answered drowsily. "What was it?"

"A list of people who went to an AIDS benefit."

Ross dreamily connected that with the restaurant business. "It's in my briefcase."

Emily went to the hallway and opened Ross's briefcase. Marjorie's envelope for her lay on top. As Emily took it, she noticed a small white box. She lifted it out, separated the tissue paper: a purple bikini? From whom? To whom? No note, of course: Marjorie was more clever than that. How dare Ross just leave it out like that, the stupid bastard! With shaking hands, Emily took the box to the bedroom.

"Going running, honey?" he asked sleepily.

She winged the box at his head. "What the hell's this?"

He stared at the object on the adjacent pillow, trying to link it with anything in the real world. Finally making a very bad connection, Ross said, "Where did you find that?"

"In your briefcase." Emily began furiously yanking on jogging clothes. "How'd it get there?"

"Marjorie must have put it there."

Of course Marjorie put it there! "You do know what's inside, don't you?"

"Men's purple underwear," Ross said. "Belonging to Dana."

Emily laughed harshly. "Oh, right."

"Marjorie and I were cleaning out his closet before Ardith arrived."

"Saving poor Ardith again, eh? Why didn't you just throw them out? Why did Marjorie put them in your case?"

"I have no idea. I certainly didn't tell her to. Maybe she was just trying to help out."

"Help out what?"

Ross realized that further answers, any answers, would only suck him deeper into a potentially fatal quicksand. "I really don't know, Emily. I'll ask when I get to the office."

"You do that." Pulling her second shoelace tight, she left the bedroom.

The rising sun bedazzled the mirrored buildings along the Charles River, creating wide bands of light that illuminated trees on the opposite bank. Emily ran along the Esplanade, where the sanitation crews were lethargically spearing rubbish from last night's rock concert, and crossed the bridge to Cambridge. Traffic was already mucked up at the end of Storrow Drive. She ran past Dana's marina, noticing his boat still tethered to the dock: so Ardith hadn't sunk it yet. She was probably too busy counting her money. Emily looped to Back Bay at Mass Ave, threading through clumps of MIT students on foot, bike, and rollerskate. A heavy mix of carbon monoxide and ocean filled her lungs.

She returned home only after Ross had departed for another long day with Marjorie, taking that little box with him. Emily showered and dressed. Brutally hungry, she went to the kitchen. Ross had eaten the last English muffin. He had saved her a half inch of orange juice. Instead of a note of apology on the kitchen table, he had left his dirty breakfast dishes in the sink. Christ! Men! She picked up the phone and called Philippa.

"What time is it?" her sister groaned.

"Eight-thirty. Did I wake you?"

"I only got to sleep an hour ago. It was the worst night of my life. All kinds of animals were scratching the windows. I swear a few mice ran over the pillow inches from my face."

"Look, I have that guest list from Millicent. Got a minute? I'll read off the people who bought tickets to the party." Emily recited two hundred names. Philippa recognized about ten, but couldn't connect any with homicidal passions.

"Isn't this rather pointless, Em? If you were going to kill me, wouldn't you use an alias?"

"No. That would look suspicious." Emily threw an orange rind into the disposal. "I want the name of everyone who's written to your fan club in the last six months. Maybe we'll find a match with Millicent's list or see some other name we recognize."

"And where's this list supposed to be sent? To my hideout in New Hampshire? What is the matter with you this morning? You're an absolute maniac."

Nothing like a few ounces of silk in your husband's briefcase to rev up the biosystem. Emily glanced impatiently at her watch; she had places to go, people to see. "I need that list right away, Phil. Think about how we're going to get it."

"Sure. Are you coming up this afternoon? Staying overnight?"

"I'll try. Why don't you go for a walk? Enjoy the scenery."

"I'll enjoy going back to sleep."

If Philippa didn't care who murdered her, why should Emily? Fed up with her sister's problems, unwilling to sit home and contemplate her own, Emily went to the post office at South Station. Astir with businessmen and vagrants, it was the perfect setting for an anonymous box; here was as good a place as any to begin testing the key that Slavomir had bequeathed her. Emily saw a long wall lined with tiny cubicles; inside them lay letters that could salvage, inspire, or destroy lives. She took Slavomir's key from her pocket and double-checked the number etched on it. Then she went to the matching box, tried the lock: Inside was a large envelope with her name on it. Emily went to a side table and tore it open.

Slavomir had left her two smudged sketches of—herself? Terribly unflattering, one. Where'd he get the wicked little smirk, the naughty gleam in the eye? Beneath that sketch, Slavomir had written *Diavolina.* The second drawing was softer, more innocent; Slavomir had titled that one *Angelina.* On the reverse was a short message in wobbly block letters: *Leo loks for you. Be carful.* That was it? Emily peered into the envelope: nothing.

Why would Leo be looking for her? Why should she be careful? What were these pictures all about? Who drew them? Emily tried to recall her brief association with the dishwasher: not much raw material there. He had never spoken directly to her, except for the first time Ward had introduced them to each other. Slavomir had dropped his spray nozzle, soaking everyone.

Thereafter, he had been drunk and totally unreliable. That last night at Diavolina, he had swilled a half bottle of port, stumbled over the gas repairman's toolbox, bumped his head, gone berserk, and rested in her office. Emily next saw Slavomir at the morgue. End of story. She stared at the sketches for a long time. Little Angel, Little Devil? And Leo, always back to the phantom Leo. How did Slavomir know Leo was looking for her? Was she that hard to find, for Christ's sake? What was Leo going to do when he found her?

Enough of this nonsense: back to Philippa. Emily found a phone and called information. "Byron Marlowe, please." Hopefully, his roommate was still alive. "Jimmy? This is Emily Major, from the restaurant." Silence. "I'm Philippa's sister. I wonder if I could talk to you." Resuscitating at once, Jimmy arranged to meet Emily at a little cafe in the North End. He liked the cannoli there.

She waited for him at a sunny corner table. Byron's bereaved roommate wasn't hard to spot: head-to-toe black, shoes shiny as his heavy sunglasses, chainsmoking. He still wore an overdose of the perfume she remembered from the *Choke Hold* gala. "Jimmy?" she called, waving uncertainly. Technically, they had never met.

"Hi." He slid into the chair opposite her and studied her face a moment. "You're prettier than your sister. She overdoes her eyebrows. You really must tell her about that." He lit a fresh cigarette, calling over his shoulder for a double espresso and cannoli.

"I've very sorry about Byron," Emily began.

"I'm not. He lied to me. Told me he was reformed. I spent an absolute fortune on that bastard's rehabilitation. I bought him clothes, food, and jewelry. What does he do first chance he gets? Dives right back into the slime. I hope he doesn't think I'm going to pay for his funeral now. I absolutely refuse. Fucking liar." A tear dribbled beneath Jimmy's sunglasses. "I hate him."

Emily ignored the two women staring at them from the adjacent table. "Were you together a long time?"

"Almost a year. I found him in the gutter, you know."

"I understand Byron led a rather bohemian existence."

"Bohemian? The man was a prostitute! I rescued him!"

A round, pleasantly bristled woman brought Jimmy's cannoli. Emily watched as he pressed his fork into one, raining crumbs over the table. "Did you find Byron his job at Diavolina?"

"No, he met Leo at a supermarket. They were arguing over the last slab of mortadella."

"What was Leo like?"

"A wild stallion. He had an eye patch. Byron worshiped him."

"Why?"

"He treated him like a son, I guess." Jimmy lapsed into a black reverie.

Emily finished her espresso. "Why would Byron start doing drugs again?"

"Honey, I don't know. He had a rotten past and a neurotic imagination. He always thought his enemies were after him."

"What sort of enemies?"

"I don't know. People from the street. Former johns."

That narrowed it down to ten thousand or so suspects. "Where would Byron get the cash for a drug habit?"

"He had a job and I gave him money, you silly thing. I spoiled him rotten."

"That night of the party, weren't you together the whole time?"

"Darling, I didn't walk around with my thumb up his butt. He had plenty of opportunity to go off with someone for a few minutes." Jimmy pulled angrily on his cigarette. "Byron was depressed after your sister's agent shat on him. Afterward, he went into the men's room without me."

"Had he been drinking?"

"This was a party, wasn't it?"

"What had he been drinking?"

"What else, darling? Vodka with dried cherries." Jimmy calmly finished his cannoli. "Byron always thought you were a very nice lady. Much nicer than your sister."

The smoke from Jimmy's cigarette was beginning to singe Emily's eyes. She paid the bill and left.

# 10

*Ah Emily, what a fine little hypocrite you are. Apparently it's all right for you to screw Guy, but it's not all right for me to screw Marjorie. I'm delighted that you discovered a pair of purple bikinis in my briefcase. Shook you up a bit, eh, my dear? Now you know how I felt finding that lovely photograph of Witten and Philippa in your back pocket. I'll bet you couldn't believe it at first. It never makes sense for the first ten horrible seconds; thereafter, it makes perfect, obvious sense, so obvious in fact that you can't believe your own stupidity. Humiliation feels terrific, doesn't it? Black, hot as tar: quite unlike any emotion you've ever experienced before. Interesting, though, how differently we reacted to it. You came flying into the bedroom, knickers in a twist, throwing that little box at my head, demanding an explanation, so delighted to discover a sin counterbalancing your own that you never stopped to think that perhaps I'm quite innocent. And now you've played your hand. The Wounded Bride probably expects me to come groveling home tonight with flowers and perfume, begging forgiveness. It's*

*not going to happen like that, darling. First of all, you have no
sin to forgive. Secondly, I'm still sitting on my own nest of rotten
eggs, hatching your punishment. It's always better to think and
wait, love. Remember that adage about revenge being a dish
best eaten cold? Obviously you don't. Women always feel better,
somehow more purified, burning their bridges. The night I discovered those pictures of yours, I would never have stomped into
the shower and demanded an explanation. Why not? Because I
know you too well: You would have left me then and there, and I
wasn't sure I wanted that. Besides, you did not deserve such an
easy out. You married a man who dislikes bedroom Armaged-
dons, who prefers less spectacular methods of evening the score.
You know I've got the patience and cunning, Emily; just give me
a bit of opportunity. We're not done with this yet.*

⚌

A legion of disgruntled mercenaries tromped briskly along State
Street, disregarding traffic lights whenever possible. As a sharp
wind blew in from the harbor, Ross once again reminded himself to wear a hat to work tomorrow morning; sunshine no
longer induced mild temperatures. As usual, he was first at his
office. Nothing had changed since he had left last night except
for the quality of light; now a fragile, yellow glow suffused the
rooms, inviting him in. He loved working here alone before
anyone else arrived, before the phone hijacked his imagination
and a thousand petty little crises chiseled his energy to dust. In
that marvelous, yellow quiet he drew his best buildings,
dreamed his purest dreams. . . . Ross's heart invariably sank the
moment he heard someone rattling the coffeepot in the kitch-
enette, for then the gods fled, demoting him from creator to
traffic controller. He didn't mind too much when Dana had
been around to insulate him from ambitious assistants and
horny clients, all gunning for promotions and seductions and
commissions that would make them famous. Without Dana, the
bickering overwhelmed him. And the fun was gone; Ross hadn't

realized until now that the fun was as important as the money. But Dana had been telling him that for years.

The fax machine trailed a long streamer of queries and quibbles. Ross stopped reading after five pages. He had little enthusiasm for business today. Perhaps it was time for him to . . . what? Retire to the cabin in New Hampshire with Emily? Chuckling, Ross went into Dana's office and flopped onto the deep, green couch where his partner had spent so many hours recuperating from six-martini lunches and extramarital fiascos. If he looked out the window from this soft vantage, all he saw was sky. No humans, no buildings, just sky: No wonder Dana spent so much time lying here. Ross ached like a defeated man. Soon he'd have to decide what to do with this office. He couldn't leave it empty too much longer. Raising himself up on one elbow, Ross looked around. What the hell was he going to do with those old books? These embroidered pillows from Dana's girlfriends? That stupid bust in the corner? And why would Dana save a pair of purple bikinis from someone named Madly? Dana had kept a lot of secrets to himself. Some damn best friend!

Marjorie walked in with a memo pad and a new blue dress with, for her, a daringly short hemline. "Good morning," she said agreeably, sitting in a chair and crossing her legs as if their tiff last night had never occurred.

Ross could see a good twelve inches up the back of her thighs. For the thousandth time, he thought about pulling her onto the couch and seeing if her legs were as strong as they looked. But that would answer only one pleasantly intriguing question at the cost of a trillion darker ones, and he was tired of those, so Ross got off the couch and went to the bronze bust in the corner. "Where did Dana get this?" he asked.

"Someone sent it to him. That's what he said, anyway."

"Why? To repay a favor?"

"You got me."

"When was this?"

"About ten years ago. Ross! What are you doing? That thing weighs a ton!" Rushing to the corner, Marjorie steadied the pedestal as Ross tipped the statue on its side.

"Does it say anything on the bottom?" he asked. "Initials? Date? Occasion?"

Marjorie peered at a patch of small incisions. "'R.W. 83.' That's all."

Disappointed, Ross rolled the bust back to its former position. For a moment there, he had thought it looked like the statue in Joe Pola's bedroom. His eyes must have been deceived by the sunlight on Marjorie's thighs. He returned to the couch but didn't lie down. "What did you find out about that chapel Dana built for Joe Pola?"

Marjorie back-paged through her memo pad. "According to my notes, Pola called here about two years ago."

"Why? Did someone recommend us?"

"Don't know. Dana's notes don't say, either. Dana drew a few sketches and construction began in September. They finished by Christmas." Marjorie handed Ross a photograph of the finished chapel. "Not much for two million bucks."

He barely remembered it. "What was I doing at the time?"

"Commuting to Turkey."

Ross took the folder. "What was Joe Pola like? You met him, I presume."

"Oh yes. Very sexy."

"Well? What the hell does that mean?" he snapped. "Tall? Short? Bald? Fat? He had to be at least eighty."

"He looked fifty. Wavy white hair, medium height, slim, tan. He wore beautiful suits."

"And that made him sexy?"

"The way he walked, the way he looked at you was . . . very attractive."

"Sounds like you had a crush on him." Ross tried to sound amused.

"He always brought me yellow roses."

"Did he ever ask you out?"

"What? Of course not."

Ross's irritation ebbed a tiny notch. "Did he ever come in here with Dagmar?"

"No. Never. My suspicion is that Dagmar didn't even know about this project."

"Why do you say that?"

"Because Joe and Dana were having too much fun. Two afternoons a week they'd drive out to the site in Dana's Jaguar and not get back until after midnight. Unless Dagmar traveled in the trunk, she didn't go along. Anyway, you've met Dagmar. Not what you'd call a blithe spirit. She strikes me as the type of wife who would have been here every day counting nails had she been in on it."

For a long moment Ross stared at the bust in the corner: *Dana, Dana, answer me.* "Well, she knows about the chapel now."

"Why are you so interested in it?"

"I'm trying to get a fix on Dagmar. She's more interesting than you think, by the way."

"You always did have a soft spot for the old ladies."

"Speaking of soft spots," Ross retorted, "what in hell possessed you to put those purple bikinis in my briefcase? I had a great time explaining them to my wife."

"But you're so good at explaining, Ross." With infuriating nonchalance, Marjorie flipped to the next page on her memo pad.

"Well? Why did you put them there?"

"I presumed you wanted them."

"Sometimes you presume too much." Inexplicably enraged, Ross jumped off the couch. "Cancel my appointments until this afternoon."

"Where are you going?"

"Errands."

Outside, the sun had gotten higher but the earth had not gotten warmer, so Ross took a cab to Newbury Street. He got out at a shop wedged between a furrier and a goldsmith. As he entered, the tinkling of the bell above the door was immediately stifled by the plush rugs. Potpourri overwhelmed oxygen. Along the dark green walls, tiny pools of light played on briefs and bras as if they were Grecian urns or the Star of India. A salesman whished over. "May I help you, sir?"

Ross took the little white box from his coat pocket. "I have a problem," he said, laying the purple bikini on a cushion. "I can't seem to remember who gave these to me. Most embarrassing."

The salesman studied the label. "How long have you had them?"

"I don't remember that, either. I found them in a back drawer. Nothing about them rings a bell." As the fellow inspected the briefs under the light, Ross spotted a bit of black stitching. "Would it be possible to look up that monogram?"

"That's not a monogram, sir."

"What is it then?"

"I'd say it's a pitchfork." The man looked slyly at Ross. "Does that ring any bells?"

"No. You can't look a pitchfork up?"

"This was not done by us. Furthermore, we discontinued this style over five years ago."

Ross put two fifty-dollar bills on the counter. "Try to find something for me, would you? I'll call in a few days."

Why hadn't Dana told him about Madly either? Had she been another heavy like Philippa? Ross walked agitatedly to Beacon Hill, angry at all the secrets everyone was keeping from him. Neither Emily nor her car was at home. As he backed his Saab onto Joy Street, Ross wondered whether that was something to worry about. Hell, of course it was. Everything she did was something to worry about now. He threaded through midday traffic to Storrow Drive, then to the turnpike heading west.

As he drove over exactly the same route his wife had taken a few days earlier, Ross thought about Dagmar. He kept seeing her still, intent face as she led him through the apartment her husband had kept to himself for so many years. He tried to comprehend what Dagmar had felt upon discovering it for the first time: impossible. How had she managed to survive betrayal of such magnitude? By forgiving and forgetting? Ross needed to ask, to learn, although in comparison to hers, his little problem with Emily was a joke. Not even a joke, a pun. He wondered if

Dagmar had any children, and if that had mitigated anything. He admired her fortitude, or, equally as important, her bravado. He wanted to know her better. Deep in thought, Ross zipped right past the monastery and Dana's chapel in the woods. Soon he saw a neat white sign for Peace Power Farm. WE LOVE VISITORS, it said. We'll see, Ross thought, pulling into the overgrown driveway. He parked near several other cars and studied the nearby farmhouse. An undistinguished structure in the first place, its charm was further eroded by chipped paint and a sagging porch. Dead leaves blanketed the half-dead lawn. The pickup truck that had rammed Guy Witten's front window rested behind an oak. Ross walked over, checked the license plate: yep, same vehicle that had shattered the window of Cafe Presto the other night. Someone had ineptly hammered the dents out of the front fender.

A collie bounded over, yapping as if he were a thief. "Stop it, Fidel," someone called from the porch. "Fidel!"

Fidel understood the tongue of Ross's shoe a little better than he did English. Ross went into the barn, where the odor of hay and rotting wood enveloped him. No cows therein; instead, one end had been converted into a slipshod farm stand. Ross saw a very big woman behind a counter piled with eggs and cheese. Well, he was almost sure she was a woman.

"Yes?" she demanded.

Had she appeared in the least helpless or frightened, he probably would have bought some eggs and gone home. However, rising to meet her hostility, Ross said, "I noticed a few dents in the pickup truck outside. Perhaps you could help."

"Who are you?"

"For the moment, let's just say I'm a neutral witness to an accident."

"Fuck off, buddy. I don't need this shit."

"You probably don't. That's why you should tell me why you drove through the front window of Cafe Presto a few nights ago. You sent two people to the hospital."

"I didn't send anyone anywhere. I was here making goat cheese."

"But you know who was driving and why. Tell me and I'll leave you alone." Ross smiled sweetly over the counter as the woman's imagination filled in the Or Else.

"Swine," she muttered after a moment. Lifting the tray in the bottom of her register, she placed a little red card on the counter. "Ask there."

Ross's smile sagged when he read the card. Diavolina? What the hell did Diavolina have to do with this? Was Emily involved? Was she playing some sort of smoke-and-mirrors trick on him? He gently pushed the little red card away. "Ask whom there?" he echoed softly.

"Ward. Now get out."

He wandered east, back to the office.

Startled by a branch hitting the roof of the cabin, Philippa woke up around one in the afternoon. It was bright but cold in the bedroom; were it not for exigencies of stomach and bladder, she would not have gotten out of bed at all. She dashed to the bathroom, raising great roiling clouds of steam before stepping into the shower, then raided Emily's drawer for socks and sweaters. After breakfast, when the vapor had left the bathroom mirror, Philippa inspected her face, and groaned. In no way could she be seen like this: Her bruises still looked too much like a face lift. She watched television for a while, catching up on the activities of other actresses who had less talent but better agents. It was hard to believe the world contained so many blond bombshells, with more being born every day. When even the commercials began to upset her, Philippa switched off the TV and tried to read a book. Unfortunately, the shelves contained only biographies of serious people.

Desperate to amuse herself, she bundled up in lumberjack gear, found a large stick, and began walking to the liquor store: Her scotch reserves were down to half a bottle. It was a clear, blustery day, and Philippa enjoyed the exercise for the first two miles. Thereafter, her enthusiasm waned as she realized that for each step forward, she'd eventually have to take one in reverse, lugging an armful of booze. Twice Philippa came to a complete

halt, almost in tears; only the specter of an evening without alcoholic consolation impelled her forward. Finally she arrived at
a small store named Marty's. A wizened man stood at the register. He looked as if he hadn't shaved for a month but had only
been able to sprout a few grungy millimeters of beard in the interim.

"Why hello, Emily," he said. "What happened to your pretty
little face?"

"My name is not Emily," Philippa snapped. "And nothing
happened to my face. I am expecting an important guest this
evening. Please deliver three dozen oysters, one pound of prosciutto, and a few bottles of French champagne to my premises.
I would also like a gallon of your best scotch to take home with
me now."

After a moment's acute contemplation, the man answered in
a completely different tone of voice, "You're in New Hampshire."

"Yes, I'm perfectly aware of that. Would you have any single
malts available?"

"I told you this is New Hampshire," he repeated. "You'll have
to go to the state liquor store for the hard stuff."

"Goddamn it! How far is that?"

"Fifteen miles." Seeing the negative effect of his news, the
man added, "I can sell you some beer or blush."

"That pink swill? I wouldn't even douche with it!" Spying a
rack of paperbacks, Philippa bought the two fattest ones with
the raunchiest covers. She looked disdainfully at the local newspapers stacked next to the register. "I suppose you're all out of
Wall Street Journals."

The man glanced out the window. "It's a nice day for a walk. I
suggest you go back where you came from."

Had she been wearing boots instead of sneakers, Philippa
could have stomped out with much more authority. Now she
had to settle for a flyweight slam of the screen door. Fueled by
frustration, she returned to the cabin with good speed. It was
lunchtime. Philippa drank several martinis with her tuna fish
sandwich. Finally, maddened by the sounds of her own chewing

and swallowing, she phoned her agent, who should have left New York for California last night.

Simon picked up after one ring. "You stupid bitch! I don't know what kind of stunt you think you're pulling, but I'm not amused."

"The hell with your amusement," Philippa retorted. "I'm in hiding, if you really really want to know. My life is in danger."

Simon laughed for almost a solid minute, but he had just levitated his mood with a generous dusting of cocaine. When he finally got his post-hysterical wheezing under control, he said, "I recommend you come out of hiding by tomorrow night. You've got a date with a Czech director. Here."

"That's impossible!" Philippa screamed. "I can't be seen like this!"

"Seen like what? You didn't get a skin peel without consulting me, did you?"

Damn, damn. She had never told him about her face; now it was a little late. "Who's this director?"

"Name's full of Zs and Cs. He's some kind of big cheese in eastern Europe and he's got bucks. He's seen your films and is thinking of casting you in a biblical epic."

"Why me?" Philippa asked, suddenly suspicious.

Simon had no idea; his office had gotten a cold call from this stranger yesterday. "Why you? Because I've been working my tush off since the fall of the Berlin Wall trying to arrange it! Now are you going to be at Luco's at eight o'clock tomorrow morning or am I going to have to suggest someone else?"

"I'll be there," Philippa said. "What about you?"

"Wouldn't miss it for the world, darling. You know I adore power breakfasts."

After hanging up, Philippa calmly took three empty liquor bottles outside and flung them as far as possible into the lake. They made a few circles in the water, then vanished without trace: There was a lesson in that. She stood for a time thinking about what she wanted, where she was headed, and whether those two lines might ever intersect, nay, come within light-years of each other, before she died. Lately, she had begun to doubt it. Worse, she had almost begun to accept the doubt. Totally deflated, she went inside and opened one of her paperbacks.

Around four that afternoon, as Philippa was dozing over page thirty, Emily arrived. "Having fun?" she called, dropping her suitcase with a thud.

Philippa followed her sister into the bedroom. "Ah, Em—before you unpack, could we talk? Something's come up."

"Something good?"

"I think so." Philippa sat on the bed. "I called Simon this afternoon. I know, I know, I shouldn't have! But I didn't tell him where I was! He thinks I'm stashed with a lover someplace."

"No such luck, of course."

"No." Not yet, anyway. "He's arranged a breakfast meeting with a Czech producer tomorrow. Wants me to be there."

"So you told him to postpone, right?"

"Of course not. Em! You've got to do it for me! One last time!"

"Oh Christ! Not again, Philippa!"

"You don't want to help me?" Philippa mumbled piteously.

"It's not a matter of helping! Don't you realize someone's trying to kill you?"

"No, I don't. I think your chef OD'd all by himself and maybe you've let your imagination run away with you. Maybe someone murdering me is just wishful thinking."

"How could you say something like that? My own sister!"

"Sorry, it slipped out. I get crazy up here in the woods. Listen, Em, I've thought of a plan. Fly to L.A. tonight. Have a quickie with this producer. You'll be back by tomorrow night."

Emily stared at her sister. "You can't be serious."

"You know I'd do it myself if I had half a face! Did you have something more important to do tonight or tomorrow?"

"I was looking forward to a little fishing, to tell the truth."

"Fishing? Do I mean less to you than a fucking trout?"

Emily put her arms around Philippa, who had broken into sobs. "Shh. Let me think about it. I just got here, you know."

"You have no idea what an easy life you have," Philippa wept.

"You've got money, a husband, houses, pension plans, family doctors, and a career you can shove. I'm all by myself. I have to fight for every little crumb that any schmuck throws at me. And they only throw it once. No one protects me from anything. Everyone lies to me. I wish I had your life."

Emily went to the bathroom and ran a facecloth under cold water. She returned to the bed and daubed her sister's red eyes. "Why don't you retire? Open a bookstore or something."

"I need a man, not a bookstore! And I'm not ready to throw in the towel yet. Say you'll go, Em. I have all the clothes you'll ever need right here."

"I think you're forgetting something. If someone's trying to kill you, they might kill me while I'm out there eating breakfast."

"You're perfectly safe. None of my enemies would think of getting up before lunchtime."

Emily hesitated. "I guess I could drop in on your fan club and get that list we need."

"Right!" Sensing victory, Philippa went for the coup de grâce. "Luco's is one of the best restaurants in town. You must try their Lobster Baked Alaska."

For a number of reasons involving escape, retribution, curiosity, and suicide, Emily finally agreed to go. While Philippa packed her suitcase, she booked her flight and hotel. She took a brief swim in the lake before phoning Ross. "I'm at the cabin," she announced.

Ross could tell from her tone of voice that Emily was still burned up about the purple bikinis she had found in his briefcase. He decided to respond with urbane indifference. "That's nice. How's Philippa holding up? Any booze left?"

"I'm going to Los Angeles tonight."

Ross's indifference vaporized. "What the hell for?"

"Breakfast."

"Three thousand miles for breakfast? Whose idea was this? Yours?"

"Philippa's. I'll be back late tomorrow."

"Is she going with you?"

"Of course not."

"You don't mean to tell me you're playing dress-up again." Hearing no response, Ross capitulated. He had no choice. "Have fun, then, dear. I'll be here when you get home."

"See what I mean?" Philippa cried as Emily hung up. "You have a perfect life. Your husband lets you do anything."

Realizing that she had just handed her husband a free night with his secretary, Emily snapped, "Just shut up! You have no idea what you're talking about!" She grabbed her sister's suitcase; better leave before she changed her mind.

"I really appreciate this," Philippa said, following Emily to her car. "You're the best sister in the world. Let me know if you want to stay out there for a while."

"As in trade places?"

"It's crossed my mind."

Emily tried to smile as if such a suggestion amused her. "By the way, what am I supposed to do with this producer?"

"Just be yourself! Have fun!" Philippa began to cry a little. "Be careful."

"Likewise. If you need anything, call Ross. He's number six on the speed dial." Emily put the car into Reverse. "If I die with a mouth full of pancakes, you'll know I wasn't making this up." Waving, she drove off.

Philippa waited for many minutes, listening to the soft whoosh of leaves. Finally confident that her sister would not be returning, she went to the cabin and forced a half-hour delay with cable news. Then, using her credit card, she phoned Boston. "Guy Witten, please."

"Emily?" said a voice. "How are you? It's Bert!"

"I couldn't care less who this is. Is Guy there? It's rather important."

"Hey boss! Get the phone!"

Philippa's heart thumped harder with each passing second. You are out of your mind, she thought just before Guy said hello. "Have you forgiven me yet, dear?"

He hesitated a few seconds, torn between hanging up and forgiving her. As usual, the sound of her voice withered all his manly resolve. "Of course I haven't forgiven you."

"Were you hurt the other night?"

"Only a sprained wrist and thirty-seven stitches. Not worth mentioning. I take it you escaped without a scratch."

Philippa laughed caustically. "Tell me that to my face, you cocksucker."

Emily had never called him that before, even in jest. Guy did not find the endearment attractive. "What's the occasion, Plum?"

"I'm at the cabin in New Hampshire. You know where that is, don't you?"

"Seeing as I've never been invited there, no."

Damn! "Well, look on a map," Philippa said. "Endicot Lake. It's the big house with lots of glass brick and a red door. I must see you tonight. Right away."

"You mean just a few hours from now?"

"That's correct. And I'd appreciate you bringing along a bottle of decent scotch." Stung by the ensuing silence, Philippa said, "I'm leaving tomorrow and never coming back. I would like you to hear a brief confession before I go."

"Never coming back? Where are you going, Filene's Basement?"

"How dare you make fun of me! Go sprain your other wrist!" Cursing, Philippa slammed down the phone. That conversation had not turned out correctly at all. What had made her cut Guy off like that? Now he'd never visit her. And he didn't even know where the place was? What kind of inept affair was her sister conducting here? Philippa toppled impotently onto the couch. So much for coming clean. She was an idiot for even having considered it.

Philippa revived when a thunderclap shook the cabin. Pelting rain quickly followed. Her stomach wobbled: Guy was driving north. She felt it. About now he would be passing Emily on the opposite side of Route 95. If he drove fast, estimated time of arrival would be about nine o'clock. What would she say to him? What would she wear? In a welter of generosity, Philippa had just sent her best outfits, not to mention her diamonds and makeup, to Los Angeles with Emily. She ran to the bedroom and tore into her remaining suitcases. Soon a large mound of feathers, sequins, and stretch lace covered the bed. Philippa ran to the mirror and studied the rich violet splotches all over her face. Horrified, she took another boiling shower, then dressed in Emily's baggy farmer clothes. She ran to the stereo, looking for background music. Bruckner? Mahler? Where the hell was Sinatra? Philippa had to settle for something called *Bolero*, which she vaguely remembered from another beach movie. Lightning fulgurated over the lake as she turned off the lamps and poured a glass of vodka to steady her nerves. Each time Philippa tried to compose a confessional speech, she began to quiver terribly. What if Guy beat her to death here in the woods? Left her body on the deck for the wolves to devour? She was about to call the airport and intercept Emily when she heard a car rolling into the driveway. Philippa doubled over with fear as a door slammed outside. She heard quick, crunching footsteps on the porch, then rapping on the cabin door.

"I'm here, Em," Guy called. "Open up, baby!"

His voice melted her paralysis. Philippa's desire to see him overcame her desire not to be seen by him. She flung open the front door: There he stood, smiling and mythical, exactly as she remembered him. "Took you long enough, dear boy."

In the steady rain, Guy stared at her battered face. "Plum?" he whispered uncertainly.

Something spit from the shadows. Guy fell to the ground.

# 11

Moments after Emily had told Ross she was going to Los Angeles, Marjorie walked into his office. Ten steps away, she could feel the black waves throbbing from his brow, flooding the room. Marjorie couldn't tell whether his mood had been caused by the recent phone call or their argument over the purple bikini this morning; after disappearing half the day, Ross had holed up in his office, barely speaking to anyone. Finally, unable to avoid him any longer, she had tiptoed in. "Everything all right, Ross?" she asked.

"Yo." He looked at the papers she had brought. "What's all this?"

"Letters of understanding. Sign here. And here." She pointed him through the pile. "Will you be able to do some drawing tonight?"

Ross smiled wanly; that was Marjorie's nice way of asking why the hell he hadn't been drawing like a good boy all day. "I plan to." He capped his fountain pen. "Thanks."

She smiled wanly back; that was Ross's nice way of asking her to leave. "I'll be here until six. Let me know if you need any-thing."

He had seen Marjorie's legs almost every day for the last fif-teen years. Still, Ross watched them as Marjorie left; they were a necessary pleasure, food for the eyes. And, like a mother's love, they were a constant. Why had he blown up at her this morning? "Falling apart, old boy," he heard Dana whisper in his ear. How true. But that was because he couldn't grasp the links between current events. Ross found himself thinking constantly about Dagmar, who was connected to Joe, who was connected to Dana: What had gone on there? Information incomplete, so he passed to Peace Power Farm. It was somehow connected to Diavolina to that woman named Ward to Emily. He wished he had listened better to Emily's brief adventures at the restaurant, but they had only been recounted tersely, late at night, in a wash of more agitating topics. Pass again. Now his wife was sud-denly going to California. That sequence involved Philippa and, somehow, Guy Witten. It had to. Emily claimed that the trip was Philippa's idea. What was so important that Philippa had to send her sister three thousand miles to breakfast? Perhaps Emily was fibbing. Perhaps the trip was her idea, and Guy Witten was going with her. One way to find out.

"Where are you going this time?" Marjorie cried as Ross sailed past her desk.

"Out for coffee." Ross ducked around the corner to Cafe Presto. Inside, a few weary shoppers sat eating pie while, behind the counter, cranky old Bert was cleaning up. This was the time of day when customers gravitated toward bars, not coffee shops. "Hi Bert," Ross said, asking for a cup of decaf. "Holding down the fort, I see."

"Of course! Everyone around here takes off whenever they like. One of these days I'm going to do the same." Bert placed a cup on the counter. "This must be Mr. and Mrs. Major day at Presto. Your wife called a while ago."

"No kidding." Ross forced himself to swallow some lukewarm brown liquid. "What for?"

"Don't know. She talked to Guy."

"Maybe she wants her old job back."

"Maybe. But he might not give it to her. She called him a cocksucker. Shouted it so loud I heard it and I was standing two feet away. Then she hung up on him." Bert shrugged. "Emily's been pretty uppity lately, if you ask me. You can tell her I don't appreciate being talked to like a servant."

A moment's incomprehension, then, Eureka! Philippa! Ross nearly cried with relief as much mud became crystal. "Sorry she bothered you," he said. "Is Guy around? May as well apologize to him, too."

"Guy took off. I'm alone, I said. Lazy bunch of shits working here, if you ask me."

Ross went to a vacant bench outside Quincy Market and thought very heavily about driving to New Hampshire. It had to be Philippa up there now, yes? She had sent Emily to California on some wild goose chase so that she could do a little more fishing with Witten. Evidently her last meeting with him at Cafe Presto had only whetted her appetite; Ross could just imagine Philippa waving good-bye to Emily, watching her drive off, waiting a safe interval, then calling Witten with some maid-in-distress folderol. This very moment, he was probably speeding up to the country with a bottle of scotch and an umbrella-sized erection. Ross flirted with a perverse desire to walk in on the two of them tonight. Philippa, consummate liar, would never be able to explain herself. And Guy . . . here Ross's enthusiasm cooled. Merely embarrassing the man was insufficient compensation for the destruction he had caused. Guy would only laugh at his mistake, hatchet Philippa, and home in again on Emily. She'd forgive him, of course; they'd reconcile . . .

Ross distractedly left the bench. Forget driving to New Hampshire; winning that skirmish would lose him the war. Better to hope Philippa drowned Guy in her own intrigue. Ross thought briefly of going to the airport with an armload of roses for Emily, who thought she was doing her sister a favor, poor thing. Eventually, she would discover the truth. Ross was uncertain whether he should look forward to that day or pray that it never came. In any event, Philippa's game could not go on much longer. What did she hope to achieve, anyway? Guy was not a total dunce. What would he do upon discovery that he had been taunted and wounded by a parody of his beloved? If Guy were any man at all, like Othello, he would murder Philippa. On the other hand, what if he decided that Philippa was an acceptable consolation prize? Christ! What if he and Philippa actually hooked up? Married? *Brother-in-law!*

Ross began walking rapidly down Tremont Street, toward a secondary nest of riddles that had to involve Guy Witten. He arrived at Diavolina as the bar was beginning to clog with war-weary businessmen and an assortment of adults who had not accomplished one iota of what they had set out to do that day. For a long moment Ross stood at the entranceway, observing the decor. The little sconces, the layout of glass racks above the bar, the turquoise-heavy color scheme looked like early Dana, or a ripoff thereof. He'd have to ask Marjorie about it. Ross took a seat at a vacant section of bar, waiting as the she-Atlas behind it tapped a few beers. Her body fascinated him, as it did many other patrons: Were the muscles between her legs anything like her biceps? What if she decided to hook her ankles around your back and squeeze? That had to be Ward, Ross thought as she dropped two olives into a glass. Emily hadn't been exaggerating about her fearsome size. Once upon a time, Ward must have had a nice face. Now . . . well, maybe it was the steroids.

"What'll it be, dear?" Ward said.

"Knockando straight, please." Ross chewed a few peanuts while Ward found the bottle. As she was placing it in front of him, he said, "Thanks for firing my wife yesterday."

Ward paused, processing the data. Reaching an ambiguous conclusion, she returned to Ross's place at the oak bar. "You're Mr. Emily, I take it." He didn't obtest. "Care to explain that remark?"

"Nothing to explain. Thank you for firing her. She needed a rest." Ross sipped his scotch. "I'm curious, though. You seem to have gone to a bit of trouble to hire her. Why did you can her after just a week? She wasn't stealing provisions, was she?"

"I get it. You're going to sue me," Ward said. "Go ahead. I don't care."

"Why should I sue you? You've done me a favor." Ross saw several more people sit at the bar and look expectantly at Ward: He would have to strike quickly, blindly. "You've done me two favors, in fact. Thanks for taking out the front window of Cafe Presto."

Ward's fingers quietly wrung her service towel; for a moment, Ross thought she was going to reach over the counter and do the same to his neck. Instead, Ward looked into the dining room, where a man was walking slowly from table to table, inspecting place settings. "Zoltan," she called, barely raising her voice. The man came over at once. Ross tried not to stare at his surreally painted face. "I'll just be a minute," Ward told him, then looked at Ross. "You, come with me."

Downing his drink, Ross followed her to a disheveled office. The shades were drawn and the walls seemed to throb under the fluorescent light. On Ward's desk, tall piles of papers leaned slightly this way and that, awaiting the one good sneeze or door slam that would level them. Last year's calendar hung on the wall above a file cabinet that may have been dropped from a helicopter. Barbells and free weights dotted the carpet. There was no space in this room to think, let alone work, yet Ross remembered Emily saying that Ward stayed here all day long. The air was already giving him a slithery, hallucinogenic headache, as if he were wearing someone else's eyeglasses.

Ward cleared a place for him on the love seat by tossing away a sweatshirt. She sat behind her desk and studied him for a long moment. "So you're Emily's husband," she said. "No wonder the poor thing wanted to work all day and night." She pulled a bottle of crème de menthe from her desk. "Drink?"

"No thanks."

Ward replaced the bottle. "How did you know about Cafe Presto?"

What? No hedging? This woman was kamikaze; the least a gentleman could do was respond in kind. "I happened to be standing outside and got the license plate of the truck. I went to the Peace Power Farm this morning. Someone there sent me here."

"Standing outside Cafe Presto, eh? I didn't see anyone."

"I was in a little alcove across the street."

"And what were you doing there at that hour? Looking for meteors?"

"I was watching Guy Witten." That didn't sound too swift, so Ross added, "I have a score to settle with him." That sounded even worse. "It's a business matter."

After a moment, Ward retrieved the liqueur from her drawer. Her Adam's apple jerked up and down a half dozen times as she swallowed the thick, emerald liquid. "I just wanted to wreck his window," she said, wiping her mouth. "I had no idea he was sitting inside." A terrific smile lit up her face. "That was a bonus."

When the smile didn't go away, Ross became uneasy. "I take it you have a score to settle yourself."

The smile vanished. "Right. And you'd better not horn in on me, buster. I've been waiting too long for this."

For what? Ross didn't care. He had just seen God. "He sprained a wrist, you know."

"I can read the newspapers." Ward's smile returned. "The wrist was for warm-ups."

"If you'd like a word with Guy," Ross said slowly, because this woman was out of her mind, "I have an idea where he might be tonight. We have a little cabin in New Hampshire. I think he's meeting my sister-in-law there."

"Oy! You don't mean that cheap blond whose date dropped dead in my restaurant."

Ross winced: Dana. "That's the one. I think Guy's been seeing her."

"The bastard. Always looking for fresh meat. Although I wouldn't exactly call your sister-in-law spring lamb. Where is this place now?"

Ross drew her a map. "This isn't one hundred percent certain, you know."

"I'll take that chance." Folding the paper into her pocket,

Ward studied Ross for a long moment. "Why did you come here? Sheer curiosity?"

"Only as far as my wife is concerned," he answered. "What's the connection between you, Cafe Presto, and Emily? She's not involved in your end of this, is she?"

"Nope. I only hired her to aggravate Witten. Steal his chef. Drives people nuts."

"But then why'd you fire her?"

"Because people started dropping dead after she got here. That's bad karma. I don't take chances with that. Anyway, she served her purpose."

"Your purpose, you mean. What about Emily? She didn't enjoy getting the boot."

"She didn't argue much, mister."

Ross stood up: Marjorie was probably waiting for him with a baseball bat back at the office. "Thank you for being so frank."

"Why not? You want what I want except I have more balls than you do. Or maybe less to lose." At the door, her hand crushed his. "And I doubt you're going to turn me in."

Ross nodded tiredly; women were always so right. "Say hello to Guy for me."

Ward's wide, grotesque smile returned. After Ross had gone, she had a few words with Zoltan. Then she left Diavolina.

The next morning, a limousine pulled up to a posh Los Angeles hotel. Philippa's manager hopped out of the backseat and phoned Emily from the lobby. "Ready, Phil?" he asked, anxiously studying his cravat in the smoked mirror. Perhaps he had knotted it a centimeter too tight; instead of camouflaging the extra folds in his neck, the tie created a half-inch bulge along its upper perimeter. "I don't want to be late for this one."

"I'll be right down."

Emily got to the lobby as Simon was retying his fifth knot. He appraised her hot-pink-and-orange pantsuit as she walked toward him. "Not bad," he said, studying the deep V-neck. "I see you're finally getting some business clothes into your wardrobe." He inspected her face. "Could have worn your false eyelashes,

though. You look a little washed out." He took her elbow. "Let's
go. Why the hell are you staying in a hotel? What happened to
your apartment?"

"A friend's using it," Emily lied, ducking into the limousine.

"Ass first, Phil! Lead with the ass, not the nose! Don't you
ever listen to me?" Simon dove in after her. As the car pulled
away, he lit a cigarette. "First of all, let me get something off my
chest. Disappear like that ever again and we're finished. You left
me holding the bag with the entire NYPD. They accused me of
every fucking crime in the book. I had nothing to do with that
faggot who offed himself, and everyone knows it."

"They let you go, didn't they?"

"Shut up! I can't have talent disappearing into the woodwork
like a termite! If you hadn't called in, this meeting never would
have happened. And you'd be unemployed for another six
months. Where the hell were you hiding, anyway?"

"In the country. So who's this Czech producer? What's he got
in mind?"

"That's what breakfast is all about, darling. His office was very
coy on the phone. I got no details whatsoever."

Emily's stomach gently turned. "You've never met him before?
How do you know he's not going to pull a gun on me and blow
my brains out?"

Simon looked at her in surprise. "Why should he do that,
Phil? Then no one makes any money. Put some rouge on, would
you?" As Emily was reddening her cheeks, he said, "And get the
name straight. Vitzkewicz. It's a tongue twister. Mr. Vitz-ke-wicz.
I don't want you mushing it up after a few Manhattans like you
did last time. And don't sit in his lap unless he invites you. You
weigh five times as much as Shirley Temple."

Emily snapped the rouge case shut. Her enormous blond wig
was already beginning to melt brain tissue. "Any more hot tips?"

"No. Just let me do the talking." Simon spent the rest of the
journey jabbering a bizarre tide of molasses, arsenic, and
baloney into the mobile phone. When he hung up and began
poufing his hair, Emily knew they were almost at the restaurant. "Best behavior, now," Simon instructed as the chauffeur

slowed to a halt. "Don't order anything more than two inches long. I don't need you slurping noodles all over the tablecloth like you did last time. And keep your knees together when you get out of the limo! People are watching!" He sprang from the backseat to the sidewalk. Grandly extending his arm, he guided Emily into the light of day.

The decor at Luco's was Tinseltown Buddhist, that is, bare white walls, Bauhaus chairs, sexually explicit flowers, and lots of cutesy angles. Emily and Simon cut quite a swath through the dining room, kissing affectionate strangers who called their names. The maître d' finally seated them at a balcony table with a regal view of the dining room. Awaiting their mimosas, Simon reeled off the birth names, sexual orientation, and net worth of the people they had just embraced. "Where the hell is Witcovich?" he snarled after scarifying nearly everyone in sight. "Waiting more than ten minutes is an insult."

A waiter came their way carrying what looked like a small plastic pillow. "Good morning. My name is Franco. I've been asked to deliver this," he said, placing it on the tablecloth. "The other party couldn't stay."

"What other party?" Simon asked, screwing around in his chair: too late.

Franco paused until he had regained Simon's full attention. "There's a message. Filming begins in two weeks. The other party is looking forward to working with Miss Banks." He smiled at Emily. She turned superciliously away; the man's mouth reminded her of Guy's.

"Great. Thank you," Simon grunted, slipping him fifty dollars. "You wouldn't be able to give me a visual on the other party, would you?"

"I'm afraid not." Franco had obviously collected a higher tip therefrom. "But she had diamonds as big as her eyes."

"She?" Emily said after the fellow had left. "I thought Vitzkewicz was a man."

"Of course it's a man," Simon snapped. "Ever hear of delivery girls?" He stared at the package on the table. "Look at that wrapping job. You'd think it was the Crown Jewels or something." He thoughtfully swallowed most of his champagne and orange juice. "Usually I have to get them drunk and half laid before they even think of hiring you. This one just threw the script at us. Who's complaining, though? Your price just tripled."

Emily frowned. "What kind of movie gets cranked up in two weeks?"

"Phil, you know better than that. Actresses quit, get sick, get fired, gain weight. . . ."

"I don't trust this."

"Baby, neither will I until the check clears. Meanwhile, drink up. You're back in business. Once again, I've saved you from denture commercials."

"Come on! You haven't even read the script! What if it's a snuff movie?"

"Then we'll negotiate." Simon paused as Franco recited a list of arty omelettes and flapjacks. "I don't think we're staying," he said afterward. "Just bring the check."

"Wait a minute, I'm hungry!" Emily cried. "I came here all the way from New York to try the Lobster Baked Alaska."

Simon leaned over the table. "Listen, Phil, it'll cost a fortune," he whispered. "And Witkovish isn't picking up the tab." Simon magnanimously paid for their orange juice. They paraded back through the tables, exchanging rouge with effusive, emoting friends: Here the gods were rolling film and everyone wanted the lead. Out in the parking lot, Simon ripped off his cravat. "Whew! Quite an outhouse in there today. Where are you headed, Phil?"

"Your office," Emily said as Simon's limousine rolled to the curb. "Thought I'd check on the old fan club."

"We're going in opposite directions, then. You don't mind taking a cab, do you, sugar?" Simon posed the question from the backseat of the limo.

"What about the script?" Emily called as the vehicle pulled away.

"Let me take a look first, baby. Call me tonight. I'll let you know if it's doable." Simon's dark window rolled shut.

Fortunately Emily's cab driver, an unemployed actor, knew the location of Simon's office on Wilshire Boulevard. Throughout the ride, believing he was ferrying Philippa Banks across town, he talked about his upcoming auditions and his great manager and how driving a cab was just an interim job. The pathetic spiel sounded so much like poor dead Byron's that Emily stopped listening; tales of failure, like tales of success, had a certain repellent monotony. Leaving a charitable tip, Emily entered a futuristic black building.

"Good afternoon, Miss Banks," greeted an armed guard.

"Good afternoon, Miss Banks," said an armed attendant at the elevator.

"Hello, darling," Emily responded to both. Her cheeks hurt from so much damn smiling. Her feet creaked with every step in these high heels. And people were watching her every second. How did Philippa stand it? "Beam me up to Simon's, would you, sweetie? Thanks so much."

As the car ascended, Emily desperately tried to remember the name of the president of Philippa's fan club. Angus? Anson? When the doors opened on the twentieth floor, she strode to the office at the end of the hallway. In a way, it looked like Ross's office on State Street, except this one had tackier furniture and more succulent plants.

The receptionist made a flash reconnaissance of Emily's hair, makeup, and pantsuit. "Hi, Miss Banks."

Were that Marjorie, Emily would be answering fifty questions about Vitzkewicz and filling in an expense report. "Hello, dear. May I have a word with the fan club?"

"Sure." Careful not to chip her nail polish, the girl pressed a button on the switchboard. "Aidan? You've got a visitor."

Within seconds a young man in a canary double-breasted suit, bulky or tight in all the correct places, appeared. A deep marigold necktie complimented his tan. Eight rings in his left ear did not quite distract attention from a mustache the size and shade of an industrial broom. "Banks!" he cried, taking her arm. "How's your arm? You have some autographing to do for me."

Emily followed Aidan to his little office. "How's business?"

"*Choke Hold* is taking off. I told you it would." He planted Emily in a chair and brought over a pile of photographs. "Start signing."

Emily hesitated. "What should I write?"

"What you always do. No! Not with a ballpoint, Philippa! You know better than that!" Aidan gave her a purple felt-tip pen. "You got a great review in New York."

He handed her a scathing, insulting article skirting a fine line between parody and libel. Each sentence felt like one more twist of a tourniquet around her stomach. Finally Emily let it slip to the desk. "You call that a great review?" she whispered.

"What's the matter with it?"

"I don't believe what I just read."

"Neither could Si. He couldn't have bought better publicity. I just love this line." Aidan snatched the article. "'Miss Banks acts with the dignity of a stegosaur caught in a tarpit.' Gad! I have to take that guy out to lunch."

Emily began writing Philippa's name on dozens of photos as Aidan brought her up to date on a particularly active fan club in Little Rock, where Philippa was considered to be one of America's greatest dramatic actresses, right up there with Jayne Mansfield and Raquel Welch. "Would you be interested in leading their Thanksgiving parade this year?" Aidan asked. "They'd really appreciate it."

"Sure, what the hell." She scribbled blithely on. "Any interesting letters come in recently?"

"Just the usual proposals of marriage and requests for money. You now have official dues-paying fan clubs in eighteen federal penitentiaries."

"Would you mind running me a printout of everyone who's written in the last six months?"

"What for?"

Shit! Shit! Emily squeezed her brain unmercifully, finally eking out a tiny, hard turd of an idea. "I went to my psychic last night," she began.

"Zilda?"

"No, Carmen." Oh crap, now she'd have to tell a second lie

to explain the first! "I had a gift certificate. Anyway, Carmen told me that my future husband had written to you recently. I thought it would be interesting to read over your fan list and see if anything vibrated."

Finding no problem whatsoever with that story, Aidan soon had the computer churning page after page onto the floor. "I had no idea I was so popular," Emily said.

"Phil, you're not popular at all. You've just got a great sales force." Aidan laughed sort of sincerely. "I've been in the office at seven in the morning for the last three months."

As soon as possible, Emily left. She swung by her hotel, ditched Philippa's wig and fluorescent pantsuit, and went to the airport. A Boston flight was just leaving; Emily eked aboard. Suddenly she was anonymous again. It felt odd not to have people stare at her; over the last few hours, she had grown quite accustomed to peripheral curiosity and admiration. Now she was just another drone? Blah. High over Colorado, as she was consoling herself with champagne, Emily took Aidan's printout and began skimming through the names on his fan-club list. He had meticulously logged the date and content of each inquiry, as well as his response to it. Someone had sent Philippa a hand-crocheted bra? A trivet made out of bobby pins? Emily turned page after page, trying to picture the Jo-Lynns and Arnies from towns she had never hear of, in states containing the Mississippi River. Virgils, Nelsons, and Platos were easier to imagine since they wrote from prison. Many of them had asterisks beside their names. What did that mean? Emily turned to last page: Aha, they had proposed marriage to Philippa.

She had skimmed two lines beyond Charles Moody when her subconscious tugged her back to his name. Something about it had seemed familiar. Her eyes traveled across the page, her stomach rolled: He occupied P.O. Box 274 at South Station. Charles Moody: how vapid, pseudonymous. No asterisk beside his name. According to Aidan's records, Moody had received an announcement of the *Choke Hold* opening in New York. Emily let the printout drop to her lap. Had this person been there? If so, he hadn't introduced himself. She read the postbox number again, not quite believing it. No need to panic; maybe someone named Moody had vacated the box a month ago and Slavomir had chanced to occupy it next. Things like that happened all the time. In the movies, anyway.

No other names or addresses meant anything to her so Emily put the list away. Wait until Philippa heard that this trip had been totally unnecessary, that the role had been in the bag all along, and shooting began in two weeks. She had probably been up all night worrying about Emily's portentous breakfast with Simon and The Producer. By now the poor thing was probably surfing between soap operas, drinking back-of-the-cabinet crap like Cinzano as she tried to figure out who could have slipped those four cherries into her drink the other night. That episode with the mad dentist had definitely shaken her up; ever since the attack, Philippa had been oddly subdued. Emily worried about that. Perhaps tucking her in the woods, alone with her thoughts, had not been such a great idea. Philippa never did well contemplating life, tortuously gleaning wisdom from the ether. She preferred to frame her fan mail.

As an in-flight movie blurred across the screen, Emily wondered how Ross had entertained himself last night. All he'd ever confess to, of course, would be work. Had he taken another of those long midnight walks, careful to return by two o'clock, in case she called? Or had he just thought, The hell with it, and slept at Marjorie's? Emily would never know; she had not had the courage to call. What would Marjorie be like in bed? Stenographer or nymphomaniac? And what would Ross be like with her? Emily chuckled acidly. Excellent, no doubt. He made love the way he drew buildings, elegantly, presciently: science advancing art. Marjorie was going to get a piece of that? Christ! She'd never let him go! Maybe Emily should corner her at the water fountain and convey a friendly female warning, whatever that was. Maybe she should smother Ross with kindness instead, make him feel so horrendously guilty that the sight of his secretary instantly squished any erection. And maybe she should just let it happen, swallow the consequences. God knew these things were fairly unavoidable, a sudden conflagration of desperation and longing. Look at her and Guy. Could Ross have prevented that? No. But ultimately, by his simple presence, yes, he had ended it. Emily could at least have the grace to return the compliment. Would it kill her to let him run loose for a little while? Marjorie was not serious competition. She was probably disease free. So Ross slept with her a few times, big deal. It wasn't the end of the world. Emily stared miserably at the white, billowy clouds beneath the airplane. From this distance they looked so dense, so magically strong; just like her fifteen years of marriage.

Beneath the clouds, all was rain. Landing in sheets of wind and water, Emily's flight wobbled to a halt at the terminal. She wearily deplaned, suddenly and violently hoping that Ross would be inside to greet her. No way, of course; life never glittered like the movies. Emily called the cabin. Nearly eight o'clock: Philippa should be in a frenzy by now. Emily waited as the phone rang and rang. Where the hell was her sister? Swimming? Finally she hung up and called home. Got the damn machine. In a fit of bravado, Emily called Ross at the office. "Enjoying the sunshine?" he asked cheerfully.

"What sunshine? I'm at the airport."

"Great! When's the flight getting in?"

"It's in, Ross. I'm at Logan."

"Which terminal? I'll pick you up."

"Don't bother. My car's in long-term parking. I think I'll go up to the cabin tonight. Keep Philippa company."

"I wouldn't, darling. She's gone."

"What! How do you know that?"

"Because I took her to the airport last night. She took the late flight to Kennedy."

"Where'd she go from there?"

"I got the impression she was going to take the first thing anywhere."

"And you just let her do that? Do you have any idea what you've done?"

"I'd say I drove all night in the pouring rain to indulge a raving lunatic. Look, I'm trying to wrap up a long day. See you in an hour or two."

Philippa had called *Ross*? And he had actually gone to New Hampshire to pick her up? Feeling faint, Emily went home.

Ross shuffled in around ten o'clock, inexplicably jovial. When he saw his wife waiting for him with a pitcher of martinis, he hugged and kissed her for a long time. "Tell me about your trip," he said, taking his first icy swig of gin, blessing the genius who had invented distilled spirits. He led her to the couch.

"Not much to tell," Emily replied. "I slept in a noisy hotel for three hundred bucks. Then Simon took me to an incredibly phony restaurant for breakfast. This Czech producer never even showed up. A waiter threw a script on the table and said that shooting began in two weeks. Simon was too cheap to spring for food, so we left. I went to his office and checked in with the president of Philippa's fan club. Then I came home."

"That's it? Why did you go out at all?"

"Philippa thought this producer wanted to meet her before making an offer."

"Something odd there," Ross said helpfully. "Kind of a wild goose chase." He let that petite stink bomb roll around a moment. "What were you doing with the president of Philippa's fan club? Forging autographs?"

Had he not gently mocked her, Emily might have told him about Charles Moody. But that would have involved an explanation of Slavomir, postboxes, and her Mad Stalker theory. Ross would have laughed some more. So she changed the subject. "What happened last night? I can't believe Philippa called you from the cabin."

Ross refilled his glass; he was about to enjoy himself. It was really quite a hilarious story if one knew all the facts. Poor Emily didn't, of course. That made it doubly hilarious. "I got a call at the office around nine-thirty," he began. "Philippa was nearly incoherent. But we have to remember she'd been drinking our booze for days. 'Ross! Help! Someone's outside trying to kill me!' she was blubbering."

"Poor thing. What did you do?"

Actually, he had laughed. Ward was probably outside the

cabin throwing rocks at the roof, waiting in ambush for Guy Witten, scaring Philippa out of her mind. "I tried to calm her down," Ross said. "Told her she was imagining things. She didn't like that, of course. Became quite abusive."

"Oh stop. What did she say?"

"Really want to know? She said, 'Listen, you motherfucker, if I'm lying here in a pool of blood tomorrow morning, it's all your fault.' I heard some thunder in the background and she screamed like a crow. A wild sound. So I told her I'd be right there. I came home, got the car, and drove up. The cabin was completely dark. I pounded on the door but she wouldn't answer."

"I would have been scared stiff!"

"Emily, there was nothing to be afraid of. She probably heard a moose outside and let her imagination run away with her. Anyway, I unlocked the door and turned the lights on. Your sister was lying under the bed whimpering like a puppy. Quite a mess."

"I don't believe it! What could possibly have happened?"

"She wouldn't tell me." Ross smiled to himself. Guy Witten had probably shown up for a romantic little tryst and gotten tackled by Ward on the front porch. After exchanging a few black eyes, they had both staggered home. End of story. "Once she recognized my shoes and came out from under the bed, Philippa began packing her suitcases, demanding that I take her to the airport. I wasn't about to argue with her in that condition."

"What did she say on the way back to Boston?"

"What could she say, Emily? That she was having an attack of DTs? She turned the radio on very loud and kept changing stations every twenty seconds. Didn't say two words to me the entire trip. It was a miserable ride, pouring rain, accidents everywhere. At the airport, she said she'd call you. Then she ran into the terminal. Wearing all your clothes, by the way."

"What about her face?"

"What about it? It matched her outfit."

Emily frowned. "You seem to think this is funny."

*God yes!* "Of course I don't, darling. It was just so . . . theatrical, that's all. I'm sure Philippa will call in the morning full of
apologies. She's got to be curious about your trip, at any rate."
Putting down his drink, Ross loosened his tie. "Is that dinner I
smell, sweetheart?"

The next morning Ross crept out of bed, careful not to wake
Emily, who was curled in a ball, snoring femininely. Now that
nights were becoming cool, she was wearing pajamas again; rutting season had ended, snuggling season had begun. Another
winter already? Seemed like only yesterday she had tucked her
flannels in the bottom drawer. Ross prayed that the weather
would remain mild for another month or two, in which case
she'd wear cotton nightgowns with nothing underneath. Easy to
push up. Nothing to pull down, unbutton, wriggle out of . . .
weren't women supposed to be the ones with an extra layer of
insulation? Yet they insisted on wearing pajamas to bed whenever possible, claiming to be cold. Ross remembered a discussion
with Dana upon this topic last autumn, when Emily had returned to her fleecy armor. Not to worry, Dana had said, pajamas were mere props in a seductive obstacle course. Ladies
loved to be stripped slowly naked. Until they became wives, of
course. Then their metabolism plummeted, modesty skyrocketed; achieving nudity required an entirely different approach.
Dana hadn't quite figured out a reliable strategy here, but he
was married to Ardith, Queen of Glaciers. Left to his own devices, Ross was forced to rely on his two old mainstays of cold-
weather seduction, down comforters and patience on Sunday
mornings.
He tiptoed into the shower, dressed, and went to the kitchen.
Ross missed his wife at breakfast; he had become accustomed to
reading the newspaper to the sound of her crunching toast
across the table. Perhaps she'd come downstairs when she
smelled the coffee. He ground a double dose of beans, put the
kettle on, and went to get the paper from the front stoop. It was
a cool, foggy morning, thick with the ocean and incipient winter; one was tempted to hibernate with the bears. Ross waved to

his neighbor, a surgeon at Mass General who did all the society bypasses. Returning to the kitchen, he toasted the last two slices of bread in the house and opened the paper.

The international news, an ongoing *opera buffa* composed by an amateur, hadn't evolved much since yesterday; Ross read a few headlines and kept turning the page. He decelerated somewhat at the business section and obituaries, then read in microscopic detail about the Red Sox, who were tormenting their fans with another peek-a-boo pennant race. The team had a genius for floundering like a gasping fish on the brink of elimination, sending the local sportswriters into a frenzy of hopeful speculation. Eleven more wins—*eleven*—and the Sox were in the playoffs. Once again, as he had for the last forty-odd years, Ross allowed himself to believe that a fundamental dearth of cunning, speed, and power could be miraculously overcome by the wishful thinking of five million baseball fans.

Ross was still plotting the ultimate pitching rotation as he skimmed over the New England news briefs, a last-minute assortment of stabbings, fires, and moose sightings tucked in the rear of the paper. He was an inch into the article titled ACCIDENT CLAIMS RESTAURATEUR before he realized that Guy Witten was dead. Suddenly out of breath, ill almost, Ross put down his coffee and stared at the words in front of him. Guy? With full attention this time, he reread the small paragraph: The other night, in the rain, a few miles north of Boston, Guy had hit the median on Route 93 and spun into a ditch. Police were investigating whether he had died of injuries sustained in the accident or of abdominal wounds he had apparently received prior to the crash.

"Hi, bubbala," Emily said sleepily, padding into the kitchen, kissing the top of his head. "I smell coffee."

He only stared, torn between telling her the bad news himself or scuttling away to the office and letting her trip upon the article the same way he had. Ross wasn't really afraid to tell Emily that Guy was dead; he was only afraid of her reaction. Was he better off abandoning her to her grief and guilt, letting her privately swing in the wind? Or was it better to play Mr. Rock of

Ages and be there to catch her? Oh Christ! He wished she had never met Guy Witten! With him alive, now even with him dead, things would never be the same. Ross watched his wife pour a cup of coffee and slosh into the chair opposite him. Her glasses tilted across her nose, her hair skittered against the laws of gravity. She looked like a girl, a daughter—his: no way could he leave her alone with news like that and still call himself a man. Ross waited until she had taken a few sips of coffee, then said, "I'm afraid there's some bad news in the paper today, darling."

She knew that tone of voice, and braced herself. "What's that?"

"Guy Witten was in a car accident. He's dead." As he said it, Ross recalled Emily breaking the same news to him about Dana just a while ago. Had they come full circle, then? Back to the starting line, minus a few competitors? How odd that they continued to live while others died in midstream, without goodbyes forever. It wasn't as if the ones left behind had escaped, either. Each disappearance ripped and nicked, degrading the survivors' ability to float in that giant, storm-tossed lake called Time. Perhaps their one small hope was to cling together, risk their fates on the other's buoyancy, and pray that the monsters beneath the waves would gorge themselves elsewhere.

Emily didn't move as two tears dribbled under her glasses and trailed slowly over her cheeks. "Oh dear," she said softly.

"It says he drove off the road in the rain. The article doesn't have much detail." Ross watched her shuffle to the window and stare at the downtown skyline. He gave her a half minute to launch a volley of arrows to the other side, wherever Guy might presently be, before joining her. "I'm sorry, baby," Ross said, folding her in his arms. "What can I do for you?"

Aside from raising Guy from the dead, nothing. Sniffling, Emily returned to her chair. She couldn't let herself fall apart in front of Ross. "He was a good man," she said finally. That seemed the appropriate thing for a former employee to say about her late boss.

"Did he have a family? Wife? Children?"

No, just her. Lot of good that did him. "A sister in Winchester," she said. "Did the article say anything about the funeral?"

"No. Maybe there'll be an obit tomorrow."

Emily wiped away a fresh tear. "I wonder why no one from Cafe Presto called me."

"They're probably in shock. People don't generally like to call with such bad news."

"Bert would." She sighed. "I just don't believe it."

Ross hung around solicitously for a while, then left for work. At the first pay phone, he called Diavolina. "I'm looking for Ward. Is she in?"

"Sure she's in," answered Klepp. "Who are you, the steroid salesman?"

"Just put her on." Ross waited a long time before she picked up. "I've got to see you right away."

"Sure." Ward yawned. "Come on over."

"Not there. Anywhere else."

She suggested a Hispanic grocerette a few blocks from the restaurant. Ross cabbed over. Despite the early hour, a half dozen customers queued at the lottery machine. The store smelled of dried meat and room freshener. He found Ward sniffing some hirsute roots in the vegetable section. She was wearing sweatpants and a mottled blue-black T-shirt that matched her tattoos. Seeing him, she put the roots down and calmly blew the dirt off her fingers. Something about her had changed. Not outwardly: Ward still hadn't bathed. She just seemed . . . happy?

Ross noticed the people in line staring at them: His suit and Ward's body didn't exactly blend into the Wonder bread. No background music, no wayside conversations: This was no place to hear about a murderess's trip to New Hampshire. "I saw the article in the paper," he said softly.

Now Ward was fingering some tiny purple peppers. "What'd it say?"

She didn't know or she didn't care; both possibilities worried him. Ross bought a paper and motioned Ward outside. They walked in silence down a side street with undulating brownstones and a little park in the middle for drug dealers. He sat on an empty bench and opened the newspaper. "Read this," he said.

She did, slowly. Chuckling, she put the paper aside. "I should know by now that nothing ever goes according to plan."

"What the hell did you plan?" Ross snapped.

"I was going to throw him off the Tobin Bridge."

After a moment, Ross realized she wasn't joking. "Tell me what happened the other night."

"I drove up to your cabin and waited in the rain for Lover Boy."

"Where'd you park the car?"

"Way out of sight, up the road. What do you think I am, an idiot?"

"I have no idea," Ross replied, watching the veins in her neck swell into relief. Maybe she was a cyborg. "Keep talking."

"He showed up around nine o'clock with a bottle of booze. Walked right up to the door and pounded on it. Must have been drunk or high on something because he shouts 'I'm here, Em! Open up, baby!' Moron couldn't even get her name straight."

"Did she open the door? Philippa?"

"Sure, after a while." Ward looked kindly, trustfully at him, the way Emily had this morning. "I shot him before he went inside."

"Christ! Are you out of your mind? Everyone within five miles must have heard the gun!"

"No one heard anything. I shot him with a crossbow. He went down like a ton of bricks."

Crossbow? Wasn't that something they used in the Middle Ages, like catapults and racks? For a tiny second, Ross thought he felt the park bench levitate, the way objects sometimes did in dreams. "What did Philippa do? Scream?"

"Please. That worthless tart slammed the door shut so hard I thought a gun had gone off. She just left him lying there."

"Wasn't the first time. She left him in a pile of glass when you drove through the window of Cafe Presto."

"And he still wanted to see her? Gad, she must fuck like a dog!"

Again Ross felt the bench levitate. "What did you do then?" he whispered.

"I waited. Witten didn't move, the door didn't open. Finally I went to the porch and pulled my arrow out of the door frame."

"You shot a second arrow?"

"No, the first one went right through him. It's bad form to leave them lying around." Ward fell into a short silence. "Anyway, he came to as I was walking away. Dragged over to the door and started whimpering for Emily. It was pathetic. After half an hour he finally pulled himself together. Staggered to his car and drove off."

"And you waited around all that time? Why?"

Ward shrugged. "Guess I was admiring my handiwork."

"Weren't you afraid that the police might show up? What would you have done then?"

"Split, I suppose. But they never showed up. I had a feeling that bitch hadn't called them. And I was right." Ward watched a dog struggle to defecate as the man attached to its leash studied the shrubbery across the street. "After Witten left, I left. It was pouring rain and I was soaked. I had no idea he killed himself driving home."

Ross looked harshly at her. "With a little help from you, of course."

"Don't be so modest, chum." Ward patted Ross's thigh. "Don't worry. No one will ever find out unless you tell them. Or your sister-in-law does." She guffawed. "I would not want to be stuck on a desert island with that dame."

"What about the arrow wound?"

"What about it? No one knows where or how he got it. I used a broadhead with two carbon steel blades. Witten's got an inch-wide slit in his back and his stomach. It will look like he was stabbed with a long sword. I must have nicked his liver or something. He probably died of internal bleeding." Ward peered at Ross. "Does Emily know anything about this?"

"She knows he's dead. She's crushed." Ross kicked at an optimistic pigeon. "May I ask a stupid question? What did Guy Witten do to deserve this? Steal your lasagna recipe?"

Ward became very still. Nothing moved but the veins in her neck and, once, her eyelids. "He killed my sister."

"How?" Ross demanded ruthlessly, angry at all she had done. "Gun? Poison? Bare hands?"

"He broke her heart, dear. She jumped off a building."

Jump, jump. Emily had recently asked him about someone jumping off a building. She had seen an old clipping on Ward's desk. Yes, that was it, that silly little girl who had jumped off the Darnell Building years ago must have been Ward's sister. "I'm listening," Ross said. "Go on."

"Her name was Rita. She was five years younger than I, smart, bubbly. . . . I adored her. So did everyone else. Rita followed me to Boston and worked as a waitress in Leo's restaurant while she went to art school." Ward's face condensed into wrinkles and hatred. "After a few months I noticed that she began sneaking around at odd hours, coming home late, lying about where she had been, starting to drink. . . . It got worse and worse. One night I followed her to school. She came out holding Guy Witten's hand. They sat in a sleazy little diner for two hours and my sister cried the whole time. Witten was married then, of course. He just put her in a cab and went home. Two weeks later, she jumped off a building. All she left on the balcony, tucked in a plant, was a note saying that she couldn't go on like that anymore. She wore one red shoe. They never found the other one."

Ross stared at Ward's elaborate, writhing tattoos. "You've been planning your revenge all this time?"

"That's right." Ward chuckled again. "And I almost got it."

"Almost? You got it, ma'am! You nailed him!" Ross shook his head. "And I helped you."

"Now you're sorry? Don't make me laugh. If you need sympathy, go cry on your sister-in-law's shoulder."

Ross stood up. "I don't think we'll be meeting again."

"Maybe not." Ward suddenly grabbed his hand and kissed it. "Don't look back, Major. You're safe. Thank you for rescuing me. I mean that."

He walked quickly away.

# 12

*Guy's dead. I don't believe it yet. But I will.
Serves him right, really. No one poaches my wife and gets away
with it. But a broadhead through the liver? Jesus, that must have
hurt. Ward must have been only fifty feet away when she fired
that crossbow. Brilliant choice of weapon: powerful and accurate as a rifle, only no report. And she's got the muscles to load
the evil little contraption. Where'd she learn to use one, though?
She's damn lucky the bolt didn't go through Guy into Philippa.
Fine bloody mess that would have made on my front porch! Almost worth it, though, to have them both down for the
count . . . but I mustn't be greedy. One is enough. In this case,
one is actually better. Cleaner. Ward was right: No one knows
Guy went to New Hampshire. No one has any idea where or why
he got hit. And the only witness isn't going to be spilling the
beans; she's too afraid of Emily. What kind of fool story is
Philippa going to feed her sister this time?*

*I wonder if Philippa saw the arrow in the door frame. Maybe
not. Broadheads are small as pencils. It was dark and rainy. The*

*whole thing must have happened very fast. Philippa must have been half plotzed. She probably had the lights down low and her face wrapped with scarves the way she did for her little tryst with Guy at Cafe Presto. But why slam the door shut? She must have heard him whimpering out there in the rain. Why not call the police or an ambulance? Why call me instead?*

*Because she's a fiend. Poor Guy, oh God, poor Guy. What a way to go. Dead of internal bleeding? And how.*

Emily sobbed for a long time after Ross had left for work. Guy gone? Wrong, insanely wrong. She wasn't half finished with him yet. As Guy's voice vibrated in her ear, she thought of the unreturned phone calls, anguished silences, their peremptory parting: That was it? The book would stay closed at such an awful chapter? Then the loose ends would beget more guilt than their adulterous knots ever had! The newspapers must have made a mistake. Guy did not crash cars. He was a cautious driver. Emily reread the small article several times. What abdominal wounds? Old ones, from that hit-and-run at Cafe Presto? The night Guy died, she had been on a plane to L.A., watching a movie, dozing. She had heard no psychic howl at the moment of his death. Emily smiled bitterly: Perhaps he had not called her name.

Philippa phoned once, horrendously cheerful, wondering how the breakfast meeting had gone. Emily's mouth, not her brain, maintained a shallow conversation. She waited until ten o'clock, when the morning rush was over, before going to Cafe Presto. Back in operation after the recent damages, the place smelled different: new chef, new spices. Lois, as always, sat behind the cash register, frowning at customers incapable of coming up with exact change. Bert rushed around the croissant racks, anxiously replenishing the baskets up front. The fullback behind the counter must be Lina, Emily's replacement. From a distance the scene looked perfectly normal; Emily half expected Guy to stroll in at any moment.

The first sign of disaster was Lois's coiffure, which had not received its diurnal shellacking with hair spray. Perhaps she had not combed it at all. Then Emily heard Bert calling the croissants cocksuckers, a word he had never used before. No one even noticed her until she stood in front of the muffins. "Hi guys," Emily said.

Lois burst into tears and ran from the register. Emily followed her to the kitchen. "What happened to Guy?" Emily wailed.

"No one knows anything," Lois wept. "Except he was in an accident."

"Why didn't anyone call me?"

"We didn't think you cared."

"That's ridiculous! Where'd you get such a stupid idea?"

"Bert overheard you two fighting on the phone the other day."

"That was someone else," Emily rasped. "I haven't talked to Guy in weeks." Had he found a new woman already? Of course he would have; a swarm followed him everywhere.

"Bert said it sounded like you."

"Bert needs a fucking hearing aid." Emily was furiously pouring herself a cup of coffee as the culprit entered the kitchen. She was about to lash into Bert when she saw the Swedish chef, then Detective O'Keefe following a few paces behind. Emily froze as the detective's eyes found hers. Her face burned, as if he had caught her filching scones from the cabinet.

O'Keefe regained his bearings first. "I'm Detective O'Keefe," he announced. "I'd like to ask a few questions of you all regarding Guy Witten."

Lina frowned at Emily. "Who is this woman?"

"The lady who made pistachio buns," Lois answered.

O'Keefe took Emily's elbow. "I'll start with you, if you don't mind." He walked Emily into the dining room. "We really must stop meeting like this, Mrs. Major."

By chance he took her to the same table Philippa had used the morning she had revealed her affair with Dana Forbes; since then, Emily's life had been a dominoes of disasters. "I read about Guy's accident in the paper this morning," she explained miserably, eyes filling with tears. "I had to come here."

Against his will, O'Keefe defrosted slightly. "You didn't know?"

"I've been in California. Just got back last night. What happened to Guy?"

Her grief was no act; O'Keefe's distrust fizzled. "Lost control of his car and ran into a ditch. But he appears to have been stabbed beforehand. He probably passed out at the wheel."

"Who would do that to Guy?"

"I was hoping you might know the answer to that. You worked with him for six years. I presume you knew him better than you did Byron."

Sensing mortal danger, Emily pulled herself together; O'Keefe noticed that. "Guy had no enemies that I know of," she said. "Even his ex-wives liked him."

"Did Guy have any favorite hangouts? Bars? Discos?"

"He went to Toto's Gym every day."

"What did he do at night?"

"Read books. Modeled for an art school. Went to the theater."

"Alone? Did he have a girlfriend?"

Her rhythm bobbled. "None that he told me about."

"Do you have any idea where he could have been the night he died?"

"No. After I stopped working here, we lost contact."

"When was that?"

"Two days before I started working at Diavolina." Emily tried to count. "About two weeks ago." Seemed like two years.

O'Keefe watched a saucy lady walk by outside. "Why did you quit here?"

"I needed a change."

"Were there any hard feelings?"

Emily went brain dead. After a moment she said, "Guy was very understanding."

O'Keefe nodded, factoring in the tiny lines around Emily's eyes. "Heard from your sister lately? She never got in touch with me, by the way. I'd still like to ask her a few questions about Forbes."

"She's been very busy with her new movie."

"Aha." O'Keefe's fingers drummed the table. "How long were you in California?"

"About fifteen hours. I just flew out for breakfast." Emily caught herself. "A job interview."

"Going to take it?"

"No." His questions were beginning to dizzy her; soon she would topple through the thin ice separating half-lies and half-truths. Emily almost didn't care anymore.

"Did your husband know Guy Witten?" O'Keefe asked.

"Ross ate at Cafe Presto a lot. We all met socially now and then."

She answered so simply, without the least stress, that O'Keefe momentarily doubted his triangular theories. "What was your husband doing the night Guy had his accident?"

He was schlepping a catatonic Philippa to the airport. "Working," Emily said.

"You're sure?"

She frowned; why all these questions about Ross? "That's where he was picking up the phone. Since Dana's death, he's been putting in a lot of hours at the office."

With his secretary, no doubt. "So you don't think that Guy had any serious business or personal enemies?"

"No. Could he have been mugged?"

"Of course. There were a few new bumps and bruises in addition to injuries from the hit-and-run at his place last week. But he had his wallet with him, full of cash."

Emily withered. "Guess I'm not much help," she said, blowing her nose again. "Sorry."

O'Keefe walked her to the door of Cafe Presto. Her silences maddened him. Emily was the type of woman who only revealed herself when she was inhabited by a man. Coincidentally, he wanted to inhabit her very badly, get beneath those heavy layers of rectitude to the molten core of her. He suspected that Guy Witten had been there; so had her husband. Lucky men. "It'll be all right," he said. Idiot, that wasn't what he meant at all.

The wind lifted her hair as she walked away. O'Keefe returned to the kitchen, where Bert and the new chef were waving croissants at each other.

"That's how they're made here, Lina," Bert admonished. "Little crescents. We can't suddenly start making them into squares now. People won't know how to dunk them in coffee. Guy would never approve. This isn't Sweden, you know." Fuming, Bert picked up the phone jangling at his elbow. "Cafe Presto." He listened a few seconds. "You would, eh? Well, that's tough shit! He's dead! Don't call again!" He slammed down the phone.

"Who was that?" O'Keefe asked.

"The bitch who bothers him all the time."

"Did she leave a name or number?"

"You've got to be kidding. 'I would like to speak with Guy Witten,'" Bert mimicked in a domineering drawl. "God forbid she says please. Who the hell does she think I am, the butler?"

O'Keefe invited Bert to the dining room. "How long has that woman been calling here? A long time?"

"No. Two weeks. She was Guy's new girlfriend."

"What makes you say that?"

"The way he talked to her. Half angry, half gaga. And he usually took off after she called. She was probably married and telling him the coast was clear."

"When was the last time she called?"

Bert thought a moment. "Two days ago, about four in the afternoon. Guy ran out of here like a dog in heat. I was left high and dry with all the late customers. Like Mr. Major."

"Ross Major? Emily's husband?"

"Sure, he drops in all the time. His office is right around the corner."

"What did he want?"

"Decaf, what else? I told him his wife owed me an apology for being rude on the phone. I had mixed up her voice with that bitch's. It was all a mistake."

"What did Ross say to that?"

"He laughed and said Emily was in California. I felt like a real jerk."

O'Keefe did not argue with that. "Mrs. Major left Cafe Presto rather suddenly, didn't she."

"You could say so."

"Any idea why she left?"

"Said she had to help out a friend in an emergency. Emily's like that. Then we got stuck with Lina. Things haven't been the same around here since." Bert's lip twitched. "Now they'll never be the same."

"Did Guy have any enemies? Any recent blowups?"

"Only with that stupid bitch on the phone."

"And thanks to you, she won't be calling back." O'Keefe could already read the handwriting on the wall: *Case Unsolved Forever.* Man with no obvious enemies takes a drive, maybe stops to help a disabled vehicle, gets knifed by some drug-crazed scum. Happened all the time now. "Thanks, Bert," he said, rising. "You've been very helpful."

After conferring with Ward the Archer, Ross walked agitatedly back to State Street. He didn't want to go upstairs, where his appointment book awaited him, where he would have to order his thoughts and talk business with ambitious, focused professionals. Instead he wanted to walk down to the harbor and watch the boats, planes, and clouds. Avoid ceilings. He felt he should go home and comfort his wife, leap into the void he had unwittingly created. He wondered how everyone at Presto was coping with the sudden removal of the boss. They'd cope, all right; employees were the most resilient animals on earth. Look at his office: After a few days of respectful paralysis following Dana's death, one and all had plunged back into their routines, with even more vigor than before since a new space now glistened at the top. Two weeks after his demise, Dana had become nothing more than a historical figure, like Christopher Columbus, the fellow who had discovered the New World for everyone else but no longer partook of it himself. Employees walked past Dana's name on the door, his bronze bust in the office, and knew that he had somehow made their jobs possible. But they were no more grateful for the agonies involved in that than they were for sunrises: someone else's creation, now public domain.

Maybe a little walk around the block would reconcile him to another day upstairs. Ross was almost out the revolving doors onto State Street when Marjorie spotted him across the lobby. "Ross!" she called. He steeled himself as her heels clicked over the marble floor. "Where were you off to?"

She was wearing a new houndstooth suit with another short skirt. The orange flecks in the wool almost matched her hair. Ross waited a second for her light, floral perfume, the same she had worn every day for the last fifteen years, to waft over to him: ah, there it was. Ross realized with a pang that, all things considered, he should have run away with Marjorie last month. "You're early," he observed curtly, pressing the elevator button.

"Today's going to be a killer." Inside the empty elevator, Marjorie opened a white paper bag. "Here's some coffee. Want to hear about all the fun you're going to have?"

No. Now that he could never leave his wife for Marjorie, Ross wanted to stop the elevator between floors and tear her clothes off, end the constant low-frequency coveting and step up to actual possession. After a long, difficult silence, Ross said, "Fire away."

He stood in the pale light as his alternate wife reviewed familiar lines; his job was nothing but a long-running play wherein occasional players changed. Ross would have to concentrate on making this just another day at the office, with one small exception: He didn't have to agonize about Emily screwing Guy Witten anymore. That was a serious gift, perhaps the gods' propitiation for robbing him of Dana. Was he safe again? Would his life return to normal now? When the elevator door whooshed open, Ross dreamily followed Marjorie to the office, devouring her legs as she ticked through this afternoon's schedule, leaning toward her as she unlocked the door.

She suddenly stopped. "What is it?"

He hadn't realized he was so close: Ross slowly ossified from Troubadour to Boss. "Thank you for the coffee," he said, flicking on the office lights. "Marjorie, do you remember anything about

that girl who jumped off the Darnell Building years ago? Someone mentioned it to me recently. It's all rather hazy."

She reverted to executive secretary and began speaking in
codes. "You were in Korea when it happened. I'll pull the Darnell file for you."

Ross went to his drawing table. As the sun withdrew fog from
the surrounding skyscrapers, he sketched with that rare fluency
borne of an interlude with death. After an hour or two, feeling
the office begin to throb, Ross put down his pen. He called
Emily and got the machine. Damn it, where was she now? "Just
checking in," Ross said, cursing his own weakness, wondering if
he would ever stop suspecting his wife of adultery every time he
got his own answering machine. Probably not. Trust was like
virginity: once breached, never recovered.

His intercom light blinked. "Ross, it's Dagmar Pola," Marjorie
said. "She insists on speaking with you."

"Hi, Dagmar."

"Good morning. Would you be free for lunch today? I'd like
to see you."

He had originally planned to lunch with his grieving wife,
but she was out doing God knew what. The hell with her. "That
would be nice. How's twelve o'clock?"

"I'll pick you up downstairs."

"Fine." Already feeling better, he went to the coffee machine.

Philippa awoke in Orlando, Florida. Long after opening her
eyes, she stared at the blasé pictures on the walls, the white ve-
neer furniture, and the air conditioner huffing into the gray/
pink draperies, computing only that she lay somewhere with
room service. Was she doing interviews for *Choke Hold* here?
Impossible: no floral arrangements in sight. Had a flight somewhere been bumped? No, that didn't feel right. Had she
checked into a clinic of some kind? Philippa was dying of
hunger. What time was it? Rolling over, she squinted at the
clock radio on the other side of the huge bed. *Two-thirty?*
Cripes! She sat up. At the foot of her bed lay a pile of dark,
heavy clothing. It wasn't hers. Philippa panicked: Had she

picked up a stranger last night? A dentist, maybe? Was someone in the bathroom? Then she looked down at her plaid flannel pajamas: Emily's. Memory surrounded her like a mud slide.

Yesterday had been one of the worst days of her life. It had started off innocently enough: gorgeous New Hampshire morning, long walk, late lunch. Philippa should never have called Simon, never been told about some stupid breakfast date in California. She had cajoled her poor sister into taking her place; once Emily was fifty feet out the driveway, even more grandiose plans had seized Philippa's fevered brain. Must have been Ross's damn Cinzano; every time Philippa drank that, she did bizarre things, like marry or invest in Broadway musicals. This time, she had called Guy Witten. True to form, he had shot right up to the cabin, knocked on the door . . . here Philippa's thoughts went black: She was about to enter an evil forest. With great care, wary as a mole, she inched into her memory, feeling rather than seeing details. She remembered him pounding on the door, shouting, "Open up, babe!" Philippa sighed, wounded: He had called her Emily. It was raining, thundering, as she unlocked the bolt. For a second or two, they had stared at each other. Guy hadn't liked what he saw of her ruined face. Maybe he thought Ross had beaten her up. But then his eyes had widened from concern to surprise; he had jumped, skewing strangely to the side, grabbing his back. Then he had collapsed at her feet. In the gloom, Philippa thought she had seen blood oozing through his shirt. She had definitely heard a taut *poing* in the trees just before he fell.

Philippa cringed in shame, remembering how she had slammed the door: That had been the most subhuman act of her life. Why? Simple survival instinct: She hadn't wanted to get bloodied next. Something had hit Guy in the back; she'd probably get it in the face. Philippa recalled rather calmly thinking, No more beach movies; in the space of a microsecond, deciding to sacrifice Guy, she had bolted the door and hidden under Emily's bed. While that poor man lay out on the porch whimpering for her, eons bled by. She had heard light, quick footsteps in the rain, maybe some low laughing; then she heard stumbling on the porch. "Emily!" Guy had screamed once in a terrible voice, a sob really, "Goddamn you!" Then she had heard a car roar, rocks fly in the driveway: silence.

Philippa had crawled out from under the bed and, by some miracle, remembered Ross's number on the speed dial. Hearing his calm voice, knowing that he was safe in his office while she was about to be pickaxed, she became hysterical. "Ross," she had screeched, "Someone's outside trying to kill me!"

He had laughed. "I think you've got the wrong number."

"Wait! Don't hang up, damn you! It's Philippa! I'm at the cabin!"

"Oh. Hi. Is everything all right?"

"No! I wouldn't be calling otherwise!"

"Phil, would you mind speaking a little louder? I can hardly hear you."

"I can't talk any louder! I'm under the bed hiding from a maniac! You've got to get up here right away and rescue me!"

"You must be imagining things. No one's been butchered up there since nineteen thirty-four."

"Listen, you motherfucker, if I'm lying here in a pool of blood tomorrow morning, it's all your fault!" Thunder struck and she had screamed. "Help! I'll do anything you want!"

"Calm down," Ross had sighed. It sounded as if he were rolling up blueprints. "I'll be right up. Should I bring my ray gun?"

"This is no joke! Don't be surprised if you find a body on your front porch!"

"A body? Are you throwing a party or something? Never mind. I'll get there as soon as possible. You'll be waiting for me under the bed in about two hours?"

"Two fucking hours? I'll be in fifty pieces by then!"

"That's nonsense, Philippa. Simple decapitation would be sufficient." Ross had hung up.

Except for the rain, all was quiet outside. Tiptoeing to the kitchen, Philippa had grabbed a kitchen knife and squeezed back under the bed to await either her rescue or her execution.

Every snapping branch, every thunderclap outside, detonated throughout her nervous system.

After a century, the bedroom lights clicked on. "Philippa?" Ross had called. "You can come out now." Instead, she had taken a swipe at his shoes with the kitchen knife. "Hey!" Ross had snapped, peering under the bed. "What the hell is the matter with you?"

"Is he still out there?" she had whimpered.

"Who? Where?"

"There's no one outside?"

"Absolutely not. Come out from under there." Ross extended his hand and pulled her to her feet. "Good Lord," he said, brushing the dustballs off her sweater, "your face is a mess. Tumble in the bathtub, Emily told me?"

"No! A dentist did it!" Philippa had cried, disoriented with shame and fright. She had begun stuffing her suitcases as Ross watched bemusedly from the dresser.

"I think you need a drink," he said finally, going to the living room. "What would you like, dear?" he had called, clanking the bottles. "Cinzano or Amaretto? That's about all I can offer at the moment."

"Nothing!" Philippa lugged her suitcases to the front door. "Just take me to the airport!"

Ross had calmly turned down the heat and switched off the lights. As he was locking the front door, he paused. "Eh, what's that?" he asked, picking up a brown paper bag. "A bottle of scotch? How did that get out here?"

Philippa had snatched it away. "It's mine. I left it outside to cool."

Smiling in that private, infuriating way of his, Ross had put her suitcases in the car. "Are you sure you want to go to the airport at this hour?"

"Yes! Yes!" Philippa swallowed a sloppy mouthful of scotch. "As fast as you can!"

Ross backed ever so slowly out of the driveway. "Emily's going to be disappointed."

"She'll get over it! Tell her to visit me in L.A.!"

"She's already there, I thought."

Was this Ross's Saab or Dante's Inferno? As the specter of Dana Forbes filled the car, Philippa retreated into a giddy, fearful silence, alternately punching the radio and guzzling scotch as Ross drove through puddle after puddle, spewing cataracts into the night. It was a horrible trip, fraught with that silent, molten rage endemic to families wherein two kin realize that, were it not for the indissoluble ties of blood or marriage, each would gladly exterminate the other. At the airport, Philippa's door was wide open before Ross's car had even come to a stop.

"Tell Em I'll call her," she had cried, leaping out. "Thanks for rescuing me, darling!"

Except for cleaning ladies, Logan Airport was deserted. Philippa had taken the next few flights anywhere, eventually stopping in Orlando. Another German tourist had just been murdered in Miami, precipitating another slew of cancellations, so she had no problem getting a room at the airport hotel. Philippa remembered taking a long, loud shower, then toppling into bed. She had slept with the lights on.

What day was this now? Somewhere in late September. Philippa called room service. "This is room three-seventeen," she said. "I would like some breakfast."

"We're serving lunch now, ma'am."

Philippa almost divulged her name; that was usually good for breakfast twenty-four hours a day. But, having checked in as Emily Major, she decided to remain so. "Then send me whatever lunch tastes most like breakfast." She called the hotel travel agent. "Book me on the first nonstop to Los Angeles, please. First class, window seat." That way, only half her battered face would show. "Nine o'clock tonight? How am I supposed to amuse myself for seven hours in this godforsaken hole? You've got to be kidding, I couldn't care less about dolphins! Golf? Please!" Her third husband, George, had been a third-rate golf pro; the only thing he had done with absolute consistency was miss easy putts. "Never mind," she sighed as the woman suggested a bridge tournament in the banquet room. "Just send up my ticket. Thank you."

She studied the clock: two-thirty here, eleven-thirty in Los Angeles. Emily would just have wrapped up her power breakfast with that Czech producer. Soon she'd be calling the cabin in New Hampshire with a report. Getting no answer, she'd probably think Philippa was out swimming, walking, doing healthy things . . . ah, damn. Suspecting nothing, Emily would catch a flight back to Boston. She'd call the cabin again, still get no answer; then she'd probably call Ross. *Ross!* Philippa groaned; he'd blab every humiliating detail.

She dialed his office. "Mr. Major, please. This is his sister-in-law. It's an emergency."

After a long wait, he came on the line. "Well, well! Where are you calling from, Baghdad?"

"As a matter of fact, I'm in Orlando for a few days. Interviews. Listen, Ross, would you mind not telling Emily anything about last night? It would just get her upset."

"What do you suggest I do instead? Let her drive all the way to New Hampshire and find an empty cabin? That's not very nice."

"Can't you just make up a story then? Tell her I had to stand in for someone. Just don't get her worried about me," Philippa wailed. "She's already worried enough."

"Why? You're a responsible adult, aren't you?"

"This is an absolute secret. You must tell no one what I'm about to tell you." Philippa inhaled dramatically. "Someone's trying to kill me."

To her irritation, Ross burst out laughing. "You? What for?"

"Things you wouldn't understand," she said darkly. "Just promise me you won't upset Emily when she gets home."

"Tell you what," he said, still chuckling. "Give me your phone number. Emily can call you herself when she gets in. By that time, I'm sure you'll have come up with an excellent story."

"That's impossible. I'll be long gone by the time Emily gets to Boston."

"Gone where? Didn't you just say you had interviews in Orlando?"

"Orlando is my first stop," Philippa sniffed. "Forget I asked."

"I'll do what I can," Ross said. "By the way, you really should sue that dentist."

Philippa ate a cold lunch containing too many eggs. She took another long bath; perhaps in a former life, she had been a fish. At least her face looked less purple today. Soon she'd be ready for public consumption again. Cheered, Philippa passed the time watching pornographic movies; many of her costars had either begun or ended their careers in this genre, and it was always amusing to see them huff and puff in faux rapture. She got a manicurist to come to her room and, chatting in a French accent, convinced the woman that she was a princess from Palm Beach. Philippa only started to drink when a late afternoon thunderstorm swept through Orlando. The driving rain against her window tore her right back to the cabin in New Hampshire; she could almost hear Guy Witten muttering deliriously outside her door. Where had he gone, a hospital? Home? For the first time, Philippa thought about the consequences of having left Guy out on the porch last night. He would never speak to Emily again: The hatred in that last howl had been irrevocable. What would Guy do when one fine day, missing him so much that she no longer cared what people saw or thought, Emily innocently returned to Cafe Presto? Philippa shuddered, condemned; had she just hauled Guy inside the cabin and confessed everything, he and she could have devised a way out, maybe even laughed about it. Philippa would have had to let Guy go, but she would still have had Emily. Now she would lose them both. Suddenly Philippa began to cry, for once with absolute sincerity. Life without Emily? Unthinkable. Emily was her rudder, her lodestar, wellspring, conscience, *twin!*

Almost in a trance, she vibrated with each long rumble outside. Finally, when the storm had trundled off to Walt Disney World, Philippa sat up, burping champagne. Her suicidal mood had faded with the thunder. Wrapping her face in veils, Philippa checked out of the hotel and caught her plane to Los Angeles.

A large, voluble crowd met her at the baggage claim. At first Philippa thought they were her fans; then she saw a dozen banners bearing the name of a rock star who had evidently been on her flight from Orlando. As Philippa walked insignificantly past, the crowd began screeching at the object of their adoration, a middle-aged man who had been sitting across the aisle from her, reading investment reports. Apparently, having outlived his vocal rivals from the sixties, the fellow had connected with a second, maybe third or fourth, generation of teenagers. He waved as calmly as a pope at them before disappearing into a limousine. Damn! Couldn't Aidan or Simon have organized a little reception for her as well? Philippa yanked her blue bag off the luggage carousel. This time the fault was hers; no one even knew of her arrival back in town. What a colossal blunder to have holed up in the woods just when *Choke Hold* was hitting the charts! Those three days in New Hampshire had probably cost her millions in lost opportunities.

She should never have listened to Emily's tales of murder. Nevertheless, apprehensive about going home alone, Philippa checked into a hotel in Santa Monica, whence she phoned Simon. It was almost one in the morning; he'd be either groggy or manic depending on the chemicals he had ingested for supper. The phone rang a half dozen times before a sleepy bimbo answered. Odd; Simon was very touchy about other people picking up his telephone. It was private property, like his Retin-A cream. "Put Simon on, please," Philippa commanded.

"He's in the hospital."

"What? What's the matter with him?"

"He got sick."

"How sick? Heart attack? Bleeding hemorrhoids again?"

There was a short pause; hopefully, the girl was thinking. "I don't know."

"When did this happen?"

"Eh, ah—I'm not—sure."

"Which hospital then?"

Another space. "I forget."

This dame was about as swift as the silicone in her boobs! Philippa called Aidan, who was in bed himself, although with rubber, not plastic. "That you, Phil?" he said. "We've been trying to find you all day! Where were you? Playing with Carmen's crystal ball again?"

Who the hell was Carmen? What crystal ball? "None of your business. What happened to Simon?"

"No one knows. He was sitting in the back of his limousine and began to choke. The driver got him to the hospital just in time. They think it was an allergic reaction to breakfast. What did you eat at Luco's anyway?"

"Lobster Baked Alaska," Philippa guessed. That was what she had told Emily to order. "Is Simon all right now?"

"He's flat on his back. They're going to run tests for another few days."

"Eh—did he say anything about my new movie with that Czech producer?"

"Yeah. Someone stole the script out of the limousine when they were schlepping him into the E-room. He's pissed."

"What's his number at the hospital?" Aidan gave it to her. Simon answered after half a ring. "Hi," Philippa said. "Hear you had an exciting day."

"Exciting my ass! I came within an inch of buying the farm! There I am minding my own business, trying to get an honest day's work done when *wham*, I begin to choke. Like someone was trying to strangle me with my tie."

"Maybe it was something you ate."

"Very funny, you bitch!" She was trying to make him feel like a cheapskate for not buying her any breakfast. "This deal isn't in the bag yet, you know. It could all turn to shit at any moment."

"But didn't we do well at Luco's?" Philippa asked uncertainly.

"Are you out of your mind? What was there to do?"

Philippa realized that she would have to talk with Emily before asking Simon any more questions about that breakfast meeting. However, her curiosity verging on heartburn, she asked, "The script got stolen? How'd that happen?"

"Couldn't tell you, darling. At the time, I was unconscious on the backseat of the limo. This town's full of thieves who'd steal your balls if they weren't attached."

"Did you read it? How'd it look?"

"I hardly read two words before I got sick. Damn thing was wrapped in fifty layers of plastic, like a preemie in an incubator. You saw it. Took ten minutes to saw all that crap off with my emery board. I read the title page and began to choke. That's all I remember. No, I remember pounding on the partition. The driver nearly rammed a tree when he saw the look on my face. He floored it to the hospital. Shit! I stood up an important appointment because of this!"

"Don't worry," Philippa replied. "She's still sleeping in your bed. What was the title of this script?"

"I don't remember. *The Devil's Toy* or something. Probably a bad translation. It really stank."

"How would you know if you didn't read it?"

"I mean it smelled disgusting. They must use paper made out of turnips over there. Maybe that's why it was wrapped up like that. Personally, I think Vitzkovich typed it in poison ink. I have a few serious enemies in Prague. Crap, here comes the nurse. She's been trying to give me an enema since I checked in. Call me tomorrow, would you?"

After hanging up, Philippa lingered a few moments at the phone. Odd that Simon hadn't mentioned the mysterious producer at all. Bad-mouthing every human on the planet was the joy of his existence. Now he hadn't even told her the man's sexual persuasion; that was like not collecting his 20 percent commission.

Philippa dozed off during a late movie about Prohibition, awaking briefly during the heavier gunfights. Her wake-up call came promptly at six; strangely bright and sharp, she called her sister in Boston. There it was nine in the morning; Ross would have gone to work and Emily would be putzing around the house, looking for things to do. "Hi Em," Philippa chirped. "Get back in one piece?"

After long silence, a pale voice said, "Oh yeah."

"What's the matter? Emily! Are you all right? Say something!"

"Where are you?"

The quaver in her sister's voice broke Philippa's heart. "Back in L.A. Tell me what's wrong, honey."

"A good friend of mine died. I just read it in the paper."

Philippa's guts became sawdust. "Who was that?"

"Guy Witten, my boss at Cafe Presto. He was in a car crash. No one even called to tell me."

Philippa's lungs finally got a little air moving through her larynx. "But you were away!"

"I have an answering machine. Ross said there were no messages." Emily's voice rose to a half wail. "Why wouldn't anyone call? They knew how close we were."

"No one wanted to break the news. People are odd like that. They don't like to congratulate you and they hate to tell you that your"—here Philippa caught herself just in time—"your friend died. It's perverse, but true."

Emily blew her nose. "The article said he had injuries prior to the crash. I don't understand what that means."

"Didn't he have an accident at his place last week?"

"How'd you know that?"

Damn! Damn! "Ross told me on the way to the airport," Philippa lied. "When was the car crash?"

"Tuesday night, when I was flying to California."

"Where'd it happen?"

"On Route Ninety-three right outside Boston. Guy lost control of his car. Ross says it was a rainy night."

"It was a horrible night. Visibility zero. I'm so sorry, Em. Was he special?"

*Was!* "I don't know how I'm going to get over this one."

"You will, honey. Ross will help you." Philippa flushed at her own supernal hypocrisy. Thank God for the camouflage of telephones!

Emily sighed, at one with the dead. "Why did you leave the cabin?"

"I was frightened by a storm. My nerves weren't used to days of silence, then all that noise. It was like ten horror films at once. Ross was a dear to take me to the airport. Did he tell you about it?"

"Not much. You called him at the office?"

"Yes. It was quite late. He was still working, poor man."

"He said you were pretty shaken up."

"I was somewhat out of control by the time he got there. I had let my imagination and a few swallows of Cinzano run away with me. Would you believe I ended up in Disney World? I holed up there for a day then flew to L.A. last night. My face is looking much better." Philippa had to pause for breath; her lungs still weren't doing too well. "How was your breakfast with Simon?"

"It was a nonevent. We didn't eat and this mysterious producer never showed."

"How'd Simon get the manuscript, then?"

"This was weird, Philippa. We're sitting at Luco's at eight in the morning. Simon's getting ticked waiting. Then, instead of the producer, a waiter comes over with a script wrapped in plastic. People are staring as if it were the head of John the Baptist. The waiter puts it on the table and tells us that Vitzkewicz can't come but he wants a yes or no in twenty-four hours. That was it. Simon didn't want to stay, or should I say, pay, for breakfast. So we left. The whole episode took fifteen minutes. I never even got to try the Lobster Baked Alaska."

"That cheap schmuck! You'll be pleased to know he ended up in the hospital. Passed out in his limo just as he was beginning to read the script. Then as he was being hauled into the emergency room, someone stole it out of the backseat. Simon's now ranting about poison ink and paper that smelled like turnips." Philippa sighed. "A brilliant day at the races."

The sisters, mired in their separate catastrophes, did not speak for several moments. "What are you going to do now?" Emily asked.

"I'm not sure. Lie low for another day or two, see if this script turns up again. I get bad vibes about the whole episode. What about you?"

"I don't know. Don't know at all." Emily blew her nose again. "I visited Aidan and got your fan-club list. Do people always send you things like trivets made out of bobby pins?"

"Gifts from the heart," Philippa replied. "Very touching."

"Does the name Charles Moody mean anything to you?"

"No. Who's that?"

"Just a fan who's got the same post-office box as the dead dishwasher at Diavolina."

"Dead dishwasher? What are you talking about?"

"Dana was not the only casualty that night. The dishwasher drowned in the Fenway a few hours later."

"What does that have to do with anything?"

"I have no idea," Emily replied. "Probably nothing. He was a wasted old alcoholic."

"Why would a loser like that share a postbox with a fan of mine? It makes no sense."

Emily yawned, tired of love and vanity. "Where can I reach you, Phil?"

"I think I'll stay at this hotel for one more night. You've got me a little afraid to go home alone now. Say! Why don't you come out here for a few days? We can go to a spa."

"That might be a good idea."

After hanging up, Philippa went to the bathroom and vomited. Guy dead? Then she was an accessory to murder! If only she had dragged him into the cabin and called an ambulance, he might be alive now. *But that would have been inconvenient!* Damn, she was in trouble, with the law, with the Furies, with her sister. Emily must never, ever find out. If Philippa wanted to save her skin, she'd have to pretend Guy had never been to the cabin. She had never seen him in her life. *Never!* She drooped over the toilet, remembering the night Guy had swept into Dana's chair at Diavolina and touched her cheek: instant possession. She remembered Guy's wooing voice, his mouth on her neck at Cafe Presto. He had had such beautiful eyes, sensual hands . . . and he had wanted her. Now he was dead? *No!* More likely Emily had found out about her little intrigue and was playing a practical joke in retaliation. After an hour's deliberation in the bathtub, Philippa called Cafe Presto. "I would like to speak with Guy Witten," she commanded.

"You would, eh? Well, that's tough shit! He's dead! Don't call again!" shouted that same insolent twerp, hanging up on her.

Philippa collapsed in tears on her bed.

Precisely at noon, Dagmar Pola's maroon Lincoln rolled onto State Street, slowing to a halt in front of Ross's office building. To his surprise, she was driving. Today Dagmar wore pale green linen with her pearls. Her small feet just about reached the gas pedal. "Good afternoon, Ross. You're looking well."

Why not? He had just regained his wife's undivided attention. "Likewise."

"Any suggestions for lunch?"

"Out of town," Ross said. "It's a great day for a ride."

"How much time do you have?"

"I'm free until two. That's good enough for a hot dog in Providence." He looked over. "Would you like me to drive?"

"Please." She slid over to the passenger seat as he walked around the front of the car. "I must confess to having called you completely on the spur of the moment."

Smiling, Ross headed toward the expressway. "What spurred the moment?"

"Oh—a pilgrim's progress. What have you been doing with yourself lately?"

Oh—inciting weightlifters to homicide, investigating the origin of purple bikinis, spying on pathetic old actresses, lusting after a secretary's perfect legs, wondering how to reclaim a lost wife . . . "Working," Ross said. "It's been a circus at the office since Dana died."

Dagmar didn't say anything for a long while. "It must have been terribly hard for you."

"Dana was my best friend. We had known each other since we were little boys. He was more than a brother to me." Ross began to tell Dagmar about Dana, beginning with Cub Scouts, working through the football team, college, their first building projects, their last commission; someone besides Emily had to hear this, had to appreciate the size of the hole in Ross's life. Dagmar listened with patience and, evidently, perception, judging from her occasional questions. They were almost in Providence before she asked, "What was Dana's wife like?"

Ross was temporarily speechless: Ardith unfailingly wrecked a good story. "She was his childhood sweetheart."

"Dana married only once?"

"Yes. But you probably have some idea of what Ardith's life was like."

"Actually, I wouldn't," Dagmar replied icily. "Joseph never made an ass of himself in public the way Dana did."

"I'm sorry. I didn't mean it that way." Ross touched Dagmar's hand. "You were married for a long time, weren't you?"

"Thirty-five years."

Cold fact chilled the air for a mile. "How did you meet?" Ross finally asked.

"At the Athenaeum. A lecture on American poetry. He swept me off my feet. We were married six months later."

"That's quite romantic."

"Not really. I was quite pregnant."

Cripes! "Ah, so you have children?"

"No." Dagmar did not elaborate. "Do you?"

Ross slowly veered around the Providence exit. "Not yet."

"What does your wife do?"

"She's a chef. Between jobs at the moment." Between lovers, between husbands . . .

He took Dagmar to a restaurant that Dana had used for high-risk liaisons: The wine list was long, the service quick, and across the street was a motel. Ross discovered that Dagmar had grown up in the town next to his on the North Shore. Just like him, she was an only child. They had both played the cello, gone to Ivy League colleges, and studied in Europe. On Friday afternoons for the last thirteen years, Dagmar had been sitting in Symphony Hall just a dozen rows away from Ross; perhaps that was why they felt they knew each other from somewhere.

Speaking with her was so easy; the more Ross spoke, the more he wanted to tell her, the more she seemed to know already. She was soothing as a mother, invigorating as a sister: the age gap between them came and went, like a desert mirage. On the return trip to Boston, breezing past trees that were just beginning to redden, they talked about everything but their marriages: Why corrode a sweet afternoon with reality? Ross was back on State Street just a little after two. "Thank you, Dagmar," he said as she slid to the driver's seat. "That was really marvelous."

"Yes, it was." She drove away.

Ross went upstairs. His sunny afterglow did not escape Marjorie, who had been shoveling garbage on his behalf since noontime. "And how is Dagmar?" she asked, glancing up from the word processor. "Ready for her ground-breaking ceremony?"

Not once over the course of lunch had Dagmar and he talked about Joe's art collection. "I think so," Ross said, shuffling through his message slips. "Anything critical here?"

"Not particularly. Emily called. Said she'd be back from New York late tonight."

What the hell was she doing in New York? "Right," he said noncommittally, as if he and his wife had thoroughly discussed the topic at breakfast. Almost at once, a little headache sprouted just behind his eyes, driving out concentration. Marjorie had to explain a few messages twice.

She was reminding him of a dentist appointment tomorrow when Detective O'Keefe entered. His raincoat, hanging raggedly open, looked more like a canvas tent with a half dozen unnecessary buttons. He needed a haircut. "I was in the neighborhood and thought I'd follow up on a few things," he explained, scanning Marjorie's desk. "Got a minute?"

Ross wondered if O'Keefe had seen him leaving Dagmar's car downstairs. The thought displeased him immensely. "Sure. Let's go to my office. This way."

O'Keefe glanced into Dana's office as they walked by. It looked barren and stale. Refusing an invitation to sit in the chair opposite Ross's desk, the detective said, "I have just one brief question, actually. I was wondering if any more of Dana Forbes's pill bottles had turned up."

"No, we haven't seen anything," Ross answered. "Marjorie and I cleaned out his office quite thoroughly. Dana's wife came by last week to pick up his personal belongings. Still haven't found that fancy antidepressant you think he was taking, eh?"

"Iproniazid. No." O'Keefe had searched Dana's boat, Dana's house: zilch. One of these days, he'd ask Philippa Banks about it again. "By the way, what were you doing last Wednesday night?"

The night Guy had died: The question caught Ross so off guard that he could only stare.

"We were working," Marjorie answered for him.

"You were both here?"

"Yes, of course."

"How late?"

O'Keefe saw Marjorie shoot a laser glance at Ross. "Ten or eleven o'clock," she said. "Why?"

"I was walking by and thought I saw your lights on." O'Keefe smiled at Ross. "Just games we detectives play with ourselves. Thanks for your time." He left.

Marjorie stared at Ross. "He looked up forty-eight floors from the sidewalk and thought he saw our office lights on? That is bizarre."

Ross went to the window and watched a small airplane flit above the harbor. He didn't know how or why, but he knew O'Keefe was after him. The detective had probably been snooping around Cafe Presto this morning. Perhaps Bert had told him of Ross's late afternoon visit the other day and gotten a few suspicious wheels turning. Had someone at Presto dropped a few hints about Emily and Guy? Had O'Keefe actually gotten a confession out of Emily? Goddamn it! Why had she disappeared to New York just when Ross needed to ask a few critical questions? "Marj," Ross said softly because his headache was killing him, "were you able to get that file on the Darnell Building?"

"Yes. Just a minute." When she returned and saw Ross sprawled on his couch in a five-aspirin pose, she quickly detoured to the washroom. "Here you go," she said, sitting beside him, handing him a glass of water and a pill bottle. Her rear end almost touched his side.

"Thanks." Ross studied a brochure of the Darnell Building, a glitzy commission they had received during the eighties boom.

He and Dana had fought over those cute little balconies on the upper floors. Dana had won. "Do you remember anything about a girl jumping off?"

"Sure. It happened during the dinner that Dana was awarded Architect of the Year."

"Where was I again?"

"In Korea."

"You were at the dinner, weren't you? Tell me about it."

"It was a typical blowout in the upstairs ballroom. About three hundred people came. The only indication that something had happened was a few cops walking through the back of the room during Dana's acceptance speech. Afterward, there was dancing. I left early." That was because Ross had not been there to dance with her, of course. "There were lots of police cars and an ambulance outside. I heard that someone had jumped. The next day they came to the office with photographs of the girl. No one recognized her. Then the police thought that she had been a waitress. It turned out that she had talked her way past a guard, somehow gotten to one of the balconies, and jumped. She left a note behind blaming a failed love affair. I didn't follow the case too closely. It was a hectic time here."

"How would she have gotten to a balcony?" Ross asked. "That's not exactly public access."

"Maybe she sneaked past a cleaning lady. Or she was involved with someone in another office upstairs." Marjorie fixed Ross with an even gaze. "Where there's a will, there's a way."

Ross was suddenly aware of her knees just inches from his chin. He could so easily reach over, slide a hand along her smooth thighs . . . Christ! Why must she sit so close all the time? Ross raised his hand; by a supernal effort of will, he found a way to bypass Marjorie's knees and cover his eyes instead. One more complication in his life and he might jump off a balcony himself.

"Thanks, Marjie."

She left. He began to draw.

# 13

*How many seconds elapsed between balcony and pavement? Three? What kind of thoughts would have gone through that girl's head as she sailed through the air? Those of blazing, final triumph? Blind despair? I wonder if she was pretty; that would have made the final gore all the more horrific. Brains, guts, all over the sidewalk . . . pity the poor pedestrian out for a nice evening walk when* whap, *a monster falls from the sky. How did the police ever identify her? Forget the face. Dental records? First they'd have to find her teeth. Jewelry? I doubt there was a wedding ring. Clothing, probably. Shoes. No, only one shoe, Ward said. It probably didn't look much the worse for wear. Shoes survive falls, they survive getting run over, a week in the ocean. . . . Shoes always come back, the better to lead feet into mischief. I wonder what the suicide note said. Would the police have given it to Ward or do they keep that kind of thing in their files forever? Three seconds and no turning back: Where did she find the courage to jump? Was the love of a man worth her life? Yes, I can see that.*

*But what about Guy, the cause of it all? Did he feel bad? Christ, I wish he were here to ask! Maybe the girl was a psycho; look at her sister, Ward. What if she was some muscle-bound gorilla chasing him around, phoning at all hours of the night? Then he couldn't possibly have felt bad. Maybe she was just a friend who never declared herself; then he might have felt a modest twinge. I wonder where they met. Ten years ago, was it? Guy was married then. The girl must have been a fling who had delusions of becoming more than a sideshow.*

*They're both dead now and I'm so curious. Ward's the only one with some answers. But I'd better stay away from her for the moment; instead of regretting her crime, she feels cheated that she didn't get to chuck Guy off the Tobin Bridge. And O'Keefe makes me uneasy as well. He's got to be wondering who would hate Guy enough to kill him. He'll never find Ward; the trail is too old and fuzzy. Unless she does something rash, of course. I worry about that. And there's always Philippa . . . but she'll never confess a thing. Emily might have forgiven her for Dana, but she won't forgive her for Guy, so chalk Philippa off the worry list. I suppose, if O'Keefe is any detective at all, I'll become his number one suspect. He's already tipped his hand by coming here this morning. Good luck, buddy. You'd like to solve a murder; I'd like to keep my wife. No contest.*

*Poor Guy! What did he do to deserve this but love one woman, not love another!*

⹀

It was a brilliant autumn morning, invigorating and crisp, same as the morning after Dana had died, only twenty degrees cooler: lecherous winter panting after Boston. The sun burned from a pellucid sky. After her chat with Detective O'Keefe, Emily wandered from Cafe Presto to the North End. Her other senses having fled, or collapsed in shock, she was all nose today, cogently aware of aromas seeping to the street from the tiny Italian bakeries and groceries. She walked up a steep, narrow rise to a hilltop park overlooking the harbor: Guy and she had occasionally come here after a long day at Presto, when they were grimy and tired but somehow not quite ready to go home. As always, the sight of graceful, white sails on the water soothed her; how lovely it must be just to drift with the breeze and tide. She sat for an hour, throbbing numbly for Guy. Eventually a huge cloud devoured the sun. Emily left the park.

She walked to South Station and Slavomir's mailbox—hey, it was something to do with her legs besides watching the hair grow. The final wave of rush-hour commuters was whishing through the terminal as otiose benchwarmers observed them. Constant announcements of trains and platforms cut through the jostling. Emily walked past the food stalls to the post office behind the station.

In Slavomir's box was a large pink envelope, bent in half, addressed to Mr. Charles Moody. PHOTOGRAPHS DO NOT BEND, Emily read, then saw the return address: Philippa Banks International Fan Club. She laughed out loud, as if someone had sent her a hilarious card. Emily opened the envelope and removed a sheet of pink paper with an ornate silver letterhead.

> Dear Mr. Moody,
> On behalf of Miss Banks, I would like to thank you for your lovely note of 9/20. We are so happy that fans such as yourself take the time to express concern for Philippa's safety. Sad but true, in this day and age no one, not even the President of the United States, can truly claim to be totally safe from fanatics and evildoers. However, please rest assured that Miss Banks takes all proper safety precautions in public and would never want to jeopardize the happiness of her loyal fans by exposing herself to dangerous situations.
> In appreciation of your concern, Miss Banks would like you to have her latest snapshot, which she sends with her love and gratitude.

The letter was Very Sincerely signed by Aidan Jackson, President of the PBIFC. He had enclosed a picture that Emily had autographed just the other day. Aidan hadn't been kidding when he told her that Philippa had an efficient sales force: Moody had received a reply to his letter within four days of sending it. Emily returned to the station and drank a slow cup of coffee. Then she phoned directory assistance in Los Angeles. It was around seven-thirty in California; were Aidan's recent assertions about his workday true, he had been slaving in the office for half an hour already.

"Good morning," he answered. "World headquarters of the Philippa Banks International Fan Club. This is Aidan speaking."

"Just checking up on you, shithead."

"Hey! Phil! What are you doing up so early?"

"I'm calling about that printout you gave me the other day."

"Don't tell me you found your next husband already!"

"Well, I've come up with a name. I get strong vibrations with Charles Moody."

A long pause. "Are you sure about that, sweetheart? He wrote a very rocky letter the other day. Very rocky."

"No kidding! Could you read it to me?"

"It's still in the Out bin. Hold on. Okay. Here goes: 'Dear Miss Banks, I must warn you that you are in danger. I feel there are people about who would greatly harm you. Would it be possible to hire a bodyguard? Please be very, very careful, and warn your sister as well. Sincerely yours, Charles Moody.' No wonder you got strong vibes about this guy, Phil. I was considering taking the letter to the police, but it's not really threatening. It's just a warning. But you never know how these psychos work. He could be warning you about himself. And what's this about a sister? I didn't know you had a sister."

"No one does," Emily replied, trying to laugh. "So what did you do?"

"I sent him a polite pooh-pooh back with a picture. If he writes again, I won't be as nice."

"He's written before?"

"Off and on. Christmas cards, birthday cards."

"He knows my birthday?" Emily cried.

"Of course, Phil, it's a matter of public record. All the as-trologers have it. The day's right, but the year is fudged. Moody's been paying fan-club dues since day one. He's a charter member. That's why I can't figure out this dire-warning bullshit. Maybe he's having a midlife crisis. All those years fantasizing about you have finally put him over the edge. Want me to fax the letter to you? You're home, aren't you?"

"No! No!" Emily almost shouted. "Maybe I'll drop by in a few days and check it out myself. Don't discuss this with anyone, all right?"

"You're not going to call the guy, are you, Phil? Consult Zilda the Gypsy a few more times before making your next move, promise? There are lots of nuts out there. By the way, *Choke Hold* just got another great review. Want to hear it?"

"Later. I'm going to bed now. Aidan, thanks for everything. I wouldn't be where I am without you."

"Do you realize this is the first time you've ever thanked me for anything?"

"I'm a beast! I know it! Forgive me! I love you! I mean it! Bye-bye, darling!" Breathless, Emily hung up. So many eyes in the terminal; surely a pair of them observed her now. Who was Charles Moody? How did he know of her existence? Why write such an urgent note to Philippa? Why not just go to her movie openings, her parades and local appearances, go to Simon's of-fice for cripe's sake, and deliver his message in person? Obeying her feet rather than her brain, Emily boarded a train about to leave for New York. She took a window seat and stared out the window for most of the journey. The earth was so beautiful today, yet Guy would see it no more; she couldn't understand that. The more she tried, the more illusory the union of flesh and time seemed. Her spirit, alone on a stark promontory, howled for him: There was the reality. The rest was just poor transubstantiation.

Emily half awoke in New York, where time was God. She cabbed from Penn Station to Ditzi's, a popular cafe on the East Side. The place reminded her of an overpriced, pretentious Cafe Presto. The counter help was young and snotty, averse to handling anything less than one-hundred-dollar bills. Emily waited at the counter as the people ahead of her bought teensy lamb chops and overcomplicated salads. "I'm interested in some catering," she said when one of the girls finally deigned to assist her.

She was led to a small, bright office. A fiftyish woman, dressed with the extravagant, lupine authority of an Upper East Side realtor, stood up. She stared a moment at Emily, nearly recognizing her face. "I'm Florence." She smiled, beckoning to a chair on the other side of her desk. "How may I help you?"

"Mrs. Charles Moody," Emily replied. "I understand Ditzi's catered the AIDS benefit at the Remus Theater recently."

The woman's smile vanished. Emily knew at once that the police had been here asking many questions about her menu, particularly in the area of dried fruits. "That is correct."

"I was there and thought it was absolutely superb," Emily gushed. "So much so that I am considering having you cater my husband's birthday party next month."

Florence's metallic smile returned. "Let's talk about it, Mrs. Moody. When is the date?"

"October fifteenth."

"How many people will be invited?"

"Two or three hundred. I haven't decided about the in-laws yet."

"Where will this be?"

"Either on our yacht or at the Museum of Natural History. It all depends on the weather." Emily looked around Florence's small office: tight as a submarine. It would be difficult to dig any information out of here. "My husband is very fond of pheasant, cockles, and black raspberries. Could you organize a menu around those items?"

"Certainly," Florence said, writing a few four-digit numbers on a pad.

"I'd like a cocktail hour beforehand, exactly the way you did at that reception."

"Fine." Florence's pen continued hemorrhaging zeros.

"Do you supply the serving staff as well?"

"Of course. We use only our own people for these occasions."

Emily tantalized Florence with the most esoteric menu imaginable, insisting upon things like olives from a special grove in Greece and stupendously expensive champagne from a tiny French vineyard. "You certainly know a lot about food, Mrs. Moody," Florence said at one point, awed less by Emily's erudition than by the bill she was running up.

"My husband and I are very particular," Emily replied, then ordered a birthday cake involving one hundred pounds of Belgian chocolate. They spent another half hour discussing flower arrangements down to the last stamen. "All right," Emily said at last, glancing at her watch. "On to the serving staff. I would like thirty tall women with red hair." She smiled at Florence. "They must all be able to sing 'Happy Birthday' and dance a small routine that I have choreographed."

By this time, Florence didn't think that was a strange request at all; it would just cost a little more. Pulling a folder from her file, she began to study a list of names, putting little checks besides a few of them. "I have only six tall redheads on my staff at the moment."

"Six?" Emily snatched the list away and ripped down the names with checks beside them. There was one Agatha, last name Street. She lived on the other side of Central Park. "You'll have to find twenty-four more, then. And I don't want any wigs or henna rinses. My husband detests dyed hair." Emily returned the list to Florence and made a few ridiculous closing requests. She gave her a bogus address and phone number.

"This is going to be a terrific party," Florence said, beaming, as she walked Emily to the curb. "How old is your husband going to be, Mrs. Moody?"

"Ninety-three. Thanks for everything! Bye-bye!" Emily walked quickly away. After several blocks, she stopped at a phone booth and got Information. Then she dialed Agatha.

"Sorry, she's out of town," drawled a roommate.

"Any idea when she'll be back?"

"A week or so. It depends on her boyfriend."

"Aha. I'll try again. Thank you." So much for impulse investigations. Emily glanced at her watch: five-thirty. Sunlight was fading and a mass of cold air had begun to slither between the skyscrapers. The warmest way back to Boston would be a cab to the airport. After a long wait, she finally got one to pull to the curb.

"You an actress?" the driver asked, observing Emily in his rearview mirror.

"No."

They said no more. Emily got to Beacon Hill around eight-thirty and found Ross at the kitchen table with four cartons of Chinese food. "Hi," she said, sniffing them. "What are you doing home so early?"

Ross noticed that Emily's eyes still looked pretty terrible. She had been crying. He kissed her and poured some wine. "Making dinner. How are you feeling?"

"All right," she lied, sitting at the table. "I went to Cafe Presto this morning."

"That must have been tough."

She only shrugged. "I ran into Detective O'Keefe."

"Really? What was he doing there?"

"Asking questions. He said Guy had been stabbed. He probably passed out and his car ran into a ditch."

"Who would stab Guy?"

"That's exactly what O'Keefe asked."

"What did you tell him?"

"That Guy had no enemies I knew of. He asked what I had been doing the night Guy died. I told him I was in California at a job interview. Then he asked what you were doing."

"Me?" Ross laughed thinly. "What do I have to do with this?"

"Nothing. I think O'Keefe was either trying to undermine my story or get a witness." Emily twirled some noodles around her chopsticks. "I said you were working late at the office. Hope you don't mind if I didn't mention your driving to the cabin. I didn't want Philippa brought into this."

"Fine with me." Ross petted his wife's hand. "It could have been a random mugging, honey. Happens all the time."

"But O'Keefe said that Guy had a wallet full of cash in his pocket."

Damn! Ward had slipped up on that one! "Maybe he fought back hard enough to scare an attacker off." Ross slowly chewed a shrimp. "When's the funeral?"

"Don't know. I'm don't think I'm going." Emily finished her wine. "I've been meaning to talk to you about something."

*Here it comes. She's going to confess about Guy then she's going to divorce me.* "What's that, darling?" Ross's voice capsized halfway through the last word.

An awful eon passed. "I think someone's trying to kill Philippa," Emily said.

Eh? Was he spared? "Whatever would make you think that?"

"This goes back to the *Choke Hold* party in New York. You know that Philippa's favorite drink is iced vodka with four dried cherries. Well, I ordered one but gave the cherries to Byron. He died of a heroin overdose shortly afterward. It was in the dried cherries."

"Are you sure?"

"Not entirely. Apparently Byron was drinking lots of vodka with cherries. But it's my gut instinct."

"Who else knows this?"

"Only Philippa. That's why I stashed her in the cabin for a few days."

"So Philippa was alone in the woods convinced that someone was trying to kill her? No wonder she went crazy." Ross grinned in delight. "Did you discover anything to back you up?"

"Yes and no. I went to New York today to try and find the waitress who served those drinks to us at the party." Emily told him about her little skit at Ditzi's. "But she's run off with a boyfriend."

"You suspect the waitress of trying to poison Philippa? Wouldn't the New York police have nailed her already?"

"Maybe she talked her way through an interrogation. She seemed to be an actress. Don't laugh, Ross. They try to kill each other off all the time. Philippa told me."

"My little Sherlock." Ross returned to his butterflied shrimp. "Why didn't you just tell the police right away?"

"Maybe I should have. Now it seems a little late."

"It's a wild story," Ross agreed. "Heroin in the cherries? Why not just whack Philippa over the head with a crowbar?"

Emily scowled. "Last week Philippa got a letter warning that someone was trying to kill her."

"Not surprising. Her fans must be deranged people to begin with."

"This letter told Philippa to warn me as well."

Ross stopped chewing. "How did this person know Philippa had a sister?"

"I don't know."

"Where's the letter? I'm taking it to the police."

"Ross, don't be silly. Everything's under control. I'm going out to California tomorrow to do a little more investigating."

"Are you out of your mind? I forbid it. You're not going anywhere near your sister." He fished in a carton for another shrimp, couldn't find one, and finally threw the chopsticks aside. "Why didn't you tell me any of this before?"

"I didn't want to get you upset."

"What? You'd rather get yourself killed first? Christ, Emily! Think these things through to their logical conclusion!"

"I'll be perfectly safe," Emily said. "Philippa's hiding out in a hotel in Santa Monica. No one will find us there."

"Did you hear me? I said you're not going."

Thank God she hadn't mentioned Moody's postbox at South Station; Ross would chain her to the bed. "I can't just abandon my sister like a sitting duck."

"Why not? She's always preferred to be the center of attention." Ross shoved an enormous load of noodles into his mouth, damming the temptation to tell Emily all about Philippa and Guy: That would put an end to this bail-out-Philippa nonsense. "Why don't you tell her to hire a private investigator?"

"Because I'd rather do it myself."

"Em, it's too dangerous! Don't you care if you get yourself killed?"

She became very quiet. After a moment, he heard her swallow. "No, not really."

Ross sighed: Guy again. He wondered if his wife would ever get over him now. Probably not; the affair had not died a natural death. He took Emily's hand. "Well, I care."

"Let me go to California," she pleaded. "I need to get away for a little while."

Torn with guilt and anxiety, Ross could only stroke her hand. Finally he said, "All right. But promise me you'll be careful. Take no chances. I'd be completely lost without you."

She smiled wanly. "That's nice to know."

The next morning, against his better judgment, Ross took Emily to the airport. He had not slept all night worrying about her. At breakfast he had almost begged to come along to California, but caught himself just in time: better to let her grieve in private for her lover and perhaps miss her husband a little. About the Philippa-related aspects of this trip Ross had everything and nothing to say; as a result, he said nothing. Fifteen years of marriage had taught him that Emily would not be listening anyway. At the terminal, he took her hand and tried to appear cheerful. "You have a battle plan, I take it?"

She half rose from a profound silence that had overtaken her after reading Guy's obituary at breakfast. "I'm going to grill Philippa and try to sort out that strange fan letter."

Then what, invite the guy to a pajama party? "How long will you be gone?"

"Just a couple of days. What will you be doing?"

"The usual. Maybe I'll go up to the cabin this weekend if you're not back. Plant a few bulbs."

A nearby policeman pointed to the car and shouted, "You! Move!"

Ross kissed the shell of his wife, wondering if she'd ever return. "I love you. Please be careful."

Emily nodded obediently, then got her suitcase from the backseat. "Bye, darling." She faded into the terminal.

Ross slugged through tunnel traffic back to State Street.

About a block before reaching the underground garage, he suddenly picked up the car phone. "Hi, Marjorie," he said. "I won't
be in for a while. I've got to go to a funeral at ten. Where's
McAllister and Sons in Winchester?"

She flipped through a phone book. "Right on the main street.
Should I send flowers?"

"Don't bother. Anything of interest happening over there?"
Not that Ross cared to know; he just needed to hear a female
voice to stoke his courage. Marjorie kept talking, distracting,
until he got to the funeral home, a large Victorian residence
with a gigantic porch. Guy was probably lying in the front parlor. Quite a number of cars already filled the lot; to his relief,
Ross did not see a white pickup truck among them. Desperately
needing a drink, he opened the glove compartment. Hallelujah,
Emily had left her flask from Dana's funeral! He finished off the
last two inches of gin and took a deep breath. "Okay Marj, I'd
better head in."

His head began to ache as he walked up the steps. What was
he doing here, representing his wife or gloating over his work?
Ross unsteadily signed the guest book and entered the crowded
parlor. Guy was lying, sort of really asleep, among the ferns. He
looked terribly young and very handsome; who could blame
Emily for wanting him? After a moment's fascinated horror,
Ross turned away, glad that his wife had not come along.

"Hi Ross," said Bert, the pastry chef, appearing at his side.
"Where's Emily?"

"She had a family emergency in California."

"You mean she's going to miss the funeral? Sheesh! Would
Guy be pissed!" Bert looked softly at his former employer. "He
doesn't look too bad, you think?"

He looked grotesque. Ross nodded toward a tall woman with
eyes like Guy's. "Is that his sister?"

"Yep. Ursula. There are his parents sitting near the back. His
poor mother."

Steeling himself, Ross walked over and waited for Ursula to
finish talking with a few friends. "I'm Ross Major," he said, of-

fering his hand. "Emily's husband. I'm sorry she was unable to come. I would like to convey our sincere condolences."

Ursula looked a long moment at him. Did she know that her brother had been in love with Emily? Of course she did. Everyone in the room knew. Everyone in the room probably knew that Ross had killed him, too. "Thank you for the beautiful flowers," she said. "Guy loved roses."

Emily must have sent them yesterday. "We'll miss him very much," Ross said.

Ursula brought Ross to her parents. "Mother, this is Emily's husband, Ross."

"I'm sorry she couldn't be here. She had a family emergency in California," he repeated. "She's quite heartbroken."

"Yes," Guy's mother said. "We all are."

Before taking a seat near the back of the room, Ross chatted with Lois and a few of Guy's former rivals from the restaurant business. He was staring at the enormous bouquet of roses next to Guy's coffin, wondering whether he had the guts to walk up there again and read the little card, when Detective O'Keefe slid into the chair next to his. "Hello, Ross."

"Hi."

"Is Emily here?"

"She's in California with her sister."

"Didn't she just get back from California?"

"Yes." Ross looked slowly at the detective. "Philippa is more demanding than I am."

They observed the still life with ferns for a few moments. Ross wanted to ask how O'Keefe's investigation was going but knew he'd get no answer; obviously the detective was continuing his research at the funeral. Similarly, O'Keefe wanted to ask how Emily was doing but knew that Ross would never say anything but "Fine." So O'Keefe said, "Was Guy a friend of yours?"

"He was more a friend of Emily's. We saw each other off and on. Tennis, cocktails, culinary events, things like that."

Ross's voice was so even, so nonchalant; could it be possible that he suspected nothing of his wife's affair? "How long had you known him?"

"About seven years."

"Did he ever discuss business or personal affairs with you?"

"Not with me. Maybe with Emily. She always thought of him as a brother."

Brother! "Did you like him?"

"He was a good man," Ross said. "We'll miss him."

Odd; he meant it. O'Keefe was about to ask when Emily would return when Ward walked into the parlor. She was wearing what looked to be a heavy black tablecloth and black knee boots. Had she been wearing a helmet, Darth Vader would have been out of a job. Ross and O'Keefe watched as she paid her respects to Guy's family, then walked sedately toward the coffin. She paused long enough to verify that Guy's soul had left his body, then headed toward a seat on the other side of the aisle. Suddenly she saw Ross and O'Keefe.

"Hello, Detective," she said, shaking his hand, sitting in the row ahead of them. Ross she ignored totally. "How's it going?"

"Fine, thanks." O'Keefe thought Ward looked remarkably well compared to the last time he had seen her at Diavolina. Maybe she was even sober; that orangey smell could have been mouthwash or perfume as easily as Grand Marnier. "You were acquainted with Witten?"

"We worked out at the same gym. Sometimes I ate breakfast at his place." She nodded toward the coffin. "He doesn't look too bad, considering he was in a car crash. Hey, how's my dishwasher doing?"

"He hasn't gone anywhere."

Ward scowled. "You don't do too well by the victims of random violence, do you."

"We try our best, Ms. Ward."

"Try a little harder, will you? Hey, there's Bud Haskil. Haven't seen him in years. Excuse me." She left.

"Do you know who that was?" O'Keefe asked Ross.

"No idea."

"The famous Ward, manager of Diavolina. I thought it best not to introduce you."

"Thanks." Ross glanced coolly across the parlor. Ward was

joshing with two men in suits. "Emily said she was big, but not that big. What was that about a dishwasher?"

"He drowned in the Fenway a few weeks ago. Drank a gutful of grain alcohol and tried to walk on water. Ward thinks that's somehow unusual." O'Keefe's eyes began to wander. The room was filling with mourners, perhaps murderers. He stood up. "Give Emily my regards, would you?"

Ross sat stuporously through the service, which was shorter but much more wrenching than Dana's, since Guy's friends had truly loved him. He followed the hearse to that gigantic, incomprehensible hole in the earth. He said good-bye to Guy's family and walked back to his car, nodding to O'Keefe, who observed all from the periphery. Ward hung around talking somberly to strangers, as if this funeral aggrieved her. She glanced once, casually, in Ross's direction as he pulled away. Driving past a long forest, Ross pulled into a picnic area. He walked into the woods, found a clearing, and lay down on the dead leaves. Then he sobbed at the sky because he was totally lost again. He missed Emily and he really missed Dana, who would have listened to his confession, absolved him, and told him how to proceed. After a long while his tears dried. No one had heard him but the squirrels, and now he was hungry. Ross peed on a tree and drove back to the office. "I'm here," he buzzed Marjorie. "Come in when you have a minute, eh?"

Today she was wearing a white blouse with a slim gray flannel skirt well below her knees. He could barely see four inches of shin. "Ross, what's that all over your coat? Leaves?" Marjorie took a few steps forward and started vigorously brushing them off. "Where have you been? They're all in your hair, too."

She was flicking them out when he put an arm behind her waist and pulled her in—ah, there was no consolation like a woman. He held her tight, smelling her hair, her skin, branded by the indentations her body made on his; perhaps he could absorb some of her life force as well. But for that he'd need his mouth. Ross hesitated, clairvoyant and terrified for a tiny second. Then he kissed her. Finally he broke away and sagged into his chair.

Marjorie gently resumed picking little bits of leaf out of his hair. "Rough funeral, eh?"

He nodded. "I'm sorry." Then he chuckled. "No I'm not."

Marjorie took a seat opposite his desk. Her face looked young, elfin almost: After all these years, she was finally sure that he loved her. "Dagmar called," she said. "Wants to discuss a few more details of her museum with you."

"Tomorrow."

"You've got to see Billy Murphy this afternoon at two. There's a staff meeting at four. By the way, when we were cleaning out Dana's office, I remember seeing a program from his Architect of the Year banquet in one of the boxes. Would you like me to find it for you?"

"That would be great."

She left, in a little rush, as if she were suddenly shy about her rear end in that tight skirt. Ross made some phone calls, sketched for Dagmar, and went to meet Billy Murphy at a Quincy Market bar. Lunches with the building inspector were anything but social occasions, as Ross was discovering. He not only had to match Murphy scotch for scotch as the man delivered a two-hour monologue on current construction in Boston, but then Ross had to sift a mountain of hearsay from innuendo from actual fact. How the hell had Dana managed that? Fairly drunk, Ross returned to the office just minutes before his weekly staff meeting. He tried to keep the proceedings civil, make note of every gem from Murphy's mouth, and keep his eyes off Marjorie, with mixed success. The meeting ended on time because four of the combatants had tickets to a Red Sox game. Finally, only Ross and Marjorie were left at the long table.

"I'm still looking for that banquet program," she said. "There are just two boxes left."

Ross stared at his memo pad. About fifteen minutes ago, he had stopped writing; now he was trying to decipher what he had written. His mind was rejecting words in favor of images: Guy under a ton of dirt, Ward dancing on his grave, O'Keefe bursting into the office with an arrest warrant, Emily shot with a crossbow. . . . She really should not have left him alone, tonight of all nights. "Keep looking, then," he said calmly. "I'll wait."

Ross didn't wait long. "Found it," he heard her call from Dana's office. Marjorie returned to the conference room with a folder. "Terribly pretentious," she said, sitting next to him. "What did you want to see here?"

"I really don't know." Ross watched her slim fingers open the booklet. "Read it to me. Top to bottom."

"'Ninety-eighth annual Spring Banquet of the Boston Architectural Society, April twenty-eighth, nineteen eighty-three, seven o'clock, upper ballroom of the Darnell Building. Opening remarks by George Kravitz, Invocation by Harold Morse, Dinner'—oh look at this ridiculous menu, I don't have to read that to you—'Remarks by the President of the Traub Theater Restoration Project, Presentation of Architect of the Year Award, Remarks by Dana Forbes, Closing Remarks by Nat Posner, Dancing and Open Bar.'" She looked at Ross, who seemed to be sleeping. "Told you it was boring."

"Do you remember anything about the speeches?"

"They were all too long except for Dana's. His was funny. Should I read the next page? It's got board of directors, credits, patrons, all that."

"Why not." Ross listened as Marjorie's voice rippled over the names of friends, enemies, strangers, the dead: Perhaps life was just one long bedtime story. He opened his eyes when she read special thanks to Guy Witten Catering. "Let me see that."

"Right there." Marjorie pointed. "You know him?"

"I went to his funeral this morning."

"Oh." Marjorie perused the rest of the program as Ross went to the window and began studying reds in the sunset. "Guess who was on the Traub restoration committee," she said.

Amy Vanderbilt? Fred Flintstone? From the window, Ross shrugged.

"Dagmar Pola."

"She's probably on fifty committees like that."

"It's an interesting coincidence."

Maybe Dagmar had gone to the banquet while Joe entertained in his little loft on Commonwealth Ave. Guy must have been going nuts in the kitchen; what a bad time for Ward's sister to have shown up, wanting to see him. She must have been either desperate or extremely sure of herself. "Guess I missed one hell of a party," Ross said, turning from the window. He looked across the room at Marjorie. All that rifling through boxes had pulled her blouse a few inches out of her skirt. Dishevelment suited her. Ross made a small charade of gathering his pad and pencils from the table and heading for the door. He heard Dana's voice saying, "Rule number one: Never shit where you eat." What a stupid rule!

Suddenly, as if the idea had just occurred to him, Ross asked, "Are you free for dinner?"

"Yes."

"Let's go somewhere, then." He shuddered a little as he wrapped Marjorie in her coat.

# 14

Philippa was just stepping out of the bathtub as Emily arrived at her hotel in Santa Monica. It had been a trying day, spent almost entirely on the telephone with Simon, who was still in the hospital, becoming increasingly irate that Philippa seemed unwilling to visit him. Unconvinced by her tale of stomach flu, he accused her of ditching him for another agent now that *Choke Hold* was doing so well at the box office. When he started in on breach-of-contract suits, Philippa retired to her bath with a bottle of champagne, there to contemplate her toes and possibly masturbation. She hadn't had a man in almost two weeks and was feeling vaginally congested. At last came the knock on her door.

"Thank God you're here," she cried, dragging her sister in. Emily's puffy face looked about as bad as her own. Crying over Guy Witten, no doubt; Philippa put that unfortunate thought out of her mind. "Long trip, honey?"

"I watched a few movies," Emily said. Both had had car

crashes. "It took two hours to get here from the airport. Where'd you find this dump?"

"I used to meet Terrence here." That was Philippa's second husband, the one whose divorce from his first wife had dragged on longer than had his marriage to Philippa. "They have good afternoon tea. I'll order you some."

"Thanks." Emily went to the bathroom. "Hey! You've got champagne!"

"Help yourself, darling." Philippa ordered tea for two and another bottle. "How long can you stay?"

"As long as I want."

"Really? How'd you talk Ross into that?"

"I told him everything."

"He knows there's someone out there trying to kill me? Emily, that was the stupidest thing you've ever done!" Philippa burst into the bathroom. "All he's got to do now is hire a hit man!"

"I think he's got more pressing things on his mind, to tell the truth." Emily flushed the toilet. "How's Simon?"

"Still in the hospital. He's trying to talk the doctors into letting his plastic surgeon do some quickie rehab work as long as they won't let him leave. He is not in a good mood."

"Did that script ever turn up?"

"You've got to be kidding. It's probably in production already in someone's basement." Philippa emptied the last of the champagne into her glass. "The Czech director has disappeared into thin air. Simon doesn't know whether to be embarrassed or outraged."

"He should be glad he's alive." Emily inspected her sister's face. "I think you're ready to go out again. Those bruises could pass for a fading suntan."

"You think so? Simon's got me on three talk shows tomorrow. I'm not sure I should do them." Philippa waited hopefully for her sister to volunteer for the opportunity to get shot on national television.

"You'll be fine. How's *Choke Hold* doing?"

"Unbelievably well. Don't ask why. Maybe I've become part of the nostalgia craze."

Their tea and champagne arrived. Noticing Emily slip into a quiet abyss, Philippa jabbered on about movies and rivals, makeup, diamonds, anything but Guy Witten; she did not want to be in the position of having to comfort Emily for a death she had directly caused. "How's Ross?" she asked finally.

"Getting by. He misses Dana, of course."

Philippa smiled wanly. Lately she had missed Dana herself; he had had one of the world's great tongues. "What's that bitch Ardith doing with herself now?"

"She's in Europe for a month."

"Prostrate with grief, no doubt. I take it she dropped that stupid lawsuit."

"Who knows." Emily switched from tea to champagne. "I went to New York yesterday to try and find the waitress who served us at the *Choke Hold* party."

"Why, Em? All she did was schlepp the tray over."

Emily frowned; Ross had said more or less the same thing. "Hey! Just trying to help! I'm just an amateur with silly hunches." And this whole trip was just an amateurish excuse to miss Guy's funeral. She stood up. "Maybe I'll go for a run. Some brilliant idea might come to me."

Philippa studied the bubbles in her champagne as her sister changed clothes. "Say Em," she said finally, "as long as you're going out, maybe you could drop in on Simon. His hospital's only a few miles away. He's pretty hurt that I haven't visited him."

"What excuse did you give him?"

"Stomach flu. He didn't buy it." Philippa gave Emily directions to the hospital. "Just stop in for a few minutes. It would mean so much to him."

Translation: I need this man to stay employed. "I'll try," Emily said, pulling on a baseball cap. "See you in an hour."

Cars of all vintages jammed the streets. The sun was hot, the air foul; in this city, running was probably more carcinogenic than smoking. A half dozen people called "Hi, Phil" as Emily ran by. She twiddled her fingers at them and continued on, making a long loop that eventually brought her past the hospital. She went inside and asked for Simon's room.

"Go right up, Miss Banks," the nurse told her.

Emily did so and discovered Simon copulating vigorously with a redhead. The room was crammed with enough flowers to make a Rose Bowl float. "Hi guys," Emily called after a moment's indecision, tossing her baseball cap onto a chair. "I was cruising by and thought I'd drop in."

"Philippa! What the hell are you doing here?" Simon cried, shoving the lady off his narrow bed.

"I just told you," she said as the redhead rearranged her long, filmy skirt. It was Agatha Street, the missing waitress. "Auditioning for a job, dear?"

"Be nice," Simon warned. He patted Agatha's milky forehead. "It's okay, baby. She's just making a little joke. Damn it, Phil, do you always drop in without an invitation?"

"Don't give me this shit, Simon. You've been begging me to drop by for days." Emily smiled at Agatha. "We all met in New York, didn't we, Hot Pants?"

"Her name's Agatha," Simon snapped. "Phil, you have the memory of an elephant. And the manners of one, too. Since when do you jog, anyway?"

A nurse walked in. "Time for your medication, Mr. Stern." She looked apologetically at the ladies. "Excuse us, please. This will just take a moment."

Emily led Agatha into the hallway. "I've been meaning to talk with you."

"Me?" the girl cried. "Do you need an understudy?"

"No. Now listen. I'm going to ask a few questions. You give me straight answers and I'll let you get back to screwing Uncle Simon. All right?" Agatha nodded, mesmerized: Philippa Banks was her idol.

"You were a waitress at the *Choke Hold* opening in New York, correct? You brought me an iced vodka with four dried cherries. Where'd you get it?"

"From the bartender."

"Did you see him mix the drink?"

"Yes."

"How'd he do it?"

"He stirred some vodka and ice, strained it, and put in the cherries."

"And you brought it directly to me?"

"That's right."

"That's wrong. It was warm when I got it."

Agatha's face fell. "I brought it over as fast as I could. But that lady held me up."

"What lady?"

"She just stood right in my way and put a bunch of dirty glasses on my tray like I was her maid or something. I told her to take them off because the tray was for you and I wanted it to look neat. She said 'Oh, excuse me, dearie,' and took them all away."

"Were the glasses empty?"

Not as empty as Agatha's face. "I would think so. Otherwise why would she put them on my tray? I'm really sorry, Miss Banks. I didn't mean to bring you a warm drink. Ugh!"

Emily patted Agatha's vacant head. "Never mind. It was still vodka. What did this woman look like?"

"She wore heavy makeup and jewelry, and an expensive suit with fat buttons. She could have been a fag hag."

Emily had no idea what that meant but nodded anyway. "What color was her hair?"

"Black, I think. So were her eyebrows. She was wearing a black turban and thick glasses. And awful perfume. Probably cost a fortune."

"How old was she?"

Agatha shrugged. "About Simon's age, I guess. Thirty-five."

Emily tried not to laugh. "He told you he was thirty-five?"

"Shhh! It's a secret!"

The nurse left Simon's room. "What are you two doing out there," Simon called tetchily. "Someone get in here and fix my blankets."

"Do you have any more questions, Miss Banks?"

"No. Go fix Simon." Emily watched the girl dotingly rearrange her Svengali's covers as he cursed nurses, doctors, and hospitals. "So what's the matter with you, Si? Tertiary syphilis?"

"You're a real hoot, Phil. There's something wrong with my blood. It's got strange crystals in it that no one can figure out. No one believes me when I tell them it was that script from Vitkovich on polluted paper. They keep asking me if I ate moth-balls and weed killer for breakfast." He snorted. "Morons. I'm not staying here one more day. This place is the Enema Capital of the universe."

Emily retrieved her baseball cap. "Nice seeing you, Agatha. Good luck in Hollywood. I'm sure Uncle Simon will take good care of you for a few weeks."

"You'd better be sharp for those interviews tomorrow," Simon snapped. "I called in ten thousand favors to get them."

"Why thank you, darling. Let me know when Mr. Vitzkewicz turns up."

Emily ran back to the hotel, where she found Philippa curled up on the bed, lacquering her toenails. "Great news, Phil," she said. "Agatha the waitress was visiting Simon at the hospital. We're not imagining things after all. Your enemy is a middle-aged bitch in a black turban, glasses, and awful perfume. I'm going back to Luco's tomorrow. The waiter's got to remember something about that script." Emily looked over at her sister, who just sat on the bed blowing her toenails dry. "Well? Aren't you excited? Say something!"

Philippa finally took her toes out of her face. "How old is Agatha?"

"Who the hell cares about Agatha?"

"I do. Look Em, I can't stay holed up like this anymore. I've got to get back into the dogfight before ten Agathas get ahead of me. I can't disappear just when *Choke Hold* hits the charts. That's suicide."

"But someone's trying to kill you."

She shrugged. "So let them! An eye for an eye!"

What the hell did that mean? "Just let me run with it a little, all right?" Emily said. "You do your interviews tomorrow. I'll go to the restaurant and maybe drop in on the fan club again."

"What for?"

Emily began stripping off her running clothes. "It's kind of fun pretending to be you. Like dressing up for real. Maybe someday you can pretend to be me. If you ever want to, that is."

Philippa's face turned a violent red. Luckily, Emily was already in the bathroom. They ordered in Chinese food and watched three videos; afterward, crazed, they jumped into the hotel pool. Only as she was shutting out the lights did Philippa realize that Emily had not called Ross, nor he her.

Still functioning on Eastern time, Emily popped wide awake at five o'clock in the morning. Her sister snored lightly from the other bed. Careful not to disturb Philippa's beauty sleep, Emily dressed and got into her car, looking for breakfast. Although dawn was just unhinging the night with a wedge of gold at the horizon, traffic already overran the roadways. Commuters here drove as if they had been ordered to, or from, an earthquake. Emily joined the herd and crawled across town, arriving much later at Luco's, the restaurant she had recently visited with Simon. It would open at seven for breakfast.

Sitting at a bus stop, Emily watched the staff slowly piddle in. Finally she saw the fellow who had served them the other morning. "Yoo-hoo!" she called, chucking a burrito into the garbage. "Franco!"

He stared; without their makeup, jewels, and pushup bras, many actresses were nondescript as guppies. "Philippa Banks," he said after a few seconds. "You're up with the sun. Looking gorgeous, I might add."

"Cut the shit. It's too early." Did this town contain one honest person? "You brought a script to my table the other day. It was all wrapped up in plastic."

"That's right. You were with Simon Stern. He didn't leave much of a tip."

"You didn't serve much of a breakfast. Who gave you the script? I need to know. It's very important."

Franco hesitated, uncertain whether he should ask Philippa for money or for a date. On one hand, she was the star of that campy new sleeper, *Choke Hold*; on the other hand, her breath smelled like onions. "It's a little hazy," he said.

"You told us she had diamonds as big as her eyes and filming began in two weeks. Does that ring any bells?" Emily dug in her purse. "Look, I'm desperate. Here's all my money and three tickets to the Massachusetts Megabucks. The jackpot's up to seven million and the drawing's on Saturday."

"Forget the money!" Franco said. Maybe it was the wind in her hair. "It's coming back to me now. It was a lady with Coke-bottle glasses and a black turban. She looked like a Gypsy wearing her own little crystal balls."

"How old?"

"Anywhere between thirty and sixty. You just can't tell these days."

"Was she alone?"

"Yes. She put two C-notes on the table and asked me to deliver the script and a message to you. She seemed nervous. Smoked constantly."

"Was she dark or light?"

"Dark."

"Did you notice anything else besides her rings? Like warts? Bracelets?"

"I didn't have much time to look. She was in and out in ten minutes."

Emily scribbled a phone number on one of the lottery tickets. "If you think of anything else, call me here in the next few hours. Ask for Emily Major. I really appreciate it." She returned to her car and drove to Simon's office, arriving shortly before eight. Aidan nearly dropped his croissant when she walked in.

"My God! What are you doing up so early?"

"Working, dear. I don't want to look as if I just rolled out of bed for those three interviews today." Emily helped herself to a corner of Aidan's croissant. "What's new?"

"*Choke Hold* was fourth at the box office last week and moving up fast."

"Any reason why?"

"Never ask, Phil. Just count your blessings. Simon's getting a lot of phone calls about you."

"Really? He didn't mention shit when I saw him yesterday." Too busy with Orifice Agatha. Emily peered over Aidan's desk. "How's my fan mail? Heard anything more from my friend Charles Moody?"

"No. You're still getting vibrations about him?" Aidan frowned. "Get a second opinion, would you? Carmen isn't the most reliable astrologer in town, you know."

"You told me that Moody's been a member of the fan club for almost twenty years," Emily said. "Has his address always been the same?"

Aidan's frown deepened. "You're not going to visit him, are you?"

"Good God, no! I just want to know where he's from. Carmen told me never to marry a man from a state with only three syllables."

Aidan bought that; Emily didn't know whether to be pleased or insulted. "I'll have to look in the old card file," he said, taking her to a back room. "We keep all the precomputer records here." He pulled open the Mi–Mo drawer and located Moody's small card. "Here's your boy."

Until eight years ago, Charles Moody had been receiving the Philippa Banks newsletter at Sheafe Street in Boston. Then he had switched to the box at South Station. "Well, I guess he passes the test," Emily said.

"You're not going to marry him just because he lives in Massachusetts, are you?" Aidan cried, snatching the card away. "That's absurd!"

"It's not just a question of the state," Emily protested. "Carmen's got to know the numbers and letters in the address so she can add them up and divide according to the phase of the moon. Then we'll see." She looked at her watch. "How do you suggest I dress for these interviews?"

"Wear the orange suit with your diamonds from Cornell." That was Philippa's fifth husband. "And see a hairdresser as soon as you can, Phil. You're about five shades off the blond your fans have come to know and love." Aidan walked Emily to the door. "Don't forget the nail polish!" he shouted as the elevator swallowed her.

Outside, the sun had begun to bake thighs, fanny tucks, and silicone. Emily crawled from red light to red light, arriving an hour later at Santa Monica. Her room was as dark as when she had left it at sunrise. "Wake up, Phil!" she called, raking aside the thick curtains. "Breakfast."

The mound on the bed slowly stirred. "What time is it?"

"Nine-thirty. You've got an interview in two hours."

"Crap! I won't have time for a bath!" Philippa began poking through the bag Emily had brought from a nearby bakery. "Where have you been? Jogging again?"

"I went to Luco's."

"And you didn't bring back any Scallop Hash? They do take-out, Em!"

"I wasn't there to eat." Emily recounted her little chat with Franco the waiter. "Sounds like the person who switched drinks in New York was the same one who sent that bogus script to the table."

Philippa took a mighty chomp into a croissant. "So I should be on the lookout for a frump with heavy glasses? That's a big help."

Emily followed her sister into the bathroom. "I dropped in on Aidan this morning."

"Again? And got away with it? Jesus, you're getting good."

Emily sat on the toilet seat as steam slowly shrouded the bathroom. "Do you realize that bad things have happened whenever you've eaten somewhere?"

Bad things had also happened whenever Philippa had met Guy Witten but she didn't point that out to her sister. "What are you getting at, Em?"

"Think back to your dinner at Diavolina for me, okay? Do you remember seeing someone there with a turban and heavy glasses?"

"Afraid not. Dana had my full attention."

"Was there anything he ate that you didn't eat? Anything he touched? I know we've been through this before, but try again."

Philippa tried. "We switched steaks. Mine was almost raw. That moron of a waiter screwed up."

The steaks were fine; Emily had watched Byron make them. "Did anyone odd come to your table, or leave anything on it?"

"Someone sent us a bottle of wine. But we both drank it. That weird-looking ghoul with the orange face showed up with a few drinks from someone at the bar. Two vodkas with cherries. I told you that already."

"Refresh my memory," Emily said. "Who sent them?"

"Ardith's aerobics coach. You and I never figured out how he got there. Then Jack-o'-Lantern chewed the fat with Dana a little."

"His name's Zoltan. What did he say?"

"Something about not seeing Dana since the renovation. Then Dana asked what had happened to some statue behind the bar."

Statue? "And?"

"I'm trying to think, Em. This happened a long time ago." Philippa tried to shampoo her memory back. "Right! The feminists took it down." Philippa emerged from the shower and, as was her habit, studied her body in the mirror. "This goddamn potbelly! You'd think I had six kids!" Philippa turned ninety degrees. "My nipples are beginning to point up. That means everything else is starting to sag." She began toweling herself off. "Have you noticed that your periods are getting shorter?"

"A little."

"How about your cycle? Is that getting shorter too? Mine's down to twenty-five days."

Emily didn't even remember when her last period had been. Sometime before Dana's funeral. "You still keep track of that sort of thing?"

"Of course! I don't let Simon schedule any interviews the week before my period. It would be suicide. I'm really cranky if I can't fit into my leather pants." Philippa slathered her face with a heavy white cream. "You mean you don't keep those little charts for your temperature anymore?"

"No. Ross got fed up with screwing on command."

This time, Philippa did not make any wisecracks about other volunteers who might like to step into the breech. "So stop demanding," Philippa said, flipping on her hair dryer. "Go on a vacation together. Ross is still crazy about you. I bet if you picked up the phone and asked him to take the next plane out, he would."

"I wouldn't dream of asking him to do such a thing."

"No, you probably wouldn't. That's how you've managed to stay married for fifteen years." Philippa began tissuing the white slime from her face, finally aware that Emily would never tell her about Guy Witten. It was probably better that way. But Emily still needed advice; her lover was gone. If Philippa had learned anything from her five marriages and twenty affairs, it was that once they were over, they were over. Emily didn't have the experience to know that brooding over the Dearly Departed was about as productive as scolding a hurricane. "Look, I'm no Einstein, but I can see that you and Ross are having a rough patch lately. I'm sure it's my fault. I should never had laid a finger on Dana Forbes. But I did and I'm sorry." Philippa looked at her lovely, trusting sister. "No, I'm not sorry. I don't regret one minute. You've just got to pick up and go on." Satisfied with her sermon, she sailed out of the bathroom. "What do you think I should wear today?"

Emily watched her dig through a tumble of lingerie. "Aidan recommends the orange pantsuit. He told me that *Choke Hold* is fourth on the charts and moving up fast."

"Hot shit." Whistling, Philippa got a pair of gold sandals from the closet. "God, it's great to be alive!"

The phone rang. Emily picked it up. "Hello?"

"This is Franco. You spoke to me this morning at Luco's."

"What's up?"

"I was wondering if you were free for dinner tonight."

"Do you have something to tell me? We can do that over the phone."

"No, we can't. I want to see you again. I know I'm just a waiter. But don't say no."

Emily thought a moment. "Come to room four-sixteen at eight tonight." She hung up. "Did you hear that?"

"Of course I did. More mystery witnesses?"

"No, your dinner date." That sounded more romantic than bodyguard.

"What about you?"

"I'm going home," Emily said. "Try not to make me fly out here in two days for your funeral, okay?"

# 15

*If hell exists, I deserve to go there. In the space of three days, I've murdered Guy and slept with Marjorie. A superthorough job as always—I've not only deprived my wife of her lover, but I've taken one of my own. Worm! How can I ever look Emily in the eye again? What about Marjorie? Oh God, she was so sweet, butter and roses in my arms . . . and I truly wanted her that night. But the morning after was awful for both of us. She was embarrassed to be naked with me; by day, after all these years, I'm still Mr. Major the architect and she's my organizer. You don't sleep with the people who are supposed to organize you. It disorganizes them. I should never have stayed overnight, never. But I couldn't face an empty bed at home; Guy would have been in the shadows, knifing my dreams, looking for Emily. I still can't believe he's dead. So he slept with my wife! In the big picture, what's a couple inches of trespass? I forgive him now! If it was anything like my interlude with Marjorie, it was half innocent, a spontaneous detour, a sudden alignment of the planets. . . . How could I have been so paranoid? Was I that afraid of losing her?*

*Of course I was. I still am, in fact, much more than before. If she ever finds out what I did to Guy, she'll leave me. Why the hell didn't I think about that before handing Ward a road map to the cabin? All right, Major: You've dug the hole, poured the concrete, now get your feet out of it. First I'll have to end it with Marjorie. She'll probably quit. Agh, that hurts. Then I'll have to get to Emily, somehow start over, treat each day with her as if it were my last. It could very well be. I'm sorry, Guy. Very sorry. I don't know what I'll ever do about you. Any man at all would confess and blow his brains out. But I lost my honor the minute I discovered that a small, sweet corner of my wife's heart belonged to you. Funny thing is, it still does, it always will, even though you're gone. I'll never get it back now. I should never have tried; should have been content with my ninety percent and given my wife credit for the other ten. I should have taken a cue from Dana, who once walked in on Ardith in bed with her aerobics coach. Did he reach for his hunting rifle? Call his lawyer? Of course not. He left fifty bucks on the dresser and thanked the guy for working overtime on her rear end. Why couldn't I have done something like that?*

*Because I could never have pulled it off, that's why. Not with Emily. She's not into recreational sex; she'd only sleep with a man if she thought she loved him. There's comfort in that if you're the man she's sleeping with; if you're not, the desolation is total. It's the risk you take marrying a moral woman. Maybe I should never have presumed, trusted, so much. I should have kept a little cynicism in reserve, like Dana, who had a healthy respect for human frailty. He once told me that his greatest disappointment in life was having failed Ardith. At the time, I thought he was referring to his own screwing around. In retrospect, I think he was referring to her screwing around: A good wife wouldn't do that unless her husband had somehow not made the grade. And that's where I hit the wall: Guy was proof of my own inadequacy. It was a terrible shock to realize that, far from being my wife's alpha and omega, I was just her roommate.*

*So I retaliated and now Guy's dead. But Emily still loves him. What was gained?*

=

Dagmar Pola awaited Ross with coffee and rolls at her Commonwealth Avenue apartment. It was a mild, sunny morning, perfect for sitting on the veranda and inhaling early autumn. Today Ross would be showing her a few sketches of the new gallery. As she brought silver and china to the outside table, Dagmar smiled; she was far more interested in the sketcher than in his sketches. It had been many years since a man had intrigued her like Ross. Something dark lurked there, something insulated and electric that had flashed more sharply with each meeting, tingling a responsive current. Dagmar needed to get her teeth into that voltage; some alien life-form breathed there. A kindred spirit for her final years? She hardly dared hope for such a miracle; were it not to be, the disappointment might kill her.

Ross arrived on time, but not quite in order. He looked a little rusty around the eyes and ever so slightly uncombed. Maybe it was the wind. "Good morning," Dagmar said, taking his hand. "Did you walk over?"

Had he been at the office, yes; but Ross had come directly from Marjorie's place in Cambridge. "I should have," he answered. "How are you today?"

"Very well." Dagmar brought him to her balcony. They ate under a canopy, talking about the weather and crew teams. Although Ross kept up his end of the conversation, he did so without that easy intimacy she had detected the other day. Nevertheless, she could barely take her eyes off him: Ross was also delicious cold.

He showed her the sketches he had brought, watching her face as she studied them. Once or twice, her mouth lifted into a smile. Dagmar's many pearls glimmered in the diffuse light. They were exactly the color of her hair. Ross admired her complex, wise features; Dagmar was still a very handsome woman.

Forty years ago, she must have been exquisite. Why would Joe Pola screw around when he had such a wife? Ha, who was he to ask?

"They're good," Dagmar said finally. She questioned him about several details. "Do you mind if I keep these for a while? Reconcile myself to the idea of a gallery?"

"You're having second thoughts?"

"I've been coming here every day, trying to be objective. But I finally realized that I wasn't looking at an art collection. I was reading Joseph's love letters."

Ross suddenly took her hand. "How did you survive it? Did you forgive and forget?"

"Are you joking? Never. Absolutely never."

"But affairs can happen despite everyone's best intentions."

"I'm afraid I'm not the forgiving soul that you are, Ross."

Heavy blood boiled to his face. "But Joe's dead now."

"Is he?"

Temporarily speechless as yet another pat answer was rammed back down his throat, Ross could only return to his coffee. "No, I suppose not. I'm sorry, Dagmar." He watched a boat drift beneath the Longfellow Bridge. "Take all the time you need with the sketches."

"If I sold everything, I could commission you to build me a palace." A twinkle returned to her eye. "Or another chapel."

"Dana built the chapel, not me," Ross said, eyes following the boat. If his partner were alive today, he'd be out sailing too. "I was going through Dana's papers the other day and came across his Architect of the Year program. I noticed your name on some organizing committee."

"That was quite a few years ago, wasn't it?"

"Almost ten. Were you at the banquet?"

She thought a moment. "Where was it?"

"The Darnell Building. Dana supposedly gave a funny acceptance speech."

Dagmar smiled. "I was there. You're right, it was a funny speech. Joseph laughed a lot."

"Your husband was there?"

"Not willingly. But after Dana's speech he walked right up and introduced himself. I think he and Dana saw each other regularly after that." She noticed Ross staring at her. "You didn't know?"

"I, eh—no. I didn't." He flushed again. "I was abroad at the time. Tell me something. Do you remember anything at all about the food at that banquet?"

"Good heavens, no. It was banquet food."

"Do you remember anything about a girl jumping off the balcony that night?"

"Something to that effect, yes."

"You didn't notice anything?"

"She didn't scream 'Geronimo' as she jumped, if that's what you mean. What brings this macabre subject up?"

What could he tell her? That he was second cousin to a suicide? "My secretary was reminiscing about the banquet. Funny how one room can be full of people having a great time while right under their noses, a girl jumps to her death."

After a few moments, Dagmar came to the balcony and stood with him watching the sailboats on the Charles. "I think we had salmon with asparagus," she said softly.

Abducted by the past, they watched the river and the sky. "Thanks very much for breakfast," Ross said eventually, leaving the railing. He closed his briefcase. "Take all the time you need to decide about this, Dagmar. I'll call you tomorrow in any event."

"Just checking in?"

"Something like that."

Dagmar watched him go. After the door had shut, she felt very old.

Instead of returning to his office, Ross walked a few blocks to the main library at Copley Square. He went to the media room and began fanning through microfilm files of newspapers around the time of Dana's banquet. Soon he found the articles he had been looking for. Since this had been a rather mundane suicide, involving neither lawsuits, conspiracies, nor celebrities, it re-

ceived only four inches of coverage, two inches on the first day
to report that an unidentified woman had leaped off the Darnell
Building leaving a note behind, and two inches the next day to
identify the deceased as Rita Ward, age nineteen, no foul play
suspected. A minuscule obituary a few pages hence mentioned
that the victim had been a student at the Academy of Art, that
she was survived by parents and a sister, Drusilla, and that funeral arrangements would be private.

Ross walked to the art school, a decrepit building near the
Combat Zone. Drunks vied with pigeons for the sunniest places
on its front steps, impeding the paths of students who, even for
starving artists, replumbed the concept of grunge. The school's
façade had probably not been washed since—Ross looked for
the stone—1901. Once upon a time, this building had probably
looked like a place of higher learning. Now it looked like a
halfway house for flies aspiring to be Kafkas. Ross went to the
dean's office and, after a short exchange with a secretary, was
taken to a dark office that smelled of very old dust. He introduced himself to a middle-aged study in gray and yellow sitting
behind a monolithic desk. "Ross Major, the architect?" the man
asked, shaking his hand. "What can I do for you?"

"Sorry to drop in on you like this," Ross said. "I'm interested
in a student who attended classes here about ten years ago. Her
name was Rita Ward."

"Ah, Rita. I remember her well. Very talented. Quite popular
with the boys. Lovely girl. She committed suicide, you know."

"No!"

"Just before graduation. Quite unexpected."

"Poor thing. Had she been depressed?"

The dean shrugged. "Every artist goes through a period of depression. It's part of the learning process."

"Maybe it was a man."

"As a matter of fact, she left a suicide note to that effect. But
no one ever saw her with a boyfriend. Rita was a very private
person. Only two people here really knew her. Guy Witten and
her teacher."

"Guy Witten? The caterer?" Ross croaked.

"Yes. He just died in a car accident." The dean sighed. "He was a model here for years."

Ross blinked a few times, rolling with the punch. "He knew Rita well, you said?"

"He was like a big brother to her. I doubt it was a romantic relationship. Guy had just married a beautiful actress. Didn't last, of course."

That must have been Guy's first wife; Emily would probably know all the anguished details. "Perhaps I could speak with Rita's teacher," Ross said carefully. "I'm quite interested to know more about her work."

The dean's smile plummeted. "I'm afraid her teacher would not be of much assistance. He retired the year Rita died and fell into extreme dissolution. I recently read his obituary. A very sad case indeed. His name was Dubrinsky."

A muffled bell tolled in Ross's memory. Why was everyone dead? Rising, suddenly desperate to escape this shabby man and his shabbier stories, Ross put his business card on the dean's desk. "I believe we have a sculpture of Rita's in our office. I always like to know about the provenance of company artwork."

"One of her mobiles?"

"No, a bust of my partner. Quite lifelike."

"I see. Have you ever thought about teaching architecture? We would be honored to have you on the faculty. Well. It's been a pleasure meeting you, Mr. Major."

Autumn had begun to leach all the heat out of the sun, and Ross had not worn a coat. He walked briskly toward his office, trying to stay warm. Strange things had happened at that Academy of Art, and the dean wasn't going to be filling in any holes: more trivial secrets, no doubt. He was so damn tired of them. He missed Dana terribly. He missed his wife. They were his only sounding boards; without them, ideas didn't bounce, they just rolled aimlessly around the inside of his head, too weak to hatch. And the longer they were trapped inside, the more of them were slowly eaten by viperous guilt. He had to snap out of this coma before it consumed his existence. It would have been easier twenty years ago, when he had more energy, less experience: Work would have been the answer. Now Ross didn't need the money or the ego jolt that came with building skyscrapers. He had done so many of them that the trek from drawing board to real estate was no longer miraculous; it kind of happened, like the phone bill. Ross squinted at his haggard reflection in a storefront window. Burnout had intersected midlife crisis: wonderful. Were it not for the riddle of Guy's death, he'd have nothing to get him out of bed in the morning.

Downtown Crossing thronged with office workers on their lunch breaks and teenagers on leave from the pressures of single parenthood. As Ross cut through the crowd, he began to think about Marjorie. He was a little afraid to see her, to read in her eyes that last night had not been a dream after all. His heart sank when, getting off the elevator at State Street, he saw her sitting at her desk; he had been hoping that she would take the day off, give them both a chance to contemplate their sins. She looked quite normal and calm, however, just as she did yesterday. Maybe even a little brighter than yesterday. No one in the office would ever guess that she had been heaving naked with Ross all night long. When she looked at him, his stomach turned; he wanted her all over again.

"Hi," he said softly. No one was around. "How are you?"

"Fine," she answered equally softly. After a moment she remembered today's play, today's theater, and changed to speaking voice. "Care to hear your messages?"

He watched her mouth and eyelashes as she recited them. No one important had called. There was nothing important to do this afternoon. Maybe they both could go to the lake. When Marjorie began asking him about a few faxes that had come in, he held up his hand. "Come to the office a minute."

In the hallway, they talked business. In the office, Ross sat on a chair rather than his couch, where Marjorie might sit beside him. "So," he began officiously, then dwindled to silence. She was wearing another of her short skirts, maybe to torment him. He stared at her for a long moment. "I have no idea what to say to you, Marjorie."

"What's to say? I'm a big girl. Would you do it again, now that your curiosity has been satisfied?"

Yes. Immediately. He watched her cross her long legs. "Would you?"

She didn't answer at once. "It would be suicide, Ross. Both professional and personal. You know that."

"Does that mean no?"

"I think so. I love my job. You know I love you." She let that hang in the air a wondrous moment; he would not be hearing it again. "There's no way I would be able to handle an affair with you. What do you say we quit while we're ahead?"

Ross suddenly shut his eyes. Christ! Had Emily posed the same question to Guy a few weeks ago? Of course she had! And Guy had answered incorrectly, because Emily had quit working for him. He must have said, "No, once was not enough." Took guts, that; but Guy had guts. Ross sighed, fighting an insane desire to carry Marjorie to the couch. But she had asked a question to which there was only one sane answer. So he said, "That's a good idea."

Tears welled in her eyes. "As easy as that, eh?"

"No, goddamn it! Not easy at all!" He went to the window and glowered at the millions of people out there who managed to lead uncomplicated, successful lives while everything he touched turned to shit. "I should be grateful to have had one night together with you. It was an island in a cold sea."

She came to the window and put a finger on his lips. "I know." Then she left him to his work.

Emily's flight from L.A. landed in Boston around nine in the evening. Ross was waiting for her at the gate with a dozen roses. "Hello, darling," he said, kissing her. "Case solved?"

"We're getting there." Emily sniffed the roses; Ross was either welcoming her home or feeling guilty about Marjorie. "How sweet."

Ross had made late reservations at a restaurant overlooking the Common. It was one of those places where the chefs tried to compensate for puny portions by making the food look too pretty to eat. Ross liked the decor, a busy meld of Aztec and Third Reich, and the wine list. Over a great bottle of burgundy, he listened to the details of Emily's interview with Agatha the waitress. "So you think the waitress was only the messenger?" he asked. "Another woman switched drinks at that party in New York?"

"Yes. And the same woman sent Simon a poisoned script in L.A."

Ross listened quietly to his wife's outlandish tale. It made perfect sense, as did voodoo and reincarnation, to those who believed it. "So who is this woman?" he asked finally.

"No idea."

"How are you ever going to catch her?"

"We don't know."

"I wouldn't wait for her to nail you first, Em. Maybe you and Philippa should set a trap. Grab this thing by the horns."

"What do you suggest?"

Ross thought a moment. "Get Simon to set up some kind of party like the one in New York. That wouldn't be too difficult, would it?"

"Actually, it might. Do you know that *Choke Hold* is the fourth most popular movie in the country? Philippa's the hottest ticket in town."

Ross looked out the window for several moments before finishing his wine. "I take it she's recovered from her fright in the woods, then."

"I think so. The bruises on her face are almost gone. She's ready to beat the bushes again."

"She's not afraid of this woman who's after her?"

"Philippa's not going to let some lunatic cramp her style. Especially a woman."

Their food arrived. Suddenly very quiet, Ross concentrated on cutting his exquisite food with exquisite precision. Then, in midmouthful, he asked, "What about that fan letter warning that someone was trying to kill the two of you?"

Emily had to answer this one carefully. Ross had gotten quite feisty when he first heard about Moody's note; if he learned that the man was right here in Boston, he'd saddle her with a round-the-clock bodyguard. "Oh, that was a false alarm," she said. "The note was meant for the Pointer Sisters and got sent to Philippa by mistake."

"How do you figure that?"

*Damn!* "Because the Pointer Sisters got a letter about *Choke Hold.*" Noticing Ross's frown, Emily quickly added, "The president of their fan club called the president of Philippa's fan club. They all had a good chuckle once they figured out the guy had screwed up his word-processing program."

Ross studied his wife's face, trying to understand why she would lie to him about something as serious as a death threat. For the moment, he'd back off; tonight Emily looked frazzled, slightly insane. But he'd get to the bottom of this. At least she was home, safe with him. He was going to forbid any more excursions to Los Angeles. Ross took her hand. "I'm glad you're back, darling."

"I am too." She smiled. "What have you been doing with yourself? Business as usual?"

"I went to Guy's funeral yesterday." Was that his imagination or were her fingers becoming cold?

"Was everyone there?" Emily asked.

"More or less."

"I just couldn't face it."

"I know."

Her face softened a little. "You took time off from work."

"No problem. I just stayed later that night." He took the office to bed with him, in fact. Dropping Emily's icy hand, Ross returned to his dinner. "This morning I had a meeting with Dagmar Pola."

"The Pretzel Lady?"

"Would you mind not calling her that? She's actually quite wonderful. I'd like you to meet her one of these days."

"Sure. Invite her over. I'll make lasagna. Easy on the dentures." Suddenly Emily sat upright. "By the way, you never told me that Dana had done renovations at Diavolina."

His fork paused in midair. "What are you talking about?"

"The night Philippa ate there, she said that Dana was talking with the maître d', who said they hadn't seen him at Diavolina since the renovations."

Hell! Now what mischief had happened while he was out of the office? "You got me," Ross said. Maybe Marjorie knew. The thought of her filled him with equal doses of love and regret. "Em, let's get away for a while. Forget the last month ever happened. What do you say?"

So he had finally slept with his secretary. Emily recognized the postcoital guilt all too well. Anger flared and subsided: Ross and she were even now. Nothing would be gained by forcing this game into overtime. "Ready when you are," she said.

"You decide where and for how long. Then let's do it."

Ross signaled for the check. Back home, as Emily dawdled through a world atlas, suggesting destinations, Ross dawdled a finger in her hair. It was like old times, but older. They went to bed early, clinging to each other like two half-drowned passengers who, through no cleverness of their own, had managed to survive the *Titanic*.

Early the next morning, after his usual communion with the editorials and the obituaries, Ross left for work. Emily went to the North End, where the mad fan Charles Moody had once lived. Narrow, cobbled Sheafe Street was behind the park where she and Guy had frequently watched the ships in the harbor. A battery of old Italian women, leaning over their ground-floor windowsills, observed Emily as she walked by. She was not familiar so they did not smile. Emily poised a finger above the four doorbells on Moody's apartment building. She was about to press the second bell, roust the new occupant of Moody's apartment, when she read the name next to the little black nipple: LEO CULLEN.

Emily blinked in dismay. Leo from Diavolina? After a moment's hesitation, she rang the doorbell. Futile, of course: If Leo were in town, he would be at work. But she had to do something in front of all those staring old ladies. Emily rang twice,

waited, then walked to the nearest crone. "Hello." She smiled,
to no avail.

"You are an actress."

Emily kept smiling. "I'm looking for Leo Cullen."

"Away."

"Have you lived here for a long time?" Shrug. "Do you remember someone named Charles Moody? He lived here before
Leo." Another shrug, more emphatic. Emily gave up. "Thank
you."

She went to the park. Surrounded by sailboats, a big cruise
ship floated across the harbor. Maybe the passengers were
throwing gold doubloons overboard. What the hell did Leo
have to do with Charles Moody? Taking over his apartment
couldn't be just another coincidence like Slavomir taking over
Moody's post-office box. The three of them were connected and
Emily had only one option now: return to Diavolina. Oy! Ward
again? That would be like revisiting a lion's den. Maybe she
could ask someone else. Emily looked at her watch: Klepp would
be taking his cigarette break out back in half an hour. She'd try
him.

Emily walked to the South End. Except for the meter maids
and a few floral deliveries, Tremont Street slept. Little red neon
loops still spelled *DIAVOLINA* in the restaurant's front window.
Still in business: Emily stared a moment, just an iota disappointed that they had managed to survive without her. She
stepped into the driveway and waited behind a Dumpster for
Klepp to emerge.

Precisely at ten, as was his habit, Klepp slapped open the door
and sat on the rear steps of the restaurant. When Emily heard
the click of his lighter, she peeped around the Dumpster. "Psst!
Klepp!"

His face broke into a leer. "Playing hide-and-seek today,
Major?"

He obviously wasn't going to come to her, so Emily took a
few steps closer to the landing. "How's it going?"

"Great. No one's kicked the bucket here in over a week. And
you?"

"I'm fine."

"Really? You look like hell."

"A friend of mine just died."

"Another one? I'm impressed." He pulled on his cigarette. "So what brings you back to the scene of the crime? Looking for a letter of recommendation?"

"I was wondering if Leo's turned up."

"Nope. I'm running the kitchen. It's going well. No tantrums, no prima donnas."

Maybe everyone else had quit. "How's Ward?"

"Something happened to her about a week ago. She suddenly snapped out of her funk. Quit the booze and started taking showers again. I figure she must be getting laid."

"That's nice." Enough small talk. "Has anyone named Charles Moody ever worked here?"

Klepp's eyes narrowed to slits. "Why do you ask?"

Why lie? The truth was ridiculous enough. "He wrote a bizarre fan letter to my sister. Philippa asked me to look into it. I found out that he used to live where Leo lives now."

"Must have been some fan letter," Klepp said. "Hope she doesn't want to marry him."

"Why not?"

"Because he's off limits, Major. You remember Brother Augustine, the mushroom man?"

"That's Charles Moody?"

"Was, was. They change their names when they mend their ways."

Emily remembered O'Keefe telling her that everyone who worked at Diavolina had spent time either in jail or in criminal court. "Mend what ways?"

"Can't help you there, sweetheart. Only Leo knows that. And the mushroom man himself, of course. Why don't you ask him why he's writing fan letters to bimbos instead of illuminating manuscripts like a good boy?"

"My sister's not a bimbo," Emily snapped. "Hasn't Augustine been a priest for a long time?"

"As long as I've known him. That would be about fifteen years."

"Then how do you know his name was Charles Moody?"

"Aha. You do remember our poor dead dishwasher? Every time Augustine walked in here with a basket of mushrooms or fruitcakes or whatever, Dubrinsky would start mumbling. In Russian, of course. I was the only one who understood what he was saying. It was mostly gibberish about statues and jail and Leo and some kind of fight. I think that once upon a time our little Augie beat someone to death." Klepp tossed away his exhausted cigarette. "Since it was none of my business, and I was really eavesdropping on the drunk's Russian, I never asked. Leo's a good man."

Emily watched Klepp's cigarette smolder helplessly in the dirt. "The night my sister ate here, Slavomir hit his head."

"Par for the course, Major. Besides dishes, his favorite thing to crack was his skull."

"As you were taking him to my office to lie down, he looked into the dining room and shouted something. Do you remember what that was?"

"Something like 'She's here. The devil's here.' Dubrinsky thought most women were devils."

Emily scowled. "Why would he call my sister one?"

"I have no idea, Major. My mind was on other things. You might recall we were flat out thanks to that stupid faggot getting everyone all steamed up about his special dinner." Klepp stood up. "I'd better get back to work. Give those morons five minutes alone and they'll burn the place down."

"Thanks, Klepp. Nice to see you again."

"Yo." He paused on the landing. "By the way, thanks for the job. I love being chef." He went inside.

Emily stepped on Klepp's cigarette, putting it out of its misery. She retreated to Tremont Street and began walking home, looking constantly over her shoulder for a cab. None, of course; all hacks were down in the financial district. After passing the little park where Ross learned that Ward had shot Guy Witten, Emily cut over toward Copley Square. It was that peaceful time of morning when the commuter rush was over but the stores were not yet open. No one was out but tourists and meter maids. Emily finally found a cab to Beacon Hill. Five minutes later, she was backing her car onto Joy Street.

Twenty miles west of Boston, the trees were totally bare. Frost had withered the fields. After an hour, Emily got to Hale. Two foxes darted into the brush as she bumped down the driveway to Augustine's monastery. It had turned cloudy and quite raw; as she stepped out of her car, bits of rain fell here and there, as if the heavens were taking careful aim at her and just missing. In the distance, faintly, she heard barking from the kennels. Emily opened the massive front door of the main building, rather surprised that it was unlocked, and entered the foyer. It felt even colder in here than outside; the silence was intimidating. She felt like an intruder.

Emily tiptoed to the side room where Augustine had once served her coffee. Today no one had stoked the fireplaces. "Hello?" she called at the back door. An old nun answered. "I'm looking for Brother Augustine. He's not expecting me." No? Maybe he was. "I'll wait out in the grape arbor."

After a long time, Augustine appeared at the hedge. His robe fluttered at his heels as he walked toward her. "Hello, Emily," he said, taking her cold hands, scanning her face. "I'm happy to see you."

"But not surprised."

After a moment he said, "No. Come inside. You're cold."

This time they went to a tiny side office that, once upon a time, could have been a linen closet. The walls were lined with books with gold lettering. They sat on a leather sofa that just about obliterated all walking space. Instead of coffee, Augustine offered her sherry from a decanter on the shelf. "Have you had lunch?"

"This is fine, thank you." Emily took a long sip, wondering where to begin. Augustine sat on the opposite end of the couch, waiting. "Charles Moody," she said finally.

He exhaled slowly, perhaps sighed. "Go on."

"Box two seventy-four, South Station." She finished her sherry. "Please tell me what's going on."

Augustine got up and refilled both their glasses. His hands were shaking a little. "How much do you know about your mother?"

He could have flung a bucket of ice water in her face with equal effect. "In what way," Emily whispered.

"Did your uncle ever talk about the circumstances of your birth?"

"He said our mother died shortly after we were born." She felt her heart thumping slowly, laboriously, pumping slag instead of blood. "That's all."

"You were born in this room," Augustine said. "I delivered you."

Emily leaped off the couch. "I don't believe you."

"You don't have to. It's not really important in the big picture."

"How did my mother get here?"

"Leo brought her."

"Is he my father?"

"I'm afraid I can't tell you that."

"Why not? Don't tell me that would violate the sanctity of the confessional."

"Something like that, yes."

Emily left the room and walked in large, noisy circles around the foyer. When she returned to the little room, Augustine was still on his end of the couch. She sat down again. "Just tell me whatever you can. I'd appreciate it."

"I've known Leo since we were five years old," Augustine began. "We were rough boys growing up in a rough neighborhood, spending more time at the police station than we did at home. Not surprisingly, we ended up in prison. That's where we met Slavomir Dubrinsky."

"Statutory rape. I know."

"He was an artist, she was a young model. Her parents didn't approve and successfully pressed charges." Augustine lapsed into a brief silence. "Slavomir had already had quite an eventful life.

He was a fascinating, if somewhat unstable, man. Leo and I became very attached to him. He turned the two of us around. When we got out of prison, I became a divinity student and Leo started working in a restaurant."

"What happened to Slavomir?"

"He served another five years. During this time, he learned that his young lady had married someone else. When he came out, he was a broken man." Once again, Augustine fell into a melancholy reverie. "I went away to school. Leo stayed in Boston. He fell in love with your mother."

"Did you know her?"

"Only from what Leo told me. He kept her all to himself, or tried to. I think every man in town was after her. She was studying to be an actress, as you know."

"Only too well." That's where Philippa had gotten the idea for her lunatic career.

"After I became a novitiate at this monastery, Leo and I were out of touch for almost two years. One night in the middle of winter, he turned up with your mother. She was in labor and not doing well at all. Leo was nearly dead himself. I thought at first that they had been in a car crash."

"Why didn't they go to a hospital?"

"They didn't want the police involved." Augustine would not tell her more. "The rest you know. Your mother died the next day. Leo was lucky to escape with the loss of an eye."

The sherry was finally beginning to anesthetize her. Emily ran a hand along the sturdy brown couch: some delivery table. "Why didn't Leo adopt us?"

"A convicted felon? Not possible. Your uncle Jasper came for you and your sister." Augustine poured himself another dose of sherry. "Once you two left here, Leo did not pursue you."

"And you never told him where we were?"

"To what end, Emily? So that he could torment himself? And the two of you? From what I understand, your uncle treated you both well."

Jasper had spoiled them rotten. But he had had help from a few thousand girlfriends who had hoped to win the bachelor's heart through his adoptive daughters. Philippa could not have had better, or worse, acting teachers. "Well, Leo's looking for me now. I presume he knew better than to ask you for directions."

Going to the bookshelf, the monk pulled an envelope from the missal. "I got this a few weeks ago."

"'Charles,'" Emily read, "'I must find the girls first. Leo.' What does this mean?"

"I don't know." This time the monk was telling the truth. "When I first saw you at Diavolina, I thought that Leo had found you and explained everything. But that was obviously not the case. You had ended up there totally by chance."

"What does 'first' mean? Is someone else involved in this scavenger hunt?"

Augustine shook his head. "I can't help you, Emily. It would be pure conjecture and probably mistaken at that. I can only warn and pray."

"How about point? Could you manage that?"

He smiled; she had sounded just like her mother. "I'd stay where you are. Leo's bound to find you fairly soon."

"What about Philippa? Is he going to find her before this maniac does? Someone's been trying to kill her, you know." Emily briefly told the monk about the problem Philippa had had lately keeping her dinner dates alive. "You have no idea who's doing this?"

"I couldn't say."

Damn clerics, always outsmarting you with their exactly truthful words with opposite meanings. She shouldn't be mad at him; forty years ago poor Augustine had been minding his own business when two, then four, uninvited guests had popped in at the monastery. Emily got up from her delivery table and put her empty glass on a bookshelf. "Thank you for taking care of my mother."

"Thank Leo, not me."

He walked Emily to her car. The rain wasn't falling any faster, but the drops were bigger. One hit Emily on the cheek as she said to Augustine, "If I hadn't come here, would you ever have told me?"

"I try to keep my promises."

The hell with them, and him. Emily drove back to the main road with one hand on the wheel, one hand on the mobile phone. She screwed up Philippa's number three times before finally getting a ring on the other end. The voice on the phone was so deep and groggy that Emily thought she had misdialed. "Philippa? Is that you?"

"One moment," said a man.

A lighter, although no less dopey, voice said, "Hello. Em? You're calling so early."

"Come on, it's almost ten o'clock in the morning. You should have put five miles on your treadmill by now. I have some incredible news."

"Well, so do I. Franco and I are getting married. Did you hear that? Emily!"

"You just met the man two days ago, Phil. Remember? I introduced you."

"What do you want, a thank-you note?"

"I wasn't asking for thanks. I was referring to the brief number of hours you've actually known each other."

"How long do you need? A four-year engagement, like you and Ross? And still look what happened!"

"What the hell does that mean?"

"Nothing! Just a little joke! I'm hardly awake!" Philippa's voice suddenly became fifty shades sweeter. "Darling, could you squeeze me a little fresh grapefruit juice? Don't worry, it's just my sister. Thank you so much. I love you, too." After a long moment terminated with gluey smacking noises and a door slam, Philippa said, "So what's on your mind, Em?"

"I just learned that we were born in a monastery in Hale, Massachusetts."

This news engendered a long silence. "I thought you were working on death threats, not birth certificates," Philippa replied at last.

"Aren't you excited? Doesn't this fill in a hole or something?"

"Sure, sure." According to Philippa's résumé, she had been born in an exclusive hospital on the East Side of New York, not in some medieval cloister in the middle of the woods. "I hope our father's not a priest."

"I think he's a chef. His name is Leo."

"For Christ's sake, Emily," Philippa finally exploded. "Keep this to yourself, will you?"

"I don't believe this! You mean you don't care who your father is?"

"Jasper's my father! He was a great father! I don't give a shit about someone called Leo!"

"Maybe you'd be interested in your mother, then. She and Leo turned up at the monastery in the middle of the night. A priest delivered you on a couch. She died the next day." Emily couldn't go on: end of information. "I'll know more once I find Leo," she faltered.

Philippa sighed. Although the tale contained some juicy elements of scandal, she still preferred the East Side hospital version. "Why don't you just wait until Uncle Jasper gets back from his trip? He'll tell you the whole story again. Forget this Leo character. What a terrible name. He's probably fat as a goose."

"But Uncle Jasper's not getting back for another month." Every decade or so, their adoptive father investigated a new religion. This time he was trekking across India with a few ladies who either claimed to be disciples of Hinduism or tolerated the concept of harems.

"Do what you have to do," Philippa sighed at last. Maybe Leo would take her sister's mind off of Guy Witten. "Say! *Choke Hold* is number three and still going strong!"

For the moment, Emily abandoned genealogy. "You haven't gotten any phone threats or oddball deliveries or anything?"

"Nothing. Franco's protecting me 'round the clock. Here he comes. He's balancing a tray on one hand, just like a waiter. Except he's naked. Aren't you, darling?"

Philippa was in heat. Nothing short of an atomic bomb would pry her off Franco's horn. "I'll call you later," Emily said. "Congratulations on the movie."

"Pretty amazing how things can change from one week to the next, isn't it?"

"Remember that next week," Emily said, hanging up. Then she realized she had forgotten to tell Philippa about Charles Moody. Oh well. Philippa wouldn't have been interested in more priests anyway. Besides, Augustine had simply brought them into the world, assisted with the production; another man had written the script. Why the bloody ending, though? Why didn't her mother just go to a hospital to have the twins? Or marry Leo? Her head full of desperate images, Emily drove past miles of barren fields. Then she called Diavolina.

Ward answered. Emily tried to keep her voice casual, businesslike. "This is Emily."

"Major? I'll be damned. What's the occasion?"

"I'm looking for Leo."

"What for? He's not going to hire you back."

"I just want to talk to him."

"About what? Severance pay?"

"No, nothing like that. It's personal."

"I haven't heard from him," Ward said. "But I'd be delighted to pass on your message, whatever it is."

"Just tell him I'd like to speak with him. Tell him to call me. You know my number."

"How could I forget?" Ward hung up.

Too late Emily realized that, instead of speaking with Ward, she should have intercepted Klepp on a cigarette break. Of course Ward would be suspicious of a fired employee suddenly wanting to speak with the boss. But the woman had indeed sounded cleaner, more lucid: Klepp was right, something had changed there. It wasn't a lover, though. Ward's voice hadn't gone softer. Its alcoholic haze had somehow burned off, that was all. Emily drove back to Boston, wondering why her mother would not want to survive with her children.

# 16

Guy Witten's death had disturbed Detective O'Keefe. First of all, Witten had been murdered. Second, in his gut, O'Keefe knew that it had not been a random act of violence. Third, he knew that unless he got very, very lucky, he'd never find the killer. At Witten's funeral, he had sensed that diabolical black energy in the room with the corpse and the hundred mourners: who, though? O'Keefe had talked to family, friends, ex-wives, and all had said the same thing. Guy did not have any enemies. Again and again, perhaps because Emily was so often on his mind, O'Keefe found himself thinking about Ross Major, the only suspect with half a motive. But nowadays husbands didn't murder their wives' lovers, for the simple reason that a wife was no longer considered a husband's property. There would be no honor in such an act; rather, it would be seen as a ridiculous display of petulance, like shooting the neighbor's dog for peeing in your azaleas. Besides, O'Keefe was not even sure that Ross knew about his wife's affair with Guy Witten. And he wasn't about to get Emily into trouble by asking Ross nosy, leading questions; the lady had suffered enough. Maybe he should ask Emily the questions instead. But that would be a very delicate course indeed, one to be pursued only in the event that all others failed. Before resorting to that, O'Keefe would browse around the places Guy had frequented and hope that a few shards of hatred, or love, glinted at him from the muck. When money was not involved, people rarely murdered for less.

He went to Toto's Gym, where Guy had spent a lot of time hoisting weights. At seven o'clock in the morning, the place was packed with all kinds of bodies in rigorous pursuit of either more muscles or less flab. O'Keefe found Toto, a hefty black man with a gold ball in his nose, at the juice bar watching a girl clamp her thighs around a contraption with springs. Each time her knees got within six inches of each other, the springs would sigh. Toto finally tore his eyes away and asked O'Keefe if he would like anything to drink.

"Black coffee, thanks."

Toto shook his head. "Bad for the kidneys, man."

Apparently the leather belt cinching Toto's waist to Scarlett O'Hara size was excellent for the kidneys. "Never mind, I just had a cup," O'Keefe said. "I'm investigating the death of Guy Witten, as you know. Could you tell me anything about him?"

"He was a regular from the beginning. That was about ten years ago. Came here almost every day before work. His place is right around the corner. Did his routine and left."

"Were you friends?"

"We talked about weights and hunting, stuff like that. Guy kept pretty much to himself."

O'Keefe watched a well-built fellow amble over to the girl torturing her thighs. She had started grunting with the springs, perhaps unaware of the effect on males within earshot. Seeing the fellow looming over her, the girl slowed the squeaking down to an excruciating whinge as they talked. "Did Guy try to pick up any women here?" O'Keefe asked.

"Didn't have to. They were usually all over him."

"Did you ever see one with long brown hair, nice eyes, sort of tall and quiet?"

"Sure, that was his last one. They were nuts about each other."

Ouch. "What makes you say that?" O'Keefe asked.

"I saw them together once or twice. She called him here all the time. He'd drop the weights and run to the phone like Baa-baa Black Sheep."

"When was the last time she called?"

"Oh, two, three weeks ago. It suddenly stopped. He was not a happy camper."

"Did another woman start calling then?"

"Nope. No one."

But someone had continued to call Guy at Diavolina, O'Keefe thought. And that person was the key to Guy's murder. Unfortunately, Toto couldn't help him there. "Are you acquainted with a woman named Ward?" O'Keefe asked. "She was at Guy's funeral. Claimed to be a friend of his."

"Sure, she's famous. Went from a hippo to a knockout." Toto sipped a little celery juice. "Then she went a bit overboard, but that's only my opinion."

"Did she know Guy?"

"I think so. They were here a lot together. When she's lifting weights in a little red bikini, she's hard to ignore."

If Ward were Guy's friend, O'Keefe wondered, why would she steal his chef? But that was naive: Of course people stole their friends' chefs. Everyone stole anything from anyone they could. That was why he was working an eighty-hour week. "Did Guy have any enemies?"

"No."

"Why do you think he came here?"

"To stay in shape. He was a model, you know."

"For what? Underwear?"

Toto laughed out loud. "Naked, man! Artist model!"

"Where did he do that?"

"Some art school in town."

O'Keefe remembered Emily mentioning an art school. Bah, he was losing it. When the girl with the thigh press finally moved on to another mat, he stood up. "Thanks for your help."

Toto shook his hand. "You catch that sucker and I'll give you a year's membership free."

O'Keefe smiled thinly: fat chance. He walked a few blocks to Cafe Presto and got a cup of coffee with a lemon pastry that the new chef had made. "It's not as good as Emily's pistachio twist," Lois the cashier told him as he went to pay. "Maybe you'd like a muffin instead."

"Next time," O'Keefe replied. He hadn't come here to eat. "How's everyone doing?"

"Lousy. Bert's about to quit. He and Lina don't get along. The customers are grumpy. They liked to see Emily and Guy. I don't know what's going to happen to this place." She gave him a few coins' change. "I think Emily should come back. Ever since she left, it's been downhill."

"Why don't you suggest that to her? She's not too busy these days, I hear."

"She's not at that new place anymore? Great. I'll tell her to get Ross to buy this joint. Guy would approve, I'm sure."

O'Keefe slid the change into his pocket. "I understand he was a model."

"Sure. For years. We all kidded him about it. Called him Flasher, Freezeball, things like that."

"Why'd he do it? Exhibitionism?"

Lois looked insulted. "Before he went into the food business, Guy was an art student. He modeled to help his old school out. It was sort of like donating his organs while he was still alive."

O'Keefe nodded somberly. "Where was this?"

"The Academy of Art downtown. Guy always gave the food for their graduation ceremony. He was very generous." Lois's lip began to quiver. "Who would hurt him?"

O'Keefe patted her shoulder and tried to look sorrowful. For Lois, Guy's death was a personal trauma; for O'Keefe, it was a professional insult. He took his food to a shelf and ate quickly. Lois was right; the pastry was a little dry. Waving at the cashier, he left.

After a brief walk, he was standing in the dean's office at the Academy of Art. The unrelieved seediness of the place depressed him. The dean looked as if he had started working here only after flunking out of mortician school. "What can I do for you, Detective O'Keefe?" He smiled, tapping his yellowy fingernails against the desk.

"I understand that Guy Witten had been modeling here for some time."

"Years. His death is a tragedy. We'll never replace him."

"Did you know him well?"

"I knew him since his student days. He was quite talented. But practical. He knew the artist's life was not for him."

"Did he have any problems here? Make any enemies?"

"On the contrary. Everyone was crazy about him. Ladies and men."

"Any steady girlfriends?" Desperate, O'Keefe added, "Boyfriends?"

The dean thought a moment. "No."

O'Keefe felt like heaving his chair through the dean's filthy window. His investigation was getting nowhere. Soon he'd have to concede defeat; there were just too many other corpses piling up at the morgue, screaming for attention. O'Keefe stretched his hand across the dean's desk. "I appreciate your help. Here's my card, if you think of anything later on."

The dean lay O'Keefe's card next to another one on his desk. From long habit, the detective glanced at it and nearly turned to sand. *Ross Major, Architect?* What the hell had Major been doing here? "Having some renovation work done?" O'Keefe asked casually. "Major would be the man for the job."

"I agree. Unfortunately, he was here on other business." The dean led O'Keefe to the door. "Ever been interested in art yourself?"

"Eh—I took a few anatomy courses once." That was so he'd know where to shoot to kill. "Very stimulating." O'Keefe walked, squinting, into the September sunlight.

Ross was sketching at his desk when he heard clinking and gushing at the coffee machine: Marjorie had arrived. He went to his doorway and looked down the hall. She was wearing the houndstooth suit with the short skirt today. Her hair was up in some kind of twist. She had probably daubed her neck with a few drops of that perfume that he would forever associate with her smooth white thighs. Either unaware of him or ignoring him, she stood rinsing out the coffeepot. He walked over, keeping just out of arm's reach but within sniffing distance of her perfume. "Good morning."

"Hi." Her face was very pale, her freckles almost invisible. "Working hard?"

They were doing pretty well, all things considered. A casual observer would scarcely detect the stricken undercurrents in their voices. "I have another research project for you," Ross said. "A while ago, Dana renovated a restaurant in the South End. It's called Diavolina now. It may have been called something else at the time."

"You probably mean Angelina." She filled the coffeepot with water. "That was about ten years ago."

"Where was I this time? Commuting to Jupiter?"

"I think you were doing office parks for Atkins."

That was a shyster developer who had finally gone bankrupt. His wife Janelle was famous for her mink coats dyed to match her little sports cars. "Aha. Would you mind bringing me the files? Thanks." Ross watched Marjorie's legs as she walked off. If he were never going to touch them again, the least he could do was look. Already his night with her was receding into the realm of dreams; he didn't know whether that was good or bad.

"Here you go," she said after a while, walking into his office carrying a file and two cups of coffee. "It's coming back to me now. Someone named Leo Cullen had a statue that he wanted Dana to put in the middle of his dining room. The man was extremely attached to it. Dana finally talked him into putting it behind the bar. Look, there's a picture of the place when Dana finished. The statue looks nice lit up in that alcove, doesn't it? Nothing like a naked lady under a few soft lights. The sculptor was"—she flipped a page—"Slavomir Dubrinsky."

Ross stared. "Where'd Cullen get it?" he said after a while.

Marjorie rustled through the papers. "Doesn't say. But he called it Diavolina."

Little she-devil: Ross wondered where the statue had gone. That little alcove was full of highball glasses now. "Did Dana and Cullen get along?"

"Very well. I remember Dana having a lot of fun with that job. He was at the restaurant all the time. You know what that means, of course."

Far, far back in his brain, two tiny cells that had been floating in a sea of billions of other cells suddenly collided. Ross began to feel a little ill. "I hope not," he said, slowly pushing the file aside.

Marjorie opened her appointment book and recited the day's events. Ross worked with her until the other employees arrived and the fax machines began raining acid on everyone's parades. After Marjorie returned to her desk, Ross picked up his phone. He knew Dagmar's number by heart now. "Would it be possible to get together today? Late afternoon?"

"I could meet you at Joseph's apartment," she said.

"Your apartment, you mean. Four-thirty? I won't take too much of your time."

He scraped through the day on automatic, visiting a few sites, smiling at all the right faces. Business was booming, as if Dana were still alive. On one hand, it was a relief to stay busy; on the other hand, it was a little insulting to his partner's memory. Ross spent hours trying to remember what Emily had told him about Diavolina. She had mentioned someone named Leo: wasn't he the chef who ran away? There was Ward. Ross didn't want to think about her at all. Then there was Byron, the OD'd sous-chef. There were a couple of rejects floating around the kitchen. They served weird food and were very popular with the smart set. That was all Ross remembered. If only he had listened better, asked a few more questions, while Emily was working there!

At four o'clock, he buzzed Marjorie. "I have to see Dagmar for a few minutes."

"Again? Is she trying to adopt you or something?" Hearing no answer, Marjorie sighed. "You've got the Turners coming in at five-thirty. Don't forget."

"I'll be back in an hour." Ross walked briskly through the Common. The late afternoon wind was stripping trees with increasing ease and squirrels were beginning to scrap over the acorns. At Dagmar's building, the doorman led Ross directly to the elevator; by now he knew that whenever Mrs. Pola went upstairs, Ross soon followed.

"Hi, Dagmar," Ross said, kissing her cheek. "Sorry to have disturbed you."

They went to the big room with the little love seat and those splashy pillows. No coffee today; on the table was a decanter of scotch. "Something's bothering you," Dagmar said, pouring a glass. "Tell me about it."

"It has nothing to do with work." Ross swallowed and waited for the soft, warm bloom in his gut before putting the glass down. "Would you mind if I took another look at that statue in the bedroom?"

Her eyebrows lifted ever so slightly. Maybe her white nostrils flared, as if she smelled something burning. "Of course," she replied. "You know where it is."

Ross crossed the hallway and slowly opened the door to Joe Pola's bedroom. The statue of the woman standing at the window had not moved; only the light behind it had changed. The marble seemed to glow in the crepuscular shadows. As he was circling the sculpture for the fifth time, willing it to come alive, Dagmar appeared in the doorway.

"What do you know about this?" he asked. "Anything at all?"

"No." Dagmar sat on the bed, steadying herself against a post. "I wish I did."

"It's got a sister called Diavolina. Inspiring a restaurant of the same name."

"I've eaten at Diavolina," Dagmar said. "There was no statue there."

Ross pulled the snapshot of the restaurant interior from his pocket. "Same model, same artist, or I'm blind. The pose is a little different, of course."

After a long moment, Dagmar handed the picture back. "Where did you get this?"

"My files. Dana did renovations for a man named Leo Cullen. It was his statue. The sculptor was Slavomir Dubrinsky."

"Why don't you ask Cullen about it, then?"

"He's disappeared. And Dubrinsky's dead. Did you know that he taught at the Academy of Art? Do you know anything about his pupils? Anything about his models?"

"No, I don't know a thing about him. What's the matter, Ross? I've never seen you like this."

He sat on the bed and put his face in his hands. After a long time, he said, "A pupil of Dubrinsky's committed suicide about ten years ago. I need to know about it. It's very important."

"What was her name?"

"Rita Ward."

Ross felt Dagmar stop breathing. "Wasn't that the girl who jumped off the Darnell Building?" she asked.

"Yes. It was over a man. I need to know who that was."

"Why?"

Because if it wasn't Guy Witten, then Ward had avenged herself on the wrong target. "For my own peace of mind." Ross looked out the window, toward the sailboats, aching for Dana. "Have you ever hated someone enough to kill him, Dagmar?"

"Oh yes. Very much so."

"What did you do about it?"

"Waited and hoped for an opportunity."

"Did you ever get one?"

"Several. Each time I failed."

"Your nerve failed?"

"Lord no! My plans failed." Dagmar put a hand on Ross's shoulder. "Don't ever apologize for exacting your own justice, Ross. Another opportunity will present itself."

Something inside of him collapsed: Dagmar understood, and had already forgiven him for whatever he had done. Did he dare tell her the truth? He longed to; Ross was desperate to find another Dana. "The opportunity did present itself," he began. "I'm afraid my aim was a little off. Someone got hurt rather badly." He looked in her wise eyes. "I don't know what to do about it."

She held his gaze for an electric, ecstatic moment. "I'd say aim a little better next time."

Speechless, fluttering between joy and horror, Ross looked away. Dagmar touched his elbow. "Let me look into this. Something will turn up, I'm sure."

He thanked her and left.

Giddy with strange news, Emily called Ross's office the moment she got her car into the woods beyond Brother Augustine's monastery. Should she blurt out the story of her mother and Leo now, or should she just tantalize him with a few details until she could get back to the office and tell him in person? Neither, it turned out: Marjorie picked up the phone. "Where's Ross?" Emily said curtly. Damn, this was a private line!

"He's visiting sites all afternoon. He should be back around five-thirty."

At least he had left Marjorie back at the office. Emily tried to match the secretary's starchy tone. "Just tell him I called, please."

She drove back to Boston, exiting at the expressway. Traffic was just beginning to pile up along Albany Street, where five lanes had to squeeze into two after an excruciatingly long red light. Cabs and buses, with neither mufflers nor suspensions to lose, usually led the pack racing ahead after the light turned green. Diavolina was just a few dozen potholes away. Emily cut over to Tremont Street, parking up the block. She called the restaurant, praying that Zoltan would pick up the phone. He usually did this time of day, taking reservations while the kitchen staff battled over dinner and Ward began hitting the gin reserves.

"Diavolina," he said.

"This is Emily. I have to speak with you right away. Could you get away for a few minutes? I'm parked about a block up the street."

"What is this about?"

"Leo. Please, it's very important. I won't be long."

"Just wait there," Zoltan said, hanging up. Presently he

hopped in the passenger seat of Emily's car. "I told Klepp I'm buying cigarettes."

That was good for about five minutes. "You're supposed to know everything at Diavolina. Have you heard from Leo?" Emily asked.

Zoltan's dark eyebrows wrinkled. "No. Have you?"

"Of course not! Why the hell should I? You've got to tell me what's going on here." As the maître d' stared stonily out the window, Emily continued, "I know about him and my mother. But not enough. I know that they were in some kind of trouble together." She was not getting through to Zoltan, Emily saw; he was protecting old secrets, older friendships. "I talked to Augustine this morning."

His eyes finally met hers. "What did he tell you?"

"That I wasn't born in a hospital, that my mother died, Leo's half blind, and no police were involved." Emily grabbed Zoltan's withery hand. "Did you know my mother?"

His Adam's apple skipped an inch up and down. "You look like her," he said. "Sometimes you even talk like her. I recognized you the moment you walked into Diavolina."

Emily bit her tongue, waiting: Zoltan was choosing words, one by one, from a musty, abandoned cellar. What had O'Keefe told her about the maître d'? That he had murdered his wife and not been caught? Or not murdered her and been caught? It was fairly easy to imagine Zoltan's hands twisting the life out of a woman's neck as expertly as he twisted the cork from a bottle of champagne. It was more difficult to imagine the woman who would become Zoltan's wife.

"Your mother and I were onstage together several times," he finally began. "Little parts, but she always stole the show. She had many admirers. Finally she fell in love with one."

"Who? Leo?"

"No. Someone else. For a while she was very happy. Then she became pregnant. He wouldn't marry her."

"Why not?"

"Perhaps he was already married. Leo looked after her then. She was not having an easy time, as you might imagine. In those days unmarried women were viewed quite differently than they are today. She lost work, she lost her apartment. She was frequently ill. It made Leo crazy. Late one night your mother called. She told me that Leo had gone to a club downtown and that there might be trouble. I went down immediately and saw him sitting in the shadows watching another man across the room. It was quite apparent that this was the villain who had ruined your mother."

"What did he look like?"

Zoltan shrugged disdainfully. "A typical man. He was with another woman. I sat at the bar for an hour or two, waiting to see what would happen. Finally the man left with the lady. Leo followed. Out in the street, they exchanged a few words, then a few punches. They ended up in an alley. It was a long, bloody fight. They were both quite strong."

"You didn't try to stop it?" Emily cried.

Zoltan looked haughtily, perhaps murderously, at her. "I wouldn't think of doing so. Honor was at stake."

"What about the other woman?"

Zoltan opened the window and spat. He rolled it shut and swallowed noisily. "She tried once to interrupt. The man threw her into a brick wall. Perhaps he wanted to fight as much as Leo did. After a very long time, they were both lying unconscious in their own blood. I pulled Leo away from there. He was seriously hurt. The other man looked dead." Zoltan's mouth twisted into a harsh smile. "By the time I dragged him home, your mother was in labor, quite beside herself with fright and worry. Leo somehow packed her in a car and drove away. That's the last I saw of her."

Emily watched a man up the block casually drop a candy wrapper into the wind. After a few feet it fluttered to the dirt. So her father hadn't wanted her either; somehow, she had known that for forty years. "Did the other man die?"

"There were no newspaper reports of a death."

"What happened to Leo?"

"I didn't see him for a long time. He lost an eye. He was never quite the same. Quieter."

"Did he ever talk about me or my sister?"

"Never."

Why should he? They weren't his. Neither had their mother been. At the end of the day, all he had gotten for his trouble was a glass eye. "I think he's looking for me now. Would you know why?"

"Maybe to settle an old score."

Thick air here: Emily opened her window. "What does Slavomir Dubrinsky have to do with all this?"

Zoltan's eyes widened, as if he had just sat on a thorn. "He was an artist," he said carefully.

"Don't act dumb. I know he went to prison for statutory rape and Leo met him there. Before Slavomir died, he gave me a key to a post-office box. Inside were a few sketches. At first glance, I thought they were of me."

"He recognized you too." Zoltan smiled wistfully: Emily was so clever, just like her mother. "He was commissioned to make a statue."

"By whom?"

"Your mother's lover, I would guess. She posed for Slavomir three times a week before her delicate condition became obvious."

"Where's the statue now?"

"I have no idea."

"What did it look like?"

Zoltan's eyes closed. "Her naked. It was quite beautiful. After your mother died, Slavomir made a second statue for Leo."

"A copy of the first?"

"Not quite. Slavomir called the first statue Angelina. The second he called Diavolina. Leo got that one."

"What for? A souvenir?"

"A token of gratitude. Leo has always looked after his friends." Zoltan opened the car door. "If he calls the restaurant, I'll tell him you're here." He walked quickly away.

In a daze, Emily drove home. She called the office again; Ross was still out. She poured herself a stiff scotch and lay on the couch in the atrium, watching clouds and tiny airplanes drift across the sky. It was always helpful to look upward, at limitless clear expanses, when her past threatened to pull her into bottomless muck. It didn't happen very much anymore, but when it did, she felt as impotent and ignorant as she ever did: a mother again? For years, Emily had thought about her mother every day, felt her presence, sent her daily messages; having never seen her mother dead or alive, nor having experienced the downside of maternal rule and discipline, the child in Emily believed that her mother was exactly like that beauty in the photographs on Uncle Jasper's piano, forever mysterious and feminine, immaculate. That theory had suffered heavily when Philippa had started posing for publicity photos, and Emily saw the discrepancy between actress and actual woman. She had stopped idealizing her mother and, for a number of years, became fairly angry that her mother had not had the brains to get herself married before getting herself pregnant. That anger finally ran its course as Emily realized that every adult on the face of the earth was annoyed with his or her parents for something and that in many cases, parents who had remained alive had done much more damage than those who had had the grace to exeunt during the prologue. Over the last decade, thoughts of her mother had receded to a benign, diffuse fog as Ross and then Guy had overtaken her imagination. She would have been content to leave it that way.

Until today, when Augustine had exhumed all the sleeping demons, seducing her with tales of love and gore and, most astonishingly, extant human participants. Part of her wanted to know everything. But was it wise to replace fog with a willful mother, an unwilling father, and a third wheel named Leo? So she had been born on a couch in a monastery: so what? Wasn't that her stupid mother's fault? She could have gone to a hospital and had a safe delivery. She could have married Leo, whoever the hell that was, and gotten on with her life. Why should Emily get all roiled up about a father now, why presume that after forty years a stranger's silence would suddenly blossom into love just because an illegitimate daughter showed up? Uncle Jasper had been parent enough; maybe she should be thankful for that blessing and let the other ghosts rest in peace. Pursuit of this tawdry little history treaded a fine line between curiosity and masochism, and to what end? She wasn't about to write it down in a family Bible for future generations to read. Did she hope that getting to the bottom of this story would fill in some of those psychic craters? Dream on: Life was one huge crater, dug in secret, ended at random, no matter who one's parents were.

Emily was staring at the long, plush contrail of a silver airplane, thinking of Guy, when the phone rang. Perhaps it was Ross; she needed him here, now. "Hello?"

Santa Monica police: Philippa had been shot twice at close range by an unknown assailant. She was in the operating room now, playing dead. The man told Emily that his office had booked her on a flight leaving Boston in forty-five minutes. If she missed it, there was another at six o'clock, but he didn't recommend that one. Emily slammed down the phone. Flinging clothes into a suitcase, praying for time to stand still, she gunned her car down Joy Street. The hell with the dead; they had waited for forty years. They could wait a little more.

Late in the afternoon, when Ross returned to the office from his site visits, several messages awaited him. The only ones of interest came from the shop on Newbury Street and his wife. Ross returned her call first: no answer. Couldn't have been terribly important. Maybe she was just checking in to see if he had been free for lunch. Ross decided to go home early tonight. They could spend another pleasant evening with atlases and escapist fantasies, the wilder the better; this could be the year he finally talked Emily into the Paris-Dakar road race. Ross shut his office door before calling the shop on Newbury Street. "Were you able to find anything for me?" he asked the salesman investigating the purple bikinis.

"Yes, sir. Fortunately, our recordkeeping is meticulous." Of course it was; how else could the man earn thousands of dollars on the side looking up suspect lingerie purchases? "As I told you, many customers bought that particular bikini. It was very popular with power dressers of the early eighties. Red and purple were the big sellers. Had it not been for the monogram of the pitchfork, my search might not have been successful. But I was able to contact Heddi, the woman who does all our custom embroidery. She remembered the job. The purchase was made by Rita Ward." He couldn't resist adding, "Does that name ring a bell?"

"Vaguely," Ross replied.

"She paid fifteen dollars for the monogram."

"Any particular reason for the pitchfork?"

"I asked Heddi that exact question. All she could remember was that it had to do with devils rather than farmers. By the way," the man said just as Ross was about to hang up and stagger to the liquor cabinet, "Heddi said that you're the second person who's asked about that monogram. She remembers a woman coming into the store with the bikinis a week after the purchase. Quite angry."

Ross sighed, guessing the scenario. "What happened?"

"I told her nothing," the man said.

That's because Ardith had slipped Heddi, not him, the hundred bucks. "Did the woman find out about Rita?"

"There is a remote chance that she did," the man lied.

"Does Heddi remember what she looked like?" Ross asked, just in case he was on the wrong planet.

"She says the lady wore a hat and a wedding ring with three marquise diamonds. She was rather unpleasant."

Ardith, all right; even ten years ago, she knew her marriage was a travesty. "Thank you," Ross said. "It's all becoming clear to me now." He hung up.

After a moment's paralysis, he bounded out of his chair and went across the hall to Dana's office. "Marjorie! Could you come here a second, please?"

She found him struggling with the bronze bust. "Finally chucking that thing out the window?"

"Don't make stupid jokes," he snapped, tipping it on its side. "Read me the initials on the bottom again, would you?"

"'R.W. 1983.'"

"Goddamn it! Nobody tells me anything around here!"

Marjorie closed the door. "What's going on, Ross?"

"Don't think I'm nuts," he said, pacing agitatedly in circles, "but I'm fairly sure that the girl who jumped off the Darnell Building was the same one who made this statue of Dana. Rita Ward was her name. She was the one who gave him that purple underwear. They probably met while he was doing that renovation at Diavolina. The affair really went down the tubes."

Marjorie watched him pace for a quarter mile. "So what?" she asked finally. "They're both dead."

What was he supposed to say to that? So is Guy Witten? "It's been on my mind," he rasped, walking around a few more circles. "Dana never told me about it."

"You couldn't have prevented anything."

"But that girl killed herself! For nothing!"

"Says who?"

"I don't understand! Why didn't Dana tell me? Didn't he feel bad about it?"

"Either no, he didn't, or yes, he felt so bad that he couldn't ever speak to you about it. Why should Dana confess, anyway?"

"Catharsis. Forgiveness. If he had just said something to the family," Ross said, almost talking to himself. "Apologized or something. Not left them in the dark with no idea whom the girl had killed herself over."

"Are you joking? Can you imagine Dana going to the grieving parents and saying something like 'Hi, you don't know me, but I was screwing your daughter and she couldn't handle my wife and two kids'? That's almost beyond fiction."

"If he wanted to forget about it, why save the underwear? That bust?"

"Souvenirs of the good days, I'd say."

Dana had always been very clever about props; that bronze bust had probably provided the perfect excuse for artist and model to get together three afternoons a week for months. When Dana first installed the sculpture in his office, he had explained that it was a trade for services. Ross hadn't even asked what the services had been. Now he sat on Dana's soft couch, wondering if Rita had sat there once, whispering as she stroked

Dana's hair. "Do you think it was a crime?" he said softly. "Is that why he kept his mouth shut?"

"I'm not familiar with the Massachusetts laws on fornication and adultery," Marjorie said archly. "But if unrequited love were illegal, half the world would be in prison." Rising, she put a hand on Ross's shoulder. "Let sleeping dogs lie. In Dana's case, the less we know, the better."

He watched her lovely legs waft her toward the door. After several moments alone with the cold, mute bust of Dana, Ross called Diavolina. "Ward, please," he said, then waited a long time. "I have to see you."

"Again? You're not about to start blackmailing me now, are you?"

"Don't be asinine! Where and when? Preferably in the next half hour."

"This must be an emergency. How about the waiting room at Back Bay Station?"

"Twenty minutes."

Ross methodically cleared his desk, as he did every day before going home. Then he took the subway to Back Bay and waited in the crowded Amtrak lounge, where lots of actor types with gorgeous hairdos and cheap luggage awaited the next train to New York. Ward finally swept in with the same voluminous cape she had worn to Guy's funeral. Heads turned as she cut a grand swath through the crowd. Ward had gotten her hair trimmed and curled. It looked rather cute. She had stenciled her eyes with heavy liner that imitated the flow of her cape. Smiling like a debutante, she sailed past Ross out to the sidewalk.

He followed her to a park bench across the street. "I hate the smell of old coffee," Ward remarked, pulling up her hood. "Getting a little nippy out here, isn't it? What's on your mind, Major?"

She spoke so vibrantly that he sighed; why ruin another woman? Why not let sleeping dogs lie, as Marjorie had said? For a few moments, struggling, Ross said nothing. Then he thought about Guy bleeding to death alone, in the rain. "Just a few minor points," he began. "One, you really should have stolen

Guy's wallet. Made it look more like a robbery. O'Keefe's very suspicious about that."

"O'Keefe's pissing in the wind. He doesn't have a speck of evidence."

"What did you do with the crossbow?" Ross asked.

"Threw it off the Tobin Bridge. Small consolation, all things considered."

Poor, poor Guy. He had died abandoned and betrayed, whimpering Emily's name: no consolation for that, none at all. Ross pulled a small card from his breast pocket and handed it to Ward. "Recognize this?" he asked softly.

As Ward stared at the word *Madly*, the bloom left her face. "Where'd you get it?"

"Dana's closet. My dead partner Dana. The stiff in your restaurant." As Ross saw the old, dull look fleet across Ward's eyes, pity supplanted his anger; she had been happy for such a short time. Perhaps it was fitting that, having made her happiness possible, Ross should also be the man to snatch it away. That's how it worked in love, why not in war? "Dana did a renovation at Diavolina about ten years ago. Was your sister working there then?"

"Yes. As a waitress. While she was going to art school."

"I think they were lovers."

"What? No way."

Ross shrugged; what did he know? "Dana kept a bronze bust in the corner of his office. On the bottom it says 'R.W. 1983.' Once, when I asked him where it came from, Dana told me that someone was repaying a favor. I believed him. What kind of favor are we talking about?"

Ward watched a torrent of commuters emerge from the Back Bay Station and scatter like wind-up soldiers in all directions. When they had all gone, she said, "Just before her last year, Rita got an anonymous scholarship to the Academy of Art. She never told me where it came from. Maybe she didn't know. But after that, she started sneaking around at night, disappearing in the afternoon, acting sly as a juvenile delinquent." Ward held up the little card with the one small word in its center. "What's this?"

"When I was cleaning out Dana's closet, I came across a little box from a shop on Newbury Street. Inside was that note and a pair of men's bikinis embroidered with a little pitchfork. I brought it back to the shop and made a few inquiries."

"Why?"

Because cuckoldry metamorphosed a decent man into a suspicious little varmint forever. "I wanted to know why Dana would keep such a dangerous souvenir. The statue would have been enough. It is your sister's handwriting, isn't it?" Ward didn't have to answer. "I went to the Academy of Art."

"That was incredibly stupid. O'Keefe's going to latch on to that like a heat- seeking missile."

Ross almost didn't care. "The dean told me that Guy Witten had been a model there for years and years," he continued. "He was married at the time your sister was falling apart. Did you ever consider that he was just a confidant? From what my wife tells me, he was an excellent listener."

"He listened an awful lot, then," Ward said, without conviction. "He was at her place all the time. Evidently he had a key to her apartment. The night Rita died, Guy went there and cleaned out his things."

"Like what?"

"I don't know. The landlady saw him leaving with a couple of duffel bags."

That wasn't too hard to figure out, if you knew Dana. But Ward didn't. "If I were Dana, having an affair with your sister," Ross said slowly, "I would have called Guy the minute I heard that Rita was dead. I would have known Guy was her best friend. I would have given him my key to her apartment and cried and begged for mercy and talked about the scandal my wife Ardith would have to face and maybe I would have given Guy ten thousand bucks to get my things out of Rita's apartment before the police showed up."

"And why would Guy agree to do such a thing?"

"Because he would know that Rita would have wanted it that way."

Ward's hulk had sagged deep into the park bench. "This is not good news."

"I agree. You've possibly killed an innocent bystander, not to mention your sister's one true friend."

The old fire flashed in Ward's eyes. "And I've possibly not killed Rita's one true murderer."

"That's all you can say for yourself? And you call Philippa a beast for letting Guy bleed to death out on my porch? The both of you are inhuman!" Ross spat into the gutter. "Thank God Dana's dead! Otherwise, you'd have to go out and buy a new crossbow!"

"No kidding." Ward laughed hideously. "I've been robbed."

"So has Guy! So has your sister! So have I! So has Ardith! So has half the human race!"

"Get hold of yourself, Major. People are beginning to stare."

Ross swallowed a sea of bile. "I think I'm right about this, and you know it."

"I don't understand you, mister. You sicced me on Witten. I took care of him for you. Why'd you have to tell me about Dana? Why not just let me live with my delusions?"

"Because, unlike you, I feel Guy's blood on my hands. And don't give me this Poor Deluded Ward bullshit. If Dana were alive, you'd be only too happy to knock off a second Romeo."

"Seems to me you're the only one who's come out of this ahead."

"You're dead wrong. I've lost more than you will ever know."

They both glared into the passing traffic. "May I keep the note?" Ward asked finally.

"Take it. And you can have the bust of Dana, if you like."

"I don't think so." Their conversation over, Ward burrowed into her cape as Ross pulled a pair of gloves from his pocket. "Be careful, Major. I don't want to go to jail for nothing."

"Nothing?" Ross smiled, too weary to generate even mild outrage. "Don't worry, O'Keefe won't be getting any hints from me."

Ward took Ross's arm as they meandered to the corner. She looked a little lost. "How fast did Dana die, you suppose?" she asked as they waited for the light.

He thought a moment. "About as fast as your sister did."

"Funny, that doesn't make me feel any better." Slowly disengaging from his arm, like a ship that had slipped its moorings, Ward wandered a few steps away. "Know something, Major? In your own way, you're worse than all of us."

"Probably." But he was the only one to have successfully avenged himself. The light changed and Ross walked quickly home. He needed to hold his wife, his hard-won prize; inhaling her skin might make the specters go away. That lovely woman had no idea how much murder and mayhem had transpired on her account, and he intended to keep her unaware forever. He had to, really. His life depended on it.

Ross unlocked his front door and called into the empty house. "Emily? You home, babe?" No answer, and he didn't smell dinner. He trudged inside, anxious for any sound at all. Instead of his wife, Ross found a note on the kitchen counter: *Back to L.A. Will call.* Goddamn it! What was she doing out there now? Incensed, Ross took a long walk along the river. He ate a miserable microwave dinner. Finally, pouring himself a drink, he plummeted to the couch and turned on the news, only half listening to accounts of the same old wars and hurricanes; one way or the other, he knew his taxes would end up paying for them. Then Philippa's picture came on the screen. Petrified, Ross watched as the newscaster informed him that his sister-in-law had been shot twice by an unknown assailant. He winced: must have hurt. Must have bled a lot, too. Poetic justice there; he wondered if Philippa had thought of Guy as she fell.

He called Philippa's home; answering machine, of course. What the hell was her manager's name? Simon something, one syllable beginning with *S. Surf? Stir?* Damn! For years he had automatically clicked off whenever Emily started talking about her sister. Ross began phoning hospitals in Los Angeles, dashing another inch of scotch into his glass after every few dead ends.

He finally located Philippa in Malibu. "Put me through," he growled. "I'm family."

"What's your name, please?" the receptionist asked skeptically.

"Ross Major."

"Another ex-husband?"

"No! Brother-in-law!"

"Miss Banks can't speak to you right now. She's in the recovery room."

"Fine! Leave her there! I'm looking for her sister, Mrs. Major. My wife." Ross heard the PA system summon Emily to a phone. Finally a fatigued voice answered. "How's everything out there, darling?" he croaked. "I just heard about Philippa on the news. Should I come out?"

"No, we're just sitting around. She's all sewn up now. Both bullets went right through."

"What the hell happened?"

"She was out for a drive when her car got a flat. While Franco was changing the tire on the side of the road, the woman in the turban pulled up and shot her."

Ross was impressed. "The woman from breakfast and the reception in New York?"

"Looks that way."

"Who's this Franco fellow? The chauffeur?"

"No. He doesn't even know how to drive. He's Philippa's new boyfriend."

"Aha. How'd the lady in the turban get away from him? They're not a team, are they?"

"No, she knocked him out with a crowbar before she shot Phil."

"Are you sure? He's not just pretending, is he?"

"He's got about forty stitches on the back of his head. They look pretty authentic."

Ross thought a moment. "You mean this dame knocked out the boyfriend then walked to the driver's seat, shot Philippa twice, and disappeared? In the middle of Los Angeles?"

"This didn't happen in L.A. Phil and Franco were driving

along the coast to some romantic lunch spot." Actually, they were driving somewhere to elope, but Emily let that pass. "After a while, Franco came to and flagged down a car to the hospital."

"So he never got a license plate?"

"No. He was concentrating on the flat tire. Franco thought the lady drove a white Mercedes. But Philippa was ranting about a white pickup truck when they wheeled her into the operating room."

White pickup truck? Like the one that drove through the window of Cafe Presto? "Maybe she was delirious," Ross said, feeling his heart freeze. "What else did she say?"

"Mostly nonsense. Sounded like a nightmare about a thunderstorm."

"The poor thing's incoherent. How long will you be baby-sitting?"

"That depends on Philippa."

"She's got this new boyfriend to hold her hand, doesn't she? Why should you have to stick around?"

"I've got to be here when she wakes up, Ross."

He tried another angle. "What's to prevent this dame in the turban from coming to the hospital and finishing the job?"

"The place is crawling with reporters and fans. There's a cop standing outside the door. I'm perfectly safe."

"Just be very, very careful, all right? I don't want this lunatic shooting you by mistake. Where are you staying?"

"At a hotel across the street."

"Maybe I should come out."

"And do what? Stare at Philippa's catheters?"

No, eavesdrop on Philippa's ravings. "Never mind," Ross sighed. "You've told the police everything?"

"Everything I could."

Tired of half-truths, tepid lies, and his wife's abiding secrets, Ross simply said, "I want you home again, Em." Then he went to the atrium and stared at the stars nestled in perfect silence against the night sky. Twice he fell asleep, only to be wakened by Guy's voice whimpering in the rain for Emily.

# 17

*I can just picture it now: Emily's going to be in the hospital room, holding her sister's hand, when Philippa begins moaning for Guy. Plenty of screwball screenplays to choose from: She can regurgitate that evening at Diavolina, when he first came to her table and stroked her cheek; she can whimper some more about their tryst at Cafe Presto, when that white truck slammed through the window; or she can relive that night at the cabin, when she left Guy out on my porch bleeding to death. None of it's going to make much sense to Emily unless Philippa blurts out all the details, which I doubt: Subconscious alarms will cut through her delirium, chopping up her stories, mixing in a few red herrings . . . Emily's not going to know what to think. If anything sane emerges, she'll probably wait until her sister regains her senses, then ask a question or two. Philippa will laugh and spout a plausible lie: case closed. I should be relieved. On the other hand, would it be so bad for Emily to know what Philippa's done? Taste a little treachery herself? Then she could join me in the Cuckold's Club, distaff section, spend the rest of her life wondering whether Guy knew he was seducing her sister by mistake. . . . Interesting penance, that. Almost as excruciating as mine.*

*I suppose the only thing I have to worry about is Philippa blabbing that Guy was murdered; then Emily's conscience might override sororal loyalty. What would she do, though? Call O'Keefe two weeks after the event and nail her sister for obstruction of justice, just when Philippa's miserable career is making one last stand? And what could O'Keefe do that he hasn't done already? He's already sifted through the crowd at Guy's funeral, to no avail. He's questioned all Guy's friends and gotten nowhere. He knows I was in the office with Marjorie the night Guy died. All he's going to get is fresh evidence of a hunting accident. Emily will have wasted her time.*

*Poor thing. What goes around, comes around, eh, darling? As for Philippa, mutter on: May your bushwacking tongue drive my wife back to me. I miss her so.*

⚌

Detective O'Keefe sat in a luncheonette in Dorchester, munching a heavy doughnut as he read about the attack yesterday on Philippa Banks. So someone had finally shot her: no surprise. She was one of those women whose very existence produced trouble, sort of the way a Lamborghini produced speeding tickets. Look at her effect on Dana Forbes and Byron Marlowe, both suddenly dead. And look at *Choke Hold*, the stupidest movie he'd seen in years, now number two at the box office: pollution. O'Keefe still felt foolish about having bought a ticket, but he had been in an escapist mood last weekend, needing a few hours' respite from real-life crime, where the victims didn't look at all like Philippa Banks and the perpetrators were rarely caught. The only thing he had liked about *Choke Hold* was the scene where the cop had taken Philippa swimming under a full moon, artfully combining interrogation, cavity search, and breast stroke. Maybe someday he could try that on Emily. As he sipped his third cup of coffee, O'Keefe wondered who had finally shot Philippa. A woman, the article said; no surprise there, either. A jealous wife, a shafted actress . . . the list of suspects would be miles long. And Philippa had no idea who the assailant might be? Come on. Ten to one she was sleeping with the lady's husband.

As he drove to Diavolina, O'Keefe thought about Emily. No doubt she was at her sister's bedside. That would make three trips to Los Angeles in the last two weeks: Emily was certainly keeping herself occupied since leaving the restaurant. Maybe this time she'd stay in California long enough to make her solid ass of a husband nervous. Fat chance, of course; nothing fazed Ross Major. He was one of those rare men exuding total confidence in his position and his possessions, wife included. O'Keefe itched to take him down a few hundred pegs, if not remove him completely. From Emily, anyway.

Pulling into the narrow driveway of Diavolina, the detective parked next to the Dumpster out back. Halfway up the steps to the kitchen, he paused, listened: shouting within. If noises like that came from an apartment, the neighbors would be calling 911. O'Keefe charged inside. "Good morning!"

Various combatants armed with lard and dead chickens immediately fell silent. "Why, hello, Detective," said Klepp pleasantly, displaying teeth. The effect was less a smile than the carnivorous smirk of a weasel. "May I offer you a cup of coffee?"

"No, thanks. I'm looking for Ms. Ward."

"At seven in the morning? That's rather inhuman."

"She's here, isn't she? I'd like to ask her a few questions."

Klepp tossed his service towel on the counter. "I'll see what I can do." He went to the office, returning after many minutes. "I'm afraid she's sound asleep."

"When does she normally wake up?"

"When she has to. Maybe I can help you."

The kitchen doors blew open and Ward stomped in, hot and heavy as a derailed locomotive. Her complexion looked like liverwurst. Little Os of skin peeped through ruptured seams in her pants and top. Yellow morning light iridesced the purple tattoos on her shoulders. "Whaddya want now, O'Keefe?" she barked, reeling toward the coffee machine.

The detective only stared: This was not the woman he had seen at Guy Witten's funeral. Across two butcher blocks, he could smell the scotch on Ward's breath. "I'd like to ask a few questions about Guy Witten," he said. "Maybe we could go into the dining room."

"Dining room's closed." Ward slid a cup under a boiling stream of coffee. "Ask your questions here."

"He was a friend of yours?"

"We knew each other from the gym."

"How good a friend was he?"

"We didn't fuck, if that's what you wanted to know."

Titters seeped from various corners of the kitchen. Instead of concentrating on his questions, O'Keefe found himself staring at the implements in each cook's hand, wondering what his chances of survival would be if the whole crew turned on him with their vegetable peelers and wire whisks. "How long had you known him?" he continued.

"Six, seven years."

"What did you think of him?"

The little tendons in Ward's neck emerged as she ground her jaws together. "Nothing much," she replied at last.

"No? Why'd you go to his funeral then?"

"Professional courtesy."

"I guess it was the least you could do after stealing his chef." The kitchen became ominously quiet. O'Keefe glanced over his shoulder, checking the distance between himself and Mustapha, the two-hundred-pound cook with the rolling pin.

Ward carefully drank some coffee. When she next spoke, her voice was calm. "I left my card at five restaurants. Witten's chef came here two hours later begging for the job. Ask her yourself."

Not necessary; O'Keefe knew Ward was telling the truth. "Why'd you fire her after only a week?"

"What the hell does that have to do with anything?"

"Just curious."

"Curious my ass. Your tongue's hanging down to your fly."

After the kitchen staff had quit laughing, Ward said, "Major didn't fit in here and everyone knew it."

O'Keefe accepted that. "What were you doing the night Witten died?"

"No idea. What night was that?"

"Wednesday, September twenty-first."

"Wednesdays I'm here tending bar."

"Any witnesses?"

"Yo," Klepp said, raising his hand. "Wednesday nights are always busy after the Enablers Anonymous across the street lets out."

"She was working, man," said the pastry cook with the rolling pin. "I remember because it was my friend's birthday and he got a double margarita on the house."

Knowing he was defeated, O'Keefe bowed to Ward. "Appreciate your time. I'm sure you'll let me know if anything else comes to mind."

Ward bent over the sink, as if she were about to throw up. "What about those fucking orange tassels in my dishwasher's pocket?"

"Sorry, no new leads. Did anyone else here know Guy Witten?" No answer, not even a grunt. "Thank you all, then." O'Keefe quietly closed the door and left.

Ward stood motionless until her nausea had passed. "Much obliged," she said to the crew.

"Don't mention it, ma'am," Klepp replied, hammering a few veal cutlets. "Why don't you go lie down until you feel better."

As Ward was shuffling back to her office, O'Keefe was driving across town, wondering what had happened to her. She had looked so sturdy at Guy's funeral. One week later, she was a liquescent King Kong. Gambling debts? Tax evasion? AIDS? Whatever it was, Ward had hit the dirt. Probably wasn't the first time, either; women who packed on muscles like that did so at the behest of an inner demon, and Ward's was now trying to reclaim her. That missing guy Leo who had hired her to run Diavolina, actually manage people, had to be out of his mind. But that restaurant was a nuthouse; O'Keefe wouldn't be surprised to learn that the kitchen staff had roasted Leo alive several weeks ago. They had probably been plotting to dice Emily into shish kabob when Ward had fired her in a drunken, probably jealous, pique. Why did she keep bugging O'Keefe about that sot of a dishwasher? The man had drowned with a paycheck from Diavolina in his pocket and his pants still on: Not even the homosexuals cruising the bulrushes had been tempted to lay a finger on him. Odd that Ward should keep needling O'Keefe about the matter each time she saw him. Perhaps one day, when his spare time outsized his homicide file, he'd ask her about it. O'Keefe knew he'd get nowhere asking the kitchen staff at Diavolina.

He drifted through the commuter rush to State Street and took the elevator to Ross's office. Marjorie remembered him, of course. "Detective O'Keefe," she said with a mannequin's smile, rising from her desk. "Was Ross expecting you?"

"No. I was in the neighborhood and thought I'd drop by." O'Keefe belatedly realized that this was the same line he had fed Marjorie last time he had barged in. "Is he free for a moment?"

"He's drawing." Marjorie pressed a button on her phone. "Ross? Would you have a moment to see Detective O'Keefe? He happened to be in the neighborhood again." She listened to a few imprecations then hung up. "This way, please."

As her pretty legs preceded him down the hallway, O'Keefe wondered how long he'd be able to hold out if Marjorie paraded them in front of him forty hours a week. Even after two minutes, the dichotomy between her austere business suits and those voluptuous calves just about fried his libido; which would she be like in bed, the business suit or the legs? Half in a trance, he followed her into Ross's office. "Sorry to interrupt," he said, shaking Ross's hand.

Ross gestured to his couch, where he had just been napping. He hadn't slept at all last night, waiting for a call from Emily: silence. That could only mean that either Philippa, or his marriage, had taken a sharp turn for the worse. "What can I do for you, Detective?"

"It's about Guy Witten."

"How's your investigation going?"

"We're making progress," O'Keefe lied as Marjorie went to get coffee. "I was down at the Academy of Art the other day. The dean told me that Witten had studied there."

Ross felt his hair stand on end: O'Keefe knew he had seen the dean. His heart began flooding his brain with fresh blood. "I had no idea Witten was an artist," Ross replied calmly. "Unless you call volume cooking an art form."

"Witten also modeled for the students."

"An exhibitionist, eh? I never would have guessed. Maybe my wife would be able to help you there. But she's in California at the moment."

"I read about her sister in the paper. How's she doing?"

"So-so. She's got a couple of nasty bullet holes." Ross cast an intimate look at Marjorie as she brought in two cups of coffee. His eyes lingered on her legs as she left. "They have no idea who did it. But I guess that's typical in this day and age."

"You'd be surprised what the cops already know from just a couple of bullet holes. Ballistics has become an amazing science." O'Keefe sprinkled fake sugar into his coffee. "Take the case of Guy Witten. Do you know what killed him?"

"Car crash, right?"

"Wrong. He was shot by a crossbow. The arrow went clear through him."

Ross placed his mug on the desk. "Pardon my ignorance, but didn't crossbows go out with Robin Hood?"

"Apparently not. In the right hands, they're extremely lethal weapons."

"Are there a lot of them floating around?"

"Not compared to handguns, no. They take a lot of strength to operate."

"Do you need a license to own one?"

"In some states, yes."

Ross shook his head in dismay. "How barbaric. Emily will be horrified."

O'Keefe could just imagine Ross blithely announcing the details to his wife. "When do you expect her back?"

"That depends on her sister."

"Would you mind keeping this under your hat for the moment? It's not public knowledge."

"I won't breathe a word. The poor woman's upset enough about Philippa."

The intercom on Ross's desk beeped. "Coco Pflaume's here, Ross."

"I'll be right there, Marjie." Ross looked steadily at the detective. "Is there anything else I can do for you, Detective?"

O'Keefe hesitated: Ross had not in the least risen to his bait about the art school or crossbows. Obviously the man was much more interested in putting an arrow into his secretary's quiver. "I thought you might know a little about Witten's past."

"You'd be much better off asking my wife. I hardly knew the man. I'll have her call as soon as she returns." As they walked past Dana's office, Ross said, "I was down at the Academy of Art myself this week."

"Oh?"

"Dana owned some artwork by a student there. Quite good. I was thinking of donating it back to the school. Ardith apparently has no interest in it."

O'Keefe almost laughed at his own stupidity; so much for Ross's suspicious visit to the dean. "How's Mrs. Forbes doing?"

"She's been in Europe. Coming back soon, I hear."

At the door O'Keefe threw out one more desperate line. "Nude modeling. What would you think of a grown man who did that?"

Ross smiled condescendingly. "More power to him. I'll let Emily know you're looking for her." He turned smoothly from the detective to his next client, a spoiled heiress who was constantly building houses with gold-plated bidets. "Be with you in a moment, Coco."

After O'Keefe left, Ross went to his lavatory and threw up. Christ! He'd never get out of this alive!

Marjorie knocked. "Are you all right, Ross?"

He staggered to his feet. "Must have been something I ate."

She knew better. "What did that awful man want?"

"He's just digging."

"Into Dana? And that girl?"

"Something like that."

She followed Ross to his desk. "Can I help?"

"You're sweet. But I'm afraid I've brought this all upon my-self." Ross kissed her scented hand. "Go get Coco," he whispered.

He passed the morning with more of Dana's clients and their pushy wives who had yet to comprehend that it was a century too late for their residences to upstage The Breakers. To make matters worse, a thick fog had puffed in from the ocean, corner-ing him in his office with nothing to look at but a succession of women who talked, dressed, and thought like Ardith.

When the last of them had left, Marjorie buzzed. "The tooth fairy's on line three."

He picked up. "Ross? Would you have a few moments later today?" asked Dagmar.

"How's five o'clock?"

"At my place? Good."

On the way to meet Billy Murphy, he stopped by Marjorie's desk. "Dagmar is not the tooth fairy," he said.

"Surrogate mother, then?"

Marjorie would never have dared ask such a question had she not slept with him last week. "A client with a project," he replied wearily. "And a widow."

That bought about a half dram of sympathy. Ross met Mur-phy at their favorite bar and spent a few hours discussing cur-rent Boston pharaohs and their pyramids. Buoyed on a lake of single malt scotch, he walked to Dagmar's apartment. The air was cold, the shadows already long: Death and discovery stalked him tonight. He bought a dozen roses for Dagmar to sniff if his words became too malodorous.

"Flowers. How kind," she greeted him, stepping back from the door. Her mohair suit precisely matched the red petals. Dia-monds, not pearls, sparkled in the soft light; was this an occa-sion?

Ross followed her into the large room overlooking the

Charles. "You really must throw a Fourth of July party here," he
said, dropping onto the sofa, losing himself in the pillows.
"Think of the fireworks."

"I might." Dagmar proffered a tray of shrimp sandwiches.
"You probably don't want any more scotch right away."

No condemnation there, only a tacit nod to reality and a
dash of maternal sympathy: Ross wondered how much that
would degenerate if he ever slept with her. "It's brutal trying to
keep up with the building inspector. Dana could do it much better than I."

Their eyes met for a long moment. "I've been thinking about
you, Ross."

Cripes! Another vamp? He smiled emptily, waiting for the ax
to fall.

"You asked me about the statue in Joseph's bedroom last time
you were here. Could you explain why you need to know about
Rita Ward?"

"It's not a pretty story."

"I expect not. But I would like to hear it." She lit a slim black
cigarette. "I assure you I've heard worse, darling."

The *darling* put him over the edge. Ross wanted to climb onto
her lap, cling to her neck, hear a few lullabies, confess, be forgiven. "A few weeks ago, I learned that my wife was having an
affair. I was distraught, to say the least. Destroyed is more like
it."

"It must have been the first time." Dagmar clucked. "The first
time you found out, that is. Poor man."

"My wife's a chef, I told you. The fellow in question was her
boss at Cafe Presto. I came across some pictures."

"Of what? The two of them in bed together?"

No, of Guy stroking Philippa's cheek in a crowded restaurant.
Big fucking deal. "Not quite. But almost."

"Do you love your wife?"

"I adore her." He felt hollow as a cathedral. "I'm not the con-
frontational type."

"Is she continuing to see the man, then?"

"No. The man's dead."

Dagmar deftly tapped her cigarette above a crystal ashtray. "Did you kill him?"

Smart, smart lady. She understood him perfectly. "Quite by chance, I ran into a woman who wanted Witten dead. I knew where he'd be on a certain night and told her. She killed him. So I would say the answer is yes."

"Lucky man," Dagmar murmured. "I envy you."

He stared. "You've got to be kidding. I'm in hell."

"Why? Because the man's dead or because you think you'll be caught?" When Ross didn't answer, she said, "May I ask what this has to do with the statue in Joseph's bedroom?"

"It gets rather complicated. The woman who wanted Guy dead was avenging her sister's suicide," Ross began.

"You must be talking about the sister of Rita Ward."

Young women survived on looks, old women on wit; Ross suddenly perceived that Dagmar might outlive them all. "Yes. She was under the impression that Witten had been having an affair with Rita. But after Dana died, I began clearing out his office. He had a bronze bust of himself that no one knew much about. He also had a personal gift in his closet that had not come from his wife. I did a little research and found that the gift had come from Rita. She had made the bust of Dana while she was a student at the Academy of Art. They met while he was doing renovations at Diavolina."

"So you're saying that Rita killed herself over Dana, not this Witten fellow."

"That's correct."

"And her sister took her revenge on the wrong man. My, my. Did Witten have a family?"

"No. He was probably trying to start one with my wife."

"What does she know of all this?"

"Nothing. I don't ever want her to know, either."

"You mean to say that you've forgiven her?"

"I've punished her enough." Wasn't that the purest form of forgiveness?

Dagmar delicately chewed a shrimp sandwich. "And what does Rita's sister think?"

"She's upset that she didn't have a chance to kill Dana. She's not sorry about Witten."

"But you are."

"Yes." Ross desperately needed another scotch. "Very sorry. I should have let things take their natural course. I think my wife would have come to her senses eventually."

"Dropped her lover, you mean? You're such an optimist, Ross. I used to think the way you did. Joseph never came back to me. Never."

"At least you didn't run out and murder the competition."

"If I had, I would have damn sure done it solo." Dagmar eyed him with a mother's profound calm. "What's your weak link here? Witnesses? Evidence?"

Ross swore he felt the sofa rise a few inches above the floor as he replied, "The sister shot Guy with a crossbow. He made it to his car but passed out at the wheel and crashed on the expressway. The police have identified the murder weapon."

"Any witnesses?"

Only one, presently cocooned in bandages, maybe dead. Dagmar didn't need to hear about that fizzled comedy. "Not creditable."

"Any evidence?"

"No. The killer retrieved her arrow. It apparently went right through Guy's guts."

Dagmar didn't even blink. "Is she going to break down and confess?"

"I don't know," Ross said. "I wouldn't call her altogether sane. When she's not completely drunk, she lifts weights. I don't think a gorilla would want to fight with her."

"Where is she now?"

"At Diavolina. She's the manager there."

"What's her name?"

"Drusilla Ward. No one has ever called her by anything but her last name."

"Are the police suspicious of her in any way?"

"There's a Detective O'Keefe working on the case. I don't

think he's gotten very far. The loose ends are just too loose. And the motive's preposterous."

Dagmar plucked one rose from the bouquet on the table and dabbled her nostrils with it. "So what are you worried about?"

"Absolutely everything, Dagmar. Most of all, my wife finding out."

"Finding out what? That you told an unstable woman where Witten might be on a certain night? That's hardly a crime. If anyone should feel sorry about anything, I'd say it should be your wife. None of this would have happened had she behaved herself in the first place."

"I should have just let it go. Taken my lumps like a man."

"Don't be ridiculous," Dagmar snapped. "Once they start, they never stop. Eventually you would have ended up like me. Without the art collection, perhaps. You don't know how much I admire you for having taken matters into your own hands. And the risk seems to have paid off, in case you hadn't seen the forest for the trees. You've removed the lover and retained your wife. How is she reacting to her deprivation, by the way?"

"She's been quiet as a ghost. At the moment, she's visiting her sister in California. I hope she'll return home ready to start over again."

"She's a very lucky woman. Her husband has paid her the ultimate compliment." Dagmar poured each of them an inch of scotch. "Thank you for taking me into your confidence."

Ross swallowed the sweet fire. "Normally I would have burdened Dana with it."

"And what would he have told you?"

"Exactly what you did, I hope." Ross kissed her hand. "Could I hear about you and Joe someday? I'd like to know everything."

"I'm not so sure of that."

"Try me. I'm an excellent listener."

She was about to speak when the phone rang. Dagmar went to the hallway and had a very brief conversation. When she returned, Ross saw that her cheeks were as red as the roses. "Someone else knows about this place?" he asked, not pleased.

"It was a wrong number."

Lie: That conversation had lasted two sentences too long. "Aha."

"One of Joseph's mistresses, I presume. I told her the party was over." Dagmar's diamond rings quavered as she lit a black cigarette.

"How is it that you didn't know about this place, Dagmar?" Ross asked after a moment.

She blew tersely at the ceiling. "I had an idea. A fairly good idea. But what would have been the point of sending in the bloodhounds? It wouldn't have changed a thing." Dagmar's eyes glinted behind a veil of smoke. "Men are terrible with secrets. They think that silence is a protective shield when in effect it's a dead giveaway. Women do somewhat better, but their eyes and voices eventually betray them. That woman in your office, for instance. Miss Fischer, is it? She's in love with you."

"That's ridiculous," Ross sputtered.

"Forgive me, but I'm not convinced, and I've never even seen the two of you together. I've only heard her voice when she says your name."

"She's been with me for years," Ross protested feebly.

Dagmar smiled. "You're protective of the women close to you. I'm glad to see that."

Again, fiercely, Ross missed Emily. If she were on the sidewalk beneath Dagmar's balcony, he would have leaped over the railing to be with her. All this confession and dissection had created a giant vacuum in his guts: If he didn't become a husband again soon, he would collapse. Wedlock had been his natural state for too many years. He was not cut out to be a lover to Marjorie or a confidant to Dagmar. He was only good, only content, being both to Emily. Dreadfully homesick, he said, "Would you mind if I took one more look at that statue?"

"By all means."

He crossed the hallway to Joe Pola's sanctum. Frail light from the sun drew the sculpture from the shadows. "Pretty," Ross whispered, running a finger along the cool, glowing cheeks. "It looks like my wife."

"Really? You may have it, then."

He looked over: Dagmar's voice sounded exactly like Ardith's that day she had trashed the contents of Dana's office. "That's very kind. But I couldn't."

"It means nothing to me. In fact, I'd prefer it away from here. I'm quite convinced it's a statue of Joseph's first mistress. Even now I can't look at the thing without wishing I had killed her."

Quickly crossing the room, Ross embraced her. She seemed fragile as a rose, stiff as a sequoia. "Shhh. Don't talk like that."

Withdrawing from his arms, Dagmar said, "Thank you so much for coming today. No one's given me flowers in years."

"I've upset you."

"No. You've given me a lot to think about. I have to go out of town for a few days. Let's get together when I return. Bring your wife along. I'm very interested in meeting the object of your affection."

"Sounds good," Ross lied. "Where are you going?"

"New York. Estate business." As she straightened his collar, Dagmar said, "You're a brave man, Ross. Really." Her eyes glittered as she closed the door.

After news of Philippa's shooting became tabloid grist of the week, Choke Hold surged to the top of the box-office charts. Crowds camped out on the hospital lawn beneath her window, whence Aidan Jackson delivered hourly bulletins on the victim's condition. Enough flowers for fifty funerals arrived. As videos of Philippa's films became scarce as great screenplays, theaters across the country began planning retrospectives. Simon's office received more inquiries in one day than it had in the last year. Unfortunately, lying in a stupor, the star was in no condition to enjoy this midlife rush of popularity.

Emily's appearance at the hospital had nearly sent Simon back to his bed at the Enema Capital of the Universe. "Who are you? What kind of joke is this?" he had shouted when she had taken off her scarf and sunglasses. "Police! Get this woman out of here!"

"I'm Philippa's sister, Emily," she had said, going to the bedside. "Who are you?"

"Her manager, Simon! She never told me about a sister!"

"You've talked to me on the phone on several occasions," Emily reminded him.

"That was with her baby sister!"

"I'm eight minutes younger." Emily took Philippa's hand. It felt dead. "How's she doing?"

Simon slumped into a chair, overwhelmed with double vision. "She's barely making it."

"How's Franco?"

"Fine. That dipshit could wait tables tonight if he wanted to."

"Have the police found anything?"

"No." Simon looked more closely at Emily. "You're Phil's sister who lives in Boston? Now I see why she never introduced us."

Emily lay her cheek on Philippa's hand. "Has she talked to you?"

"No. She's been out cold." Simon's mobile phone rang. "Yes? Hi Marv. You do, eh? Send it over. I'll take a look maybe next week. No, that's the soonest I can get to it. There are hundreds ahead of you in line, believe me." He hung up. "Christ, Phil had better snap out of this. I've got enough work to keep her going until the next century." He sank into a chair. "Why'd she have to get shot in the gut? Why not a little nick in the arm or something? Crap! By the time she's back on her feet, she'll look like Norman Bates's mother! Did you ever take any acting lessons, Emma? Maybe talent runs in the family. Obviously looks do."

"Why don't you go home and rest," Emily said. "I understand you've been under the weather lately."

He paused, confused; that voice, that inflection: stress was playing tricks on his hearing. "I'll be back tomorrow," Simon said. "I think I need a good night's sleep."

After he had left, a nurse came to check Philippa's vital signs. Eventually a doctor appeared and reviewed the gory details. Philippa had been shot twice at close range with a .40-caliber pistol. Miraculously avoiding serious organs, both bullets had plowed through her side, exiting cleanly into the car seat; had they exploded into any bones on the way in or out, Philippa might have gone to the morgue instead of the hospital. But she had barely survived the loss of so much blood; sheer willpower, it seemed, had kept her heart beating those last few miles in the ambulance.

Since Philippa's grip on life was still precarious, Emily was allowed to stay with her at the hospital. The first night was bad. Philippa groaned terribly, then lay so still that Emily thought she had stopped breathing. The second day was the same, but with little snorts and starts: Philippa's body was adjusting to two ragged tunnels. As she lay comatose, invaded by dribbling tubes, Simon visited, saying little but staring a lot. Philippa's third husband, George, who still received generous alimony payments, checked in on his golden goose. Franco dropped by with a fresh head bandage and a photographer, to act stunned. Ross called every few hours, asking if Emily would like him to come out. No point, she replied, so he sent books instead. To pass the time, Aidan Jackson pumped Emily for intimate family memoirs for transmission to the fan club. He spent hours cataloguing Philippa's get-well cards. The police, getting nowhere with their investigation, requested that they be notified the moment Philippa opened her eyes.

"Fucking wig," Philippa snarled on the second night.

Emily went to the bed. "It's Em," she whispered. "Can you hear me, honey?"

Philippa lay absolutely still, as if she had just been disconnected from a power source. She lay that way for another fifteen minutes, then tossed her head. "The white truck! Watch out!"

That white truck again: Philippa had been raving about it when they lugged her into the operating room. The police had been tracking down every white truck in Los Angeles despite Franco's assertions that their attacker drove a white Mercedes. "Phil," Emily whispered. "Don't worry. You're all right."

Philippa dropped off again, this time until daybreak. Then she said, very calmly, as if conversing with a maiden aunt, "Oh dear. Rare steak gives me such hemorrhoids."

What could possibly be running through Philippa's mind? Unable to sleep, Emily began making notes of her sister's strange utterances. When Philippa recovered, they could amuse themselves trying to figure out what she had meant.

"I'm not a plum," Philippa snapped. "Don't call me that."

Emily's pen wobbled as she wrote the words in her date book. Someone had called Philippa a plum? That was what Guy used to call Emily. As she waited for her sister's next outburst, Emily glanced over the thirty little squares on the page in front of her: This had been the worst September of her life. Guy had been dead for nine squares. Soon it would be ninety, nine hundred. . . . Those squares would accumulate forever. She still couldn't comprehend that infinity. Emily looked for less empty squares. Oy, Ross's brother had turned fifty-three last Tuesday. Perhaps Ross had remembered to call. Her great-aunt would be eighty-nine on the thirtieth; Ross would be forty-five next week. What would she do for his birthday? Just a month ago, Emily and Dana had been discussing a surprise party on his boat; obviously that was out of the question now. Poor Ross. Poor Dana. How long had he been dead already? Emily counted: twenty squares and rising.

From long habit, she looked for the little dot on the date marking her last period. Reeling between murders and masquerades, she hadn't paid much attention to her body this month. Hmm, no dot in September. Emily turned back to . . . Wednesday, August 16; over five weeks ago. All this zipping between time zones must have discombobulated her cycle. And yet . . . Emily ran her finger down the Wednesday column, stopping two weeks after that little dot. What had she been doing the thirtieth of August? Nothing. It was just another Wednesday. Had she slept with Ross? Hadn't he been in Dayton that week? Of course he had . . . that was how she had been able to sleep one blissful night with Guy. That had been September 2. Past her prime time, as the doctors had been telling her for years. Her eggs only lasted minutes. Last month's ovum would have already degenerated into a corpus luteum by the time Guy's sperm had begun whipping down the pike. Yes?

Simon turned up around nine o'clock with a snail pizza, one

of the most popular take-out items from Luco's. "How's the patient today?"

"She talks in her sleep. The nurse tells me that's a sign of recovery."

"Great! How long before she's back on her feet?"

"No one knows."

Simon frowned. He had just breakfasted with a heavy producer who wanted Philippa to star in a vampire movie. The current leading lady, a manic depressive, had just been fired and shooting was to begin in mid-October. The producer suggested that they do the blood-sucking scenes first; that way all Philippa would have to do was lie down and writhe. When she felt better, they could shoot the more active things like Victorian swimming parties. Breathless at the offer, Simon had 99 percent accepted; every actress in Hollywood had been gunning for that role. All he had to do now was snap Philippa out of this aggravating coma.

"This morning I landed her the gig of a lifetime," Simon said. "But she's got to be on her feet in two weeks."

"I wouldn't count on it."

Simon lifted the window a crack, waved to Philippa's fans picnicking on the lawn, and lit a cigarette. "Listen, Emma, I've been thinking. Have you ever wanted to be an actress? See your name up in lights? Get hundreds of letters from people who adore you? Put an Oscar in your trophy case?"

"Not particularly."

Shit. Simon blew a ragged trail of smoke out the window. "But you must be terribly proud of your sister. She's worked very hard to get where she is."

"I appreciate that."

"It would be such a shame, so goddamn—*unfair*—for her career to suffer just because some lunatic shot her. You wouldn't want that, would you? Not if you could prevent it?"

"You want me to pretend I'm Philippa, don't you."

Simon threw the cigarette out the window. "I could have an acting coach here in one hour. In a week, you'd be as good an actress as your sister. I feel that in my bones."

"And how do you think Philippa would feel in her bones?"

"She'd be thrilled and grateful, darling. And you'd have the time of your life." Taking Emily by the shoulders, Simon turned her slowly around, studying her body. "A little work on the hair and you'd be the spitting image of the star of *Choke Hold*. In my opinion, there could be no greater act of sisterly love."

Philippa struggled with her sheets. "Damn you, I'm not your plum."

Simon looked tetchily over. "What is she raving about now? Who's a plum?"

Again Emily's thoughts suspended over a canyon named Guy. After a moment she said, "She'll tell us when she wakes up."

"She's got a little more color today," Simon observed. "I predict she'll be out of here by the weekend. That woman's got the constitution of a horse. Wish I were built half as well. That last siege at the hospital nearly killed me."

"Whatever happened to Mr. Vitzkewicz, by the way?"

"Who the fuck knows? I find him, I'll sue him." Simon looked at his watch and squeaked. "Places to go, people to see, Emma. Think about what I said." At the door, he paused. "Remember, opportunity knocks but once. You can split the proceeds with your sister."

After he left, the policeman investigating the case came by to see if Philippa were in a talkative mood. No new suspects had been found, although nine people had now turned themselves in, volunteering to have been violent criminals. When Franco and his photographer appeared for another bedside tableau, Emily went for a walk. Deprived of sleep, her body was beginning to run in a fuzzy overdrive; events seemed to register in slow motion and the gap between thought and action had widened to several seconds. Passing a pharmacy, she floated in and bought a pregnancy testing kit. It was right next to the ovulation kits she had been buying to no avail for years. She returned to her hotel and took a long, hot shower before running the old experiment with urine, tiny vials, and second hands on watches.

God! Pink: pregnant. Guy was not dead after all. New blood,

wonderful strength, immediately began to warm her veins. The life force, perhaps? Emily called her husband's office. "Hi, Marjorie. Is Ross in?"

He came on the line. "How's everything, darling?"

"Great. Would you be able to come out here? I have so much to tell you."

Communicating again? That gave him hope, like the first crocuses in spring. "How's Philippa?"

"Talking in her sleep. The doctor says she's working things out."

"Have the police made any progress?"

"No. They're looking through the computer records for owners of forty-caliber pistols."

"They're somewhat unusual. That should help." Dana had been the proud owner of a .40-caliber Smith & Wesson, which he had bought through a friend on the police force. The pistol had more knockdown power than a .357 but wouldn't obliterate the target like a .45. Dana had kept it on his boat, supposedly to shoot predatory fish. "Any other news?"

"I got an offer from Philippa's manager this morning. He wants me to act in her next film."

"You'd do that?"

Not anymore. Still, just to keep her husband on his toes, Emily said, "It sounds like fun."

After a small silence, Ross said, "What the hell, if it amuses you, go ahead. I'll catch the next plane out."

"Really?"

"I've just been waiting for the invitation, sweetheart."

Inert as a slug, Ward remained in her office for several days following Detective O'Keefe's visit to Diavolina. One afternoon Klepp walked in with a lunch tray, as if he were a nurse and Ward a patient in a mental institution. "Someone on the phone for you, ma'am."

"Whoozit?"

"She doesn't want to leave her name. Says it's important." He waited a few moments; Ward didn't budge. "Go ahead, talk to her. You could use a little diversion."

Grunting, Ward lifted the receiver. "Yez?"

"This is Dagmar Pola. I'd like to speak with you. Could we meet at your restaurant?"

"Whad you want?"

"I'd like to give you a red satin shoe, size seven, with a little black bow."

"Son of a bitch!"

"I believe I can help you."

Another good Samaritan? Like hell. "Bring me that shoe." Ward hung up. "Fuckin' termites are coming outta the woodwork."

"You've got to be ready for them, ma'am. It's the secret of survival."

"Whatr you, my mother?"

"Your friend," Klepp replied, opening a window. "Go and freshen up. You want to present a solid first impression, even to termites."

"Wha for?"

"Because you never know when the tables might turn again."

Cursing, Ward dragged downstairs to the shower. She put on a gigantic T-shirt and white chef's overalls. She combed her hair for the first time in a week. Returning to the kitchen, she invigorated her system with a megaload of coffee and mashed potatoes. Meanwhile, Klepp straightened up her office. When he showed Dagmar in, Ward almost looked as if she were in charge of the place again. As the two women surveyed each other's overlays of pearl and muscle, Klepp retreated, feeling that he had just introduced a small, smoking fuse to a ton of dynamite.

Dagmar took a red shoe from her handbag and laid it on Ward's desk. "I've been wanting to speak with you for a long time," she said.

Ward stared, shocked, at her sister Rita's missing shoe. "Where'd you get this?"

"Ten years ago, I attended an architect's dinner in honor of Dana Forbes. It was a long evening with many boring speeches.

After the third or fourth, I stepped out to the balcony for some fresh air. It had been decorated for the occasion with trees and trellises. From the fortieth floor, one had a magnificent view of the harbor. I was quite alone behind a trellis, watching the ships, when I heard two women's voices. Both were unaware of me. Once I overheard the nature of their discussion, I thought it best to remain out of sight."

Ward touched the place on Rita's shoe where her big toenail had begun to fray the satin. "I'm listening."

"They were discussing Dana Forbes. The woman objected to your sister's affair with him, for obvious reasons. Forbes was her husband. He had invited your sister to the dinner and she had come out to the balcony expecting to see him, not his wife. Apparently the woman had intercepted some correspondence as well as some silk underwear that your sister had given to him. Worse, your sister had recently written a suicide note, which Mrs. Forbes read aloud to her."

"What did it say?"

"That she was three months and five days pregnant and that Dana would lose them both if he didn't make up his mind soon." Dagmar knew those items had not made the newspapers. "I hope you believe me now."

As if in a trance, Ward slipped a hand inside her sister's shoe and held it to her cheek. "Then what?"

"Mrs. Forbes said that her husband would never leave his family for a whore. Furthermore, she had promised him a new boat if he ended the affair. When your sister said that Dana would certainly choose her over a boat, Mrs. Forbes produced what must have been a sales contract. The effect was devastating. She told your sister that she was out of her league and suggested jumping off the balcony."

"That must have been when you crashed through the trellises and tried to prevent anything rash from happening."

"No, I'm sorry to say, the indelicacy of the situation had paralyzed me. And, to tell the truth, I didn't believe that anything more serious than a few verbal insults might occur."

"Guess you were wrong."

"Terribly so. Your sister told Mrs. Forbes and her husband to go to hell. Mrs. Forbes laughed, then I heard nothing more. I waited for what seemed an eternity, then looked out. There was nothing on the balcony but that red shoe. I took it and went back inside."

"Why'd you take the shoe?"

"Because I thought your sister, in making a grand exit, had somehow lost it. It's a rather casual design and could easily have slipped off her foot. I had no idea that anyone had jumped from the balcony until I saw the ambulances in the street later that evening."

"You never went to the police?" Ward delicately replaced Rita's shoe on her desk. "I should ram this down your throat."

"Don't be ridiculous." Dagmar lit a black cigarette. "What would have been the use of telling the police this sordid tale? Mrs. Forbes would have been subjected to even further humiliation and scandal. She acted cruelly, but predictably."

"Cruel isn't the word. She incited Rita to jump."

"I would have to agree with you."

Ward went to the window. When she turned, her eyes were wide, white, and quite flat. "Why are you telling me this now?"

"Since the death of Dana Forbes, this matter has been increasingly on my mind. I do not believe that Mrs. Forbes properly regrets what she has done. She has taken not one life, but two."

"Make that three. I punished someone by mistake."

Dagmar barely raised an eyebrow. "Do you believe in vengeance?"

"A little less than I did a week ago." Ward chuckled. "I take it you've got something on your mind besides the return of missing property."

"Listen to me," Dagmar said, going to the window. "I want you to cater a reception at my home on Commonwealth Avenue next week. I live on the tenth floor. Mrs. Forbes will be there."

"You know her?"

"Not well. Our husbands were involved in business together. I will arrange that you meet her alone, perhaps on a balcony. You can ask her yourself about the details of your sister's suicide."

"Then what?"

Dagmar shrugged. "She weighs one hundred ten pounds. You could probably lift her with one hand."

"And toss her overboard? I'd be behind bars ten minutes later."

"Absolutely not. Mrs. Forbes has compelling reasons to commit suicide. Grief at her husband's death. Humiliation at his hundreds of affairs. She's been taking medication for clinical depression for years."

"Sorry, that's not enough."

Realizing that she would have to move all her eggs into one basket, Dagmar said, "She shot Philippa Banks in California last week. Mrs. Forbes was insanely jealous of her husband's last affair. The police will find her very soon."

After a moment's stupor, Ward burst out laughing. "You take the cake, madam. What's your stake in this?"

Dagmar extinguished her cigarette and looked Ward in the eye. "Everything."

Ward recognized a more cunning, more bitter, soul mate. "I'll think about it."

After a brief culinary discussion, the women walked through the dining room to the front door. "I've eaten here before," Dagmar said. "Didn't there used to be a statue behind the bar?"

"The owner took it down."

"Leo is his name, I believe. I knew him long ago. How's he doing?"

"Beats me. He's been out of town for three weeks. I'm beginning to think he's dead."

"What a morbid thought. If he returns by next Tuesday, make sure he comes to my party. I'd be delighted to see him again." Dagmar shook Ward's hand. "Take care of yourself." She left.

Ward walked back to the bar, where Zoltan stood polishing glasses. "Give me a hit of club soda, would you, dear," she asked lightly. "I'm back in training."

He placed the drink in front of her. "Who was that woman?"

"Some old tarantula who wants us to cater a party next week."

"What did you tell her?"

"Yes, of course. I'm going to charge her a fortune. Want to tend bar?"

"I believe I should remain here. But thank you for asking." When Ward had retreated to her office, there to lift weights with frightening vigor, Zoltan phoned Emily. Since she was in California, he got her machine. "Call Zoltan," he said, and hung up.

Philippa had been raving again when Ross arrived at the hospital in Los Angeles. He found Emily trying to initiate a conversation with her slumbrous sister, with no success: Philippa seemed to be shaking her head, almost physically evading Emily's questions about a white truck. Going to the bed, Ross embraced his wife, inhaled her. She looked well. Terrific, in fact. He doubted she had missed him, let alone thought about him, at all. "Hi darling," he whispered. "How's everything?"

"Much better. I think she's getting over the hump." Emily brought Ross up to speed on Philippa's condition. "She's pretty heavily sedated but I think she knows what's going on. She just doesn't have the strength to open her eyes yet."

"Maybe tomorrow," Ross said. "You've been sleeping here?"

"More or less. Phil's been blurting out the strangest things in the middle of the night. She keeps talking about a white truck, a wig, and steaks." And plums. "It's odd."

"I'm sure she'll be able to explain everything once she's feeling better." Ross glanced at Philippa's face: Was she really floating in some nether world or was she just feigning sleep, listening, preparing a new set of fables to explain the last? He couldn't tell; Philippa was an actress, after all. "Have you eaten, sweetheart? Can I bring you some dinner?"

"No, let's go out. She'll be all right for a few hours."

They went to the hotel restaurant across the street. Ross would have preferred room service and torrid sex, but after fifteen years had learned that his wife rarely performed fellatio on an empty stomach. As they wended to their table, he noticed people staring at Emily: She was beginning to walk a little like Philippa now. If her clothes and hair were just a little bit different, people would begin calling him Mr. Banks. Shuddering, Ross slid next to her on a banquette and ordered their customary round of martinis.

"Not for me," Emily said. She didn't want any wine, either. Carrot juice would do.

Ross tried to smile. "You're becoming a real Californian."

To his surprise, Emily kissed him. "I have so much to tell you, Ross. You won't believe it."

"Let me guess. You've agreed to star in Philippa's next picture. Naked."

"No! Those days are over." She kissed him again. Emily looked so happy; was he finally going to get some good news? "We're pregnant, darling."

Words, thought, fled. Ross slowly apprehended what his wife had just said: They were together again, for life. "You're right," he whispered, voice breaking, "I don't believe it."

"I just found out today. Ross, I'm so excited I can hardly sit down."

He swallowed his martini whole. The two of them kissed each other like two mooning adolescents. "Are you sure?"

"I've done the test three times already. But we can go upstairs and run it again if you want to see for yourself."

"No, no. That's incredible, Emily. I'm flabbergasted. I'm thrilled. I—" he ran out of words. "Thank you so much."

"That's not all the news." Emily paused until the waiter had taken their order and left. "The afternoon I left Boston, I learned a few things about my past. Phil and I were born in a monastery."

Ross's brain stalled once again. "What? Where'd you hear this?"

"The monk who delivered us told me. I know it sounds crazy, Ross, but it's true. Mother's friend took her to the monastery. He was an old friend of Brother Augustine."

"Who's Augustine? Who's the friend? How'd you come in contact with him? I'm totally confused. Please start at the beginning."

"I learned all of this from Klepp at Diavolina," Emily began.

Christ! Why did that restaurant keep resurfacing like a dead fish? Ross's head began to throb ever so slightly. "He called you?" he asked politely.

"No. I visited him. Remember that weird fan mail that Philippa had been getting lately? I tracked it down to a postbox at South Station. From there I got an address in the North End. The name next to the doorbell said Leo Cullen. That's the missing chef at Diavolina. So I visited Klepp and asked if he knew anything about Charles Moody. That was the name on all the fan mail. He told me that Charles Moody was actually Brother Augustine, the monk who delivered mushrooms to the restaurant on Mondays and Thursdays. Follow me?"

"Perfectly," Ross lied.

"I drove out to the monastery in Hale."

Hale hell: The pounding in Ross's temples cranked up a notch. "Sounds familiar."

"It should, I guess. Dana had built a chapel there several years ago. Anyway, I had a little chat with Brother Augustine. He told me that Leo and my mother had turned up one night, both half dead. She was in labor and Leo had just been in a fight."

"With whom?"

"My father, it seems. Augustine delivered us. Mother died the next day. Uncle Jasper came and took us to New York. Leo went back to Boston. He never got in touch with us after that. But he's looking for us now."

Ross passed a hand over his temple, as if to prevent his reason from vaporizing. "Why?"

"He thought we were in danger. He was right, as it turned out. Philippa got shot."

"How'd he know?"

"That's a mystery. When Leo finds us, he can explain everything."

"Have you told the police?"

"No. I'm sure Leo would have told them himself if he thought it would have helped. And I think I've caused Ward enough trouble with the police already. The last thing she needs is another investigation at her restaurant. I wanted to wait until Uncle Jasper got back from India before making a big deal of this."

"But this Leo fellow might know who tried to kill your sister."

"If he does, he'll eventually show up and they'll find her."

Ross shakily kissed his pregnant wife's hand. "That's quite a story, darling."

"It doesn't end there. After I got done at the monastery, I drove back and saw Zoltan, the maître d' at Diavolina. He knew Leo well. He also knew my mother. They were both actors. Zoltan said that she had an affair with a man who abandoned her once she became pregnant. Leo and he had that fight that nearly killed them both."

"You're making this up, Emily."

"No I'm not! Do you want to hear the rest of it or not?"

"Of course I do."

"Zoltan wasn't the only person at Diavolina involved in this. There was the drunken dishwasher Slavomir Dubrinsky. About five days after I started working there, he drowned in the Fenway. Zoltan tells me that Slavomir recognized me the minute I walked into the kitchen."

For a second Ross's system shut down. "What was his name?"

"Slavomir Dubrinsky. He was a sculptor before he was a dishwasher. Leo and he had been in prison together. When Slavomir got out, my father commissioned him to make a statue of Mother. After she died, Slavomir made another one for Leo. I'd really be interested in seeing that someday."

Ross shut his eyes; the table had just levitated an inch from the floor. "What was your father's name?"

"Augustine won't tell. Zoltan doesn't know. Slavomir's dead and Leo's gone." Emily shrugged. "What does it matter? He didn't want me anyway."

Ross sat lifeless as the sculpture in Joe Pola's bedroom. Then, slowly as a wounded animal, he placed a hand over Emily's. "Forgive me, sweetheart. All this news at once is just overwhelming."

# 18

*I must see Dagmar or I'll lose my mind. Is that statue in Joe's bedroom really of Emily's mother? Yes, of course it is. I should have figured that out the moment I saw it: same nose, mouth, breasts. . . . Paranoid little cuckold that I am, I thought the statue was of Emily. I even thought that she had been one of Joe's mistresses. Fool!*

*The story confuses me. Like all tales of adultery, it's a dark confection, devil's food. Joe gets Emily's mother pregnant and bails out, but not before capturing her in marble. Leo tracks Joe down and they nearly beat each other to death. Why were the twins born in a monastery, for God's sake? Was the mother trying to hide them from someone? She might have survived had she delivered them in a hospital. And what's this about Brother Augustine writing letters to Philippa, signing them Charles Moody? He must know so much more than he's letting on; priests always do. Then Joe builds that chapel for him: either a bribe or a payoff.*

*Poor Dagmar. I keep seeing her hard eyes as she says she's barely able to look at that statue without wishing she had killed the woman. Just wait until she hears that my wife is Joe's illegitimate daughter! Wait a moment: Does she know that already? Does she know everything? Is she drawing me into some sort of trap? Dagmar is so cunning, so much smarter than I. Why invite me to that apartment, lead me to that statue in the bedroom? She didn't bat an eyelash when I confessed about Guy Witten. And her advice was ruthless:* Take better aim next time. *God, I must think about this some more. I've known her for such a short time. Why did Dagmar pick me to build a gallery for her? There are plenty of other architects in town. Our friendship grew so fast, almost like a cancer. Wasn't she the one calling me most of the time? And I was desperate to talk to someone. Now I've handed her my balls on a silver platter. I wonder what she's going to do with them.*

*Odd that her first request was to meet Emily. The object of my affection, she called her. Well, that's not going to happen until I get to the bottom of this mess; there are too many bodies, dead and alive, floating in this river. I don't completely believe anybody's story anymore. Ever since Guy Witten, I've been unbalanced, suspicious of every other name in the phone book. Perhaps Dagmar's ignorant of this whole affair; Joe may have been just a few points smarter than his wife. And perhaps not. If only Dana were here to tell me what Joe was really like! But he's gone, Joe's gone, and I'm not taking any chances with Dagmar. Emily is expecting a child. We're going to start over again and make up for lost time. There's a killer loose out there. Should I tell my wife about Joe Pola? I don't think so; not yet. I'll let her digest the first gush of surprises before hitting her with her father's identity. She's got enough on her mind with her sister and our baby.*

*Where, who, the hell is Leo?*

—

Eventually Philippa opened her eyes and saw Emily over by the window reading a magazine. The *Wall Street Journal* hid whoever was seated in the other chair. Bouquets crammed the room, not quite camouflaging an aroma of disinfectant and instant chicken gravy. Philippa turned her head, saw IV tubes, and realized that she had been involved in something a little more drastic than a nose job. "Say Em," she said. "Would you mind bringing over a mirror?"

Her sister rushed to the bed. "You're awake! How do you feel, honey?"

"Like shit." The man behind the newspaper turned out to be Ross. "Where am I?"

"In Malibu. You've been shot. Do you remember?"

Philippa closed her eyes. "How bad?"

"You've got three belly buttons. You'll be all right."

"How's my face?"

"Looks great. Really. Your bruises have all gone away."

"Where's Simon?"

"He comes by twice a day, praying for you to wake up. You're a very hot ticket now."

"How's *Choke Hold?*"

"It's number one. That's worth waking up for, isn't it?"

"Definitely." Philippa smiled, aware that she had nearly died; Ross would never have come to her bedside otherwise. "How long have I been out?"

"Three days."

The policeman on the case walked in. "Up and about, I see? My name is Detective Hobson."

Philippa appraised the attractive man at her bedside. "So who shot me, darling?"

"We were hoping you could tell us that."

"You don't know? Son of a bitch!"

"Easy, Phil," Emily said, patting her hand. "There weren't many clues besides bullets."

"Could you describe the shooting, Miss Banks?" the policeman asked. "Any detail would be helpful."

Philippa sighed, but not for long, because that hurt. Instead she shut her eyes. "I was reading a road map. My friend was changing a flat tire. Someone pulled up behind us, to help, I thought. A woman."

"What was she driving?"

"A white Mercedes."

"Are you sure? It wasn't a white truck?"

Ross glanced quietly up from his newspaper as Philippa's face turned pewter. "It was a white Mercedes," she repeated.

"What did the woman do?"

"I'm not sure. I don't generally pay much attention to women. I thought she was chatting with Franco. Next thing I know, she's leaning over the window with a gun."

"Describe her."

"She was about medium size. Her face was all covered up. She wore a wide straw hat with an attached scarf so it wouldn't blow away. Big, dark sunglasses and atrocious orange lipstick. Middle-aged, I think. She had a thin mouth. And a white linen blouse of no particular distinction."

"Did you see the gun?" Hobson asked after a pause.

"I guess so," Philippa replied. "But a gun's a gun. I could describe her ring a little better. It was a square-cut emerald surrounded by yellow diamonds. Set in platinum. Nice hunk of change."

Ross put down his newspaper. He remembered Dana coming into his office years ago with a ring exactly like that, whining that in his hand was the equivalent of a thirty-foot sloop. He would have had the boat had Ardith not discovered a bra in the glove compartment of his Jaguar a week before their anniversary.

"Any other unusual items?" the policeman asked, marveling that a woman staring death in the face would remember little but her assailant's baubles. "Earrings? Brooches?"

"No. But her hands were shaking. Obviously she was a terrible shot." Suddenly Philippa realized that no one had mentioned the man who had last been seen changing her tires. "My God! Did she kill Franco?"

"No. He got beaned with a crowbar. He's all right."

Philippa frowned. Where the hell was he, then? "I see."

As the detective began asking Philippa for possible suspects, Ross slipped into the hallway and found a phone. "Hi Marj," he said, praising God for the greatest miracle in all creation, a steadfast female. "How's everything?"

"Fine." She ran down a long list of business events, finally saying, "Dagmar's throwing a party tonight at her apartment. Starts at eight."

Her secret nude apartment? "What's the occasion?"

"Maybe it's her ninetieth birthday. Think you'll be back?"

"Tell her I'll be there. But late." Ross nodded across the hallway to Detective Hobson, who was leaving Philippa's room in pursuit of a suspect wearing a ho-hum linen blouse and spectacular jewelry. "Say, do you think Ardith's back from Europe yet? I was thinking I should stop in and see her."

"Funny you should mention it. She came by late yesterday with a beefcake named Rex. They went into Dana's office and carted away that bust."

"What? Without asking me? You let her do that?"

"Of course I did! It's hers, isn't it? She was stinko, Ross. I wasn't about to make a scene in front of clients."

"I suppose you're right," he said, feeling his stomach twirl. "Any other good news?"

"Someone named Brother Augustine called again. Wants to see you as soon as possible. Should I know him?"

"It has to do with that monastery Dana built for Joe Pola," Ross said so lightly that his voice shook. "The roof is probably leaking."

"Aha. I'll book him in later in the week. How's the actress?"

"She'll be back making mischief in no time." Ross saw two men in foulards and goatees walk into Philippa's room. "Getting herself shot was a great career move."

"Did they catch the guy yet?"

"No." Ross's head ached with leaden premonitions. "I'll try to get the next plane."

He returned to Philippa's room as Simon, unaware that Philippa was only pretending to be in a coma, introduced Emily to the producer of the vampire movie. As Emily sat smiling from the bedside, Simon delivered a superb sales spiel, pointing out how much prettier Emily was than her sister, and how much more cooperative she would be on the set. Simon was well into the shooting schedule when Philippa finally opened her eyes. "You bag of shit," she said. "I should sue you for fraud."

Ross beckoned his wife into the hallway as crude epithets began jagging among the three cineasts. "That was not nice," he admonished.

"Oh come on! We were just having a little fun."

Ross kissed her. "Listen, darling, I have to get back to Boston. There's a catastrophe in the works. Will you be all right here by yourself for a day or two?"

"Sure. Sounds like Phil's recovering fast. What's the matter?"

"I'm afraid a big job is going down the tubes."

Emily walked Ross back to the hotel. One hour later, he was in the air.

A chill wind wracked Boston Common, nipping pedestrians. Ross walked quickly down Beacon Street, inhaling sharp, fresh oxygen and the moldering perfumes of autumn. His knees hurt from the airplane, from the cold, from spying and age. Now that the Red Sox had once again been eliminated from the pennant race, the sky no longer glowed over Fenway Park. No one seemed to be out but dogs, their scowling owners, and students majoring in beer. Garbage cans, raided by rodents and scavengers, creaked from black alleys. Around ten-thirty, Ross halted at Dagmar's apartment on Commonwealth Avenue. Double-parked cars lined the street. He glanced up: Yellow lights blazed from the tenth floor. He felt uneasy, mildly betrayed.

"Evening, Mr. Major," greeted the doorman.

"I understand there's a party on." He frowned, entering the small elevator.

"Quite. I'll let Madame Pola know you're here."

The brass cage inched upward. When it finally petered to a halt, Dagmar was waiting outside the doors. She wore black silk and luminescent pearls matching her soft hair. Her eyes glittered, feral but composed; he knew that whatever might happen tonight, Dagmar had willed it.

"Hello, Ross. I'm so glad you're back."

"You look beautiful." He kissed her cool, dry hand. "What's the occasion?"

"Utter amusement."

Ross smiled dubiously; Dagmar could have amused her friends at her home in Weston. "I'm sorry my wife couldn't make it. She's still in California."

Dagmar took his arm. "Would you mind being my chaperone, then?"

"My pleasure." Dagmar led him to Joe's salon, where several dozen guests had already disposed of several dozen bottles of champagne. They all looked like people who would either buy art or ruin artists. A saxophonist, singer, and pianist crooned to each other in the corner, forming a salacious undercurrent to the conversations and laughter breaking giddily over the room. Ross recognized no one: This was Dana's sort of crowd.

A small, ferocious butler appeared, bearing champagne. Ross took a glass and accompanied Dagmar, watching and listening as she spoke with her guests. She seemed to enjoy confining everyone to scholarly discussions of specific artworks rather than answering questions about the impetus behind this vast cache of nudes. When a pair of inebriated curators expressed surprise that Dagmar had never mentioned the collection to them before, she replied that it had been Joseph's harmless little hobby. She introduced Ross to everyone as an architect, without mentioning any plans for a museum. No problem; he was glad not to have to talk. Each time the little man came back with champagne, Ross took a glass.

Dagmar approached a slim, expensively maintained woman who was studying a gouache. After she introduced Ross, the lady said, "Ah, you must be Ardith's husband's partner."

"That's correct," Ross replied, affixing his most wooden smile. "You're a friend of hers?"

"Yes, yes, for years. She's here somewhere."

"Is that so? I'll look for her." Ross cast his eyes about the room and saw, across the hallway, a figure quietly emerge from Joe Pola's bedroom. *Ward? Impossible!* What could she be doing here? What could Ardith be doing here? He looked, ashen, at Dagmar, who patted his arm and turned to her guest.

"It's so nice to see you, Caroline. We really must try to get on the same board again." Caroline gushed about an upcoming benefit for a ballet corps, then asked who was responsible for such exquisite barbecued shrimp. "Diavolina," Dagmar said. "That whimsical little restaurant in the South End."

"I should have known!" Caroline cried, relating her own fascinating horror story about caterers.

Ross didn't register a word. When the woman finally wandered off, he whispered, "What's going on, Dagmar?"

"Something perhaps beyond us," she replied. "Don't leave me, please."

As the evening wore on, her grip on his arm tightened; Dagmar's guests, presuming she and Ross were lovers, invited them for weekends at Nantucket and Lenox. Too preoccupied to protest, Ross smiled and waited for the skies to open. He was exchanging an empty champagne flute for a full one when a black man in tails approached.

"Excuse me, madam," he whispered to Dagmar. "There is a gentleman at the door."

"Is that so? Invite him in," Dagmar replied.

"He seems to be a policeman."

Ross's pulse faltered as Dagmar smiled girlishly at him; it was the same smile he had seen in Ward's eyes as she announced that she had killed Guy Witten, the same smile he had seen in Emily's eyes as she told him that she was pregnant. Funny that he should live for those intimate, orgasmic smiles that one day would be the death of him. Ross put his glass down: Time to take over, play Man. "Where is he? I'll have a word with him."

He was somehow not surprised to see O'Keefe waiting in the corridor. The detective's battered raincoat draped his body as if, from the neck down, he were a sculpture about to be unveiled. His eyes looked weary. "Dagmar Pola," Ross introduced, "this is Detective O'Keefe. What can we do for you, sir?"

"There's been an accident. A woman has apparently fallen from a balcony to her death. Was Ardith Forbes a guest in this apartment tonight, Mrs. Pola?"

"Oh dear," sighed Dagmar after a stunned silence. "Yes."

"May I see the rooms out back?"

Joe's bedroom was dark and quite cool. The sliding door to the balcony had been left wide open and the gauze curtains fluttered delicately toward the statue of Joe's departed mistress. On the balcony, an antique chair leaned against the railing.

Ross peered down to the alley and saw sirens, spotlights, and a small body splayed on the cement below. Ardith, all right: Even in death, she managed to look as if she were shaking a fist at Dana. He thought he'd vomit. "Don't look, Dagmar," he said, nudging her away.

"Don't touch anything," O'Keefe said sharply, picking up a small gold shoe lying beneath the chair. "How'd she get out here, Mrs. Pola?"

"The apartment was open. My guests went from room to room, looking at the artwork."

"How many guests?"

"About one hundred."

"What was the occasion?"

"Simply a party. I'm resuming my social life following the death of my husband."

O'Keefe peered at Ross. "How do you know each other?"

"Mr. Major is designing a gallery for me," Dagmar answered.

"When did you get here?"

"Around ten-thirty," Ross said.

"You weren't in the bedroom?"

"No. I haven't left Mrs. Pola's side the entire evening."

"You didn't see Ardith Forbes at all?"

"No. I wasn't even aware that she had been invited until another guest mentioned it."

When Dagmar corroborated Ross's story, O'Keefe knew he was in for a long night. "I'm going to have to question everyone here, Mrs. Pola," he said. "Sorry."

"Don't be. My guests will be thrilled. How can I help?"

"No one leaves. Could you put someone at the door while I get my assistant up here?"

Posting her chauffeur at the door, Dagmar took O'Keefe to a small study where he began asking intoxicated, pseudo-horrified guests whether they had been in Joe's bedroom. Most of them had, of course; none of them had seen anything unusual. Eventually they all went home, heady with alcohol, nudity, and violent death. "Send in the catering staff," O'Keefe said, glancing at his watch: nearly two. So much for a nice, quiet evening with beer and the pennant race.

As Dagmar went to the kitchen, O'Keefe cast a harsh eye on Ross. "What the hell's going on here, Major?"

Ross shook his head miserably. "I don't know. I got back from California and came directly over. Dagmar's a big client."

"You've known her how long?"

"About a month."

O'Keefe scowled. "Who would want Ardith Forbes dead?"

After a moment, Ross chuckled. "Only Dana."

The vicious little man who had been serving champagne entered the den and said, "Why, good evening, Detective O'Keefe. How nice to see you again."

"Sit down, Klepp," O'Keefe snapped. "Did you see anyone go into the bedroom tonight?"

"Everyone went everywhere. I just kept serving bubbly."

Realizing that Klepp would never tell him anything, O'Keefe waved him away. He next talked with a thickset black man, who said exactly what Klepp had, but more politely. The detective had a few words with a saucy waitress who perhaps remembered a woman in a white suit going into the bedroom. No one else from Diavolina could tell him anything. Finally O'Keefe capped his pen. Speaking to all these zombies from the restaurant reminded him of Emily. "Is that everyone?" he growled at Dagmar.

"One more, I think," she said.

Ward swaggered into the den. "O'Keefe! How's my dishwasher?"

The detective gaped: Humpty Dumpty was back together

again. After catering an affair for one hundred guests, Ward looked only slightly exercised, as if she had just completed the first leg of a triathlon. In no way did she resemble the wreck he had interviewed following the death of Guy Witten. "Ms. Ward," he said. "You're looking well. Have a seat."

Ward's massive body filled an antique chair. "What's up?"

"There's been an accident. A woman fell from the bedroom balcony. Her name was Ardith Forbes."

"Oy! Not that bitch who was trying to sue me!" Ward's face turned an unwholesome brown. "She's lucky I didn't meet her. I would have given her something to sue me about."

"Did you go into the bedroom tonight?" O'Keefe asked.

"Once. Klepp insisted that I see a statue. He thought it looked like one I used to have in my restaurant."

"Did you see a woman in a white suit in the bedroom or on the balcony?"

"No, I looked at the statue and split. The kitchen was busy."

O'Keefe had to buy that. "What's this about Mrs. Forbes suing you?"

"Ten million bucks' damages for serving her husband contaminated food. It was a joke." Ward's chair creaked as she crossed her immense legs. "She withdrew the case last week. Cost me ten million gray hairs worrying about it."

Perhaps that was why Ward had looked so bad recently. "Thank you," O'Keefe said. After she left, he found Dagmar. "Why did you hire Diavolina to cater tonight?"

"I had eaten there several times and enjoyed it. Their barbecued shrimp is outstanding."

"This was the first time you've used them?"

"Yes."

"Were you pleased?"

"Absolutely. So were my guests."

That was because they had no idea they had been served by a bunch of convicts. "How well did you know Ardith Forbes?"

"We met years ago at a fund-raiser for the Horticultural Society. Since then we've been on several charitable boards together." Dagmar lit a cigarette. "We were cordial but not intimate friends. Ardith was a very unhappy woman. She had problems with chemical and alcohol addiction."

"Had you been in touch with her lately?"

"Only once since the death of her husband. She seemed extremely depressed."

"Why? I thought you said she was unhappily married."

Dagmar eyed him coldly. "Why should the death of a hated husband suddenly make black white, Detective?"

He retreated, ashamed. "Did you speak with Ardith tonight?"

"Briefly. She had just gotten back from Europe."

"How did she seem? Still depressed?"

"On the contrary. She appeared unusually gay. Giddy, in fact. I had never seen her like that before."

"What did you make of it?"

Dagmar pulled heavily, almost salaciously, on her black cigarette. "I presumed that the poor woman had found romance and adventure on her trip."

Enough of acid, feminine presumptions. O'Keefe looked at Ross. "When did you last see Mrs. Forbes?"

"She came to the office about two weeks ago, clearing out Dana's belongings. She was just about to leave for her trip."

"How was she?"

Ross tried to be charitable. "Agitated."

O'Keefe sighed; poor Ardith. No one would mourn her. Maybe that was why she had jumped. "Her husband left her financially secure, didn't he?"

"Very."

Ward and her co-workers thumped by. "We'll be on our way, Mrs. Pola," she called. "The leftovers are all in your refrigerator. Hope everything was to your satisfaction. Anything else we can do for you, Detective?"

O'Keefe merely scowled. While Dagmar saw the caterers to the door, he collected his assistant from the balcony where Ardith had jumped. With a minimum of words, he left.

Ross sent Dagmar's chauffeur home then went to the kitchen. He made a pot of coffee and brought it to the den. Now that her guests were gone, her deeds accomplished, Dagmar looked a century old. Ross sat on the couch beside her and poured two cups of coffee. "Talk," he said. "Everything."

Dagmar took a few sips and replaced her cup with a delicate *chink.* "I believe Ward threw Ardith off the balcony."

"Good Christ Almighty! What for?" Ross listened, awed, as Dagmar told him about the conversation she had overheard years ago, forty floors above the pavement, and the conversation she had had at Diavolina two days ago. When she had finished, he didn't move for a long time. "Why did you do it?" he asked finally.

"To protect you," Dagmar answered simply. "Ward's now murdered twice. Her credibility is hopelessly compromised, should any questions about you ever arise. Secondly, I've avenged that poor girl. Ardith's words drove her off the balcony as certainly as if she had physically pushed her. Lastly, Ward owes me her life. She'll do anything I tell her to do now."

Ross went to the mantelpiece and fondled a tiny soapstone figure, an exquisite elf crouched with her hands about her knees. Emily often curled up like that when they sat together in the atrium after a long day. "Don't stop there, Dagmar. I think there's more to this story."

"What do you mean?"

"Slavomir Dubrinsky was Rita's teacher at the Academy of Art. He sculpted a statue just like the one in Joe's bedroom for someone named Leo. You didn't go to Diavolina just to procure Ward, did you. You went to find Leo." When Dagmar didn't answer, Ross continued, "He was in a fight with Joe years ago. Over a woman, I understand. Perhaps you were there."

Dagmar's eyes flashed. "Where did you learn this?"

"Secondhand. Then there's a Brother Augustine wanting to see me as soon as possible. It might be about a chapel that Dana and Joe built in the wilderness. Might not." Ross put the figurine down and sat next to Dagmar on the couch. "We're in this together," he whispered. "I need to know everything. From the beginning."

Dagmar's pearls rose and fell with her short breaths. Ross locked eyes with her until he knew he had won. When he took her hand, she began to talk. "Joseph was the most riveting man I had ever seen. I fell hopelessly in love with him. You would understand that fate, I think." Ross nodded; all too well. "Joseph was ambitious and smart, but penniless. I persuaded him to marry me and my money, sure that a love as strong as mine, proven with children, would conquer all. A common blunder, I'm afraid. My cause was hopeless; Joseph had already met the love of his life. An actress of some sort. He even saw her the morning of our wedding day, as I later found out. He didn't even have the decency to get me pregnant first."

"You didn't know about this other woman?"

"About a half year after we were married, Joseph and I had just left a nightclub downtown when an ugly little man accosted him and said, 'I hear Susannah's pregnant.' They had an awful fight. I made the mistake of intervening and got tossed aside."

"By whom?"

"Joseph. Whether from my own injuries or from dragging my husband out of an alley, I had a miscarriage. I never became pregnant again." Her eyes clouded with that dull resignation acquired only years after the battle, when both enemies and burning causes were dust. "Joseph stayed married to me. But every night, as the clock struck six, I wondered whether he would be coming home for dinner or whether he had finally run away with that woman. I knew there had to be an illegitimate child somewhere. I spent years trying to track them down. It became the obsession of my life."

"What would you have done had you found them?" Ross whispered.

"Something appropriately drastic."

"Go on," Ross said after a silence.

"When Joseph was quite ill with cancer, he asked Leo to find his child for him."

"How do you know that?"

"A few weeks before he died, I found the key to his desk and began going through his papers. There I found a picture of a woman with a note from a monastery in the middle of Massachusetts. Since my husband had never been a religious man, and never gave something for nothing, I drove out and saw Brother Augustine, who showed me the chapel that Joseph had built. I asked Augustine what he had done for my husband in return. He didn't answer me, of course. But when I showed him the picture, he knew that I knew."

"Do you have the picture with you?"

Ross followed Dagmar to Joe's bedroom, where she opened a night-table drawer. "It's the daughter, wouldn't you say?" she asked.

It was Emily at the cabin. She was on the deck looking across the lake, half smiling, holding her hat so the breeze wouldn't blow it away. Ross had taken the snapshot himself a few years ago. How had that damn monk gotten it? "There's a faint resemblance," he said.

"I have no doubt about it. I've spent hours here looking from one to the other. As it turned out, half my worries were in vain. The woman had died in childbirth. Augustine at least had the charity to tell me that." Dagmar dropped the picture back into the drawer. She pushed it sharply shut and walked out of the bedroom. Ross caught up with her in the den, where she was standing over the mantelpiece, shakily lighting a cigarette. "I could discover nothing about the girl," Dagmar continued. "Someone was clever enough to have hidden her birth records completely. After Joseph died, I learned about this apartment. That statue in the bedroom nearly drove me mad. I found the sculptor Dubrinsky, who had become a filthy, drunken degenerate. Yet when I put ten thousand dollars under his nose, he would tell me nothing. So I pursued the only clue I had left. Major and Forbes, architects." She looked at Ross. "Where I met you. And there the story becomes somewhat more complicated."

She seemed fragile as a sparrow, but Ross knew that was a total delusion. "How so?"

"I was in to see you one day when Dana came out of his office with that woman in the photograph. I couldn't believe my eyes. I knew it was the daughter I had been searching for all my life. Most likely Dana had met her through Joseph, who would have told him all about her when they had been building that chapel together. Dana very proudly revealed the girl's name. She was an actress. Philippa Banks. I had never heard of her, but I haven't been to the movies in years. Are you familiar with her?"

The couch began to float, buoyed by massive, inflating lies. "I think she makes beach movies and other trash," Ross said. Would Dagmar buy that? He waited a long time for her to resume speaking.

"I tried three times to kill her."

His heart lurched so violently he thought he would vomit it onto Dagmar's silk couch. "How?" he whispered.

"The first time at a movie opening in New York. She was supposed to swallow a lethal dose of heroin in a drink. Someone else swallowed it instead. The second time she received a manuscript saturated with odorless poison, the fumes of which are quite fatal for about fifteen seconds after exposure to the air. That attempt failed as well. The third time, she was shot. I'm afraid she's going to live."

"You shot her?" Ross whispered.

"Good God, no! Ardith did."

Ross became very afraid, asphyxiated. "Ardith was in this with you?!"

"Not voluntarily. She owed me a few favors in exchange for my silence regarding her involvement in the death of Rita Ward. I simply called them in. Ardith delivered the drink in New York. She delivered the manuscript in Los Angeles. She shot Philippa Banks a few days ago."

"She never went to Europe?"

"Of course not. But she proved to be a most unreliable messenger. Botched absolutely everything. Imagine standing three feet away, shooting that woman twice, and missing! Tonight she was nearly hysterical. The situation was becoming dangerous and uncontrollable."

"So you had Ward toss her off the balcony," Ross said. Fright almost gave way to awe: He was in the presence of a darker intelligence. "What makes you think Ward's going to keep her mouth shut? Or even get away with this?"

"Because there's no connection between Ardith and Ward except that silly lawsuit, which was dropped. At my suggestion, I might add. Ardith had every reason to commit suicide. No one saw her and Ward out on the balcony. We're home free, dear."

*Free?* "What about the actress? Now that your hit man's gone, you're going to leave her alone, aren't you? It wasn't her fault that she was born, was it? What harm could she possibly do?"

"Plenty. I have reason to believe that Joseph changed his will," Dagmar said. "Leaving everything to what is so quaintly called his *issue*."

"So tear up the will!"

"You're forgetting Leo," Dagmar said. "He's looking for her. I suspect the new will is in his pocket."

"Why hasn't he found her yet, then? Wouldn't she have been in every newspaper in the country after the shooting?"

"I don't know why he hasn't found her. He must be incredibly inept."

"What are you going to do about the actress?" Ross persisted.

"I'm not sure. But I'm determined to see her before Leo does."

Ross began pacing agitatedly around the room. "Dagmar, you've been very, very lucky with Ardith. She's out of the picture. This two-bit actress can't harm you. I would advise you to find Leo instead. Head him off. Buy him off."

"Are you joking? If I couldn't buy off a degenerate sculptor forty years after his model dies, what makes you think I'll have any better luck with this Leo? And who's to stop Augustine from contacting the woman? No, it's much better to get rid of her."

"Give her a couple million bucks! Buy her off! Don't try to kill her, though. It's too dangerous. She's not worth it," he concluded feebly.

"I don't think you understand, Ross. You've gotten rid of Guy Witten. Ward's gotten rid of Ardith. I've taken care of you both, yet I'm the only one who hasn't been satisfied. What makes you think my need to even the score is any less than yours?"

He dropped into a chair across the room. "But the girl didn't do anything except be born. Isn't that different?"

"Not really. The mother stole my husband. Now the daughter is in a position to steal everything I own. There will be scandalous publicity. What little consolation I've had in my social position and my possessions will be taken from me forever. I can't allow that."

"But she'll be surrounded by police and bodyguards, won't she? How would you ever get to her?"

"I'll find a way, believe me."

Dagmar looked imperturbably at Ross; for a horrifying moment, he thought she would ask him to kill Philippa for her. He owed her a favor, after all. "Have you got any aspirin in the house, Dagmar?"

Was that disgust flickering across her face? Or just that insidious, maternal tolerance that neutered all women in the end? "In the bathroom."

Ross escaped into the hallway, pressing two hands to his hammering forehead the moment he was out of her sight. He went to the master bathroom and opened Joe's medicine cabinet. There was nothing inside but a can of shaving cream and a bottle of tiny pink pills. Were that strychnine, he'd swallow it all: Ross read the label. The prescription was for Dagmar. The pharmacy was in Paris. The pills were iproniazid.

Hands shaking, he grabbed the bottle. He would fling it in Dagmar's face. Then he would fling her off the balcony after Ardith; she had just as many reasons to commit suicide as Ardith, didn't she? He'd be doing everyone a favor: Dagmar, Philippa . . . Emily. Emily: She called him back from the smoking rim of insanity, telling him he'd never get away with it. Kill Dagmar, kill himself. He'd go to prison. He'd never play with his child on a July afternoon. He'd never sleep with Emily again. Ross took the iproniazid and walked calmly back to the den.

"Did you find it?" Dagmar asked.

He sat next to her and put the little bottle next to her saucer. Ross waited several moments then, addressing the bottle rather than Dagmar, said, "You killed Dana, didn't you."

The pearls on her chest came to an utter standstill. When she spoke, her voice was hesitant and very soft; if he didn't know her better, he'd think she sounded contrite. "I was beside myself when I saw Dana with that woman at your office. When he announced to your secretary that they would be eating at Diavolina that evening, I knew that I had to get to the restaurant. I stood near the bar, which was very crowded and noisy, and watched Dana and that woman begin their meal. When they were about to eat the main course, I called over a waitress and gave her five hundred dollars to get Banks to autograph a pepper mill that I had brought. I suggested she apply a liberal sprinkling to the lady's steak. It wasn't pepper in the mill, of course."

"Wait a moment. Iproniazid isn't fatal unless ingested with cheese or red wine."

"I had sent over a bottle of chianti beforehand," Dagmar said patiently. "Everything went perfectly until Banks took a bite of her steak and stopped eating for some reason. Then she switched plates with Dana."

"And you just watched this happen?"

"There was always the hope that he'd switch plates back again."

"Where's the pepper mill?" Ross asked dully. "In your trophy case?"

"I've burned it."

"The waitress never told the police?"

"Why should she? She must have earned a thousand dollars that evening getting artifacts and autographs for Banks's depraved fans. My request was not unusual, believe me. And Dana Forbes was a notorious substance abuser. He left a long trail of pill bottles behind."

"The police never found the iproniazid."

"So what? Forbes could have swallowed the last of his prescription and tossed the bottle away."

Ross wondered why Dagmar, who had taken such exquisite care to obliterate all evidence of her crimes, should leave that bottle of pills in her cabinet. Maybe for the same reasons Ward had gone to Witten's funeral: to jeer at the gods, dare them to accelerate the havoc . . . to be discovered and executed, and perversely admired by those few honest souls who had identical urges but inferior courage. But women always preferred clean endings, neatly burned bridges; men were much more able to digest the shreds of a putrefied conscience. Ross would take no chances with Dagmar's suicidal craving for judgment: She would take him down with her. "Come with me," he said, pulling her off the couch, leading her to the kitchen. He turned on the garbage disposal, flushed it with water, and poured the few remaining iproniazid pills down the drain. He held the plastic bottle under the water and peeled off the label. Then he wadded the label into a ball and swallowed it.

"You must be tired," he said. "Wait here. I'll drive you home."

He got his car. On the way to Weston, where the Charles River ran quietly beneath a bridge, he pulled over. They both got out and leaned over the rough cement ledge. After Ross dropped the empty bottle into the water, near a wavering reflection of the moon, he said, "Leave the actress alone."

Dagmar did not answer. He put her back in the car and drove into the blustery night.

# 19

Once Philippa awoke, her recovery was swift. She told Franco to go to hell since he had not only failed to take two bullets in her stead, but he had not slept at the hospital, as Emily had. Philippa caused gridlock in the corridor when she went strolling in her extravagant peignoirs. Fans outside kept trying to scale the walls to her room. Finally, two days after Ross left for Boston, Philippa was told that if she was well enough to hurl vases at her business manager, she was well enough to go home. The hospital lawn was wrecked and the surgeons were tired of pickup trucks from Arkansas in their reserved parking spaces. Only the orderlies, who were making a fortune selling what they claimed to be Philippa's used hospital gowns, were sorry to see her go. They arranged a confetti parade in the front hall for her departure that afternoon.

Emily was manicuring her sister's nails in preparation for her first Incredible Survivor interview when Detective Hobson came to the room and announced that two boys, playing in a ravine near the accident, had discovered a .40-caliber gun. A trace of the serial numbers would identify the owner within the hour.

"Fine," Philippa huffed. "Just arrest her, please. Don't interrupt my interview. Em, what time's the plane?"

"Four-thirty."

"Crap, I'm going to have to talk fast." That afternoon the sisters would be flying to an undisclosed destination for two weeks, after which Philippa would begin work on her vampire film in Paris. That nameless destination was, of course, Boston; Ross had called yesterday with the shocking news that Ardith had committed suicide. Knowing that she must return home at once, Emily had entreated Philippa to come with her. Boston was not only loaded with doctors but it was halfway to Paris. It would be much better to recuperate there than at that flimflam holistic farm near the San Andreas Fault. Philippa finally agreed, on condition that they stay in Beacon Hill and not that horrible little cabin in the woods.

Philippa's interview ran late due to her eloquence upon the impact of bullet holes on her sex drive. Then Hobson knocked on the door. "Miss Banks," he interrupted, "may I speak with you, please?"

The journalist was reluctantly sent away and Emily summoned from her hotel across the street. "Well, what's the good word?"

"Does the name Dana Forbes mean anything to you?"

After a second's hesitation, Philippa clamped the back of her hand over her mouth. She had learned the gesture from old Joan Crawford films. "My God! Don't tell me that gun belonged to Dana!"

"It was registered in his name. You know the man?"

"I did at one time."

"Where might Mr. Forbes be presently?"

"In Massachusetts. Now and forever."

"Excuse me?"

"He's dead, darling. Six feet under."

"Since when?"

"You'll have to ask my sister. I'm terrible with dates. Some-time around Labor Day."

"Was he a good friend of yours?"

"Absolutely not. He was a lover," Philippa said. "There's a huge difference."

"Was he a lover at the time of his death?"

"No, he was eating dinner with me in a restaurant." Philippa tried to look sad, but couldn't: Dana had been out of the circuit for too long. "I believe he mixed alcohol with some fancy barbi-turates, poor dear."

"Where did this happen?"

"In Boston."

Then how the hell did the weapon get to California? "Did you ever see his gun?"

"Not the one with bullets, sweetheart. Em, did you ever see Dana with a gun?" Philippa called as her sister walked in.

"No." Emily took a seat. "Why?"

"Someone shot me with it. What was his wife's name again?"

"Ardith."

"He had a wife?" the policeman asked. "Where?"

"Boston," Emily replied. "She committed suicide yesterday. She had just gotten back from Europe, I think."

"What did she look like?" the policeman asked. "Medium height? Fair? Thin lips? Tacky blouses? Did she know about your involvement with her husband?"

"You're not saying that Ardith shot Philippa," Emily said after a silence.

"I wouldn't rule it out," he said. "The weapon in question def-initely belonged to Dana Forbes. And a woman fired it."

Philippa's manager, nearly blinded by a massive spray of gladi-olus, strode into the room. "Phil! Ready to roll?" Simon heaved the flowers onto the bed and straightened his pale blue ascot. "Where's that wheelchair? Aidan! Step on it, the entire U.S. press corps is waiting! I've planned this operation to the mi-crosecond!"

As Philippa, Simon, and Aidan fussed with a wheelchair, flowers, rhinestone sunglasses, and a gauze-swathed pith helmet,

Emily gave the detective her phone number in Boston and told him to contact O'Keefe, who would certainly know all about Ardith. "You! Emma!" Simon interrupted, handing her a chauffeur's jacket and cap. "Put this on and take the back stairs to the limousine. Get in the front seat. Now! Go! I don't want you and Phil running into each other out there! It'll cause a riot!"

"Bye-bye, Officer," Philippa called as she was wheeled into an Armageddon of flashbulbs. "Keep up the good work! I love you!"

The policeman shook Emily's hand, wondering how an identical strand of DNA could have split so unevenly. "Good-bye, ma'am. Good luck."

Emily slipped to the limousine and, through heavily tinted windows, watched her sister's departure from the hospital. After a leave-taking rivaling that of Cleopatra and fifty thousand Egyptians, Philippa and her entourage tumbled into the backseat. "What a fucking circus!" Simon cursed, tearing off his ascot. "They're animals!"

"Animals buy movie tickets, dear," Philippa replied serenely. *Choke Hold* was number one again this week. "Try to arrange a few decent interviews in Boston, would you? I'll be out of my mind with boredom."

They drove to the airport, where the twins were whisked onto a jet belonging to the producer of the vampire movie. A steward, a nurse, and a spare copy of the screenplay waited onboard. After glancing through the first few pages, Philippa tossed it aside. "I think Ardith shot me," she said to Emily. "Just gut instinct."

"If she did, then you're safe."

Philippa guffawed and said no more. Soon she fell asleep, muttering repeatedly about the white truck, not opening her eyes until the jet again touched ground. "Where am I?" she asked the nurse. Hearing "Boston," Philippa swore: the last place on earth she would ever want to be. In twenty years, this damn town hadn't been able to scrape together the minimum bodies necessary for an official branch of her fan club. The men here were either irresponsible libertines, like Dana, or immovable hulks, like Guy. She should never have listened to Emily and come back. Boston was bad luck.

No fans awaited them except Ross, who only had eyes for his wife. "Hello ladies," he said, commandeering Philippa's wheel-chair from the steward. He rolled her roughly into the terminal. "How's everyone feeling?"

"Just fine," Philippa snapped.

"That's terrific. Detective O'Keefe is anxious to speak with you immediately."

"I've just had an exhausting trip! Is this necessary?"

"Let's get it over with, Phil," Emily said. "Where does he want to see us?"

"I told him to go to the office. He'll meet us there in twenty minutes."

Philippa bitched all the way to State Street, her foul mood exacerbated by the billing and cooing of Mr. and Mrs. Major, who had obviously patched their marriage together since Emily's last trip to California. Her stomach yowled with hunger. Her stitches itched. The absolute worst thing about getting shot was that she couldn't take a bath for another week. "Goddamn it," she exploded as Ross rumbled her into the elevator, "this is in-human!"

She was taken to Dana's office, site of the largest couch at Major & Forbes. As Emily propped a few pillows behind her, Philippa noticed that the bust of Dana, his crystal decanters of scotch, and his books were all gone. Suddenly she missed him; rarely did brains, lust, and cash converge in such a delectable package. "Wouldn't happen to have any scotch in the house, would you, Ross?" she asked. He went to his office and returned with two stiff drinks. Emily got water. "What's the matter, Em? Ulcers?"

She saw her sister shoot Ross a mischievous look. "Much worse," Emily said, eyes bright. "We're pregnant."

*We?* With a twin's immediate, infernal intuition, Philippa knew that the child was Guy's. "My God, that's fantastic," she croaked at last, half exultant that Ross had been cuckolded forever and half stultified with jealousy of her sister's glorious fate. "You little twit, not telling me."

"We wanted to tell you together," Emily said.

"You did, all right! When's the blastoff?"

"Next May sometime."

Philippa emptied her glass. "I'm speechless! Congratulations, Em. All that rot with the missionary position and three pillows has finally paid off. Ross, be a dear and give me enough alcohol to make a proper toast." Ross brought the bottle. Philippa was on her third toast when O'Keefe arrived.

"Sorry to keep you up so late," he said. "How are you feeling, Miss Banks?"

"Never better, thank you," Philippa replied, rising to her elbows. O'Keefe was much handsomer than she remembered. Of course, last time she had seen him, her vision had been impaired by Dana's face in a bowl of whipped cream. "You had questions?" she asked.

O'Keefe retired to a deep, cushiony chair. "Answers, actually," he said. "All evidence is pointing to the fact that Ardith Forbes tried to kill you. She was in Los Angeles the day you were shot. We've found hotel bills and rental-car receipts for a white Mercedes."

"She never went to Europe, then?" Emily asked.

"No."

"How would she get Dana's gun through airline security?"

"She drove to California with a friend named Rex. He seems to have been completely uninvolved in all this." O'Keefe let that sink in a moment before asking, "Was Ardith aware of your affair with her husband?"

"Afterward, yes," Philippa said. "During, I'm not sure."

"Would she have known that you and Mr. Forbes would be at Diavolina the evening he died?" O'Keefe felt three pairs of lungs halt: bingo. "Who knew you'd be there, Miss Banks?"

"Emily knew, because she was cooking dinner. So did the secretary."

"That's all?"

Philippa once again tried to clarify a blur of orgasms and

boats and frilly hats. "There was someone sitting in the office when Dana announced we'd be at Diavolina."

"A man? Woman?"

"Woman. Old. Plastered with pearls. She wore a black hat with two peacock feathers. Bally shoes and purse."

Emily half opened her mouth to tell O'Keefe that that was probably Dagmar Pola, then noticed that Ross's face had turned so white that it almost looked blue. "Were you going to say something, Emily?" O'Keefe asked.

"All of Byron's friends knew that Philippa would be eating at Diavolina," she said quickly. "At least fifty of them showed up."

"It was more like a hundred, Em," Philippa corrected. "And I almost forgot Ardith's gymnastics instructor. He sent over vodka with four dried cherries. It's my favorite drink."

"What was he doing there?"

"Beats me."

O'Keefe looked very tired, as if he had just been asked to disinter an entire graveyard. "Thanks for your time, everyone," he said, rising. "Take care of yourself," he told Emily, wrapping her hand in his own.

"Have you learned anything more about Guy Witten?" she asked.

Once again, O'Keefe felt the entire room stop breathing. Why was that? He looked at Ross, who imperceptibly shook his head. "We now know that he died of internal bleeding, not from injuries sustained in a car accident. He had been shot with a crossbow."

After a small silence, Emily said, "You mean an arrow?"

"About the size of a pencil. The shaft went right through him."

"Where did this happen?"

"We don't know. We're working on it."

Emily withdrew her hand from O'Keefe's. "He was murdered?"

"No question. Unless he was wandering in the woods. Deer season just opened. No one hunts at night, of course." O'Keefe suddenly noticed that Philippa was shivering. Her lips looked a little blue. "Are you all right, ma'am?"

"Would you mind handing me that drink, please?" Philippa said. "My stomach always becomes upset after long plane trips." She tossed back the contents of the glass. "Thank you."

O'Keefe thanked them and left. After a pensive silence, Philippa sighed. "Is that man married?"

"Is that all you can think about, Phil?"

"What else should I think about?" she snapped. "That bitch Ardith playing Annie Oakley?"

"I'll tell you two what to think about," Ross said. "Getting your stories straight. O'Keefe's going to be back with more questions about that party in New York and that little breakfast in L.A. He's going to be digging like hell the next couple of days."

"So what? We didn't do anything," Emily replied.

"Just wait until he hears that you both suspect someone was after Philippa and never clued him in when that chef got nailed. He might have cracked this case weeks ago and been the hero of the police department. Not to mention preventing Philippa from getting shot and poor Ardith from jumping off a balcony."

"It's more complicated than that," Philippa cried. "You wouldn't understand."

"I understand better than you think."

"We'll just tell him about the dentist," Emily said. "None of this would have started if Phil hadn't been beaten up."

"No way! Leave the dentist out of this!" Philippa screeched.

Ross stood up. "It's late, girls. We've got a funeral in the morning."

They returned to Beacon Hill. In bed, Emily asked Ross to describe a crossbow. No one really slept.

Detective O'Keefe arrived early at Ardith's funeral, not that seating would be tight, but he wanted to speak with several mourners before they went inside the little church that, just a few weeks ago, had given Ardith's husband such a rousing send-off. It was a chill, brumous morning, clouding the abyss between the quick and the dead: perfect burial weather. O'Keefe waited, smoking, under the same tree that had sheltered Philippa during Dana's obsequies. Not too far away he saw a mound of dirt and the deep hole that would soon swallow Ardith. He found it hard to believe that a woman who had taken such pains during her life to look good—nay, perfect—would allow herself to expire looking like roadkill. An overdose of sleeping pills would have been more Ardith's style. But who was he to know, or judge, what had overtaken her on that balcony? Perhaps nothing more than a few glasses of champagne, enough to inflame guilt and rage and, worse, the specter of imminent discovery of her crime. Spend the rest of her life in prison? For Ardith, who lived to shop, the pavement was the easiest way out.

A blue car pulled up to the curb and Marjorie stepped out. Today she was wearing a black cashmere coat and black stockings over those fabulous legs. Tossing his cigarette on the lawn, O'Keefe walked over. "Good morning."

"Hello." Marjorie looked around for Ross. "I suppose I'm early."

"Very. You're the first one here. Don't go in yet." O'Keefe steered her toward a garden opposite the graveyard. "It's a shame about Mrs. Forbes."

"In what regard? That she killed herself or that she tried to kill Philippa? Ross told me about it this morning. Don't worry, I can keep my mouth shut."

"Ardith must have been insanely jealous."

"She was. What for, I don't know. Dana was no prize." Marjorie sidestepped a mound of leaves. "Neither was Philippa."

"You've met?" O'Keefe asked innocently.

"Only once. I walked in on her and Dana in his office. It was extremely embarrassing. I mistook Philippa for her sister. Dana never explained the situation. I think he wanted me to think he was kissing Emily. That was his idea of a big joke."

Funny only because he knew that Marjorie was hopelessly infatuated with Emily's husband. "You called Ardith afterward, didn't you?" O'Keefe asked. "Rex told me about it. Don't worry, I can keep my mouth shut."

"I—I wasn't thinking clearly," Marjorie stammered. "It was a big mistake."

"What did you tell her?"

"I suggested that she might be interested in going to Diavolina that evening."

Ardith had sent Rex instead. "Did you tell anyone else? Ross, for instance?"

"Good God, no."

"Why not?"

Because that would have been too blatant; much better that Ross discover his wife's infidelity from an outraged third party, like Ardith. "Because it wasn't any of my business," Marjorie lied.

O'Keefe walked her around a birdbath. "What was Ross doing the night Dana died?"

"Working with me. He had been out of the office for several days. We were catching up."

On what, business or pleasure? "How late?"

"I don't remember. Ten, eleven."

"There was an old woman in that day. Plastered with pearls. She wore a black hat with peacock feathers."

"That was Dagmar Pola. She had come to see Ross."

"Concerning what?"

"He's building her an art gallery."

Shucks, that was what Ross had said. "Since when?"

"About a month ago. It's a big project." Marjorie laughed sourly. "Since Ross wasn't in the office, Dana had to ditch the tart and entertain Dagmar. She wasn't too pleased."

"Who? The tart or Dagmar?"

"Both."

"Did Dagmar overhear that Dana and Philippa would be at Diavolina that evening?"

Marjorie thought a moment. "It's possible. Dana made a big fuss about it at my desk. I don't remember. I was pretty burnt up at the time." In the distance she saw four people from the office get out of a car. "Would you excuse me, please?"

O'Keefe watched her mesmerizing legs recede into the fog.

He ached to run his hands over them, toes to pelvis. Perhaps, once she realized that Ross was forever beyond her, once this case was closed, or abandoned, Marjorie might meet him for a drink somewhere. Standing behind a hedge, he watched a few more cars pull up to the church. The people getting out looked like architects in pursuit of promotions and women who had swatted a lot of tennis balls at Ardith. A maroon Lincoln crunched to a halt and Dagmar Pola stepped to the street.

She looked regal, omnipotent in deep black. Two peacock feathers adorned her hat. O'Keefe walked quickly over. "Good morning."

Dagmar nodded. "What can I do for you, Detective?"

Seeing that she wasn't about to take a stroll into the garden, O'Keefe skipped the mournful preambles. "You were a friend of Ardith's. Did you know Dana as well?"

"My acquaintance with him was strictly professional."

"You were in his office the day he died, I understand."

"Yes, I had wanted to see Ross."

"Did you happen to see Dana there with Philippa Banks?"

"I saw Dana there with a woman. They made quite a spectacle of themselves with that poor secretary."

"Did you hear that they were going to eat at Diavolina that evening?"

Dagmar's obelisk stare shamed him. "I am not in the habit of eavesdropping, Detective O'Keefe."

Screw dignity; one more try: "Where were you that evening?"

"At home. Since my husband's death, I do not go out much."

O'Keefe pulled a rumpled paper from his pocket. "This is a bill from the hotel in Los Angeles where Mrs. Forbes was staying. She called your apartment on Commonwealth Avenue four days ago. You spoke for one minute. You were the only person she called."

Did Dagmar's face go as white as her hair, or was that a trick of the mist? "Mrs. Forbes called to say that she would be coming to my party, " Dagmar replied. "Our conversation was brief because she was late for a hairdresser's appointment. I'm afraid I can't tell you why she made no other calls. I was under the impression that she was phoning from Europe."

O'Keefe sagged as another torch, poked into another murky catacomb, sputtered out. "Were you at Dana's funeral?"

"No. Ardith was not that close a friend. I had been to quite enough funerals lately."

If Ardith weren't such a close friend, what was Dagmar doing here now? O'Keefe had his answer as a Saab crawled by and Dagmar said, in a voice fifty years younger, "I think that's Ross."

She watched him park the car quite a ways off. Her ebullient gaze slowly turned to stone as first one, then a second, woman emerged. As they got closer, she asked O'Keefe, "Would you know who that is with him?"

"The lady next to him is his wife Emily. The other one is Philippa Banks, Emily's twin sister." What was she doing here? She ought to be in bed. "He never told you?"

Dagmar made a strange little purring sound. "I never asked." As they got closer, she leaned on O'Keefe's arm. "Would you mind introducing us?"

Ross and his two women, walking at a bride's pace to accommodate Philippa's war wounds, finally reached O'Keefe and Dagmar. The three of them looked as if they had been sticking leeches on each other all night.

After a curt nod, Ross took over the introductions. "Dagmar, I'd like you to meet my wife, Emily, and her sister, Philippa."

Dagmar's eyes finally left his. She studied the twins before extending a tiny, gloved hand. "I've heard so much about you both."

"I've seen you before," Philippa replied. "Dana's office. I'd remember that hat anywhere."

"Quite." Dagmar turned to Emily. "I understand you've been in California."

"We got back last night."

Conversation, illusions, died. Ross suddenly said, "Philippa, you must be wanting to sit down. Why don't you go inside with Emily. I'll be right there."

When the twins were out of earshot, Ross said, "Philippa insisted on coming. I'm sure her agent's got a photographer stashed in the trees somewhere. Anything new, O'Keefe?"

"Not since last night." The detective watched the two women edge away. "Looks like Philippa could use a little help getting up those stairs. Would you excuse me?"

Ross walked with Dagmar into the garden. They sat on a stone bench near the birdbath, where people were supposed to think pure, or at least poetical, thoughts. "I never once guessed that there might be two of them," Dagmar said finally.

That was because she had been dealing with a cagey husband and an even cagier monk. "My wife is pregnant," Ross said. "We've been trying for fifteen years. Don't take this child away from me, Dagmar. I'm begging you."

"My God, you ask a lot."

"I'm asking you for everything."

"There's no point in only getting rid of one of them, you realize."

"Think! Quit while you're ahead! O'Keefe's so suspicious already. Did anyone see you at Diavolina the night Dana died?"

"I'm sure everyone did. But I was wearing a turban and rather heavy glasses. The same costume as I gave Ardith a week later. If he's anything worth his salt, Detective O'Keefe has already found it at her home."

Always one step ahead of him. Ross shivered, but not in appreciation. "We should go. The service is about to start."

Halfway to the church she said, "Are you sorry you met me, Ross?"

Was Prometheus sorry he stole fire? Pandora sorry she opened that box? If he hadn't met Dagmar, Emily would have died a sudden death, and he never would have known why. Ross shut his eyes; if he didn't find Leo, she might still die a sudden death. "It never entered my mind," he replied. They went inside to bid Ardith good riddance.

# 20

*Here I am, staring at that unfathomable hole in the ground again. Dana's down there beneath my feet, inert as the deep, brown dirt. In fact I'm standing on him: sorry, friend. I wonder what he looks like now. Better than Ardith, that's for sure; she was such a mess they had to keep the coffin bolted. At least she's getting herself planted in the same color box she chose for Dana. Ardith was always big on matched sets. Agh, I don't want to think about them both down there forever. I can't look anymore.*

*I'll look at my wife instead. The poor girl's crying. Aside from Ardith's interior decorator, I bet she's the only one here who feels any grief at all. Emily is so beautiful in the fog. She's standing at the grave, head bowed, murmuring prayers with the preacher. Her hair is tumbling over her face. If we were in bed, I could push it to the side with one finger, study her eyes, lips, skin. . . . Has this woman really been sleeping beside me for fifteen years? They've gone so quickly by and it seems I'm just getting to know her. I'll probably never know her completely; that's because, in the bottom of my heart, I know I'm not the love of her life. Oh, I'm her friend, her confidant, protector, provider, but I'm not the mirror of her soul. I fall short there, always will; the most I can hope for is that the next time she meets another Guy, I'll have racked up enough Brownie points to retain possession. I'm the father of her child, after all. If nothing else, that should buy me a little breathing space: She'll be so busy with the baby for the next few years that she'll have no energy to get into mischief. And I'll be such a good father, the best on the planet. Boy or girl? Twins? God, give me quintuplets! We're going to be a family: unbelievable. Miraculous.*

*Dagmar wouldn't destroy that, would she? She's standing on the opposite side of the chasm, staring at me. No prayers coming out of her mouth, and this whole damn funeral is her doing. At least I had the conscience to get good and drunk for Guy's. She's sober as a rattlesnake. I'm afraid of her: She's a woman scorned. She's murdered before and gotten away with it. What's to stop her now? If Leo gets to Emily or Philippa before I get to him, Dagmar's got nothing to lose. I can see her killing my wife as a matter of honor. She doesn't make empty threats and she didn't promise me anything. She doesn't trust me anymore, I'm sure, not after that double whammy I laid on her an hour ago. And when there's no trust, there are no longer any rules. I wonder how much time I have before Dagmar makes her move. Should I go to the police? I don't dare: I tattle on Dagmar, she'll tattle on me. Emily would pack up and leave. Should I find Leo? Christ, I'd have better luck locating a new planet with the naked eye! Agh, what a nightmare. I'm going to have to start praying for another favor, from God or the devil. At this point, I'll bargain with either.*

═

After the funeral, Philippa was feeling faint, so Ross and Emily took her back to Beacon Hill. From the rear seat, Philippa discoursed upon the stupidity of recent events as she frowned at adipose tourists along Joy Street. "This whole thing makes no sense," she kept repeating. "Why did Ardith have to shoot me? It's not as if I were Dana's first girlfriend."

"You must have been the straw that snapped the camel's back," Emily replied.

"Come on, I was just an innocent bystander. She should have been ecstatic that Dana got knocked off and left her swimming in money! Why blow that by going after me? The woman was out of her mind."

"Obviously," Ross said, pulling into the driveway. "That's why she jumped off Dagmar's balcony."

"Even that makes no sense," Philippa continued. "Why didn't she just jump off Dana's boat? Take a few dozen sleeping pills? Such a fucking mess, throwing herself off a balcony. What about her poor kids, knowing that their mother was hamburger? Didn't she even think of them? There's something odd here. I'm going to bring this to O'Keefe's attention. What's his first name, anyway?"

"I don't know. Phil, your imagination's running away with you," Emily said, hoisting her sister from the backseat. "Let's leave this one to the professionals, all right?"

Philippa hobbled inside. "And who's this Dagmar broad, Ross?"

"One of my clients."

"She's got the eyes of a Gila monster."

"Actually, she's very sweet," Ross lied. "Very cultured."

"Believe me, the only thing cultured about her was her jewelry. What does hubby do?"

"Hubby's dead. He made pretzels."

"Pretzels! That's just a step above making suppositories! Ross, I think I could handle a glass of wine today. Just a little one." Stretching out on the couch in the atrium, Philippa invigorated herself with mounds of pasta, prattling nonstop. Finally she pushed her plate away. "That was great, Em. It's a real shame you won't be working anymore, now that you're pregnant."

"Says who?"

Ross looked at his wife. "You're not considering anything until after the baby is born, are you?"

"It's not as if you were seventeen with good elastic," Philippa agreed. "You can't go knocking around a hot kitchen with a gut the size of a beer keg. Besides, you've had rotten karma at your last two jobs. People dropping dead like flies. Your boss, Dana, that guy Byron . . ."

"Don't forget Dubrinsky," Emily replied sarcastically.

"Who's that?"

"The dishwasher at Diavolina. He was the one who sent me the note of warning and two sketches of Mother."

"What sketches? You never told me."

"Phil, I told you everything. You were preoccupied with that buffoon Franco."

"Oy, now I remember. That idiotic story with the priest named Leo."

"Augustine." Emily brought a large yellow envelope from the library. "Here are the sketches. See for yourself."

Philippa studied them distastefully for a few seconds. "A dishwasher drew these?"

"He was a sculptor before he worked at Diavolina."

"The man just gave these to you? Who's to say he didn't just draw them at home one night? Why tell you they're your mother?"

"Slavomir didn't say anything about a mother. He didn't have a chance to. He drowned in the Fenway the night Dana died."

"What, trying to take a swim?"

"He was drunk. But before leaving the restaurant, he went into my office and slipped me a key and a picture. It was in an envelope pinned to my T-shirt."

"Come on, Em! A drunken dishwasher doing all that?"

Emily went to the library and returned with a second, smaller envelope. "There you are."

"Who's this?" Philippa asked, looking at the faded brown photograph. "Looks like he was carrying it in his underwear for fifty years."

"Maybe it's his mother."

Philippa studied the old picture again. "You sentimental fool,

Em, that's the old bag Dagmar, fifty years ago. Look at that little pearl pin. She was wearing it today."

Ross's eyes lifted slowly from the newspaper he was reading. "That's quite a stretch, Philippa."

"The hell it is. Faces I can forget. Jewelry never."

"Was Dagmar related to Dubrinsky?" Emily asked Ross.

"No idea. I can ask her," he said, casually taking the picture. Dagmar, all right: Those eyes had never changed. He knew that he was staring at the inchoate shoots of his deliverance. *Grow! Fast!* "Has anyone else seen this, Emily?"

"No."

As Philippa launched a diatribe against priests, dishwashers, and illegitimate births in filthy monasteries, Ross left the atrium. He returned shortly with his briefcase. "If you'll excuse me, ladies, I think I'll try to get a little work done today." He kissed Emily's cheek. "Get some sleep, darling. I'll be back early. You two aren't planning to go out, are you?"

"Are you kidding? With half my insides in shreds?" Philippa cried.

"Keep the doors locked, then. Don't open them for anybody." Ross left.

"What was that all about?" Philippa asked, pouring herself a huge slug of wine now that Ross was gone. "I think he gets off on the idea of you locked up in the house. He'll be chaining you to the bed next."

"He's just being protective. No one knows what this Leo fellow's like, remember."

Philippa scowled at yet another reference to her tawdry birth. "Ross is an insanely jealous man, Em. Don't ever let him catch you fooling around. He'd kill the guy." Philippa finished her wine, yawned, and shut her eyes. "I suppose that's a compliment. Not many people would kill for love nowadays. Not even in the movies."

"What do you think Ardith just did?"

"That wasn't love. That was stupidity." In a few moments, Philippa had dozed off.

Emily gathered her sketches and pictures and returned them

to their drawer, there to await the return of Leo, who might explain everything. Where had he been these last four weeks? Maybe he was dead, like everyone else. As she cleaned up the lunch dishes, Emily wondered if Ward had heard anything from him. Emboldened and incisive, as people usually are for a short time after funerals, she picked up the phone. It was ringing at Diavolina when Philippa cried from the couch, "No pepper, I told you! Think of my hemorrhoids! And don't call me Plum! I'm not your damn plum!"

Emily hung up and went to the atrium. "Phil," she whispered, shaking her sister awake. "You're having a bad dream."

Philippa slowly focused. "What did I say?"

"You were crying about pepper and hemorrhoids again. One of your favorite nightmares." Philippa scowled; surely she dreamed about loftier topics. "It must have something to do with Terrence," she said. That was her second husband. "He was a nut on anal sex."

"Does pepper really give you hemorrhoids?" Emily asked.

"Of course not! Nothing does but steak tartare," Philippa fumed. "That stupid waiter at your restaurant tried to feed me raw steak, you know."

"I know, dear. You've told me many times now."

"And it was covered with pink pepper. Pink! No wonder I'm having bad dreams. That color has always made me violently ill."

"Guess what, Phil. We never used pink peppercorns at Diavolina."

"You certainly did. Ask the waitress who gave my steak a half-inch dusting. What a hopeless restaurant. You should never have taken a job there. Such a low class of people involved."

"Oh, but Simon's high class? Give me a break," Emily snapped. "And what's this about plums all the time? Why do you keep dreaming about plums?"

Philippa tried to look very, very blank. "I have no idea. I really must have a session with my analyst soon. All this obsessing with fruit and assholes! Bizarre! Where are you going now?"

"Food shopping," Emily replied, needing to get out of the house. "Go back to sleep."

She drove to Cafe Presto. The lunch rush was piddling out and Lois was gloomily closing her cash register. Seeing Emily, she brightened. "Hi! Hope you didn't come to eat!"

"Just some lemonade. If you've got a minute, could I talk with you?" Emily waited for Lois at a table by the new front window. Perhaps Guy had been sitting here when that car had come crashing through. Had she really worked here for seven years? What a long, sweet dream; like Guy, over now—on to other dreams.

Soon Lois came over with a mug of coffee. "How's everything, Em? You look great."

"Fine, thanks. Still holding up the fort?"

"Of course. Bert's leaving tomorrow. It was either him or Lina. Guy's sister, Ursula, is trying to keep the place running now. She's looking for a buyer. Wouldn't be interested in coming back, would you?"

"I'll think about it." Without Guy? No way. Emily sipped some lemonade. Lina had changed the recipe; it tasted rather weak now. "Detective O'Keefe told me that Guy was probably murdered."

"It's unthinkable. They'll never find out who did it, you know. That policeman's gotten nothing but dead ends. He can't tell where it happened, who did it, or why. Personally, I think some wacko was just having a little target practice and Guy happened to be in the line of fire. Bert's theory is that Guy was shot by a boyfriend or husband. One of those jealous-triangle things."

"Guy had a girlfriend?"

"One bossy bitch. She called him here all the time. Irritated the hell out of Bert. Guy generally took off after she called. We figured she was married and was telling him when the coast was clear. We also figured that that night the window got smashed, he was sitting here waiting for her. He was really not himself those last few weeks. And you know something? That night

Guy was killed, he got one of those phone calls and took off. We never saw him alive again."

"Does Detective O'Keefe know about this?"

"Sure. But what can he do? That woman doesn't call anymore. No one even knew who she was. She never left a name. The first couple of times, Bert mistook her for you. He said your voices were alike."

Guy had always preferred women with low voices. And he had never paid much attention to husbands. Had he replaced her immediately, then? Emily changed the subject to bingo, Lois's hobby. After a while she finished the lemonade. "Give my regards to Ursula, would you?"

"Sure. Think about buying the joint, would you, honey? We really miss those pistachio buns."

Emily went to Diavolina, where the last of the lunch guests lingered over the last inch of their cheap wine as waiters glowered at them from the sideboards. The place looked exactly the same, but smelled different: new chef here, too. Zoltan bowed from his little podium. "How are you?"

"Fine. You left a message on my machine a while ago. I was in California until last night. This morning I had to go to a funeral."

"Mrs. Ardith Forbes, yes? I saw the article in the newspaper. Terrible."

"Did you have something to tell me?"

Zoltan's orange face went quite still. "It was about an opportunity that is now past."

Emily doubted it had to do with the restaurant business. "Have you heard from Leo?"

"Not at all. I am beginning to get worried. He has never been away this long before."

"Hey Major! What are you doing here?" called Ward, stomping over from the bar. She looked great. Trim, neat . . . happy?

"I was just passing by. How's Klepp holding up?"

"Super. He's a fanatic about law and order. In the kitchen, anyway. What are you up to?"

"I was in California with my sister. You may have heard that she got shot."

"I did. Serves her right. You must have come back for Ardith Forbes's funeral."

"It was not a happy occasion."

Ward giggled. "To think I was just twenty feet away when she jumped! Unbelievable!"

"You were invited to Dagmar's party?"

"Hell, no. We were catering it." Noticing a thirsty customer at the bar, Ward headed back. "I haven't seen Leo, in case you were wondering," she called over her shoulder.

Emily took a few steps toward the door, then stopped. "Zoltan, have you ever used pink peppercorns in the dining room?"

"Never," he sniffed.

"You were an old friend of Slavomir's, weren't you?" Zoltan neither affirmed nor denied. "Did he know Dagmar Pola from way back?"

The maître d's eyes flickered toward Ward, who was aiming a stream of club soda into a large glass, laughing with a customer. "Perhaps that would be another question to ask Leo when he returns."

"*If* he returns." Emily left, knowing that Zoltan would help her no more.

After Ardith's funeral, fog had swollen into rain. Instead of going to the office, as he had announced to Emily and Philippa, Ross drove to the Academy of Art downtown. Rivulets leaking from its gutters followed ancient stains down its façade before finally becoming puddles on the stoop. The dean was thrilled to see Ross again. After the usual prolegomenous banter, Ross said, "I've been thinking about the possibility of teaching here, as you suggested."

"Excellent," the dean responded, trying to appear calm. Had someone actually swallowed the line he had been throwing into barren waters for so many years? "Naturally, we couldn't offer you too much in the way of remuneration."

"That was not my objective."

They talked about courses and students and the joy of exposing eager young minds to higher education. Ross asked a few questions about the faculty, living, before rounding to faculty, deceased. "I've just seen two sculptures by Slavomir Dubrinsky," he said. "Quite remarkable female nudes. The same model."

"Where are they?"

"Private collections. One of the owners expressed an interest in knowing more about the artist. So little is known."

"The less the better," the dean said. "Dubrinsky went to prison for twenty years for statutory rape. You know what that means, of course. The girl was willing but her parents weren't. Poor Dubrinsky didn't stand a chance. He lost his best years. And the girl was married to someone else when he got out. No wonder he went to pieces."

Ross dolefully shook his head. "Who was that girl?"

"I don't remember the name. Dagmar something. A spoiled, scheming nymphomaniac, if I may be frank. She did everything simply to annoy her parents. It was a tragedy for Dubrinsky."

Ross stayed another ten minutes hearing about the misfortunes of other faculty members. When the dean started in on the tragedy of Guy Witten, beloved model, Ross glanced at his watch; how time had flown. He had an appointment and must leave at once. After a curt good-bye, he headed west, toward the monastery that Dana and Joe Pola had built. Befogged, traffic moved slowly past the many dead animals lining the turnpike; or maybe Ross just noticed them more today. Driving conditions were even worse in Hale, where the temperature hovered above freezing. Ross saw the sign for the monastery mere yards before having to swerve into the driveway. Halfway down the rough hill, his Saab began to slide in the mud. It clunked twice in a pothole before reaching level ground.

Ross paused in the driver's seat, looking at the mansion ahead of him: an admirable if peculiar work, a cross between Stanford White and the Comte de Sade. He counted twelve statues of angels tucked amid balconies and porticos; even one hundred years ago, a client's ridiculous whims could dent an architect's better judgment. Where was Dana's chapel? As Ross got out of the car, a brown-robed monk appeared on the porch. The man was old but his eyes looked neither chaste nor serene. "I'm looking for Brother Augustine," Ross said, wishing he had worn a coat. The heavier raindrops had become sloppy snowflakes. "My name's Major."

"I'm Augustine. Won't you come inside?" The man led Ross to the overheated room off the foyer. "Coffee? Brandy?"

"Brandy." Ross took a seat. Exquisite stone, wood, and plaster work here. Once upon a time it had been the sitting room; now Augustine probably used it to sock penitential sinners for donations. Ross did not like the way Augustine looked at him, obviously sizing him up as either Dana's or Emily's partner. So instead of chatting for a few minutes about the house, he said, "I understand you visited my office a few days ago. I'm not sure whether that was in connection with Dana's chapel or the rather fantastic story you told my wife about her mother."

"Both, actually. One story grew out of the other."

"I would appreciate your starting at the beginning, then. And try not to leave too much out. I'm in no position to either judge or pass the story along. I trust you realize that my wife's life is at stake."

That got no reaction whatever. The priest began telling him about growing up with Leo. "Your name was Moody then," Ross interrupted. "Tell me about the connection between Joe, Dubrinsky, and Dagmar. I already know about Dagmar and statutory rape."

After a displeased silence, as if a naughty parishioner had interrupted his sermon, Augustine said, "What connection? Joe met Dagmar and married her."

"Dubrinsky must have really appreciated·that."

"Dubrinsky couldn't have offered her anything and he knew it."

"Why did Joe marry Dagmar if he was in love with Emily's mother? Money?"

"It's a powerful lure. So was Dagmar. No man could have resisted that combination."

"So Dubrinsky's ruined, Emily's mother is dead, Joe goes for the gold, and Dagmar becomes obsessed with illegitimate children. Great."

"Dagmar never knew about the twins."

"She knew there was at least one child, didn't she?"

"Yes. I arranged to have the twins' birth certificates signed by a doctor in New York, not here. Their mother was adamant that Joe Pola never find them."

"Did he even try?"

"Not to my knowledge. But his wife did. About twenty years ago, a woman came asking if a child had been born here at that particular time. I told her nothing." Augustine swallowed some brandy. "When Joe was diagnosed with cancer, he called Leo and told him that he wanted to see his child before he died."

"Why call an old enemy?"

"Because an old enemy is frequently one's only hope for salvation. Leo sent Joe to me. The sick old man drove out and threw himself at my mercy. I could tell him nothing either. I had made certain promises to the mother. Then our chapel burned down. Joe gave us a large sum of money to build a new one. These gifts are not without certain strings attached."

"What did he want?"

"Nothing but a picture. I went to New York and talked to the twins' uncle about it. He gave me a photograph and said the man needed to rest in peace."

"I took that picture of Emily myself," Ross growled. "What did Joe do with it?"

"Nothing, as he had promised. Unfortunately, when he was near death, Dagmar discovered not only the picture, but paperwork concerning the chapel. She put two and two together and came out here again. I told her nothing."

"Nothing can be everything. Especially to Dagmar."

"The day before he died, Joe called me to Boston. He had only then noticed that the photograph was missing and that Dagmar had probably taken it. He was afraid of what she would do. He had rewritten his will and sent Leo after the girls."

"Where'd he go?"

"I don't know. Leo didn't ask me for directions."

"Why not? He must have known that you knew where they were."

"He respects my vows of silence."

A loud lie, but that was the priest's problem. "What does the will say?" Ross asked.

"I don't know."

"Where is it?"

"In Leo's pocket, I'm afraid."

"Oh Christ," Ross swore. "Why is Leo doing all this for the man who virtually killed the girls' mother?"

"As I said, he's not doing this for Joe Pola."

"Thank you so much. That explains everything. Tell me, why did you come to my office?"

"Because you're the only man who can bring this to a satisfactory conclusion."

"Me?" Ross laughed harshly. "You think I'm some kind of knight in shining armor?"

The priest's old eyes looked into the fire. "Absolutely not."

"What do you suggest I do? Nothing's going to stop Dagmar. I don't have much time."

"God will show you the way."

"I'm glad you're so confident." Ross quickly left the room. Hotter than hell in there.

As rush hour was just getting under way a large truck flipped into a ditch aside the Massachusetts Turnpike. Trapped about a half mile back, Ross waited in the fog as police cars and ambulances screamed by; this had been a super day for fatalities. Famished and tense, he got home at eight o'clock. Philippa was nowhere in sight. Emily was dozing on the couch in the atrium, where she had slept so often these last few months. She looked serene and still . . . dead, almost. In a sudden frenzy, Ross threw himself at the couch. It bounced into the wall.

She opened her eyes. "Ross! What are you doing?"

"Sorry, I tripped."

"Where have you been? I called the office and no one knew where you were."

"I had to check on a project in Springfield," he said. "Sorry I'm so late. The traffic was horrendous. Where's Philippa?"

"She's gone to bed. Have you eaten?"

"No." Ross followed her to the kitchen, where he tiredly watched her take a casserole from the oven. Beef stew: ah, what a perfect wife. "Have a good day?"

"So-so. Philippa glued herself to the tube. I went to Diavolina."

His fork paused in midair. "What for, darling?"

"I wanted to see if Leo had been in touch. He hadn't. No one's heard anything."

Ross swallowed wine. "See all your old buddies?"

"Some of them. Klepp's running the kitchen. Ward looks great. By the way, you didn't tell me that Diavolina had catered Dagmar's party."

"Sorry, I didn't really notice the food. Or the people serving it." Ross halved a potato with his fork. "Did they offer you your old job back?"

"No. I asked the maître d' if Slavomir Dubrinsky had known Dagmar. He said that was a question for me to ask Leo. I think he's not telling me something. Everyone at that place seems to be covering for everyone else."

Ross shakily refilled his glass. "Emily, what do you remember about Dubrinsky?"

"Nothing much. He was a complete derelict. He could hardly stand up, let alone wash dishes. He was another of Leo's old friends."

"He died the same night as Dana?"

"He drowned in the Fenway. I had to identify his body."

"You never told me that."

"It happened at a bad time. I didn't want to bother you." She sat opposite Ross and picked a few peas from his plate. "O'Keefe called me one day while Ward was out and said they had just fished Slavomir from the Fenway. So I went to the morgue. I recognized him and signed a paper. That was it."

"How did he die?" Ross asked.

"Technically, he drowned. But he had been drinking pure grain alcohol. And that was after finishing off a half bottle of port at the restaurant. Poor bastard. Ward went to pieces for a while after he died. Claimed that someone had killed him. But he hadn't been robbed or raped. He just had a little bump on his head."

"O'Keefe didn't notice anything unusual?"

"Just a little orange tassel in Slavomir's pocket. The kind you see on a lampshade or a pillow. He could have picked that up from the sidewalk. An artist likes colorful things, right? I don't know why Ward bugged O'Keefe so much about it."

"Violent people think violently." Ross stabbed the mashed potatoes with his fork. "Please don't go back there anymore, Emily. It's not a nice place."

She kissed his hand. He looked so weary tonight. "I don't want to go to any more funerals for a long, long time."

Ross could think of one more funeral he would be delighted to attend. "We won't, darling." He ate slowly, letting her voice waft him to better lands.

As Ross had predicted, Detective O'Keefe called Emily around noon the next day, asking if he could stop by. He was wrapping up a few details on Ardith and needed to ask Philippa a question or two. Could they see him in ten minutes? Emily looked across the kitchen table at her sister, who had just vacated her bed and was mulling through the stack of mail that Aidan had forwarded to her. She only looked semiconscious, but perhaps that was an advantage. "Sure," Emily said, hanging up. "O'Keefe's coming over."

"Now? Before I even have my contact lenses in?"

Emily began grinding coffee beans. "What are we going to tell him about switching places with each other?"

"Nothing. Just play it by ear. Follow my lead." Philippa ran a few fingers through her tangled hair. "How do I look?"

"Ravishing."

Philippa managed to hobble to the bathroom, slather on a

few ounces of makeup, change into her favorite white peignoir, and arrange herself becomingly on the couch before the doorbell rang. "Good morning, Detective," she said, extending a perfumed hand as he walked into the den. "How nice to see you again."

O'Keefe took a seat as Emily brought coffee and a dozen packets of sugar substitute. "How are you feeling?"

"Much better! My doctors are astounded. They say I've got the recuperative powers of a twenty-year-old."

"That's nice." O'Keefe watched Emily's long, slender fingers as she poured the coffee. "I've been doing some more checking on the movements of Ardith Forbes over the past few weeks. I believe that she was at your movie opening in New York. In your statements made the night Dana Forbes died at Diavolina, you said that vodka with four dried cherries was your favorite drink. I think it's no coincidence that Byron Marlowe ingested a fatal amount of heroin with dried cherries at that party. Do you remember speaking with him at all that evening? Possibly giving him your drink?"

"Of course I gave him my drink," Philippa replied without hesitation. "He thought the cherries would bring him good luck."

"Who brought you the drinks?"

"A waitress named Agatha. She's an aspiring actress, currently sleeping with my manager in Los Angeles."

"Any last name?" O'Keefe asked.

"Street," Emily said after a ten-second silence. "Wasn't that what you told me, Phil?"

Philippa shot her sister a dire look. "I think so. Forgive me, I'm so bad with last names."

"Your manager was seriously ill recently," O'Keefe continued. "You've told the Los Angeles police that you believe he received a poisoned manuscript. How was it delivered to you?"

"We were eating breakfast at Luco's, our favorite restaurant. Franco brought it to our table."

"Who's Franco?"

"A social-climbing waiter," Philippa sniffed. "Not a very good one at that."

"Any last name?"

"Panopoulos."

O'Keefe frowned. "Wasn't that the man with you when you were shot?"

"He was changing my tire. I wouldn't waste my breath talking to him if I were you. He'll only say that a woman with a turban and heavy glasses gave him two hundred bucks to take a script to my table."

"What color turban?"

Once again, Philippa couldn't answer so Emily piped in, "I think he said black."

"Will you stop interrupting," Philippa snapped. "Let me handle this."

O'Keefe emptied a few packets of fake sugar into his coffee. "The morning after Byron's sudden death in New York, the police met you at your hotel for questioning. The report mentions that you had severe facial bruises and several lacerations on your arms."

"I had slipped in the bathtub the prior evening. Champagne sometimes makes me dizzy."

"The officer writing the report thought the bruises were a day or two old. He's seen enough injuries of this nature to know what he's talking about."

"That's ridiculous! What does this have to do with anything? So I had an accident! What's the big deal?"

"I'm just trying to determine that this was an accident and not another attempt on your life," O'Keefe explained.

"Calm down, Phil," Emily said. "This is all confidential information. Detective O'Keefe's just trying to help."

"All right, all right," Philippa muttered. "I went out on a blind date with a dentist and fell in his bathtub."

"After the *Choke Hold* party?"

Whoops. "Yes! When the hell else?"

"What was his name?"

"I don't recall. Denton something or other. It was strictly a one-night stand. We went dancing then took a bath. I'm embarrassed by the whole episode."

"Do you think this man was in any way connected to Ardith Forbes?"

"Christ! No! Of course not! That's absurd!"

"Phil, get ahold of yourself!" Emily turned to O'Keefe. "We appreciate your concern, Detective, but I think this night with the dentist was just a matter of poor judgment."

He nodded vaguely. "Were you badly hurt?"

"A small black eye! No one even noticed!" Philippa rolled to her side. "I refuse to discuss this further. It's a purely personal matter."

O'Keefe almost acceded but, hating liars to have the last word, asked, "Just for the record, where were you the night before the gala?"

Perhaps Philippa was sleeping. Finally rousing herself with a yawn, she said, "In New York. I had had an exhausting day doing interviews and went to bed early. I was not feeling well. Ever since eating that wretched meal at Diavolina, my stomach had been bothering me."

"What do you mean, 'wretched'?" Emily interrupted. "You ate everything in sight."

"What else could I do, send it back? That chef was an abomination. Rolls in the shape of swans, moldy mushrooms, raw steak, pink peppercorns . . . agh."

"No pink peppercorns, I told you, Phil. Sorry."

"Pink as those little envelopes there, damn it! All over my steak. Raw, by the way."

O'Keefe's eyes bored into her. "Did you eat any?"

"Hell, no! I gave it to Dana. He ate the whole thing."

"Who was their waitress?" O'Keefe asked Emily.

"Lola."

O'Keefe wrote a few words in his pad. "Well, that's been very helpful. Thank you both."

As he stood up to leave, Emily suddenly said, "I've been thinking about Guy Witten." Again; always. "Is it possible the same person who drove through the window of Cafe Presto shot him with the crossbow?"

O'Keefe needed a moment to flip from one frustrating, dead-end file to another. He tried to keep his voice even. "Quite. Unfortunately, we've been unable to locate either the truck or the crossbow. Not to mention a suitable perpetrator."

"What do you mean, 'truck'? I thought a car drove through his window."

"No, it was a much heavier vehicle. Left some white paint behind. The lab tells me it comes from an old farm truck. What with all the bodies piling up around you girls, I haven't really had the time to check out every dented pickup in New England. Wouldn't happen to know of any farmers with crossbows, would you?"

Emily almost replied, then thought better of it: This morning, between imaginary dentists and pink peppercorns, Philippa had sent O'Keefe on two false leads. Emily hesitated to send him to Peace Power Farm on a third. "No. But I'll think about it some more." She showed him out, them stomped back to the atrium. "What a fiasco! You're a terrible liar, Philippa! Did you notice what a bad temper he was in all of a sudden? He obviously got fed up with your tall tales."

"You fool, he was angry because you were asking about Guy Witten."

"Why should that irritate him?"

Because jealous suitors never liked to be reminded of their more successful predecessors. "Because the case isn't solved! You put him on the spot!" Philippa staggered toward the liquor cabinet. "That beast has destroyed my nerves. His insinuations make me feel like a criminal."

As she was guzzling an inch of Ross's best scotch, Emily said, "Why do you keep crying in your sleep about a white truck? You shout 'Look out, look out' as if it's going to hit you."

"How many times do I have to tell you that getting run over is a common nightmare of actresses?" Philippa thought her head would explode. For an insane second, she almost confessed everything to Emily. Her sister would forgive her attraction to

Guy Witten, her desperate meeting with him at Cafe Presto . . . but Emily would never forgive her for leaving him out on that porch to die. Never. Philippa reeled back to the couch. "Stop asking me about the truck, Emily. Please. I can't explain my dreams. If I ever figure it out, I'll tell you."

She looked feverish. Emily went to the bathroom and brought back a cool, wet towel for her sister's forehead. "Forget about the detective. You should rest."

Philippa nodded weakly. "Bring my mail, would you, sweetie?" A large package from California had arrived that morning. "Hearing from my fans always cheers me up."

Announcing that she would return by dinnertime, Emily left her sister with the phone, the soaps, and a stack of letters bearing Love and Elvis stamps. She got into her car and headed west, into the exhaust of sooty intuition, arriving at Peace Power Farm as the sun was just kissing the violet hills. The WE LOVE VISITORS sign had been removed for the season, if not forever; Emily drove in anyway. No dog came yipping and snapping as she left the car. Unswept leaves had settled around the old farmhouse, there to mulch until spring. Water and worms had finally vanquished the far end of the porch railing. The white pickup truck was nowhere in sight. Emily rang the doorbell and waited. Someone was home; she smelled a cabbagey soup.

After a long while Bruna answered, looking huge and mean as a Cape buffalo. "Hi," Emily said. "Remember me? I was wondering if you had any goat cheese for sale."

"Stand's closed for the winter. I'm only delivering to restaurants now."

"In that big white truck?"

"Nope. I lost the differential on the turnpike and sold it for scrap. I have a van now."

Emily glanced toward the side yard. "Looks like you're closing down for the winter. Even the archery range is gone." Bruna did not reply. "Still delivering to Diavolina?"

"Look, what do you want?" Bruna said suddenly. "You didn't come out here for cheese."

Two more seconds and the door would slam: Emily grabbed at a passing straw floating down the Panic River. "I—I was wondering if I could go to your school for battered women," she cried, surprised at how much she sounded like Philippa in *Choke Hold*. "I've been having trouble at home lately. You told me last time I was here that you taught women how to fight back."

"Nothing would help you but a forty-five Magnum, lady."

"What about piano wire? Electric-frying-pan cords? I'm desperate."

"Why don't you just call the police? Throw the stinker into jail."

"He'd kill me! You've got to help! I need to learn about self-defense. Wrestling. Crossbows."

Bruna laughed. "You with a crossbow? You hardly have the brawn to pick the thing up, much less load it."

Emily tried to look very, very hopeless, the way Philippa had in the more emotive scenes of her greatest movie hit. "How long did Ward stay here?"

"Almost a year."

"Did she look like me when she started out?"

"Worse. She was a total wreck. I brought her to where she is now. No one would dare step on her toes now. Go ask."

"I can't," Emily wailed. "She fired me."

Bruna scowled. "So what did your old man do to you?"

"Hit me! On my ribs so it doesn't show."

"With what?"

Emily desperately tried to think of something that Ross might hit her with. "The electric toothbrush. It really hurt. He's—he's"—a fervent line from *Choke Hold* came to her—"Satanic!"

"No kidding," Bruna said.

Emily paused, confused: Bruna had said it so calmly, as if she knew the man. "I'm almost better now," she stumbled on, "but if it happens again, I want to stay here."

"Start lifting weights, then," Bruna said. She shut the door.

Emily returned home. The soaps had ended and the talk shows were now contaminating the air waves. Philippa's mail lay all over the floor; perhaps she had been disinfecting her wounds with the half-empty bottle of scotch on the coffee table. Emily turned off the television and gently prodded her sister. "Wake up, Phil. I'm back."

"Uhhh. Get your errands done?"

"Sort of. What have you been doing? The place is a mess."

"This is all the fan mail that Aidan sent this morning. I get this much every single day. It's incredible."

Emily started picking up. "What's this?" she asked, holding a thick envelope.

"Feels like pictures. Be a dear and get a pair of scissors, Em. I didn't want to ruin my fingernails getting through all that tape. Honestly, you'd think my fans were sending uncut diamonds, the way Aidan wraps these packages."

Emily went to the kitchen and cut the side of the envelope. A dozen snapshots and a yellow note fell to the counter. *Just a reminder—still waiting for that personal thank you!! In memory of Byron. Always your devoted fan, Jimmy.* Emily looked at the first photo and felt her heart stop: Diavolina again. There was grinning Dana. There was Philippa in that stupid wig.

Emily headed back to the couch. "I forgot to give you something a while back," she called, then stopped dead, staring at the photograph of Guy Witten and Philippa with the same incomprehension that Ross recently had. What was Guy doing at Diavolina? Why was he touching Philippa's cheek like that? Why was she allowing it?

"What've you got there, Em?" Philippa asked.

Emily dropped the photo into her sister's lap. "What's this?"

One look and Philippa realized that in the next sixty seconds, she had better deliver the performance of her life. Her face remained calm as she took a few extra seconds to compose herself. She didn't blink as every brain cell in her head quietly ignited. "Looks like that great night in Boston," she said, casually handing it back.

"Who's the man?"

"I have no idea, Emily. When Dana was in the men's room, he just took over his chair and began talking to me in tones of rudest familiarity."

"What did he say?"

"Pfffuiii, I hardly listened to him. He had the audacity to call me—what was it—a pear? The maître d' sent him away at once." Philippa took another look at the photo. "Not a bad-looking man. His style left something to be desired, however. What else is in that pile? Ah, there's Dana. That poor boy. There's that lunkhead waiter. Check out that dress of mine. I really looked stunning that night, if I say so myself. Who sent these pictures? I don't remember anyone with a camera."

"His name was Jimmy." Emily walked quickly to the bedroom and began pulling open her drawers, searching for the prints that Byron had put in her pocket that last day at Diavolina. Where the *hell* had she put them? She scrambled through her underwear, all her pants, between the mattresses: finally, with a sinking heart, she found them in her night table, next to the pencils Ross always used for doing crossword puzzles. She went through the pile but found no photograph of Philippa and Guy Witten. Once more, just to make sure, she checked: nothing.

She lay down and stared at the ceiling. *Ross knew!* He had said, indicated, nothing, but he knew. Emily remembered the pain, the certainty, in his eyes the night he had asked her if she were having an affair with Dana. His suspicions had been correct; only his aim had been off. Had he said anything to Guy? No, Guy would have told her immediately. Besides, Ross was never one for confrontation. He preferred to study his enemies, know them, isolate them . . . then knock them off the board forever. Had he done the same to Guy? He had been out so late, so many nights. She had thought he was fooling around with Marjorie. Perhaps Ross had been doing something quite different. His behavior had taken a remarkable turn for the better not once Emily had left Cafe Presto, but once Guy was dead. She thrashed to her side, fighting a rush of hysteria. Ross was incapable of murder, wasn't he? And he had been in his office the night Guy was killed. Philippa had called him there from the cabin and he had gone to pick her up.

The door banged downstairs. Emily shuddered: Her husband was home. She ran to the den. Philippa had guzzled another couple inches of scotch. She looked as if the white pickup truck of her dreams had finally mowed her down. Emily gathered the photographs that Jimmy had sent. "I don't want Ross to see these. He'll be upset."

"Do us all a favor," Philippa moaned. "Burn them."

Emily was stashing the pictures in the garbage as Ross walked into the kitchen. "Hi, honey," he said. "Have a good day?"

Would he even be here if he hadn't forgiven her? Emily put her arms around his neck and held on tight.

Sure that his wife was asleep, Ross slipped out of bed, poured himself some scotch from a very light bottle, and went to the atrium. He lay on the couch where he used to find Emily around this time of night. She hadn't come out here since Guy died; no use wrestling with her conscience if the prize had been withdrawn forever. Sipping his drink, Ross looked up through the glass. No wonder she had crept out here so often: The deep sky nudged one into eonian thoughts. Clustered by a few shy stars, the moon glowed in a black infinity. Everything looked so tranquil up there. All a delusion, Ross knew: In reality, the moon was dead and the stars were violent, erupting suns. How appearances could deceive . . . and how the deceived preferred their delusions.

Emily had been uncommonly skittish tonight. Was that because of her first doctor's appointment tomorrow? Maybe it was an absorption of excess radiation from Philippa, who was either inhaling laughing gas or losing her mind. Ross hadn't seen her this manic since the night he picked her up from the cabin in New Hampshire. She and Emily had apparently had a disastrous interview with O'Keefe that afternoon. All night long, the two of them had clawed each other like a pair of cats. Then, in bed, turning out the light, Emily had said, "I wonder why Ward's sister jumped off the Darnell Building."

"Whatever brings that up?" he had asked, trying to look bemused, not impaled.

"I was just thinking of that clipping on her desk. Remember we talked about it once?"

"It was a failed romance, if I recall."

"What was the sister's name? Lisa or something?"

"Rita." Ross fussily returned to his book. He thought Emily had gone to sleep.

A while later she murmured, "It must have done a real number on Ward."

"Didn't you tell me she went to an analyst? She's probably still working it out."

"I guess so. It's too bad you two never met. I think you would have liked her."

Ross had patted his wife's shoulder. "You can introduce us next time I need a bulldozer and can't find one."

But the evening had already been ruined by a call from Dagmar, who had chatted a few horrendous moments with Emily before asking for Ross. "Hello, Dagmar," he had said, swallowing terror and bile: How dare she invade his home, speak with his wife! "What can I do for you?"

"I wonder if you could come to the apartment tomorrow morning."

"How's nine o'clock?"

"Fine. I look forward to seeing you."

He had hung up. Both Philippa and Emily were looking oddly at him. "Some clients are real pains in the ass," he explained.

"She sounded nice enough to me," Emily had said.

"She's not nice! Don't get taken in by that den-mother tone of voice!"

Philippa had delicately bitten into a corn dumpling. "I told you Dagmar had the eyes of a Gila monster. Nobody listens to me around here."

Ah, what a charming evening in the bosom of his family. Weren't people supposed to huddle together, comfort one another, after a funeral? Maybe that was only the case after burying someone they liked, in which case, Ardith's funeral definitely didn't qualify. Still, the ghost of Dana should have cowed Emily and her sister into civil behavior. Another night like this and Ross might have to move up to the cabin until Philippa left. He wasn't used to a third body in his living space;

it upset the equilibrium. Then again, he was a cranky old man, set in his ways. For the first time, Ross wondered how he'd fare with a baby in the house.

He'd be lucky if he ever got one in the house, of course. He dreaded his meeting with Dagmar tomorrow: Whatever she wanted, he probably could not deliver. She had never disguised her overriding goal in this string of atrocities: to do away with her husband's *issue*. Too bad if that involved doing away with Ross's wife as well. Dagmar could get away with it! Wherever they might hide, she would eventually find them. Ross watched the moon, praying for black inspiration. Around six, when the moon sank and his brain had become purest lead, he showered and kissed his wife good-bye. "Don't get up," he whispered. "I'll call you later."

He walked to the office and sketched as if this were a normal day. Marjorie arrived at seven in a knit dress that clung to all swells and slopes. "Ross! When did you get here?"

"A little while ago. I couldn't sleep." His ragged voice confirmed that. "Dagmar called me at home last night. Wants me to come to her place at nine. I have to go."

Something was wrong. "Is there going to be trouble with her?"

"I hope not." He put down his pencil. "I expect so."

"Can't you just drop the project? We haven't billed her anything. She hasn't offered to pay anything, either."

"This goes back to Joe and Dana's chapel. There's bad blood. It's personal."

Marjorie put a hand on his shoulder. "What could she possibly do to you, Ross?"

"I don't know. That's what scares me." He rubbed his cheek against her hand. "This is just between us, Marjie. It should blow over in a few days." *Sure!*

"I'll head off your appointments." Marjorie returned to her desk. At eight-thirty, she found Ross staring out Dana's window. "Don't let the old bag get you down," she said, accompanying him to the elevator. "Remember, you can always throw her off the balcony." She winked as the doors closed.

Ross walked through the financial district as a hostile wind whipped between the skyscrapers, knifing pedestrians. Sunshine singed his eyes. A hard frost crunched beneath his shoes as he cut across Boston Common. Promptly at nine, Ross nodded to Dagmar's doorman and caged himself in her small elevator. Before today, it had seemed to take hours to reach the top floor. Now it rocketed upward. Dagmar stood behind the tenth door. She was wearing the pearls that so perfectly matched her hair. "Good morning." She smiled.

Ross smiled back. "How nice to see you again."

She brought him to the little nook where they had first sat together. "I hope you don't mind eating inside. It's a bit windy on the balcony."

As she poured coffee, Ross looked at her jewelry. When she turned to serve him, he saw the little pearl brooch on her lapel. "What a pretty pin, Dagmar," he said. "Where'd you get it?"

"It's an old family piece." She settled back in her chair and got down to business. "I'm upset with you, Ross. You gave me a nasty surprise yesterday."

"What was nasty about it? The fact that you had no idea you were going to have to kill twins or that you only found out yesterday?"

Dagmar's slender lips curled. "You know, after your eloquence the other night, I actually considered quitting 'while I was ahead,' as you put it. But now I see that your motivation was not concern for me, but concern for your wife."

"It was for both of you."

"I wish I could believe that. But I'm now a little worried that, in order to protect her, you might do something rash."

"Like what? Tell the police? I don't think so, Dagmar. We each have enough dirt to bury the other ten times over."

"I was thinking of something a little more masculine than tattling to the police."

"Oh, you thought I'd come up here and shoot you?" Ross stood up. "Go ahead. Frisk me."

She did, slowly, lustfully. Ross thought he felt the floor rise when she dragged a hand between his legs. Finally Dagmar sat down. "I don't think you're strong enough to throw me off a balcony."

He walked to the tall windows overlooking the river, wishing with all his might that Dana were alive: Dana would have helped him exterminate Dagmar. They could have taken her sailing, gotten out the fire ax, and used her for chum. Drowned her in wet cement. Something like that. Anything. Without Dana, he was reduced to begging. "Emily won't touch you, I guarantee it. Neither will Philippa."

"You can't guarantee anything until we find Leo."

"Then we'll find Leo."

"You might have to do more than find him," Dagmar said.

Ah, there was the price tag: Leo for the twins. Ross didn't know how he could pull off a murder. He was much better at suggesting it to other, braver, people. "Where is he?"

"That's for you to discover. You have exactly three days."

Ross returned to the divan and tried to drink some coffee. "And if I fail?"

"Then I proceed with my own plans."

He dropped his cup. The coffee spilled over his trousers and the couch. "Effff! Sorry!" Dagmar went to the kitchen and brought back towels, watching as Ross vigorously swabbed the floor and Joe's silk couch.

"I'll get some soap," she said.

Ross was wiping off a pillow when he noticed that a tiny orange tassel was missing. Odd, Emily had been talking about an orange tassel just yesterday, in connection with . . . with something. Ross couldn't recall. Something lousy. A thick thread hung in the gap, as if someone had torn the tassel out. Who who who: Aha, Slavomir, the drunk who drowned. He had had an orange tassel in his pocket when they fished him out of the Fenway. *Hell!* An iceberg snapped; Dana rolled in his grave. Ross seized his miracle and yanked off another tassel.

He was tucking the pillow back in place when Dagmar returned. "No soap. Never mind. That divan's not staying anyway." She resumed her seat. "I never knew you had such delicate nerves. Here, eat something. These rolls came from Cafe Presto. I understand your wife used to work there."

So Dagmar had been studying her quarry. Enraged, burning to break her neck, Ross took a cinnamon bun. "You know," he said, calmly taking a bite, "statutory rape is such a silly crime. Why should someone go to prison for letting nature take its course? That Dubrinsky fellow, for instance. He must have lost a good twenty years of his life for no reason at all. Then to top it off, his girl dumped him. No wonder he turned into a stinking drunk."

"Who told you this?"

"Chefs, priests, deans . . . it's common knowledge." Ross took another bite. "I figure he saw you the night you went to Diavolina. Even with the hat and glasses, he recognized you. After forty years, that's some compliment. I guess you brought him up here, had a cozy chat about the good old days, showed him his statue, tried to get a fix on Leo. . . ." Ross licked the sugar off his fingers. "How'd you get him to drown, though?"

"Grain alcohol. I threw my glasses into the water and asked him to fetch. Slavomir always was a perfect gentleman. You'll never prove anything, Ross."

"I wouldn't even try." He looked at his watch. "Guess I'd better start chasing Leo. I only have until nine o'clock—what is it—Friday morning before you come after my wife." He took one last walk past Joe's beautiful women. They really were best naked. Put clothes on them, let those brains fester over honor and soured love and *issue*, and they'd eat every man on the planet. "You'll have to get me first, of course. Good-bye, Dagmar."

Outside, a breeze ruffled the trees yellowing Commonwealth Avenue. Ross walked a few blocks to a pay phone and called Diavolina. "Ward, please."

"You again?" Klepp said. "Hold on."

Ward came on the line almost at once. "Can you meet me in fifteen minutes in the Fenway? Near the Victory Gardens. Last time, I promise."

"This had better not ruin my day, mister," she said.

"It will make your day."

Ross continued up a bridge to the boggy Fenway. Tall reeds overran the park, providing cover for hedonists and stranglers. He waited only briefly before Ward appeared. She looked, literally, tremendous. With no effort, he thought, she could snap him in half. Maybe that wasn't such a bad idea. "No one followed you?" he asked.

"Please." They headed toward the bulrushes. Like most sane citizens, Ross had always avoided the area. But going in there with Ward was like going in there with Superman. When they were surrounded by reeds and muck, she stopped. "What's on your mind?"

"Slavomir Dubrinsky. Your dishwasher." Ross handed her the little envelope he had taken from home that morning. "He gave this to Emily."

Ward looked at the picture of Dagmar and the note. "I don't get it," she said.

"Neither did Emily. Dubrinsky had pinned it to her T-shirt. She didn't find it until a week after she moved out of Diavolina."

"'Leo is looking for you? Be careful?' Why didn't she bring it right to me?"

"Why should she?" Ross pointed to the photograph. "That's Dagmar Pola. Young, of course."

Ward looked again. "What's she got to do with this?"

"She was the cupcake who bagged Slavomir for statutory rape. That was before you were born. More recently, she was at Diavolina the night he drowned. At some point he must have looked into the dining room and recognized her."

Ward's face darkened as she remembered her dishwasher panicking for no apparent reason. "This is bullshit."

"I don't think so. When you saw O'Keefe at Guy Witten's funeral, you asked how he was doing with Slavomir's case. Obviously, you don't think the man drowned all by himself. Open your hand." Ross dropped the orange tassel into it. "Look familiar?"

"Jesus Christ! Where'd you get this?"

"Dagmar's apartment. From a pillow on her couch. I reckon that once she knew Slavomir had seen her at Diavolina, she invited him up and served him a bit of grain alcohol. Tried to pry a little information out of him and got nowhere. So she took him for a stroll over here. It's five minutes from her place, I just walked it. Dagmar tossed her eyeglasses into the water and asked her boy to fetch. He never made it back to shore."

Ward sagged to the ground, as if she had been punched. "Why'd she do it?"

"To eliminate a witness. Oh, I forgot to tell you. Dagmar killed Dana. By mistake, of course. She was going for Philippa. A couple weeks later she set you up to kill Ardith."

"What do you mean, 'set me up'?"

"You don't think Ardith would risk her widow's mite by killing a second-rate actress, do you? She was being blackmailed by Dagmar. When things got out of control, Dagmar played you like a violin with that story of your little sister and Dana."

"That was no story. Ardith confirmed everything."

That must have been a pleasant scene. "What did you do, corner her on the balcony?"

"I happened to find her out there staring at the moon. Introduced myself, told her about Rita and one red shoe . . . she just stood there with her mouth open. I knew it was true."

Dagmar was such a clever devil. "How did you get Ardith off the balcony without her screaming bloody murder?"

"Gave her a little chop in the back of the neck. After that, she never knew what hit her."

Ross shut his eyes. "You do realize that Dagmar owns you forever now." He suddenly squatted in the mud next to Ward. "We have got to get rid of her. Soon."

"What's in it for you this time?"

"When Dagmar gets done with Philippa, she's coming after Emily. She thinks they're her husband's illegitimate daughters."

Ward burst into that depraved laughter. "Are they?"

"I hope not. Leo's got the paperwork. Incidentally, Dagmar made me a deal. If I get rid of Leo, she'll lay off Emily. I've got until Friday morning."

"What's Leo got to do with this?"

"I'm not sure. Did he ever mention anything to you?"

"No. Leo's a private man."

"Is he dangerous?"

"No more than you, I'd say." Ward put her head between her knees for such a long time that Ross thought she was ill. "Go away, Major," she said finally. "I'm thinking."

He left the Fens.

Deep in the night, Emily felt Ross slip from the bed. She knew he had gone to the atrium, there to stare at the sky, perhaps to drift into troubled dreams. She didn't dare follow him; he might ask a few questions that she was not yet prepared to answer. Instead, she thought about Guy. Had he really replaced her so quickly with another woman, as Bert and Lois thought? If so, Emily didn't feel quite so beatific about making him a posthumous father. In fact, she would rather have an abortion, rather have no children at all, than pass off his accidental child as her husband's. The guilt of that would surpass anything she had known. Bastard! Who was the other woman? Was there one at all? Emily had to find out, and soon: The child's survival depended on it.

After Ross had crept in at dawn and kissed her good-bye, she had gone to Cafe Presto. Bert was there alone, opening up. With the keys she had somehow never flung in Guy's face, Emily unlocked the front door. "It's me, Bert," she called, walking in. "Lois told me this is your last day here."

"You're damn right. This place is hell now." He stacked a few croissants in their baskets. "Who would have ever thought so a month ago?"

Emily made coffee, just like the old days. "I've been thinking a lot about Guy lately. Did he really have a girlfriend those last few days? That's what Lois tells me."

"Sure he did. She called him here all the time. He would take off like a dog in heat."

Ouch. "What do you mean, 'all the time'? Every day?"

"Well, no. Only about five or so times in all, I'd say. I usually picked up the phone. She was an incredibly irritating slut."

"Did she call the day the truck drove through the window?"

Bert was silent a few moments. "I think so. She definitely called the night he was killed. I was left here holding the bag. I'm sure Ross got the worst coffee of his life that day."

"Ross was in?"

"Sure, he dropped by late in the afternoon. Good thing he did, too. I was bitching about how the woman sounded like you."

"Planting ideas in his head?" Emily laughed feebly.

"He told me that was impossible since you were in California. We had a good chuckle over it."

Sure. Ross never chuckled. "Did the lady go to Guy's funeral?"

"I wouldn't even know what she looked like. She never had the courtesy to introduce herself."

The front door opened and Guy's sister, Ursula, walked in. Obviously not a morning person, she somnambulated to the coffee machine as Emily watched, speechless, from behind the counter: The resemblance between Ursula and her deceased brother, while subtle, was enough to take her breath away.

As Ursula was taking her first sip of coffee, she noticed the extra body. "Emily," she called in a gritty voice, "what brings you here?"

"I just got back from California and thought I'd stop by. See how you were doing."

"I'm sure Bert's told you all the gory details. Have a moment to chat?"

Steeling herself, Emily followed Ursula into Guy's office. She sat on the nubby chair where, in simpler days, she used to spend hours talking to Guy about ovens and eggs. How many times had he shut the door and kissed her? Not enough. "Rough business, eh?" she said.

"I'm too old for this." Ursula whisked a strand of gray hair out of her eyes. "I don't know what will happen after Bert leaves.

Maybe I'll sell the place." She swallowed another dose of coffee. "Guy told me why you left. I think I understand."

What was Emily supposed to reply to that? *Hey! Great?* "Interested in coming back and salvaging it?" Ursula continued.

"It wouldn't be the same without him."

"No. But I'm sure he'd want you here."

Emily sighed. "I couldn't, Ursula. I'm pregnant."

Ursula's eyes gleamed, then clouded over as she realized that she could never ask and would probably never know whether her brother had left a child behind. "That's wonderful."

They sat wordless as two crones. Finally Emily said, "I'm sorry I couldn't make the funeral."

"It's all right. Plenty of other people did. People I hadn't seen in years. Previous wives, all wrinkled up now. Your new boss. That Ward woman."

"Guy knew Ward?"

"Not really. He was close to her younger sister, an art student. It was before your time. A sad story. She jumped off a building. Guy always blamed himself."

"Why? Was he her boyfriend?"

"Heavens, no. He was married at the time. He was just her friend. But friends of suicides always feel as if they've dropped the ball." Ursula shrugged. "The big sister certainly looked as if she had recovered. I was quite touched that she came to the funeral. It meant that she had finally forgiven him."

"For what?"

"For being involved at all. People are like that." Out in the kitchen, Bert began shouting at someone. "Lina's here," Ursula said, getting up. "What a disaster she turned out to be."

Emily cringed; all her fault, like so many other things. "Don't throw in the towel just yet. I'll think about coming back."

"In your present condition?"

Emily smiled wanly; that could always change. She was about to ask if Guy had really found another woman when Ursula said, "Thank you for making my brother's life happier. He was mad about you, you know. He was even able to laugh about the night the truck ran you both down. If that isn't love, nothing is."

*Mistake here,* Emily thought as she exited to the sidewalk. The magnitude of it didn't register until she sat at her gynecologist's office totaling all the weird phone calls, the photographs, the nightmares about trucks, dentists from hell . . . her head began to ache as thoughts tumbled toward a steep, black ravine. Surely she was wrong: Philippa could not have done this. Not wittingly. Wit, Witten, witless: oh yes, she could. Guy was a man, after all.

After her checkup, Emily walked to the North End, to the park high above the harbor, and stared at the ships. They seemed motionless, aimless almost, until one closed the eyes for several minutes and looked again; then their slow paths and far-off destinations became apparent. One needed only patience and perspective. Slowly, distantly, Emily began reconstructing Philippa's and Guy's paths, following as if they were boats meandering toward foggy ports. Finally she stood up, shaken, needing Ross; he would believe her.

Emily remembered that he had gone to Dagmar Pola's for a meeting. She looked at her watch. If she walked fast, she could get there before he left. It was a brilliant, blustery morning, conducive to speed. Emily concentrated on inhaling maximum oxygen, thinking minimum thought. She was just about at Dagmar's apartment when, across the street, she saw Ross lunge to the sidewalk. Instead of turning left toward his office and her, he took a right toward Kenmore Square. Emily could see from his taut, fast walk that something had upset him. She began to walk even faster, to catch up. Then she saw him hunch at a pay phone and speak just a few words. To whom, Marjorie? Another woman? All of Emily's blood-sucking demons returned. She followed her husband along the windy boulevard, up to the Fenway. When he stopped, she hid behind a tree; even from this distance, she could feel the sharp, black waves pulsating toward her.

Soon a stocky figure appeared: *Ward!* Ross said he had never met her in his life! When they disappeared into the reeds, Emily's heart began pumping corrosive waste into her bloodstream. Her brain burned, her baby wailed. She sank to the ground, into the whirling leaves, gasping as a maelstrom sucked her into its gigantic funnel. It was too large, beyond her; yet without comprehending the particulars, Emily comprehended the whole, in the way a drenched animal understands a flood. She was still gasping when Ross emerged from the reeds and walked quickly away.

After a very long while, Ward shuffled out, took a look around, missed Emily completely, and headed in the direction of Diavolina. Emily returned to Beacon Hill and, without entering the house, got into her car. Upstairs, Philippa was probably just opening her eyes, wondering where her coffee and fan mail might be. Block that out: Emily drove north at great speed, as if Guy sat in the front seat with her.

The trees were bare up in New Hampshire. Behind the cabin she saw nothing but naked, prickly hills. It was cold. Suddenly losing her courage, Emily continued to the general store down the road. She needed a sandwich, hot tea, anything to keep the body from consuming itself.

"Why hello, Emily," the storekeeper said, peering at her. "You are Emily, aren't you?"

"The other one was my sister."

"She looked a little bashed up."

"She got hit by a truck. Could you make me a ham sandwich and a cup of tea, Marty?"

"Coming right up." He took the cold cuts from the case to the slicing machine. "Sister, eh? She's a real whippersnapper, that one. Came here one morning lookin' for champagne and oysters and somethin' called shooto. Said she was expecting important company. Walked out in a huff when I couldn't accommodate her."

"She's not a country girl," Emily said, taking the sandwich.

"That's for darn sure." Marty related the local news as his listener ate mechanically as a cow. When she had cleaned her plate, he walked her to the car. "Will you be staying up a while?"

"No. I'm just changing the mousetraps." Emily backed onto the road. She drove to her cabin and bounced into the driveway, skidding to a halt on a bed of lichen. Somewhere over the last half mile, Guy had abandoned her: She was all alone now. She walked to the porch, not sure of what she would find, what she should even be looking for. Outside the door, she paused, sniffing the air, smelling smoke and dead leaves. A loon yodeled over the lake. Afraid to go inside, Emily stared at the doorknob, wishing with all her might that it had a memory and a voice.

The wind blew, firs moved, shadows shifted: She saw a small dot in the door frame. Emily dropped to her knees and put her face close to the little hole in the wood. When she saw dried blood and one slender splinter, she began to cry.

## 21

While Ward was meeting Ross in the bulrushes, O'Keefe paid a visit to Diavolina. "Good morning. Is the boss in?" he asked Klepp, who was tamping unidentifiable animal parts into the meat grinder.

"You mean Leo? Of course not."

"I meant Ward."

"She's at the therapist," Klepp replied. "How can I help you, sir?"

"I'm looking for a waitress named Lola."

"She should be in any minute to pick up her paycheck. May I offer you something while you wait? Rib eye and swizzle fries? Frozen mocha deluxe bombe?"

"Just coffee." It was impossible to see Klepp as anything other than a convicted criminal in chef's clothing. O'Keefe went to the empty dining room. That weirdo with the orange face was restocking the bar. What had he done? Beheaded his wife with pruning shears? "Good morning." O'Keefe smiled, taking a seat.

"You catered Dagmar Pola's party a few nights ago. Who referred her to you?"

"Her own good taste, I would say."

"Ah, you know her, then. Did she eat here the night Dana Forbes dropped dead?"

"I did not see her. But it was very busy and I was tending bar."

A young, delicious woman walked into the dining room. She was dressed as simply as a shepherdess, as if she knew that men would never pay attention to her raiment. "I'm Lola," she said, putting a mug of coffee in front of him.

O'Keefe's tongue was not obeying signals from the fore half of his brain. Finally, after scalding it with coffee, he got it under control. "Pink pepper," he said. "You covered Philippa Banks's steak with it that eventful night."

Lola tossed her hair. "Was it pink? I don't remember."

"Try to remember here rather than at the police station," O'Keefe said. "I really don't have much time."

Lola flushed. "A lady asked me to get her pepper mill auto-graphed. She gave me five hundred bucks." The money had not gone into the waitrons' pool.

"Describe her."

"She wore glasses. She was alone. Sat there." Lola pointed to a nearby table.

"What color was her hair?"

"I don't remember. She was wearing a tight scarf. Like a tur-ban."

"How old was she?"

"Sixty."

Eh? After all that plastic surgery, Ardith had looked a spe-cious thirty-five. "Are you sure?"

"I can tell by the hands. Hers had age spots. My sister's a manicurist so I know all about these things."

Damn! O'Keefe began stabbing in the dark. "Did she wear a lot of jewelry? Pearls?"

"Nope. Just gold hoop earrings."

That sounded like Ardith again. "What did she tell you to do?"

"Give the lady a load of pepper and get her autograph."

"Did you notice anything about the pepper?"

"Are you kidding? Pepper's pepper. I didn't hang around counting the little specks."

O'Keefe realized that, once again, he was treading water a thousand miles from shore. Iproniazid had unmistakably killed Dana; that insidious woman in a turban had sent Lola over to smother Philippa's steak with it; O'Keefe had found the turban and glasses at Ardith's house; she had the motive for murdering not only Philippa, but Dana, and she had impeccable reasons for killing herself; now Lola claimed the woman was old as the hills. Who the hell could that be? Dagmar? She and Ardith had talked. But why should a dowager want to kill a B-movie star? It seemed, on the surface, nonsensical; then again, irrationality was the key to getting away with murder. This was almost as frustrating as the case of Guy Witten, which had no witnesses, no motive, no weapon, and a slew of perfect alibis. O'Keefe would have given up long ago if he hadn't known, in his gut, that these two cases were somehow twins, offspring of the same diabolical parents. He'd just have to keep sniffing and hope that someone misstepped before his hope withered like a plucked rose. "Thanks for your help," he said to Lola and Zoltan. "Give my regards to Ward."

He drove to Beacon Hill and found Philippa alone, breakfasting with her fan mail. She didn't look pleased to see him, but that could have been due to a dearth of makeup. "Is Emily at home?" he asked.

"No, she's at the doctor's." Philippa took off her glasses and tried to lead the detective into the den. En route, she realized that this was the second day in a row he had seen her in the same white peignoir. "So! What brings you here?" she asked in clipped tones.

"I thought you'd like to know that I've talked to Agatha Street, the waitress who served you at the party in New York. A woman in a black turban indeed switched drinks with you there."

"Why, that's wonderful. That little twit has a remarkable memory."

"Indeed. Miss Street also remembered that she had already spoken to you about this at length while your manager was in the hospital."

Philippa laughed lightly. "I think you're right. I had forgotten. At the time I was so distraught over his illness."

"I also spoke to the waiter Franco," O'Keefe continued. "He said you had been asking him questions about a woman in a turban shortly after your manager took ill."

"Franco's hallucinating. How would I know such a thing?"

"That's exactly the question I had."

The detective's staunch stare unnerved her. Philippa wished to God Emily were around to help out with these potholes in their alibi. "Franco is confusing me with my sister," she sniffed. "When Emily came to California, she took it upon herself to run around asking silly questions. Naturally, people would get us mixed up."

A little bell chimed in the back of O'Keefe's brain. "Would she try to mix people up on purpose?"

"No! That would be outrageous! Emily knows she could never impersonate me!" Philippa sagged gingerly to the couch. "Ever since leaving her job to work at that awful restaurant, Emily has been consumed with all kinds of pish. She thinks that our father is a cook who had a fight with a priest and that we were born in a monastery."

"Where do you think you were born?"

"In a fine hospital in New York City," Philippa snapped. "As you know, we are orphans."

"Your father is deceased?"

"Our father is nonexistent! Our mother was a liberated woman! Emily just doesn't know when to leave well enough alone. She's been receiving pornographic sketches and keys from degenerates who send notes to the president of my international fan club."

O'Keefe wondered if Philippa had eaten a can of Sterno for

breakfast. "I'm afraid I don't follow any of this. Maybe I should come back when your sister's here."

"Leave Emily out of this!" Philippa screeched. "She's been in-coherent ever since Guy Witten got shot in the back."

O'Keefe was stunned. "In the back, you said?"

"Back, front, who knows?"

Wild thought: Had Philippa shot her sister's lover? Was there some kind of fatal triangle going on here? "Where were you the night Witten was murdered?"

Philippa lit a cigarette. "In California."

O'Keefe pressed on. "Where was Emily?"

After a small silence, Philippa whimpered, "With me. I was not feeling well."

She looked as if she had been shot all over again. O'Keefe felt bad for twisting the screws on her so tightly, but he was a des-perate man. "Did you know Guy Witten?"

"I never met him in my life."

O'Keefe's beeper went off: fatality on Commonwealth Av-enue. The address looked distressingly familiar. The detective dropped Philippa and sped to Dagmar's apartment. The medical examiner's car was parked outside. O'Keefe nodded to the door-man, who remembered him from the other night and packed him quickly into the elevator. On the tenth floor, he nearly kicked open the door. Two gaga policemen stood in the hallway, studying the artwork. They took him right to Joe Pola's bed-room.

On the floor, with mush for a skull, lay Dagmar. A few feet away, near the telephone, sat Ward with her face between her knees. Mud caked her sneakers. As a detective took pictures of the still life, the coroner padded over to O'Keefe. "Cause of death fairly obvious," he remarked. "Can I pack her up?"

"No." Sidestepping the wide red stain on Joe's carpet, O'Keefe went to Ward. "What happened?"

When she raised her head, he could smell the scotch. She looked completely wasted again. "She wanted to see the initials on the bottom of that thing. I began tilting it and it got away from me." Ward buried her face in her knees. "Oh, shit."

At least she didn't have the gall to ask if Dagmar were hurt. "What were you doing here?"

"Collecting my check and a few pans from the party the other night."

O'Keefe studied the small, still body beneath the marble. Dagmar looked flattened, as if the statue had been flung, not dropped. On the other hand, she was a calcium-deficient old woman. The statue must weigh a ton. And Ward was stinking drunk. O'Keefe walked to the kitchen. Yep, there were the pans. Small copper salad molds: Ward could have concealed them under her coat and the doorman never would have noticed her bringing them in. He returned to the bedroom. "How'd those pans get left behind at the party?"

"Easy," Ward replied. "My crew was in shock after you grilled them."

O'Keefe felt like kicking her. "When did the accident happen?"

"About a minute before I called nine-one-one."

"Why did Mrs. Pola have to see those initials?"

"I have no idea. When a customer hands you a check for two thousand bucks and requests a little favor, you don't ask questions."

"Let me see the check."

Ward reached in her pocket and handed it over. Today's date; O'Keefe sighed, defeated again. If he tried really hard, he might nail her for manslaughter. And he might not: no motive, no witnesses, mitigating circumstances. He'd spend a week in court hearing all about Ward's hard life and drinking problems and abuse and victimization, and at the end of it all he'd look like a schmuck for trying to escalate an accident into a prison term. O'Keefe gave back the check. "Did you like her?"

"Sure, I liked her. She ate and she paid."

O'Keefe wondered if, had Dagmar survived, she would ever have told him why Ward had flattened her. Probably not. "If you liked her so much, why didn't you roll the statue off?"

Ward laughed oddly. "Because I heard her skull crack like a coconut."

He stood up and told the medical examiner to test Ward's blood alcohol level. While she was getting her elbow swabbed, O'Keefe peered at the base of the statue. It was perfectly smooth. "Wrap the lady up," he told the policemen waiting at the door. Straining and grunting, they raised the sculpture to its feet. Rather than contemplate the mess remaining on the floor, O'Keefe stared at the statue's face. That blood-glistening mouth, those imperturbable eyes . . . Emily? O'Keefe shook his head, loosening the hallucination. While Dagmar was getting zipped into a bag, he studied the pedestal, finally locating letters and numbers delicately inscribed in the foot: *S.D. 1950.* Hard to spot; no wonder Dagmar couldn't see them.

"Take her statement," he muttered, leaving.

He dropped ten floors and flashed his badge at the doorman. Then he lit a cigarette. "Did Mrs. Pola have any other visitors this morning?"

"Only Mr. Major."

"At the same time as the woman who's up there now?"

"No, he left an hour before she arrived."

"Had you ever seen that woman here before?"

"Only the day of Mrs. Pola's party."

"Did Mrs. Pola have a lot of visitors in general?"

"No. Only two people came here to see her. Mr. Major and Mrs. Forbes."

O'Keefe nearly pinched his cigarette in half. "How often did she come around?"

"Three or four times. Is everything all right up there?" the doorman asked anxiously.

"Not quite. Mrs. Pola's going to come through the lobby in a body bag in about five minutes." O'Keefe inhaled enough smoke to kill an iron lung. "Answer any questions the officers might have, would you?"

He drove roughly to State Street. "Major in?"

Marjorie smiled nervously from her desk. "He's with a client. It might be a while."

"I'll wait." O'Keefe plopped into a chair and stared vacantly at the ceiling, as if he were on a raft, drifting toward oblivion.

All these bodies and no explanations: This case was worse than an Italian opera, and now Dagmar had taken the first two acts down with her, leaving him with only a few disjointed arias to extrapolate into a full libretto. Maybe that wasn't possible anymore.

"Ross, Detective O'Keefe's here," he heard Marjorie say at last. She listened then looked over. "Follow me, please."

O'Keefe trailed her beautiful legs into Ross's office. "Stay," he said. "You should both hear this. You were at Dagmar Pola's this morning, Ross?"

"Yes. We had a nine-o'clock appointment."

"What did you talk about?"

"The usual. Her new art gallery. I was only there about ten minutes."

"Why so short?"

"She was simply giving me the go-ahead."

O'Keefe went to Ross's window and watched an airplane lance the clouds. "There's a statue in the bedroom. A standing woman. Know anything about it?"

"Not much. Dagmar didn't like it. It was the one piece she wanted to get rid of."

"Seems the feeling was mutual. The statue fell on her. Dagmar's dead."

Ross rocketed out of his chair. "What? How?"

O'Keefe chuckled. "You remember that rather large woman from Diavolina named Ward? Said she was tilting the statue so Dagmar could read the initials on the pedestal and it got away from her. Dagmar's skull was crushed flat as a cow pie."

Ross covered his face. The tears were genuine. "How awful."

"Did she have any children? Any family?"

"Not that I know of. Excuse me a moment." Ross wandered into the washroom.

While the plumbing gushed, O'Keefe asked Marjorie, "Was there something between the two of them?"

Marjorie swallowed heavily, wondering how to steer O'Keefe as far afield as possible from the man she loved. "He was very kind to Mrs. Pola without encouraging her fantasies."

O'Keefe had to agree, remembering how gently Ross had introduced Dagmar to his wife and sister-in-law at Ardith's funeral. When Ross emerged from the washroom, he said, "Why do you think Dagmar wanted to see the initials on that statue?"

Ross blew his nose repeatedly before answering. "She was probably trying to track its provenance. She was in the process of cataloguing the art in the apartment."

"Wouldn't she have done that when she bought the art?"

"Her husband bought it. She knew nothing about that apartment until after he died." Ross plummeted into his chair. "Poor old girl. What a way to go."

O'Keefe's breath stopped: Beneath the grief, had he detected a spark of glee? Or was that just more wishful thinking, another pathetic attempt to demonize Ross Major for having it all? How many hours of sleep had he lost already trying to figure out how Major could have killed Guy Witten? How many more would he lose trying to figure out what Major had to do with the death of Dagmar Pola? Bah! He was no detective, content with facts. He was an outclassed Romeo with a vindictive imagination. Thoroughly oppressed, exhausted with losing all his games, O'Keefe shuffled to the window. "Bear with me while I run the last few weeks by, would you? Dana dies of barbiturate poisoning. He's offed by his enraged wife, but by mistake. She was going for Philippa, whose steak got peppered with iproniazid. But then the steaks got switched and Ardith becomes a widow. Make sense?"

"The pills got ground into the steak?"

O'Keefe ignored the interruption. "There's only one problem. The waitress tells me that the woman sending over the pepper was old. Sixty or seventy, she's sure of it. So I don't think Ardith did this. But let me continue. Not content with what she's done to her husband, Ardith follows Philippa to New York and California and fails both times to kill her. Causes enough mayhem to land in jail for a long time, however. The police are closing in. So she goes to her friend Dagmar's party and jumps off the balcony. Make sense?"

"Ah—sure. I guess. If you knew Ardith."

"Well, I didn't, and now I won't. Let's back up a little. Let's say that Ardith and Dagmar were closer friends than we think. Let's say that it's not Ardith, but Dagmar, at Diavolina the night Dana's killed."

Ross's eyes went round as quarters. "Why would Dagmar want to kill Dana?"

"She didn't. She wanted to kill Philippa."

"What the hell for?"

"That's where I draw a blank. But I saw your sister-in-law this morning. While not what I would call totally coherent, she did mention that Emily and she had been upset lately by threatening letters and news concerning their births. I have a hunch this is somehow connected to Dagmar. The timing is too coincidental." O'Keefe inspected his fingernails as if deciding which one to nibble first. "Any thoughts?"

Ross sat with his mouth open. "I—no. Nothing."

"Would it upset Emily to ask her about it?"

"Possibly. But I suppose you must."

"Is she home today?"

"I think so." Ross picked up the phone. "Phil? Is Em in? No problem. Have her call when she gets back, all right?" He hung up. "She's out. Philippa has no idea when she'll return."

"I'll keep trying. Did Emily talk to you about any of this business?"

Ross grinned sheepishly. "To tell you the truth, I didn't pay much attention to it. She does carry on at times."

O'Keefe didn't even try to grin back. Ross and Marjorie walked him to the door; only as he was taking a last look at Marjorie's legs did the detective notice the tiny rim of mud on Ross's shoes.

After a morning at the police station describing how Joe Pola's statue could have slipped from her hands onto Dagmar's cranium, Ward emerged into the sunshine and took a few deep breaths. Fabulous day, great for walking. She went briskly to the Longfellow Bridge and leaned for quite a while over the rough cement balustrade, watching birds and boats. Then she returned to Diavolina and took a nap. Ward was on the floor of her office, lifting weights, when Klepp knocked. "Ma'am? Chef Major's here. She'd like to see you. Says it's not about Leo. I already told her not to apply for her old job back."

"Send her in." Ward rolled to the couch. "Major! Just in time for cocktails!" Emily looked as if she had just driven nonstop from California, in a convertible. "You need one, I'd say."

"No thanks." Emily sat on a tiny, vacant corner of Ward's desk. "After I saw you and Ross talking this morning, I went to the cabin in New Hampshire. In the door frame, I noticed a little hole." She rummaged through Ward's pencil holder and took out a broadhead arrow. "About this size."

Ward sighed: Denial had never suited her. "This is between your old man and me, Emily. Stay out of it."

"Did he tell you to kill Guy?"

Acrid laughter burst out of her like pus from a boil. "Hell, no! He just told me where I might find him one night. I got a little carried away with business of my own. The wimp was horrified."

"What business?"

"I thought Witten had caused my sister's suicide. It was all a mistake. Sorry."

"*Sorry?* You think that wipes the slate clean? Do you realize what you've done?"

A slow smile stole over Ward's face. "You were screwing him, weren't you? That explains everything."

That explained nothing! "Oh, so it's all my fault? Did I fire the fucking crossbow?"

"You started the chain reaction, baby. Without you and your horny sister, none of this would ever have happened."

"Leave Philippa out of this."

"Can't. She was in it up to her neck. She was sitting with Witten at Presto when I drove that truck through the window. When he went up to New Hampshire, he thought he was visiting you. 'I'm here, Em! Open up!'" Ward guffawed. "Poor schmuck."

Emily's eyes got very hot. "I'm telling the police."

"Sure, go right ahead. Ross could use another two or three life sentences." Ward poured herself a glass of brandy. "By the way, we dropped a statue on Dagmar Pola this morning. A terrible accident. She's dead."

Emily slumped into Ward's chair. "You and Ross killed Dagmar?"

"Hell, no. Your hubby doesn't have the balls to kill a flea. He made the suggestion and I carried it out. It's our routine now." Ward swallowed neatly. "Preventative maintenance, my shrink would call it. Seems Dagmar was trying to kill you. It would only have been a matter of time before she succeeded."

"Why? What did I ever do to her?"

"You emerged live and kicking from your mother's twat, Major. Dagmar seemed to think you and your sister are her husband's bastard daughters. She didn't like that idea very much. Screws up her retirement plans. So I took care of her for you."

Joe Pola the pretzel man? Her father? Emily gripped the sides of her chair, which seemed to be undulating beneath her. "But Ardith shot Philippa."

"Yes but no. She was obeying Dagmar's orders. Owed her a few favors. Poor woman. Suicide was her only option." Ward licked a few drops of brandy meandering down the neck of the bottle. "Think about it, Emily. I lost you a lover and gained you a fortune. We're even now. I'd say your poor devil of a husband has paid off his debt to you as well. Saving your life cost him an art museum. Not to mention his self-respect forever. You really put him through the wringer."

How? By pursuing a furtive wisp of happiness? "None of this is true."

"No? Ask Ross. He took it in the neck. Better yet, ask Leo when he comes back. Whenever the hell that might be. Oh, by the way." Ward tossed an orange tassel onto the desk. "Guess where that came from."

Emily stared at it. "The morgue?"

"A little pillow on Dagmar's couch. She drowned my dishwasher."

"Why?"

"Because he recognized her the night she came here to poison your sister. Nailed Dana Forbes by mistake."

"How?"

"Did O'Keefe ever describe iproniazid to you? Tell you it was a pretty little pink pill? Sort of like those peppercorns you were asking Zoltan about the other day?" Ward lay on the couch and closed her eyes. "Go home, Major. Take a bath. Bury this conversation and get on with your life."

Emily didn't move for a long time. When she finally got to the door, she asked, "Why did you hire me?"

"The pistachio buns. They were great." Ward's biceps swelled as she raised herself up on one elbow. "I'm sorry about Witten. Really. But you've got to admit it was a blessing in disguise. What if he had lived? You'd have ended up killing your sister."

Emily closed the door.

The afternoon had chilled into evening by the time Emily got back to Beacon Hill. As soon as she stepped inside the foyer, she smelled Philippa's heavy perfume and the specters of many cigarettes. "That you, Em?" her sister called. "Where have you been all day? I've been worried sick! I was just writing you a note. My taxi's going to be here any second now."

Pen in hand, Philippa sat at the kitchen table. She was dressed in a black suit with a few dozen understated rhinestones around the collar. "Where are you going?" Emily asked.

"Paris, darling. I simply cannot lie flat on my back here one day longer. I'm getting bedsores. Besides, I'm almost well. Feel like new."

She was obviously in pain. Emily took a chair and, seeing her sister's pinched, pale face, almost let bygones be bygones. But there was something she had to know. "Tell me," she said, voice as unsteady as Philippa's hands, "what were Guy's last words to you that night at the cabin?"

Philippa's lip began to quiver. Then suppressed tears and words slipped free. "I was just sitting at Diavolina minding my own business when this stranger came to the table and ran a finger over my cheek. I thought I would die, he was so beautiful. I had to know who he was." Emily said nothing. "I came to Dana's funeral to see him. He wasn't there. I saw a flyer from Cafe Presto in the drawer over there and called him, pretending to be you. He agreed to see me—you—and then a truck smashed through the window. I ran away. What could I do, Em? Stick around and patch him up? I was pretty banged up myself."

Emily still said nothing. Perhaps she hadn't even heard. "I had to see him again," Philippa continued. "But to confess, not to—do other things. He could tell I wasn't really you. So I invited him up to the cabin. It was a rainy night. He knocked on the door. When I answered it he twisted to the side and fell."

Philippa faltered to a standstill. Emily finally stirred to life. "Then what."

"I—I wanted to bring him inside and call an ambulance but he said no, he didn't want to make a scene that might get you into trouble. He didn't seem to be so badly hurt. He just got into his car and kissed me on the cheek and said he'd call in a few hours when he got back to Boston. His last words were 'I love you.'" Philippa actually choked on her own tears. "I don't know why I did it, Em. He swept me off my feet. It's been awful beyond belief since he died. I couldn't tell anyone without getting you into trouble." Philippa rushed to the other side of the table and bawled into her sister's lap. "Please forgive me! I've been unable to live with myself. I never slept with him. I never stood a chance. The only time I even came within arm's length, he said that I had changed perfume. It was a hopeless infatuation. I'm a desperate, worthless old woman."

"Did you ever think about bringing the killer to justice?"

"Court? Juries? I couldn't bear it! Why didn't you ever tell Guy you had a twin? Were you ashamed?"

Outside, a horn tooted. Philippa tightened her clutch around her sister's knees. "Say it's all right, Emily! I won't leave until you do!"

Emily patted her sister's sprawling blond hair. What had

Philippa done but fall under Guy's spell, same as she had? Ah, how love made solitary wanderers of them all. "It's all right," she said.

The horn blared. Emily helped Philippa to her feet. "I'll bring down your things."

As the cab driver was heaving the last suitcase into the trunk, Philippa leaned out the window. "I feel so much better, Em. Maybe my nightmares will go away now."

Fat chance. "Make a good vampire movie," Emily said, blowing a kiss.

Roaring and rattling, the cab crested Joy Street. Emily was about to go back inside when O'Keefe's car pulled up. "Hi," he called. "Got a minute?"

She took him upstairs to the den. "Sorry about the mess," she said, clearing a space for him on the sofa. "Philippa always leaves in a whirlwind."

"She's gone?"

"To Paris. Her new movie starts shooting in a couple days. May I get you something?" The detective looked as if he had been cruising through a cyclone in a hot-air balloon.

"No thanks. Did your sister tell you I had dropped by this morning?"

Emily chuckled. "No, the little stinker."

"She mentioned that you had been receiving pornography and keys in the mail."

"That was a while ago. It was pretty harmless so I threw it out."

Damn! "She also mentioned threatening notes to the president of her fan club."

Emily frowned. "I think he gets about a dozen a day. Why did she bring it up?"

"I'm not sure. She seemed to be speaking off the top of her head. She said you had been looking into reports of being born in a monastery." As Emily blanched, O'Keefe took her hand. "I don't mean to upset you with this. I'm trying to see if there's any connection with recent events."

Emily went to the window and admired the Boston skyline.

Her good husband was the force behind so many of those proud, shimmering lights. She couldn't allow O'Keefe to put him in prison for a crime she had instigated. "Our mother died in child-birth. I spend a lot of time trying to find my father. It's a little fantasy of mine that one day I'll find him and we'll be one happy family again." She shrugged. "I hit a lot of dead ends."

"Like that monastery?"

Emily nodded. "It's pretty rough on Philippa. All her life, she's compensated by acting and fibbing. She doesn't mean to. She just does."

O'Keefe swallowed that: It was solid, like beef stew. He passed on to a murkier matter. "Did your husband know Ward?"

"From Diavolina? I never introduced them. Why?"

Oh, just a little mud on two pairs of shoes and a statue through a dowager's brains. "I thought they may have seen each other this morning."

He was lying: He was fishing. He had seen them. Emily had to choose, immediately, and parry. *Guy! Help!* "I don't see how," she said. "Ross had a meeting with Dagmar Pola at nine. I took him there and waited outside. Then we went to the obstetri-cian's. I dropped him off at work afterward." Emily smiled with a shy radiance, part woman, part atom bomb. "We're pregnant. It's a secret. I know I'm old enough to be a grandmother."

O'Keefe knew that he must let this case go, let it sail away from him and sink in the deep, cold sea of suspicion and jeal-ousy and unrequited lust. He knew everything and nothing: The murderers had been murdered and the witnesses would remain forever dumb because somehow, beneath the pile of bodies, scores had been settled, justice had been served. Family affairs, domestic disputes: Cops had no jurisdiction here. "That's won-derful," O'Keefe said. "Congratulations." He and Emily ex-changed a few sentences about blessed events and ecstatic fathers-to-be. He saw no point mentioning that Dagmar Pola lay in the morgue near a dead dishwasher, nor that Lola had perked up a steak with iproniazid: People were evil and nuts and no one was ever sorry for anything. They'd do it all over again the next moment temptation drifted within a mile of opportunity. Sometimes he caught them, sometimes they caught themselves, and eventually death caught them all. Tonight Emily looked, for the first time, happy. Who was he to deprive her of a husband, a child's father? She'd never look at him again. Saying good night, O'Keefe went home and watched a long baseball game.

# 22

It was another bright morning, but a little too cool to breakfast outside. Ross was reading the sports pages as Emily padded into the kitchen in her flannel pajamas. She kissed the top of his head, poured a cup of coffee, and watched from the other side of the table as he came upon the obituaries. "My God," he said, straightening his eyeglasses. "Dagmar Pola died."

"From what?"

He read a moment. "She had an accident at her apartment. Whatever that means."

"What a drag! There goes your art museum."

"What can you do."

"When's the funeral? You should probably make an appearance."

"What for? She never paid me a cent. All right, I'll send flowers."

Emily peered over the page, trying to read upside down. "Any family?"

"It doesn't say."

The doorbell rang. Husband and wife stared dully at each other: Now what? "I'll get it," he said. "Stay here."

She heard voices. Then Ross returned to the kitchen with a compact, swarthy man wearing an eye patch. Perhaps he had left his parrot and wooden leg at home. "This gentleman says he's Leo," Ross said.

She stared, but not for long; Leo looked ferocious as Klepp, sullen as Zoltan, cunning as Dagmar. "Coffee?" she asked. No. "What brings you here?"

Leo's one eye strayed to the newspaper. "That," he replied, tapping a finger on Dagmar's obituary. "I don't want there to be any trouble. Read this." He tossed an envelope on the table.

Emily opened it. "The last will and testament of Joseph Pola?" She read the short document. "Looks like he leaves everything to his two daughters, if they be found." She slid a fork under Ross's scrambled eggs. En route to her mouth, a pale yellow curd fell on Dagmar's picture. "So? Are they found?"

"Nope." Leo laughed. It was a strange sound, midway between a bark and a sob. "Joe never had any daughters."

"Back up," Ross snapped. "All the way."

Leo smiled, displaying a set of gray teeth. "Where should I begin this merry-go-round?" He nodded to the newspaper. "I guess that one started it. She couldn't just tell Dubrinsky to get lost. She had to put him away for twenty years. Rape, my ass."

"Why'd she do that?" Emily asked.

"Because he wouldn't go away. She preferred Monsieur Joe Pola, a social-climbing gigolo who made pretzels. Dagmar was nothing to him but a cash cow. Joe was in love with your mother, of course."

Emily swallowed some eggs. "Did my mother love him?"

"She played her part well. She was an actress, after all."

"But why should she act?"

"Because Joe was her oil well and she was pregnant. Not by him, though."

"Let me guess," Ross interrupted. "You're my father-in-law."

Leo's mouth twisted slightly upward. "One day Dagmar discovered a theater ticket in Joe's pocket. It was an actor's comp. She went to a show, took one look at your mother, and made the connection. Women have a sixth sense about these things. So she sent a bottle of cold cream backstage. Unfortunately, the co-star used it and lost most of his face. A chemical peel, to put it mildly."

"Zoltan," Emily sighed.

"Your mother put two and two together and ran away. She was terrified of Dagmar. So she came to me."

"Why should she come to you?" Ross said. "How do you fit into all of this?"

"I used to have a diner on Lincoln Street. It was one of the few places in town you could get a cup of chili after midnight. Your mother used to stop by on the way home from her shows. On my birthday, so did Joe."

"Isn't that nice!" Ross exclaimed. "Was he helping you celebrate?"

"You could say that. Joe was my twin brother."

Ross and Emily stared at him, filtering many causes and effects. Finally Emily said, "You must have really hated him."

"Always did. Always will. He was the favorite. We didn't even look alike. I ran away when I was twelve." Leo let that settle as he got himself a glass of water. "Joe found me in jail. Whenever he visited people would say *You're related to the pretzel man? Wow!* I changed my name the minute I got out." Leo drank heavily. "The rest you know. Your mother didn't make it and Dagmar spent the rest of her life hunting for you."

For a while the only sound in the kitchen was an occasional drip from the faucet. "Why did you disappear?" Emily asked. "Were you looking for me and my sister?"

"Hell, no. There was nothing to find."

"Didn't Dagmar know who you were?"

"Are you crazy? Joe never told her. An ex-con brother was a blot on his social agenda. He only saw me for ten minutes on our birthday. When he found out he was dying, I got a call. Joe had been obsessing over his missing children for forty years and wanted a deathbed reunion."

"Why didn't you tell him the truth?"

"That would have been too cruel."

"Too merciful, you mean," Ross guffawed. "You had all the tin soldiers. All you did was aim them at each other and evacuate the war zone until there were no more bullets and no more bodies. Now you get everything."

"So? At least I didn't kill anyone."

Drip, drip, went the faucet. Ross twisted it shut. "Who's the father?"

"Slavomir, of course. Joe should never have commissioned him to sculpt his mistress in marble. You know how it is with artists and their naked models."

"I don't believe you," Ross said. How could Dagmar have gotten it so wrong?

"No? Go to the morgue and run a DNA test. Make it quick, though. I'm burying him tomorrow."

Emily slowly swallowed the last scrambled eggs. That sot of a dishwasher was her father? That amoral wildcat was her mother? Perhaps Philippa had been right to insist they were born in an upper East Side hospital. "Why did the priest keep this all to himself?"

"Because I made sure that Joe sent a large gift to the monastery. All Dagmar's money, of course. It was a small step toward expiating her original sin with Slavomir."

Who had done nothing but fall in love with an inconstant woman. Ross stood up. "Thanks for dropping by. We love guests for breakfast."

"Wait," Emily called to Leo. "If you hated your brother so much, why did you take such good care of his mistress?"

After a long look, as if he were about to cast Emily in bronze, Leo replied, "Because that was as close as I'd ever get." He turned quickly and left.

Soon Ross returned to the kitchen. "Do you believe him?"

"Yes."

He stared at Dagmar's egg-smeared obituary. "All that fuss for nothing."

Nothing? Fall in love, take your chances. Everyone knew it

was Russian roulette with not one but six loaded chambers, and everyone played anyway, seizing the opportunity to die smiling, laughing even, as their brains hit the wall. Emily kissed Ross's ear. "Do you have time to come to the travel agent with me today, sweetheart? Let's take that trip we've been talking about."

He folded the newspaper and followed her to the bedroom.

⚌

*We're leaving tonight for Italy. Emily's never looked happier. I know that some great weight has been lifted from her shoulders, but I'm not sure Leo did the lifting. He didn't tell her particularly good news, after all. He just threw stones in a few old holes. No, it was something else. I'm not going to ask; she'll tell me if she needs to. Until then, I'm going to accept her silence. Bless it, rather.*

*Today I was sitting on the bed watching her pack all sorts of vitamins and little baby books for the trip. "I think we can throw these away," Emily said, handing me a stack of ovulation graphs that have been enslaving our sex life for years. Then she went to get the laundry. I was tossing them out when I noticed the uppermost page. It was for last August. We should save that one, I thought, put it in the baby scrapbook, just for laughs. Dana always used to joke that his eldest son had been conceived at thirty thousand feet somewhere between London and Milan and said he had the charts and the plane tickets to prove it. So I looked at the chart, following the temperature line up and down. It hit a high point on August thirtieth. Bingo, I thought, then stopped: I know I was in Dayton, Ohio, then. In fact, I had been there that whole week. Marjorie had been drilling the dates into my mind for months. She wanted to make sure I didn't schedule any vacations in the middle of a national builders' conference.*

*I just stood there for a few moments, wondering whether these charts were fubar, or Emily's cycle was. Then the truth washed over me like a warm, tropical wave: Guy had fathered this child. You just know these things, you feel them in your blood. I began to quiver, not out of anger this time, but out of awe at the mercy, the divine architecture, of it all. How often I've thought of him lying alone on my porch, in the dark, the rain, whimpering Emily's name as he bled to death. Maybe, as I watch his child grow, that ghastly image will fade, leave me in peace.*

*How fitting that he should give my wife something that I, in fifteen years, never could. Maybe that was his destiny, to fecundate her and die. Maybe the two of them were a superior melding of yin and yang, of acidic and alkaline; and maybe I was only meant to be the caretaker, never the possessor, of my wife's heart. It's not the worst of fates. Besides, I've lost my taste for absolute possession. Like a severe drug habit, it shortens the life span: Look at Dana and that poor waif Rita. Look at Guy. Even if you outlast your obsession, beat it down to a dull ache that haunts your days, you're still left with only a speck of conscience separating you from a beast. Look at Dagmar and Ward. Leo. Did they really even the score? Get what they wanted? I don't think that's humanly possible: Justice, particularly in love, is a delusion. I'm going to abandon that pursuit. Now that I have another mouth to feed, I'd rather live longer, but less madly; see more seasons change, read more books, watch Emily's hair turn slowly white. Die a quiet old man, humbled by maternal tolerance.*

*I think she knows that I put an end to Guy, and has forgiven me; she wouldn't have given me this stack of charts otherwise. I'll never learn how she found out. Did Ward crack? Did Philippa? Has Emily forgiven that worthless sister of hers, too? I can't comprehend such love. But that's why she remains the enigma, the vortex, of my life. She's my one small window to God.*

*Rest in peace, Guy. I'll remember you whenever I see her smile.*

*I am such a lucky man.*